GOD'S AVENGER

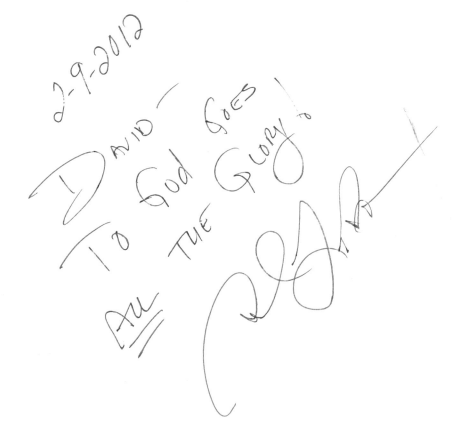

2-9-2012

DAVID —

TO GOD GOES

ALL THE GLORY !

A PRO-LIFE
NOVEL

GOD'S
AVENGER

MICHAEL, THE IMPRECATORY ANGEL

DANIEL JOHN GURA

Pleasant Word
PW A Division of WinePress Group

ISBN 13: 978-1-4141-1091-2
ISBN 10: 1-4141-1091-X
Library of Congress Catalog Card Number: 2007906579

For he is the minister of God to thee for good. But if thou do that
which is evil, be afraid; for he beareth not the sword in vain:
for he is the minister of God, an avenger to execute wrath upon
him that doeth evil.

—Romans 13:4

Dedication: In memory of the 50,000,000 innocents.

FOREWORD

IMPRECATORY PRAYERS . . . only the innocent dare pray them and only the wicked need fear them.

I have always been fascinated by the imprecatory psalms. The idea that a man, any man, can petition the Court of Divine Justice for protection and appropriate punishment for criminals is so awesome it almost defies belief.

King David, one of the greatest figures in the Old Testament, authored over thirty psalms that contain an imprecation, or curse, uttered against the enemies of God. He understood such prayers were not to be taken lightly when he wrote, "break the teeth in their mouths, O God; tear out, O Lord, the fangs of the lions! Let them vanish like water that flows away" (Psalm 58). And, "let his days be few; and let another take his office. Let his children be fatherless, and his wife a widow" (Psalm 109). Remember, these are inspired prayers, not to be taken—or uttered—lightly. I know for a fact a young woman in Texas cancelled her abortion and walked out of the clinic because of an imprecatory psalm she heard being prayed outside.

These imprecatory psalms are at the heart of my novel, yet I find that many modern Christians are unfamiliar with their message, a message of dependence on God that is as timely today as it was 3,000 years ago when they were first uttered.

David knew well that a righteous imprecatory prayer can only be said for a righteous cause. He wrote them when he was powerless and suffering terrible harm and no earthly means of relief was available. They are prayers that acknowledge God as their last and only hope.

This is much the situation pro-lifers find themselves in today. America is under the yolk of the most pro-abortion president in the history of the republic and the number of slaughtered innocents since *Roe v. Wade* has passed 50,000,000. Local politicians, beholden to well-funded pro-abortion groups, harass and oppress the faithful at every turn. The pro-abortion, liberal media has never yet told the true story of the horrors of legal abortion, and even refuses to call us pro-life, instead coining the derisive term "anti-choice." Pro-lifers are threatened with prison, financial ruin, and sometimes even harm to their person.

My story explores a scenario in which untold thousands of Christians petition God to save the lives of the unborn. They come before the Father powerless to stop evil, but—and this is very important—with clean hands. They petition God, not on their own behalf, but to give voice to those innocents yet to be born. And they do not ask God to destroy the outpost of hell—the human slaughterhouse. No, their prayers ask only for the overthrow of Satan's kingdom, and that his followers be either brought to repentance and forgiveness or that His judgment metes out the justice they deserve. Their is a cry for justice to a just God, confident that He will answer their prayers in the manner of His choosing—and in His time.

Recently, George Tiller, one of the most notorious abortionists in the world, was murdered. Was his death the answer to imprecatory prayers? I do not think so. Patience is an essential element in any prayer, but Tiller's assassination was both impatient and an act of personal vengeance. In Romans 12:19 Christ is very specific: "Dearly beloved, avenge not yourselves, but rather give place unto [God's] wrath: for it is written, Vengeance is mine; I will repay, saith the Lord."

God's vengeance can take many forms, and how it is visited upon the evildoers ranges from a Divine rebuke of their careers and lifestyles ("Saul, why do you persecute me?") to horrific death, or complete destruction of cities such as Sodom and Gomorrah.

As an activist committed to saving lives, I vigorously oppose violence. That is why it has always been my philosophy to convert abortionists. If a man dies outside of a state of Grace, Satan wins. That is not what our Father intends for any of us. So I encourage everyone to pray for the intervention of the Holy Spirit into the lives of everyone involved in the abortion industry. The Pro-Life Action League's website has testimonies from former abortion providers, including Luhra Tivis, a state officer in the Kansas Chapter of the National Organization for Women and medical secretary for George Tiller, who were saved by the power of prayer.

Pastor James E. Adams wrote in his essay, *Why We Pray the Imprecatory Psalms,*

To pray the imprecations of the Psalms is to surrender all rights for vengeance to God. It means being prepared to suffer and to endure without personal revenge or hatred as Christ did. It involves being gentle and loving even when I am reviled and persecuted. It encompasses acknowledging in all my ways that God's cause is more important than I am.

After writing my book I don't think I'll ever be able to look at an abortion mill without visualizing a one-hundred foot tall Archangel swinging his flaming sword as he metes out Divine Justice. But until that day, I'll keep praying for the salvation of the souls of everyone who toils inside its bloodstained walls . . . and for the healing of the mother's lives that they destroy.

CHAPTER 1

MODERN STEEL AND concrete office towers don't just collapse, yet everyone was staring at one that looked as if someone had sat on it—someone really big—and that didn't make any sense.

This had been an impressive building, one of a complex of eight identical glass-covered towers known as City Gate. The name was said to be a tribute to its location on the far northwest edge of the city limits, where the buildings flanked both sides of the Kennedy Expressway for almost half-a-mile. The developer said the name would serve to remind motorists driving in from the airport they were no longer rubbing elbows with the rubes in the suburbs. They were now in the big city.

OK, he didn't use those exact words, but everyone knew what he meant. City gates of old were built to keep uncivilized barbarians out. However, for those who were deemed worthy to pass through their portals, wonders beyond belief awaited. Only the most cynical thought the name sounded one heck of a lot like that of Chicago's mayor, Sidney Gates. And now one of the buildings had a problem—a very big problem.

Fred McBarker Junior had been a Chicago building inspector for more than two decades, getting his job thanks to the city's clout-heavy Democratic machine. His father worked as a laborer for Streets and Sanitation and had been a loyal precinct captain all of his life. Fred Senior took great pride in delivering the vote every election day, an achievement which made him many friends in high places. So naturally, when his son graduated from high school, he did what every connected father had done since Nimrod started building the Tower of Babel. He went to his patron to get his kid a public works job.

"Of course we got a job for your kid," Alderman Whyte told him with a smirk, "provided he voted right in the last election." Both men chuckled knowing

1

his son hadn't been old enough to vote the previous November. "So how about something nice and clean? Might even lead to a cushy office job in a few years." With a wink and a handshake, the City of Chicago hired a new employee.

Right from day one, Fred was different from the usual patronage hack's kid. He had ambition and took pride in his work. His work ethic soon caught the eye of one of the senior building inspectors who took him under wing and became his mentor. "You can do a lot better than this," he advised. "You should give some thought to enrolling in night school at a community college and study engineering and construction techniques." Fred picked up a catalog and application packet on his way home that same evening.

Attending classes part time, it took four years to graduate from Wright Junior College and another eight to earn a Masters Degree in structural engineering from the University of Illinois. A lot of his co-workers resented Fred's drive, but his supervisors were smart enough to recognize talent. More and more of the tougher assignments went his way. His hard work paid off when he was named the youngest First Deputy of the Chicago Department of Buildings in the city's history—not bad for the son of a ditch digger.

With the promotion came new responsibilities, including being on call twenty-four hours a day as the city's primary responder to "structural incidents." In a city as large as Chicago, that meant at least a couple of middle-of-the-night calls a week to inspect a fire-gutted building while the embers were still hot. Fred had just enough gray in his hair to think he had seen every possible collapse—from porches overloaded with partying yuppies that had fallen and killed twelve, to century-old, two flat apartment builings built in the post Great Chicago Fire building boom, that shifted off of their tired foundations.

But there was nothing routine about tonight's phone call. This collapse was very different. When he first viewed the structure from the police line a block away, it reminded Fred of the time his rather large aunt from Wisconsin sat on a stack of birthday presents. The wrapping paper made a loud pop as the boxes compressed and mushroomed out at their edges. His dad even caught his family's reaction on his Kodak 8mm movie camera.

What would make a building compress like a pile of cardboard shirt boxes? Fred wondered. Even though he had been only seven or eight at the time, he couldn't shake the vivid childhood image as he stared at the building. *It looks as if a giant Aunt Bertha sat on it.*

"I think we can say for certain an airplane didn't crash into this building." Billy Haynes clicked off a few more pictures.

McBarker's team was completing their preliminary inspection of the exterior of the collapsed building when Philo Clemson shouted, "Wait! I saw something move—over there! Behind the garbage carts!"

"Any idea what?"

"I can't say. I only caught a glimpse of it."

All three flashlight beams were pointing at a different dumpster. "Where? I don't see anything." McBarker swung his light along the row of carts.

"It was moving left-to-right behind that blue dumpster. Billy, shoot some pictures that way." Clemson pointed at the cart. "Maybe your flash will catch something."

"I don't know, Philo. The dust is causing funny reflections—it might be nothing," Haynes replied.

"Could be a guard dog," Clemson suggested.

"I don't know, but you're not going inside to find out," McBarker said. "Let's get moving. We've got a lot more work to do."

"Give me a second. I'll push the dumpster out of the way without going in," Clemson picked up a long piece of metal.

McBarker cautioned, "Don't get killed for some rat munching on leftovers."

"Don't worry. I'm not going in. I'll push it from out here. The floor looks crooked, so it should roll across the room." Clemson braced the aluminum bar against his shoulder and gave it a shove.

"Don't push so hard it smashes into the wall and knocks something down on you." McBarker said.

The cart's wheels squeaked as it began to roll, revealing a couple of overturned trash containers behind it.

"Oh my God!" Philo screamed as much as a prayer as an expression of shock. "There's a baby! No, more than one! Quick! Shine your lights over there!"

Their flashlight beams converged on a debris pile on the floor in front of two large green dumpsters that had tipped over. Together, they illuminated the bloody bodies of two naked babies. The rapid flashes of Haynes' camera lit up the small room.

"What are babies doing in there?" Clemson screamed.

"Get rescue over here right now! Hurry, they might still be alive!" McBarker shouted into his radio.

"I'm going in!" Haynes yelled.

"I need an ambulance! We found . . ." Before McBarker could finish the sentence, the building started to shift. The strobe on Haynes' camera continued flashing as he followed Clemson through the hole in the wall. Concrete groaned and exploded causing the gentle rain of fine dust to become a torrent of small rocks.

"Get out of there!" McBarker's command was drowned out by the noise of the building. "Get out now! It's coming down."

"I can't see them!" Clemson yelled.

McBarker could not see the men as they searched on their hands and knees. The rumble grew even louder and larger chunks of concrete rained down around them.

"Emergency!" McBarker yelled into his radio. "My men are inside!"

"Billy!" Philo screamed. "It's too late."

"No, I've got to save them! Just a few more seconds, I'm almost there!" Their voices were raised to screams, but the sounds of the dying building all but drowned out their words. Shrieks of tearing metal echoed through the building and the floor began to tremble.

"*Run! Run!*" McBarker was blinded by the rain of dust as he fought his way inside. "*Run for your lives! That's an order!*" McBarker screamed at his men.

Before they could react, the room was filled with a light so bright, so intense and pure, that the air looked clear. A heartbeat later, part of the floor collapsed causing dumpster after dumpster to fall over and spill its contents. Lifeless bodies and hundreds of pieces of tiny babies—severed arms, legs, and heads—spilled across the floor and were washed by a river of blood into the gaping hole. The three froze in shock at the horror at their feet, oblivious to the building collapsing around them. After the last of the dumpsters finished pouring out its carnage, the light turned a dazzling gold and moved into the basement. Darkness reclaimed the room. They stared transfixed into the chasm as the loading dock became eerily silent.

An instant later, they were snatched back to reality by the blare of a trumpet. It was a sound so chilling and terrifying, it caused the men's hair to stand on end and goose bumps to cover their arms. The cinder block wall in front of them disintegrated, exposing concrete columns and pillars that swayed a violent dance before crumbling. As the last notes of the horn faded, it was replaced by the thunderous roar of the building collapsing onto them. It sucked the air out of their lungs and filled their ears with its death rattle.

At the same instant each man realized he was going to die, a blinding flash of light erupted from the basement. It lifted and carried the men outside as the building began to settle into its grave.

Despite a steady rain of concrete and debris slamming into the ground all around them, none of the men was injured. Dazed, their minds fixated on what they had just witnessed. Each had seen something in the basement in addition to the slaughtered innocents.

CHAPTER 2

MAYOR GATES WAS awakened by his senior bodyguard knocking on the bedroom door. When Wilson didn't hear a response, he inched the door open and stepped inside. The only light in the room came from an alarm clock, but it was enough for him to see Gates sitting up in his king-sized bed with the covers pulled up to his chin.

"Mr. Mayor. Mr. Mayor." He whispered. "I'm sorry to wake you, Sir, but we've got a situation; 911 received a call that an airplane crashed into a building at City Gate."

"Airplane? Why did an airplane crash?" He asked.

"I don't know, Sir." He kept his voice lowered. "I don't have a lot of details, but the crash happened about ten minutes ago."

Gates held his index finger to his mouth and ssssshhhhed the officer. "Outside."

A moment later, the mayor emerged wearing a royal blue robe and gently closed the door behind him. "I don't want you to wake my wife. This is serious, isn't it?" Gates yawned.

"Yes, Sir. If it wasn't serious, I wouldn't have bothered you. Downtown called it as a 5-11 Alarm; District 3 has Battalions 9, 10, and 11 on their way; several others are standing by. They're also responding with EMS Plan III." Seeing the mayor's quizzical look he explained, "That's an Emergency Medical Services additional response. They're sending fifteen ambulances, a triage van, and a command van.

"The 12th Battalion at O'Hare has been put on stand-by, as has the Air Force Crash Team."

Gates held his hand up. "I'm sure they know what equipment to send. So cut to the chase. Who's running the show?"

Wilson replied, "I don't know, Sir, but the District Fire Chief and Deputy Fire Commissioner are en route."

"Do you at least know who saw the plane crash?" the mayor was now awake and thinking.

"A garbage truck driver. He heard a loud explosion and watched the building collapse. He told the 911 operator an airplane crashed into the top floor."

"May God have mercy. Was it one of the residential buildings? Was it a commercial jet or a small private one?"

"I'm sorry, Sir, but I don't know anything else. I got the call from CECC, the Chicago Emergency Communications Center, right after they dispatched the first units. They're sending everything out there just in case. They put the disaster plan into effect and Resurrection and Lutheran General Hospitals are preparing to receive casualties. They also alerted the blood bank in Glenview."

"Enough with the details already. Were there any survivors?"

"I don't know, Sir. A State Police helicopter is on its way to the site. They're talking to the control tower at O'Hare, and I'll be patched in as soon as they arrive."

"Let me know as soon as you have some real answers." *It's his job to know. How can I do my job if he isn't doing his?* "Is my driver ready? I'll need a couple of minutes to get dressed. What's the weather like outside?"

"He's ready, Sir. It's in the mid seventies. There's a light wind, but no rain," Wilson answered.

"It's way too early to bother my wife, so leave her a note while I put on some clothes. Let her know I won't be back in time for breakfast."

Less than two minutes after they left, all six of the mayor's telephone lines began to ring. Mrs. Gates wouldn't be sleeping in today.

The mayor's chauffeur opened the door to his limousine as soon as he saw him walking down his front stairs followed by two plainclothes police officers. They were part of a nine-man security detail that worked in three-man rotations of twelve hours on and twenty-four hours off. Their sole duty was to accompany the mayor everywhere he went. Gates wanted to present an image of having secret service agents, so he had all of his men wear matching black suits, white shirts, and narrow black ties. With a minimum height requirement of six-feet, two-inches, all towered over the portly mayor.

Gates ignored his driver's greeting like he did every morning and climbed into the backseat. The car was soon accelerating down the deserted street.

"I want to know who's in charge," the mayor said as he settled back to drink the cup of coffee his driver had waiting for him, "and I want to know what happened ASAP."

"Yes, Sir," both bodyguards responded as they began dialing their cellphones.

It was a couple of minutes before either had anything to report.

"Great. Great." Wilson said. "Sir, I've got the State Police copter. It was an office building that was hit. Building Eight."

"Give me that!" Gates leaned forward and gestured for Wilson to hand him the phone.

"This is Mayor Sidney Gates. What about the airplane?"

The helicopter pilot responded, "I've circled the building, but I can't see any wreckage. A couple of floors collapsed. Maybe it's in there. It's hard to tell because it's still dark out and there's some pretty extensive damage to the exterior."

"Well, someone must know what crashed! Call me back when you know something!" The Mayor tossed the phone back and muttered something under his breath. He turned and stared out the window as they raced west on the Kennedy Expressway.

The Chicago Police Department considered being a member of the mayor's security detail a privilege. The men assigned to it soon learned otherwise. The bodyguards found themselves treated like servants, even though they were hand picked for their experience and valor. They learned the mayor expected them to be invisible, omnipotent, and willing to take a bullet for him, yet he never bothered to learn their names. Instead, if he used any name at all, he would call them "Lucky" because that was what he considered them—lucky to be serving him instead of doing the job for which they were trained.

Several long minutes passed before the next update. Then they started rolling in one after another.

"Sir," Officer Martin Landy broke the silence. "The building was empty. There were two security guards inside but both made it out. Detectives are talking to one and the other is on his way to the hospital. No report on the extent of his injuries."

Wilson quickly followed with, "O'Hare and Midway say they're not missing any planes. Radar at Aurora says nothing is missing. They're checking with Palwaukee and the other small airports right now."

"Sir, the first fire units report there is no sign of airplane wreckage on the ground—just concrete and broken glass," Landy said.

Wilson's cellphone rang. "Uh-huh. Well call me the moment you know anything.

Yes, I'll tell him."

"Sir, the State Emergency Management Agency is sending a rapid response team in case this was a terrorist attack."

"A terrorist attack! Give me the phone, Lucky." Gates motioned him forward with his fingers.

Before Landy could comply, Wilson held his hand up and announced, "Sir, it's the pilot again. They've turned every searchlight they've got on the building, and he's certain there wasn't a crash. There's no sign of an impact. No fire. No blast marks. No wreckage of any kind."

"So why did it collapse?" Gates demanded.

"I'm putting you on speaker phone. Please repeat what you just said."

"Copy that." The pilot was hard to hear over the noise of the chopper. "I said I have no idea why it collapsed. I'm right over the building looking down. It's not leaning but all four walls are buckled. All the windows are gone. There's a lot of broken glass and concrete all over the parking lot. Man those walls are pushed way out. My guess is something exploded in the middle of the building, but don't hold me to it."

"Mr. Mayor," Landy interrupted. "A team of structural engineers has arrived at the building."

"Finally, someone who can answer a simple question. Get them on the phone."

The phones began ringing at City Hall well before anyone arrived for work. Each was answered with a recorded message that recited office hours then offered the option of leaving a message on general voice mail or, if you knew your party's three digit extension, being transferred to the bureaucrat of your choice's answering machine.

While many of the callers swore and slammed their phones down, vowing to call back after nine o'clock, more than a few left messages that would make a sailor blush. A surprising number, however, had the home phone numbers of their aldermen. A few even had the mayor's home and cell numbers. Many politicians were awakened that Monday morning by phones ringing off the hook.

"A police officer forced me and my wife to leave our home in the middle of the night wearing only pajamas and slippers." The man's voice seethed with rage. "I am a taxpayer and I demand we be allowed to return to our condominium immediately to retrieve proper clothing."

"Well, it wasn't our building that fell down, so I don't see why we had to leave." The elderly woman's confusion sounded genuine.

"I want the rude policeman who woke us up fired or at least transferred to a beat in a bad neighborhood."

Since the City Gate collapse occurred in Alderman Herbert Whyte's ward he was receiving the lion's share of the telephone calls. Between his house and cellphones, the calls were coming so fast he didn't have a chance to change from his pajamas. A lot of callers didn't even let him say hello before laying into him.

His wife Vikki could hear it all from the kitchen and stifled a laugh as he tried to complete a sentence. "I'm very sorry you and your wife were inconvenienced but . . . No, I don't know when you will be permitted to return home, but . . . I'm doing everything in my power to find out what is . . . ."

One of the biggest drawbacks of calling on a cellphone is the angry caller couldn't slam down the receiver for emphasis, but Whyte sure heard his share of swearing before the *click*.

"Don't these idiots realize the sister building to the one they live in just collapsed?" The Alderman fumed as yet another caller ended his conversation with an obscenity. "You would think they would be happy the police saved their lives," Whyte complained.

"Yes dear," his wife chimed. "Coffee's ready."

"Honey," he offered his ringing phone to his wife, "would you please answer it?" He gave a sheepish grin. "I really need a cup of coffee."

"Are you kidding?" She snickered. "I'm not their alderman. Remember, Herby, you're the one who keeps reminding me I'm just a housewife."

Now both phones were ringing. Whyte threw his arms up in defeat, sighed, and said, "Please" while motioning for Vikki to pour him a cup.

He opened the flip phone but never got a chance to say a word before the caller unloaded, "Are you aware storm troopers pounded on our door in the middle of the night and made us huddle in our robes in the parking lot? I want to get back into my condominium. No, make that, I demand to get back into my condominium immediately!"

"I'm sorry. The police evacuated the building to protect you. They're doing everything in . . . "

"Look, you overpaid flunky," the irate caller interrupted, "I'm a close personal friend of the mayor and a major campaign contributor. I don't want to hear your excuses." *Click*.

It was going to be a very long day.

Mayor Gates' limousine came to an abrupt stop a block from City Gate.

"Sir, the road is blocked by a hook and ladder."

Dozens of police and fire vehicles were marshaling outside the western entrance to the parking lot. Their emergency lights created an incredible kaleidoscope that bathed everything in a thousand shades of red and blue.

Gates leaned forward and slapped his hand against the back of the driver's seat. "Crank up the siren, Lucky. I'm not waiting for some parking attendant,"

The high-pitched wail attracted everyone's attention.

"Who's the clown?" A young cop directing traffic called out.

"Uh-oh . . . I'd recognize that limo with City of Chicago flags on the hood anywhere." Officer Stan Wazanewjeski had spent a couple of weeks on Gate's detail when one of the men got married. They were the two longest weeks of his career. "Move it! Move it!" he yelled to the driver as he banged on the fire truck's door. Right now. Get it outta the way!"

"Where?" The driver asked.

Wazanewjeski answered, "I don't care. Just get it outta here. I've gotta clear the road." He moved on to the next truck and repeated his command to move their rig.

The firefighters assumed an ambulance or some other emergency vehicle needed to get through and complied. They were not amused to see all the fuss was for Hiz Honor himself.

With every news crew, TV camera, and reporter in the city flocking to the scene, few were surprised the mayor was making an appearance.

Patrolman Bates saw Wazanewjeski salute the limo as it drove by and did the same. "Who was that?" He asked as he watched it park closer than any other vehicle in the lot. He didn't receive an answer because Wazanewjeski was now running after the black car.

"Good morning, Mister Mayor. District Three's command van is right over there." Wazanewjeski gestured towards two enormous white trucks. "The one with the doors closed."

The police department mobile communications center facing it had three satellite dishes on the roof. Its large side doors were wide open and the interior was illuminated by the glow from a half-dozen computer monitors. Four men sat at state-of-the-art workstations while talking on cellphones.

Mayor Gates was curious and walked over. *Hmmm. So this is what a million bucks buys.* He peered inside.

"I don't care if it's the middle of the night. I need those blueprints now. Then wake him up and tell him I'll have a squad car at his house in five minutes to drive him to his office to get them." A long-haired man wearing a Rolling Stones concert T-shirt threw up his arms in frustration.

Nick Sandoval's scruffy beard and casual dress made it obvious the technician was not a police officer. However, his demeanor left little doubt that he knew how to accomplish his assigned task.

The Stone's fan barked into his phone. "And tell him I want everything he has on this building—his whole work file. Everything."

The man sitting next to him held out his phone and yelled, "Yo, Nick! Problem. I've got some pinhead who says he doesn't have to cooperate."

Sandoval took the phone. "You don't know me, but I hold your future in my hand. So when my man says he wants it now, what he means is if you ever want to do business again in the City of Chicago, you will do what he says before you take another breath. So do you understand what he means when he says '*I want it now*?' Good." He handed the phone back. "Sam, I think he'll cooperate now."

Before he could sit down, his cellphone rang. "Sandoval. No, I don't know his name. I don't see what's so hard about finding the general contractor who built this place and bringing him here. And no, I don't care what time it is. I need him now. Not at 9 A.M.. NOW! Sandoval threw his arms in the air. "Idiots. I'm surrounded by a city full of idiots."

Gates stepped into the communications center. His bodyguards followed two steps behind. He cleared his throat, expecting someone to acknowledge his arrival.

The man nearest the mayor kept talking, "Chief, the City of Chicago appreciates your offer, but it looks like we won't need your fire trucks after all."

"Who's in charge here?" Gates interrupted.

The technician ignored him as he answered another phone call, "Yes, Sir, we're starting to release the ambulances." He turned and began typing. "Franklin Park," he pounded the keys until he found what he was looking for. "Franklin Park . . . here it is. They should be leaving any minute now."

The other men were also too busy talking on phones or typing on their computers to respond.

"Who's in charge?" Gates asked, much louder than the first time.

Recognizing the voice, a police officer wearing a white uniform shirt, denoting a rank of lieutenant or higher, stepped out of the passenger side door of the other van and walked over.

"Sid, what are you doing here?" Sixteenth District Police Commander Beeman asked. The two men had been friends since grammar school.

Gates didn't even say hello. "Ike, what happened?"

"They tell me a significant event caused a partial compression of the support structure—whatever that means. There are three engineers checking out what's left of the building right now. The Deputy District Chief said he was going to hold everyone else back until they say it's stable. That's all that I know for sure."

"Are they going inside?"

"Not yet, Sid. They're doing an exterior inspection first. We took two security guards over to Northwest Memorial Hospital. They were inside the tower when it collapsed. One says he has no idea what happened, and the other is incoherent. The talker said there was no one else in the building. We had a copter overhead a couple of minutes ago and I can show you the video they took." Without waiting for a response he said, "Henry, show the mayor the film."

Mayor Gates shot his men a look and both scrambled to pull a chair out for him to sit in while he waited for the techie to bring up the pictures.

"Here's the approach from the west. The camera is panning the building from bottom to top. See how all the windows are broken. We're looking straight down now. The air conditioning unit and elevator equipment appear to have been crushed. This would be consistent with a downward force being applied to the building. Even more interesting is how perfectly symmetrical the damage is. The columns are bent at the same angle. Only the rebar cores are holding them together."

The mayor looked confused.

"You can see them sticking out—the steel reinforcing rods." He pointed to the screen. "I've never seen anything like this before. Well, that's about it except for one last shot of the north side of the building. They all face the Kennedy Expressway, you know."

"Yes, I know," the mayor was curt. "Ike, you said you have three engineers at the building. Are they any good?"

"They tell me they're the best." Beeman took a small notebook out of his shirt pocket and thumbed through it. "McBarker, Haynes, and Clemson. I talked to them before they left, but they said they've never seen anything like this. They have radios, but they haven't called in yet. And that brings you up to date."

"Oh yeah," he continued, "Sid, you should know one of the first police units gave the order to evacuate the entire complex. He figured if one fell down, the others might too. The boys here," he swept the room with his arm, "got calls out to every building inspector with structural experience the city has. I don't think anything else is going to fall down, but I sure wouldn't want to make that call. There are a lot of unhappy people gathered in the parking lot across the street. We're starting to organize shelter for them right now—rooms at local hotels. There's not much else we can to do until we know the other buildings are safe."

"Let's keep them out for now. I would rather have them mad than dead," the mayor reflected.

"Yep. That's what I was thinking." Beeman looked at his watch. "It'll be rush hour soon, and we've got the highway closed. The building is set back far enough the road would be safe, but if we open it there'd be a gaper's block way past Rosemont."

"Leave it closed." Gates answered. "Is there anywhere I can get a cup of coffee?"

"I've got a fresh pot brewing in my command van," Beeman replied.

The two men walked out leaving behind the four technicians who continued working.

"Yo, Nick," Sam called out, "they found the general contractor. He lives up in Wilmette but everything's in his office downtown—plans, specs, sub-contractors bids—three file cabinets full. How do you want to get him there? A police escort?"

"Not quick enough. We need that data. Can he e-mail it?" Sandoval asked.

"We might not need that," Frank Zellner, who was sitting at the far console, interrupted. "I've got the Building Departments' permit set of blueprints coming by copter right now. They should be here in about fifteen minutes."

"That the first good news we've gotten," Sandoval said.

"Even better. There are a few dozen cardboard boxes coming with them. They grabbed everything that said 'City Gate' without worrying what was in 'em," Zellner added.

"What do you mean? Sandoval asked. "For the whole complex?"

"Don't know. They woke some guy up and told him we wanted everything they had."

The crowd at the command center continued to grow. The five-member State Emergency Management rapid-response team arrived and joined a couple of arson investigators who were watching a re-run of the helicopter video while expressing their eagerness to get inside the building.

Outside, the number of news vans and reporters also continued to grow. Each television station staked out a little piece of the parking lot where their anchorperson could broadcast with Building Eight illuminated by dozens of floodlights from the emergency vehicles glowing in the background.

The sun was starting to break the horizon over Lake Michigan. It would take a few more minutes for it to rise high enough in the sky to reflect off the mirrored windows on the remaining seven buildings. It promised to be a magnificent sight.

"I'm Nicole Marche reporting for Channel One News, your number one choice for news. I'm standing in the parking lot at the City Gate office and condominium complex. Behind me is what is left of one of the office towers."

"This is Doug Randall reporting live for Channel 3 On the Spot News at City Gate where one of the buildings collapsed early this morning."

"Good morning, Chicago, and welcome to Channel 6, Your News Source," A deep, masculine voice provided the voiceover introduction. "We're interrupting your regularly scheduled program to bring you live coverage of a developing story on the city's far northwest side."

The monotonous rhythm of dozens of idling diesel engines was drowned out by a deeper rumble—one that grew louder by the second as it rolled across the parking lot. Every head turned to see what was happening. All the television cameras shifted away from their perfectly made-up news anchors and zoomed in on the building.

An intense flash of light exploded from it, blinding everyone. The purity of the burst played havoc with the camcorders' light meters, burning out many of them. The asphalt parking lot began to shake, not a lot, but enough to get everyone's attention. Several people fell to the ground as the roar grew in intensity, battering their unprotected ears. Many more dropped to the pavement and covered their mouths with their handkerchiefs in an attempt to protect their lungs from the approaching black cloud. In a matter of seconds, the air was thick with dust and the sounds of choking and coughing. Debris rained down freely and the earth trembled.

The smart ones began to pray before they were blinded. As the ripping of metal and cracking of concrete grew louder, assaulting every ear, even the most stubborn asked God to make it stop.

And then it did. For a moment, the silence was total. There was no sound even from the dozens of diesel engines that had been idling a moment earlier. Their motors stopped when the dust cloud choked off their carburetors.

"Thank you, God, for saving us!" a woman yelled out. When the air cleared, the ground was littered with people hacking as they struggled to breathe; many were vomiting. Everything was covered with a layer of pulverized concrete.

A thick cloud of dust hovered over the spot where Tower Eight had been. Then the wind shifted and a strong gust from the east kicked up, blowing the dust toward the forest preserves. The building no longer existed.

"Chief, look!" someone shouted.

In the distance, three shadowy figures could be seen standing in the middle of the sea of debris. "We've got survivors!"

"Rescue one! Roll out!" Battalion Chief Venture shouted. The driver closed his eyes and prayed, *Please God, let it start.* The ambulance started on the first try and a cheer went up when he threw the rig into gear.

"Engine Company One, go! Go! Go!" The motors in all six trucks roared to life. Inside them firemen were breathing oxygen from tanks strapped to their backs. As soon as they drove away, Venture turned his attention to the dozens of injured news people.

"Let's get a triage set up. There's a whole lotta of people having trouble breathing."

The ambulance got within a hundred feet of the trio before debris blocked their way. The EMTs jumped out the back door and started running.

A few seconds later, the fire trucks arrived. Before they even stopped, their crews leapt off and began connecting hoses to the pumper truck. The firemen looked surreal wearing elaborate breathing apparatuses and bright yellow helmets as they unrolled their hoses towards the smoking hole. The collapse was so sudden, unexpected, and morbidly magnificent, they couldn't wait to get to it.

The inspectors watched in shocked awe as the building collapsed. They were close enough to touch it yet made no attempt to flee from the danger. A violent blizzard of paper was followed by a dense cloud of gray-black dust that blew out of a thousand cracks and smashed windows. One-inch thick steel reinforcing bars screamed as they sheared off, causing the exterior walls to collapse onto the sidewalk below. The horrific roar grew louder as interior support columns buckled then failed. Massive beams groaned as they were ground into powder.

The building's death dance accelerated. Huge chunks of concrete were thrown through the air as floor after floor slammed into each other. Everything was crushed—desks, file cabinets, and computers—as the building settled into the basement. The ground quivered as the earth swallowed the last traces of the tower.

When the roar of destruction subsided, Fred ran his hands over his face to reassure himself he was still alive. He stared as his fingers and then at his palms. He touched his wedding ring and looked at his watch—still ticking. He shook his head and started laughing when he realized his clothes weren't even dirty. "How?" He asked aloud as he looked at the ground around them. Everything he could see was covered with debris—shards of broken glass, hunks of concrete, twisted steel rods. Even the swirling cloud of filth seemed to have parted around them. Fred struggled to comprehend what had happened. "How?"

He panicked when he saw Clemson and Haynes on their knees until he realized they were praying. Billy looked at him and said, "He destroyed the building to end the killing." His voice trembled with emotion.

"You saw what I saw! I knew I didn't imagine it!" Philo jumped up and shouted. "You saw him in the basement just before the explosion. Fred, you saw him too, didn't you?" Philo grabbed him by the shoulders. "I can see it on your face. You saw him!"

Before Fred could answer, the paramedics arrived. They found the three men standing in the center of a perfectly clean circle of the parking lot.

Amazed, the lead EMT, John Anderson said, "I don't know who your guardian angel is, but I want him covering my back."

Angel? Fred was confused. *Had he seen him too?*

"We're all right. None of us is injured. Look." Philo waved his arms in the air. "There isn't a scratch on me—on any of us!" He spun around shouting, "It's a miracle! Alleluia! Hey Billy, it's like the song. We saw him 'loose the fateful lightning of his terrible swift sword.'"

Two paramedics tried to calm Philo down.

"No way. There is no way you guys are OK. You should at least be having trouble breathing. Choking . . . coughing?" Anderson persisted. "Even with masks on you had to have sucked a couple of pounds of dust into your lungs."

Fred could see the man's facemask was soiled after only a few dirty breaths.

"Honest, I feel fine," Billy stated just before a medic slipped an oxygen mask on him.

"Can you breathe OK?" Anderson asked him.

He gave a thumbs up.

Philo tried without success to keep a medic from pulling a mask over his mouth so he could tell everyone what happened. He was so excited he kept praising God even though the oxygen mask muffled his voice so much he couldn't be understood.

"Those guys were standing right here when it collapsed." Fred heard someone say behind him. He turned and saw several firefighters dragging hoses towards the smoking hole. They started back in disbelief.

"Your turn." Anderson held a mask in front of Fred.

"No, not yet. I want to call my wife and let her know I'm alive." He tried to reason with him.

"There will be plenty of time to call her later."

"Two minutes . . . please."

"Nope." He pulled the mask down tight on Fred. "You're going back to my rig so I can check you out. Then you're going to the hospital. You can call her from there. Now get on."

Fred waved off the gurney and motioned he would walk to the ambulance.

Billy also refused to be carried and Philo was so animated Anderson was tempted to sedate and strap him down. As he moved from man to man, Philo's arms flailed through the air as he pantomimed what he had just seen.

You'd be dancing around too if you saw what we just saw, Fred thought.

The two paramedics planted firm grips on Philo's shoulders and led him towards the ambulances. Another followed carrying a green oxygen bottle.

They passed dozens more firefighters rushing by in the opposite direction and arrived at the ambulances just as the first orange-red sliver of the sun appeared above the trees. Thousands of small prisms incorporated into the mirrored walls of the remaining buildings' exteriors began catching the sun's rays and showered everything with an incredible rainbow of colors. City Gate was waking up . . . at least seven-eighths of it was.

CHAPTER 3

DOROTHY PIENKOS BEGAN her Monday routine before the sun came up because it was very important for her to be on time. She must arrive no later than 8 A.M. because babies' lives depended on her being prompt. She chose her outfit with great care—a royal blue skirt with a matching blazer and a plain white blouse—wanting to convey a professional image of confidence and wisdom. A pair of comfortable shoes completed her ensemble. She looked in the mirror and was pleased. She looked more like an executive secretary, or maybe even a successful middle manager, than the retired store clerk she was.

She walked down to the corner, took her fare card out of her purse, and joined the dozen commuters waiting for a Harlem Avenue bus. Most of the crowd at the bus stop was girls going to high school. Dorothy knew how futile it was for a gray-haired lady to try to strike up a conversation with teenagers who cared for little except boys, clothes, music, and boys. She could only wonder if she would see any of them again later on in the day.

Two changes of the traffic light later, a CTA bus pulled up to her corner. She did not try to board until the gaggle of girls had pushed inside. She knew from experience they lacked the manners to let a senior citizen board first. Taking a seat in the front, near the driver, she closed her eyes and started praying as the bus rambled along. *Father, grant me the strength to do Your work today. Do not let me get discouraged. Put Your words into my mouth and make me Your instrument. Our Father, who art in heaven.*

"Irving Park," the driver called out as he approached her stop. Dorothy needed to transfer to complete her trip. She got off and hurried across the intersection to catch her next bus. This bus, however, was packed and she had to stand for the entire ride. She grabbed a safety pole, but was jostled by the ebb and flow of riders every time the bus stopped. The crowd seemed to be buzzing about something—some kind of disaster had happened early that morning. Dorothy did her best to ignore them all as she talked with God.

Fifteen minutes later the driver called out, "Elston."

"Off," several riders, including Dorothy, shouted as they began their struggle to get to the exit doors. She doubted whether this driver even heard her say thank you as she squeezed past the crowd attempting to board. Now all she had to do was walk south two blocks and she would be ready to do His work as a sidewalk counselor outside an abortion mill.

There were five women gathered on the sidewalk in front of the one-story brick building, between the "No firearms allowed" and "Trespassers will be prosecuted" signs when Dorothy arrived. Two surveillance cameras were recording their every move and the women made it a point to smile and wave to them. Their conversation was so intense no one noticed her arrival.

"It was God's answer to our prayers. And He smote it into dust just like He did in the Old Testament." Vanessa was a tomboy at heart and ground her shoe into the sidewalk for emphasis. At fifty-five, she was also the youngest of the group and favored black shoes, pants, blouses, and sweaters. Her one concession to femininity was her long, jet-black hair, which swept across her back. "Yep, He smote it into dust."

In contrast, the group's informal leader, Sandy, always wore a dress—often one she had sewn herself—and high heels. The matching hat atop her styled white hair made her look like a grandmother from a 1950s television show. She spoke next, "They had that evil looking woman from The Council of Women on TV screaming that a lifetime of work was destroyed and someone would have to pay. And I believe the correct word is smite."

"Smite? Destroyed? What happened?" Dorothy asked.

"You mean you didn't hear the good news?" Sandy asked.

"Don't you listen to the morning news?" Vanessa sounded surprised. "The biggest abortion mill in all Chicagoland, the big one by the airport, collapsed early this morning. It's gone."

"Gone?" Dorothy sounded confused. "What do you mean gone?"

"Gone . . . kaput . . . *fineto*. The big, fancy new building that is—was— the headquarters of every abortion mill plaguing this city. The one with the mirrored walls we picketed a while back is now a pile of broken concrete and smashed glass." Vanessa answered.

"What happened? Was there a fire? An explosion?"

"Well, the reporters say they don't know why it collapsed. They just keep repeating it collapsed for no apparent reason." She again ground her shoe into the sidewalk. "But we know why it fell down," Vanessa said with a smug grin.

Sandy winked knowingly at her prayer partner. "I heard that handsome young newsman say it will be weeks before they know why it collapsed. But *we* all know why it fell down."

"It really fell down? That evil building is really gone?" Dorothy still couldn't believe it was true. "I . . . I mean we all prayed they would stop killing babies there, but I never thought . . . "

"Oh, did you doubt God would answer our prayers?" Sandy teased her.

"No. I knew He would," Dorothy was firm. "But I didn't expect something so dramatic . . . so . . . ."

"So Old Testament," Vanessa said with a sly grin.

"I'm sorry I sound confused," Dorothy said, "but I don't have time to watch TV before I ride down here. And I didn't notice the newspaper headlines because I was praying on the bus. But what you're telling me is so . . . so . . . ." She searched for the right word.

"Miraculous," the Hansen sisters, Ruth and Kaye, responded in harmony.

"But if the reporters say they don't know what happened," Sandy hesitated for a moment, "why do you keep saying you do?"

"Because we do, dear. All the reporters saw was a huge flash of light followed by the building collapsing. We witnessed what happened inside. We saw Archangel Michael destroy that unholy place with his flaming sword of justice." Sandy continued, "And we watched him shepherd the souls of the slaughtered innocents home to heaven in our dreams."

"Dreams!" Dorothy gasped. "Oh my! I have goose bumps. I had the same incredible dream last night, but I was afraid to say anything because I thought you would think I was making it up. Everything seemed so real. It was as though I was standing there. I saw the warrior angel swinging a flaming sword. I saw the dead babies at his feet. I saw the bright flash and the building crumbled into dust around him." She paused to study their faces, "You're not pulling my leg, are you?"

"No, dear. We all had the same dream," Sandy smiled, "and yes, everything you saw really happened." The other women smiled and nodded in agreement.

"It's true," Kaye stated. "I had a dream where I watched Archangel Michael destroy that building with one swing of his flaming sword."

"I also saw an angel of the Lord knock it down with his flaming sword," Ruth said. "That's how I know why it fell down."

Dorothy took a deep breath. "It seems so hard to believe. I mean, we've been praying for so long. I thought the dream about an angel wearing armor and swinging a flaming sword was symbolic, like in Ephesians 6: 'And take the helmet of salvation, and the sword of the Spirit, which is the word of God.'"

"It wasn't symbolic," Ruth replied with great conviction. "It really happened. God heard our prayers and sent an angel to do His bidding."

"Archangel." Kaye corrected her twin sister. "It was Michael the Archangel who knocked it down."

"That's what I said. God sent His *Ark*-angel," she emphasized the first syllable," to smote that evil building. Then the trumpets blew and the building crashed to the ground. Like when Joshua sounded his horn and the walls of Jericho came a tumbling down. Yep, some good Old Testament smoting."

"Smiting." Kaye stated.

"Who played the trumpets?" Vanessa teased. "I'd like to hire them to serenade us here today."

The women laughed at that comment.

"Was anyone in the building?" Dorothy asked with genuine concern.

"No, the news said the security guards escaped. And it happened in the middle of the night, so no one else was there," Ruth answered.

Vanessa raised her arms, "Praise the Lord. No one died when that evil building collapsed. And no babies will ever be killed there again."

A chorus of amen's rose up.

"Well, we'd better be extra careful here today," Sandy warned. "I've been here since seven thirty and I haven't seen anyone arrive. But I would imagine they're liable to be in a foul mood what with their world headquarters being destroyed and all. Remember the Constitution guarantees our right to be here, but that doesn't mean that they won't harass us."

"I wouldn't put anything past someone who would murder an unborn baby," Vanessa said.

Sandy held up her Bible. "Let's start with some readings, then I'll close with a prayer. Jeremiah 1:5; 'Before I formed you in the womb I knew you, and before you were born I consecrated you.' Deuteronomy 30:19; 'I set before you life and death . . . Choose life then, that you and your descendants may live.'"

"Don't forget Psalm 139," Kaye said, "verses 13-16, 'For you created my inmost being; you knit me together in my mother's womb. I praise you because I am fearfully and wonderfully made . . . your eyes saw my unformed body. All the days ordained for me were written in your book before one of them came to be.'"

They then recited the Lord's Prayer with Dorothy adding after they finished, "'for Thine is the kingdom, the power, and the glory, forever, Amen.'"

"Amen." everyone repeated.

"Now let's see how many babies we can save today." Vanessa opened her large purse and took out a supply of fetal development brochures. "OK girls, you know the drill. We can break up into three teams, so let's pick partners. Dorothy, would you stand with me by the driveway?"

Kaye smiled to her twin sister who nodded back. "If no one objects, Ruth and I will take the door." They liked to stand in front of the entrance because the sight of two elderly identical twins, dressed in identical calico dresses, always made people pause. And if they paused, their baby could be saved.

"Don't forget." Vanessa said, "You can't block anyone's access."

"But we can sure talk to them as they walk in," the sisters replied at the same time.

"I don't think they have any 'deathscorts' working today," their white-haired leader said, referring to the escorts the clinic hired to herd the pregnant women through the door before the counselors could speak to them, "but I wouldn't be surprised if they showed up later."

"Well I'm not waiting for them," Sandy stated. "Krista, why don't we walk down to the corner and wait by the bus stop? So many of these poor girls ride the bus down here."

Five of the women were lifelong Catholics and each took a rosary out of her purse or pocket. They would pray the Hail Mary aloud until the pregnant women, many little more than children themselves, came to keep their appointment with the abortionist. They would offer a rosary and try to get her to stop and talk.

Sandy was the exception. She, too, was born Catholic but became an Evangelical Protestant when she discovered the saving power of Grace. Even though she was outnumbered, she testified so strongly to her faith she won the respect of all of the other members of the group. When she wasn't praying to save babies, she asked God to open the eyes of her friends to His gift of Grace. She suspected they were praying just as fervently for her conversion back to Catholicism, but took great comfort in knowing it was their common faith in Jesus Christ that united them.

Eight A.M. came and the lights went on in the Irving Park Woman's Clinic. Nowhere on their weathered sign did they even hint they were—as the Council of Women preferred to phrase it when pushed—'a pregnancy termination center.' A uniformed security guard took his usual place standing behind the bullet-resistant glass window in a little alcove next to the front door. No one could gain entry without his approval.

He always kept one hand on a red button that would immediately lock the interior door if the perimeter was breached. The last thing the clinic wanted was a blitz, where pro-lifers would swarm the waiting room, pass out literature, and attempt to talk women out of terminating their pregnancies. Some of the blitzers even tried to convince the workers to quit. Worst of all, they would refuse to leave until the police arrived. Their goal was to cause such a disruption no patients could be seen that day. Everyone knew the clinic only made money if the woman had "the procedure." The security guards were constantly threatened with automatic termination if they ever let a blitz get past them.

Kaye and Ruth made a point of waving and smiling to Bob the guard every Monday morning even though he never returned the gesture.

Ruth stared through the window trying to get Bob's attention. "I keep praying for that young man to find a better job. Can you imagine what it must be like to have to stand there all day protecting abortionists from little old ladies?" Kaye asked.

They both laughed and began praying the rosary with enough gusto anyone hiding inside would be sure to hear it.

A little after eight the first customers arrived in a beat-up old Chevy trailing a cloud of blue smoke behind it. They stopped for a few seconds in the no-parking zone in front of the clinic then pulled forward to the parking lot's entrance. They paused again and seemed confused by the ominous signs posted on both sides of the lot's open gates: No Obstructing Traffic 720 ILCS 5/12-5/A and No Trespassing Allowed 720 ILCS 5/21-3. The driver shook his head and pulled forward about a half-block until he came to an open parking space on the street.

It was a godsend whenever they parked on the street instead of in the lot because the counselors could meet and talk to the mother-to-be curbside before she could commit to entering the building. As the pregnant woman was being helped out of her car by the driver, the front door rescue team sprang into action.

"Excuse me, Mom and Dad. My name is Kaye. This is my sister Ruth. Could we please speak with you for a minute?" The couple paused. Their puzzled expressions showed they had no idea what the odd-looking women wanted.

"We would like to show you some pictures of what your baby looks like. Let's see, you look about five months pregnant. I'll bet you can already feel your baby kicking."

The woman looked very embarrassed. She had come to end an inconvenient pregnancy, not to hear how a human being was growing inside her. Her male companion stared at the sidewalk, unwilling to look at the pictures that were thrust in front of them.

"Look, you can see how developed your baby is. Look, you can see all of your baby's fingers. Is your baby a boy or a girl?" Kaye asked as she pointed to the picture. "Look at how your baby has tiny little toes. We can take you to our crisis pregnancy center right down the street. They will do an ultrasound for free, so you can see how beautiful your baby is."

"They will give you a free picture of your beautiful baby that you can show to your family and friends," Ruth added.

"Here's a picture of how your baby will look in just four more weeks . . . you can even see your baby's fingernails. Our center is only a couple of blocks away. We will give you and your baby all the help you need. We will help you after your baby is born.

We love babies at our center. But do you know what they do in this clinic?" Kaye asked.

No answer.

"They kill babies in there—beautiful babies like yours. Have you thought about what abortion does?" Kaye didn't give her a chance to reply. "Have you thought about how abortion will affect your life and your health? Have you thought about how much your beautiful baby will suffer? Did you know that there are over two dozen malpractice suits on file against this clinic?"

Ruth held out a photograph of an ambulance in front of the clinic and spoke. "We've seen paramedics take women to real hospitals after their abortions went bad. Let me show you these summaries of the malpractice suits against this clinic. These are all taken from the public records. You can look them up at the courthouse yourself if you think that one word I am telling you is not the truth. Look, here's the doctor's name, this clinic's name, the date, and the name of the young lady who had the abortion. See, it says deceased after her name. She died after getting an abortion here."

The couple seemed frozen. When they made their appointment over the phone, they had been promised a quick, simple solution to their problem. No one told them the consequences.

The young woman began to cry. "Our baby has fingers and toes," she sobbed as she ran her hands over her large belly.

Kaye and Ruth were so committed to saving the couple's baby they didn't see four police cars pull up and park across the street from the clinic.

Sandy and Krista, however, had been watching traffic and noticed their arrival. It was not at all unusual to have a couple of squad cars stop and watch for a few minutes, so they both waved to the officers. The officers often waved back, but today something was different.

That's odd, Sandy thought. *I can't remember the last time they got out of their cars.*

"Oh my," was all Krista could muster when two police officers wearing bullet proof vests stepped out of each car. "Oh my indeed," Sandy added as the policemen put on riot helmets and formed up in a line across the street.

Since retiring, Phil had little to do to keep himself occupied except watching TV, watching cars drive by, and watching people walk down the sidewalk in front his second-floor apartment. He lived across the street from the clinic, over a store that had been vacant as long as he could recall. There were many vacant stores in the neighborhood—the Mom-and-Pop grocery store closed first, then the corner drugstore. The only business he could remember opening on the block during the last ten years was that woman's clinic across the street, and they were only open one day a week. He thought it was a shame they tore down three greystone two flats to make a parking lot which they then surrounded with giant gates and a ten-foot-high security fence with large spirals of razor wire on top of it. They used to call it concertina wire back when he was in the army and it always reminded him of the Nazi death camps he helped liberate half a century ago. The entire building, in fact, reminded him of a military outpost on the edge of enemy territory, especially the way they bricked up all but one window and fortified the roof.

Phil was sad because both he and the neighborhood were getting old. He had seen many changes that made him nervous to venture out after dark. One of the few things he did look forward to was Monday mornings because there was always a group of well-dressed women his own age gathered across the street from his apartment. He told himself someday he would work up the nerve to go over and introduce himself.

When Phil saw the police cars pull up he guessed something big was up and dug out his old camcorder, a huge monster that took open-reel videotapes. The batteries were long dead, so he plugged the adapter into the outlet and began to record the scene that was unfolding right outside his front door.

Sophie always arrived late at the clinic, but she had a great excuse. Even though she was one-hundred years old, almost deaf, and darn near blind in one eye, she insisted on walking to the abortion mill using a walker to maintain her balance. It took her almost an hour to get there, including a stop at the donut store to buy a bag of goodies for her friends. She also bought a jelly-filled donut for the security guard, even though he always ignored her when she offered it to him.

The young couple Kaye and Ruth were counseling saw the police and became nervous.

"We're leaving," the man said. "My wife and I, we're leaving now."

"Wait, take this. It's a brochure telling about our crisis pregnancy center and how we can help you. We have real doctors there and we will give you free assistance with your baby. Our clinic is only a block away," Kaye said as they turned to get into their parked car.

The man grabbed the brochure and held the door open for his pregnant wife.

"Thank you . . . I want my baby to live. Thank you. We will go to your clinic," the woman sobbed as he closed the door.

"Praise God, a save," Ruth and Kaye shouted.

A chorus of amen's rose up from her fellow counselors as the wall of blue uniforms started to march across Elston Avenue. They stopped just short of the sidewalk.

Lieutenant Frank Warren knew his precinct had enough of a crime problem that they could not spare the resources to harass these old women, but he had his orders. He stood off to the side and announced on a bullhorn, "You are ordered to disburse. If you do not disburse, you will be arrested. You have exactly two minutes to vacate the area or you will be arrested." The police officers stepped onto the curb and stood toe-to-toe with the sidewalk counselors; each towered over the elderly women.

The women were too shocked to respond. Their silence was broken when Warren announced, "One minute and forty-five seconds."

Dorothy tried to control her anger as she spoke. "The Constitution of the United States guarantees our right to peacefully assemble. The Supreme Court has ruled . . .".

"One minute and thirty-seconds," he barked.

No one, including Warren, noticed Sophie as she rounded the corner. Her late husband had been a policeman, as had her oldest son, so she assumed the officers were friends from the department coming to visit. She forgot about the pain in her legs and smiled. *I would have bought more treats if I knew we would be having company . . . maybe some coffee too.*

She walked up to the one who appeared to be in charge and offered, "Would you like a donut." Something seemed to snap in the Lieutenant at the perceived insult. In front of his startled men, he grabbed Sophie, spun her around and handcuffed her in with one well-rehearsed movement, then said, "You're under arrest."

Unable to hold onto her walker Sophie fell to the pavement, banging her forehead.

"Throw her in the squad," Warren ordered, but no one moved. "I want you to arrest any protesters who are still here in thirty seconds."

Still no one moved. The officers were too surprised at what they were seeing and the counselors were too dumbfounded to respond.

When Sophie realized what happened, she struggled with the handcuffs and kicked her legs in protest. One feeble kick grazed Warren's pants.

The other six women surrounded her. "Sophie, are you OK?" they cried out almost as one as they struggled to help her to her feet. They lifted her up by her elbows because her arms were handcuffed behind her back.

"What did she do?" "How dare you do that to her!" "Don't you know who she is?"

A young woman who had stopped to watch yelled at the police, "She's an old lady . . . you can't arrest her."

"You two! Take her to your car!" Warren pointed to two of his men, "Drive her to the station *now*, I want her booked for assaulting a police officer."

Looking very embarrassed, neither moved.

"I said throw her in the squad! She kicked me . . . I want her arrested for assault. *NOW*," he screamed.

Finally, two officers walked over. They apologized for what happened as they helped her walk towards their car. "Are you OK, Ma'am? Would you like us to drive you to the hospital?"

"We can call an ambulance for you if you're hurt," the second offered.

Warren raged, "That woman assaulted me! Stop treating her like she's special! Get her to the station and book her. And if anyone tries to stop you, arrest them too!"

The remaining counselors continued their barrage of questions, their voices rising in anger as they watched the most gentle woman they had ever met being escorted away in handcuffs.

In an attempt to quiet them down, the Lieutenant said, "The security guard at the clinic called to complain that he felt threatened by your presence. Therefore, you must immediately disburse or you will also be arrested."

"Now let me get this straight," Dorothy glared at Warren, "Bob, the six-foot two-inch tall, two-hundred-forty pound security guard, who is wearing a pistol, a stun gun, and a billy club, was threatened by a five-foot tall, eighty-pound, hundred-year-old woman carrying a bag of jelly donuts?"

The other police officers tried to suppress their laughter.

"That's it. Arrest them all," The Lieutenant fumed. "They had their chance."

The women had long ago planned what they would do if the police ever tried to arrest them. They sat on the sidewalk, linked arms, and began praying as loud as they could. "Our Father, who art in heaven . . . "

Vanessa sniffled and tears ran down her cheeks. Dorothy leaned over and whispered, "Be strong, dear."

"Thy kingdom come." The Hanson sisters smiled as they recited the words; their eyes sparkled in defiance as they sat ramrod straight and prayed with vigor. *We must be as brave as Christians in the Coliseum*, Ruth thought.

This many police cars attract attention, and a crowd soon formed. Most of the people in the neighborhood had seen the ladies praying in front of the mill and many shouted encouragement. A young couple stepped off the sidewalk and joined the women sitting on the street in prayer. More than a few began to jeer and taunt the police.

"Pick on somebody your own age."

"Hey, cop, you got Bonnie. Where's Clyde?"

It took a few minutes, but the two officers were able to help Sophie into the backseat of their squad. "I'll sit in back with her." The younger officer said. A moment later they were moving.

Patrolman Walsh removed her handcuffs as soon as they could were out of sight of his superior. "Your forehead is bleeding, Ma'am, so we're going to take you to the hospital. I can't apologize enough for the Lieutenant. He's not himself today. I think he's under a lot of pressure from his boss or something. I'm sorry, but we have to take you to the station after they patch you up. Is there someone you would like me to call?"

"Well my husband is dead, so is my son—they were both Chicago police officers all of their lives you know—now all I have left is my grandson."

The driver, Rick Zelermann, was too embarrassed to turn around. He sighed and shook his head. He had twenty-five years on the force and wondered if he knew her son.

Walsh's mouth dropped and he too sighed. *I don't know what to say,* he thought.

"What happened? Sophie asked. "Someone die?"

"I'm so sorry about what happened, Mrs . . . . er."

"Call me Granny. And think nothing of it. Anybody can get a bee under their bonnet." She rubbed her wrists. "Don't feel like anything's broken."

"Would you like to use my cellphone to call your grandson?" Officer Walsh asked.

"Thanks a bunch young man. But could you please dial for me? Those numbers are so small." She recited the digits for him.

Zelermann glanced in the rear view mirror to see if he recognized her. *Where do I know her from?*

"I'm sorry, Ma'am. I tried three times but your grandson's phone is busy. Don't worry, we're almost at the hospital. I'll keep trying while you see the doctor."

Back at the protest, Phil continued to video everything, often zooming in on the lieutenant whose face was so red he looked as if his head would explode like an overripe tomato. He opened his window so he could also record the noise of the crowd as well as cop's screaming rant.

"Pick on somebody your own age!" The young couple sitting with the counselors kept screaming.

"Go arrest some real criminals!" A Puerto Rican teenager yelled as he gave the finger.

Traffic in both directions was blocked by the surging crowd, and a number of drivers started blowing their horns, adding to the noise. This attracted even more people, many of whom joined the women in singing "Amazing Grace" with great vigor. Most seemed to know at least a few words of the hymn and repeated them over and over, "Amazing Grace how sweet the sound, that saved a wretch like me."

The bystanders switched to a chant of "Let them go; let them go." The group increased in size until people lined both sides of the street, surrounding the police officers. A group of young men wearing gang colors began to rock one of the squad cars.

"Backup! Call for backup!" Warren yelled. The officers were starting to get nervous as the mood of the crowd was getting ugly in a hurry. Someone hidden from view threw a bottle that struck an officer on his back. This was followed by a hail of small rocks.

"Unholster your guns," Warren yelled to his officers. Then he shouted in his megaphone, "I order everyone to immediately disburse, or you will all be arrested."

Three different officers called in to their precinct to report they were losing control of the crowd. A steady hail of rocks flew through the air. Some missed the policemen and struck the counselors who were still praying with their arms linked. An officer jumped to the side to dodge a rock, tripped over one of the women, and fell face down on top of them.

"Officer down! Officer down! Thirty-eight hundred block of North Elston Avenue!" an officer yelled into his radio.

Lieutenant Warren tried to quell the crowd by firing a warning shot into the air.

"Gunshots fired," Patrolman Gutierrez shouted into his radio.

Chaos and confusion broke out everywhere when people trying to run away ran into those who wanted to stay and watch. Rocks and bottles continued to rain down on the crowd as yet another shot rang out. The windows of the police cars were smashed by someone with a baseball bat and one erupted in flames. A cloud of black, acrid smoke spread over the street.

They could tell reinforcements were getting close because the wail of sirens was getting louder, but the officers knew they couldn't wait. They formed a defensive circle and began to pepperspray the crowd with abandon. Innocent people, their eyes blinded, tried to stagger to safety.

The crowd scattered into gangways and alleys. One person, however, a longtime friend of Sophie's, hid behind an ancient oak tree and took out her cellphone. Her call to the local news radio station's tip desk got through just as Mayor Gates's press conference from the scene of the City Gate building collapse was starting.

Most reporters dream of the day when they can put a politician with an attitude on the spot and bring him down a few notches on national TV. It could even be their ticket to becoming a network news anchor. The room chosen for the press conference was the grand ballroom at City Gate's luxurious clubhouse and spa. It was a marble-clad two-story building located across the Kennedy Expressway from the office towers, and it was overflowing with reporters and their crews. A sea of microphones blocked the view of the podium.

Outside, hundreds of displaced condominium owners voiced their anger to anyone who would listen . . . and the pack of reporters was eager to interview them. Police tried to direct the homeowners to buses that would take them to nearby hotels, but a lot of pajama-clad people refused to leave until they had their say.

"I want to know when we can go back home," an elderly man demanded. "All of my wife's medications are up there." He pointed towards one of the upper floors in Building Two.

"I have to get into my unit to shower, shave, and get dressed! The police can't expect me to go to work in my robe and slippers," another fumed.

A middle-aged man grabbed the microphone next and announced, "With God as my witness, I will never vote Democratic again." The crowd roared its agreement.

Jackie Jefferson stood off in the shadows and studied the crowd, looking for the right opportunity. He knew both his timing and his stooge had to be perfect to become the part of a story this big. He sprang into action the moment he spotted his ticket to the microphone—an elderly woman with a cane walking towards him.

"Excuse me, Madame." He offered his arm to her. "Please allow me to assist you," Jackie smiled his sincerest fake smile.

"Why, thank you, young man. But all I really want to do is lie down. I heard there was a bus waiting to take us to a hotel."

"No problem. I can take you to the bus. But wouldn't you rather first tell your family and friends that you survived this morning's disaster?"

Inside the clubhouse, Mayor Gates's press conference began a few minutes after nine with the Fire Commissioner reading a prepared statement detailing what happened but giving very little information about why.

"As you are all aware, Tower Eight at City Gate has collapsed. This was an office building which was fully occupied by the Council of Women world headquarters and a clinic. Let me start by saying, there is no truth to the rumor that an airplane crashed into it. Bomb and arson teams, including specialists from the Federal Bureau of Investigation are combing the wreckage. However, at this time we do not have any theories on what caused the building to collapse. Fortunately, this incident occurred during the night and there were no fatalities."

The mayor took the podium and pretty much repeated what had just been said, adding extra emphasis when he thanked the heroic efforts of the Chicago Police and Fire Departments and repeating for a third time that there was not one fatality. "We got lucky today. There was a team of structural engineers from the Department of Buildings right next to Tower Eight when it collapsed, but they do not appear to be seriously injured. I have been advised they are undergoing tests at Northwest Memorial Hospital and we hope to have an update on their condition after the doctors are finished with them." He closed with, "We have a few minutes for a couple of questions."

Every reporter and news anchor's hand went up. Having an eye for the ladies, the mayor selected a long-legged blonde in a short skirt sitting in the first row who was holding a cellphone to her ear.

"Mayor Gates, Jillian Morrow, Radio News 710. Could you please comment on the riot that was sparked when your grandmother was arrested for assaulting a police officer?"

It would take a lot to get the collapse of an eight-story building off the front page of the newspapers but the late editions of the *Chicago Tribunal* screamed, "ARREST OF MAYOR'S GRANNY CAUSES RIOT" while the *Daily Sun* went with "100 YEAR OLD GRANNY GATES' ARREST SPARKS RIOT."

CHAPTER 4

WITH THE KENNEDY Expressway closed in both directions, Chicago was waking up to one of the worst traffic jams ever. It was an easy decision to use medevac air ambulances to transport the engineers to the hospital. Fred McBarker tried without success to look out the side window of the helicopter as it took off. Despite the three men's assurances that they felt fine, fire department paramedics insisted on taking them to the hospital for a complete checkup.

"You must have sucked up a couple pounds of concrete dust," was how the EMT phrased it. Now McBarker found himself strapped tight to a gurney with an oxygen mask covering his mouth. Several wires dangling from his body were hooked to a machine that made a comforting *beep* every few seconds. A clear plastic tube attached to his wrist gave him a steady drip that was making him drowsy.

He fought to stay alert. *Think, Fred. There has to be a logical explanation. There's something you're missing. You've got to remember everything if you're gonna figure this one out.*

He closed his eyes and thought back to the moment he arrived at City Gate. *There was a policeman waiting for me. He looked like a copper in an old gangster movie, tapping the palm of his hand with his a club . . . and that red hair. An Irish name . . . O'Reilly. No, O'Malley. Yep, it was definitely O'Malley. Someone must have told him I was coming.*

Sergeant John O'Malley was a gruff, thirty-three year veteran of the Chicago Police Department who still spoke with slight brogue.

"The rent-a-cop claims he has no idea how they got out." O'Malley thumbed through a small notebook as he approached the inspector. When I got here, I found one Juan Alejandro Ramirez, a twenty-five-year-old Hispanic male, doubled over, crying like a baby. He claims he was doing his job, watching security monitors, when he found himself sitting outside on the sidewalk. Says he was the most surprised guy in Chicago when he turned around and saw the building was squished—you'll love this—'like Godzilla does to Tokyo.'" O'Malley cracked the nightstick hard against his hand for emphasis, then laughed as if he didn't feel it. "Detectives are talking to him right now."

"I can't wait to see what wonders of modern chemistry they find in his urine test. We found the other guy, identity unknown, wandering around the parking lot looking all crazed . . . his eyes all bugged out. I asked what happened, but he just kept crossing himself and mumbling 'angel' over and over. As of right now, we have no idea who angel is.

"I've got men looking around the neighborhood to see if they had someone else partying with them. I would imagine two bored minimum wagers pulling an all-nighter in a clinic could find a lot to get them in trouble."

"Sarge," a young officer standing next to O'Malley interrupted. "My wife hired a gardener last summer who changed his name every week. First he was Caesar, than he was Julio. The next week he was Juan. He did good work, so I didn't care who he was. Big surprise, it turns out the guy was an illegal and got deported." He shrugged. "So maybe Juan is 'Angel' with a fake green card."

"No matter," O'Malley said, "Whoever he is, the detectives got him too."

"Can I speak with them?" McBarker asked.

"I'll check, but they're probably on their way to the hospital by now."

The honk of a car horn distracted the three men from their conversation.

"Looks like we have company," O'Malley gestured towards the white sedan with his nightstick. Even from a distance, the lack of hubcaps and black-wall tires made it easy to recognize the car as a city-owned vehicle. As it drove by, they could see a city seal on the door with Chicago's motto, *Urbs in Horto*—City in a Garden—and DEPARTMENT OF BUILDINGS, REYNOLD O'DEA, COMMISSIONER, printed in gold below it.

"Two of your guys," O'Malley stated.

A uniformed officer pointed out a parking space at the far edge of the lot amidst a sea of squad cars. An even larger pack of fire trucks and ambulances were parked nearby. Without a fire to put out, and no one to rescue, the firemen and paramedics stood around speculating on what happened to the building.

As the two casually dressed men stepped from their car, McBarker squinted to see if he had helpers or bosses. He had learned early on all Chicago departments have lots of politically connected figureheads, commonly referred to as bosses, who show up for the TV cameras, then disappear without doing any work. Even worse, however, were the ones who thought they knew what they were doing, seized command, and turned an efficient operation into total chaos. Fred had six Assistant Commissioners above him and any number were liable to be attracted by the large number of news people showing up. And then there was the ultimate camera-loving boss, the commissioner himself.

Oh, no, he thought, *the last thing I need is Rey taking over*. Fred was still about fifty-feet away and couldn't make out their faces, so he crossed his fingers and hoped neither was the commissioner. He stopped, shook his head, then laughed out loud at the thought of O'Dea arriving in anything other than his black, stretch limousine, let alone before sunrise.

McBarker smiled when he recognized the men and knew he had seniority on both of them. Better still, William "Billy" Haynes and Philo Clemson were structural engineers hired on their merit, rather than their connections. The only problem was the two young black men looked so much alike in the dim light that he couldn't remember which was which.

Billy Haynes stood next to the car and stared at City Gate Tower Eight. "Whoa . . . I've never seen a building do that." He pointed at the roof, then swung his arm in a line to the intact building next to it. "Were they the same height?" He asked.

"From what I've been told, they were all identical." McBarker replied. "And hello to you too."

Haynes was so mesmerized by the wounded building he didn't notice Fred's outstretched hand. Philo Clemson chuckled and pumped his hand. "Don't mind Billy, Mr. McBarker. He gets like that when he sees a building do something he knows is impossible."

Thank you. Billy—blue shirt, glasses.

"There could be a common design flaw," Haynes said. "Have the other buildings been evacuated?"

"All eight buildings may appear to be the same, but the four across the highway were built as high-priced condominiums," O'Malley pointed at them with his stick. "One of my men says his parents live there and he watched them being built. He says they've got real steel girders in them instead of concrete ones like that," he gestured towards the stricken building, "but I didn't want to take any chances. I've got men going door to door evacuating the condos as we speak. The other three office buildings are empty."

McBarker was impressed Sergeant O'Malley had taken control without waiting for orders. "Better to shake a slew of people out of bed than to . . . He didn't even want to finish that sentence, let alone think of how many would have died if this had happened during a workday.

"God sure saved a lot of people by letting this happen on a Sunday night." O'Malley said.

"Actually it happened Monday morning," McBarker stated as if on the record. "The call came in at 4:15."

"Whenever," O'Malley stated. "We should thank God for His mercy."

McBarker was uncomfortable. "Well, you did the right thing Sergeant. You ever think about moving up to management?"

O'Malley blushed. "Nah," he shook his head. "I'm just an old beat cop with flat feet counting time 'til I retire. Then I'm gonna sell the house, take my pension, move up north, and spend the rest of my days fishin' an' listenin' to the Cubs fold in the stretch."

"I'm a White Sox fan myself," McBarker responded with a grin.

"This is unbelievable," Haynes' excitement drew their attention back to the building. "I've seen computer simulations of a partial progressive collapse, but I've never actually seen one. I didn't think it was possible." He took a pair of binoculars out of a case and continued. "He was right about it being concrete slip-form construction. The interior columns show signs of severe compression. Man, the stress on the failed structural elements must have been incredible before the mass achieved equilibrium."

O'Malley kept quiet rather then admit he had no idea what the engineer was talking about.

"All the exterior columns are deformed. They're bowed out, a good five-, maybe six-feet, wider in the middle than the first and top floors. The degree of deflection is so uniform it almost looks as if the building was designed that way. But I don't see anything that looks consistent with a collision or an explosion. No, the girders and mullions are bent, not sheared off. Could someone have put a load on the roof heavy enough to do this?" He continued without waiting for an answer,

"The exposed rebar looks to be an eight, maybe a nine." Haynes' referred to the thickness of the reinforcing steel bars that had been imbedded into the concrete. "Whoever designed this building sure included a wide safety margin."

When they started to speculate on the bar's tensile strength, O'Malley tapped his hat with his nightstick and said, "You and your men got plenty of work to do. I'll be over in my cruiser catching up on my paperwork if you need me."

"Thanks again for all your help," McBarker said.

"Sergeant, before you leave," Clemson called out, "is there any chance someone might be still in there?"

"The security guard said no one was inside," O'Malley answered, "but we haven't verified that. The building looks so unstable Search and Rescue decided to wait until the 'college boys'—I'm not kidding, that's what he called you—said it wasn't gonna fall down go boom on top of them,"

"Fall down, go boom. At least he knows the technical term." Clemson drew a chuckle from everyone.

"Well, we're not going to find out what happened standing here, so let's get up close and personal and see what we can see. Do either of you have a camera?" McBarker asked.

"Yes sir." Haynes popped opened the sedan's trunk and rummaged around. "Canon or Nikon?" He held up two expensive cameras.

"I'm impressed. What else do you have in there?" McBarker asked.

"You name it, this car's got it," Haynes said as he pointed to at least a dozen plastic boxes. "Boots, jumpsuits, flashlights. Everything we could possibly need."

"Except an FM radio," Clemson said.

Haynes laughed. "He's right. This may be the only brand spanking new Chevrolet Lumina with an AM radio and cloth bench seats in existence."

"I'm thrilled it has air conditioning." Clemson grinned.

"OK, time to get serious," McBarker said, "We've got a lot of work ahead of us."

The inspectors each took a white jumpsuit out the trunk and began to pull them on over their street clothes. Before they finished zipping up, several anonymous arms pushed microphones in front of their faces. It hadn't taken long for word to spread through the media that the trio was going into the building and at least a dozen reporters were trying to get their attention. Reflective tape on their jumpsuits made them glow, as they became the focus of dozens of TV cameras and their floodlights.

"What happened?" "Why did the building fall down?" "Are you going in?" The reporters screamed several questions at once which made them easier to ignore. The last question McBarker heard before slipping on his hood was, "Can our cameraman come with you?" followed by O'Malley barking, "Back up and give 'em some breathin' room or I'll throw the whole lotta ya out."

As soon as it is bright enough, the sky will be filled with news choppers, McBarker shook his head. *Until then, they'll have to satisfy themselves with their telephoto lenses.*

Adjusting their air-purifying respirator masks to protect them from inhaling dust, Fred continued to ignore the cameras, not wanting to let on that he did not have the slightest idea what caused the collapse. *Wouldn't it be a hoot if the "eyes in the sky" actually found a giant fire-breathing dinosaur's footprint on the roof?*

The last thing each did after donning a bright yellow hardhat was to hold a gloved thumb up to show they were ready to go.

The first few hundred feet of asphalt were clean, but debris became more frequent as they got closer to the building. Without warning, all the overhead parking lot lights went off—Com Ed had cut the power to prevent a fire. Fumbling for their flashlights, the men turned around to see what had happened.

I wish they had told me they were going to do that. McBarker thought. They were blinded for a moment when dozens of floodlights on the emergency vehicles switched on. *And I wish they had told me they were going to do that too.* They turned and resumed their walk as the bright lights danced off what little mirrored glass was left.

"OK, let's keep moving. I don't think we have a lot of time," McBarker waved them on. With every step, glass shards crunched under the thick soles of their work boots. When they were within fifty feet, they heard a loud crack followed by a low, rumbling noise that sounded like a moan.

"That doesn't sound good!" Haynes shouted.

"It almost sounds . . . Clemson stammered, "like the building isn't very happy to see us."

"C'mon, guys, get serious. We're going on the record now," McBarker said as he turned on his tape recorder. "My name is First Deputy Fred McBarker Junior. With me are William Haynes and Philo Clemson. We are standing in front of City Gate Tower Eight. The structure has been significantly compromised and we are initiating a visual inspection of the perimeter. Most of the damage appears to be concentrated on the third through sixth floors. All of the windows in the building appear to be broken, however, the glass didn't travel very far . . . maybe one-hundred feet maximum.

Haynes documented the damage with his camera. "An internal explosion would have blown glass all over the parking lot and probably shattered every other window in the complex," he added as he shot a sequence of pictures.

A series of loud cracking sounds, followed by a large puff of dust from inside the building made the three men pause.

Haynes resumed walked towards the building while his camera clicked away. "I'm going to shoot as many pictures as I can before it stops defying gravity and falls down."

"Don't get any closer than you have to." McBarker's command was unnecessary as there's something about a creaking, groaning building that made even the bravest of men give it a wide berth. He resumed his narrative. "The first floor perimeter walls are no longer horizontal. They slope out by about ten degrees. All of the glass appears to have blown out when the floor compressed about one foot from its original height."

Fred froze. "Well there's something you don't see every day. The first floor windows have what appears to be burglar bars behind them."

"Why would you have burglar bars on an office building?' Clemson asked.

"I don't know, but they definitely look like burglar bars." McBarker answered.

Both men shook their heads. Though buckled, the bars would make entry impossible.

"And it looks like there was a wall behind them too." Clemson said.

"Somebody sure liked their privacy," Haynes added. "The windows on the side wall are ornamental, too. There's a solid wall behind each one."

"Well there's gotta be at least a couple of entrances to a building this size," McBarker said. "Let's find them."

"This must have been one dark place to work . . . like being in a basement." Clemson," said. "What kind of an office building was this?"

"The sign outside the door says it was a women's clinic." McBarker responded by shining his flashlight on a metal sign mounted on a pole about five feet from the entrance. The flash from Haynes's camera continued to light up the entire entrance area.

"What kind of clinic doesn't have any windows?" Clemson asked. "A vampire clinic?"

No one laughed.

Haynes said, "This is too strange. The front door looks like it belongs on a bank vault. Look, there's three dead bolt locks on it! How'd the guards get outta this place?"

With the exception of a peephole, the door appeared to be a single steel sheet, in stark contrast with the inviting revolving glass doors found in most office buildings. Even from twenty feet away the men could see that it was crushed in place. There was no way it would open without lots of persuasion.

"We'd need mechanical help to get in that way," Haynes stated. "But even with the burglar bars, I think it would be a lot easier to go through one of the walls. I've got a cut off saw in the car. The same kind fire and rescue uses."

"No. I don't want to chance it," McBarker replied. "We should have a set of blueprints when we get back. They might explain why this place looks a lot more like a jailhouse than a doctor's office. We'll wait until we can get a generator and more lights before we go in. I have no idea what the inside of this so-called clinic is like, and I don't want someone getting lost in the dark."

Both men nodded at McBarker's observation.

"But we still have a lot of work to do out here. Has anyone seen another door?"

They both answered, "No."

"Then let's see what the rest of the first floor looks like."

Rounding the corner cast them into darkness, as none of the spotlights were aimed at the north side of the building. As they walked, the building continued to creak and, more than once, made an almost human sigh. The men shined their flashlights into every distorted window frame they passed. Through cracks in the privacy wall, they could see a steady cloud of dust drifting down from the upper floors, covering everything like a layer of powdery snow.

When they rounded the next corner, they saw a truck dock recessed into the middle of the back wall. However, the space where one would expect an overhead garage door had been filled in with concrete blocks. A formidable-looking service door, secured with a steel bar across it, was the only means of access.

Clemson shined his light along the bar, "Look at the size of that padlock. What'd they do? Lock the security guards in for the night?"

"This building is locked up tighter than Fort Knox! Are you sure it wasn't a prison?" Haynes asked.

"I have no idea. Take a lot of pictures," McBarker said. "Because there is no way the city would ever approve any of this. Code requires at least one exit on each side of a building of this size . . . and emergency lights. There are no emergency lights anywhere."

The rapid flash of Haynes's camera's strobe light illuminated the area.

"Let's keep moving. And watch where you're stepping."

"Hey, I found something," Clemson yelled. "Over here . . . I found a breach in the wall. This must be how the security guards got out." His flashlight illuminated an unobstructed opening about fifteen feet further down the wall. "It looks big enough for a man get through."

"After you, Mr. First Deputy," Clemson offered.

All three men laughed nervously as they knew that it was far too dangerous to venture in. Besides, the room only appeared to contain several garbage dumpsters. A concrete block wall with another solid door blocked their view any farther into the building. It too was secured with a thick steel bar padlocked across it.

McBarker asked, "What's with the steel doors?"

"It looks wedged in place, Clemson said.

"I think you're right. The frame looks bent. We're going to need hydraulic jacks—big ones—if we're going to get it open."

"It might be quicker to knock a hole in the wall." The beam of Clemson's flashlight outlined a spot on the wall.

"No. It might be holding something up, so I wouldn't want to open it until we had some cribbing—make that lots of cribbing—to shore things up." McBarker shined his light around the room. "We'll need portable flood lights too—and a crew with a torch too for those locks.

"Shoot a series of pictures of this room. Make sure you get some close-ups of that door."

"There must be another way inside." Clemson said. "There's no reason for security guards to be in here unless they were guarding garbage." He criss-crossed the floor with his flashlight. "And I don't even see a chair in there."

"I think you're right," McBarker said. "Sergeant O'Malley said the guard claimed they were watching security monitors, but I don't see any in here. If he was telling the truth, they must have been out front near the lobby. That way the guards could monitor access to the building while watching the cameras."

"That's the logical place for a guard post. But we haven't seen anything that looks logical so far." Haynes said.

"Well, we've walked the east, north, and west sides, so let's go look on the south side for another way out," McBarker directed. Just as they were about to leave, a flashlight beam caught a movement in the shadows.

Fred opened his eyes and looked around the helicopter, unsure if he wanted to remember what happened next.

Mayor Gates had been simmering ever since that woman reporter ambushed him during the City Gate press conference. The mere mention of the word *riot* caused his bodyguards to spring into action. The media called them the "Blues Brothers" after the likewise attired characters in the 1980 John Belushi movie. The way they took off running confirmed the nickname was not a compliment.

One dialed a direct line to police headquarters, known to the force as eleventh and State, and confirmed a "significant incident" was taking place in the seventeenth District but the scene was being secured. At least a dozen people had been arrested and another dozen taken away in ambulances. Further details were sketchy, but shots had been fired and there might be fatalities.

The other bodyguard slipped away from near the podium, ran straight to the mayor's limousine, and told the driver to turn the radio to AM 710. They caught the dramatic end of a replay of their listener's phone call.

"It's unbelievable . . . I can see the police clubbing someone . . . [Cough-cough.] . . . Teargas is drifting this way and I'm having trouble breathing. [Cough-cough.] there's a lot of smoke coming from burning cars. [Cough-cough.] More police cars are pulling up . . . people running all over . . . there's police chasing them. [Cough-cough.] Lots of police now . . . two of them are pointing at me . . . I don't want to get arrested so I'm going to try to walk away . . ."

"You with the phone, drop it and put your hands in the air," a voice boomed in the background. It was followed by sounds of a brief scuffle, then a scream. Seconds later, the phone went dead.

"We have been unable to reestablish contact with our 'Eyewitness on Chicago' at the riot on Elston Avenue. We hope she is all right," the radio newscaster stated. "For those just tuning in, I'll recap what we know. Approximately five minutes ago, a listener called in a tip to our news desk that police were attempting to break up a protest in front of the Irving Park Women's Clinic on North Elston Avenue. The situation appears to have deteriorated and violence ensued. Our monitoring of police radio frequencies confirms additional resources were dispatched to the scene after shots had been fired. In a bizarre twist, we are also trying to verify our caller's claim that the melee was touched off when the Mayor's grandmother was arrested. We will continue to monitor the situation and bring you more breaking news as it becomes available."

Gates attempted, without success, to regain control of his press conference, but was deluged with demands that he answer the question about Granny. Shouting almost incoherently, invoking made-up compound-syllable words, and violating every rule of grammar, the Mayor handed the microphone to Commander Beeman and stormed away.

As Gates fled into his limo, his guard said, "Mr. Mayor, that reporter's radio station claims your grandmother was taken away in handcuffs. I called a friend at seventeen," he said, referring to the police department's seventeenth District—Albany Park, "and he confirmed Granny was taken by squad car to First Presbyterian Hospital with a head injury."

"Head injury! Hospital!" he shouted. "How bad is she?"

"She's been admitted to the Emergency Room, but he didn't know the extent of her injuries. I'm waiting for a call back from the hospital."

The mayor was breathing heavily as he slid into the backseat. He lost it again when the radio personality stated they would have a riot update after the commercial break. "Drive me to the hospital and turn that garbage off!" he fumed.

That day's traffic jam was one for the record books. The Northwest Tollway carried tens of thousands of cars and trucks every morning from the suburbs to the city. So too did the Tri-State Tollway. Both intersected with the Kennedy Expressway, I-90, just east of O'Hare Field, within sight of the City Gate complex.

With the Kennedy closed, Illinois Department of Transportation workers set up detours, causing massive backups in all directions.

Once word of the closure got out, suburbanites began taking every possible alternative route into the city, creating an invincible gridlock. To make matters even worse, scores of reverse commuters trying to get to work in the suburbs locked bumpers with curiosity seekers from all over Chicagoland who were trying to negotiate unfamiliar side streets to get a closer look at the City Gate complex. The whole mess ended up competing for pavement space with the locals who were trying to go about their normal day.

No longer needed, dozens of fire trucks, ambulances, and rescue vehicles were released from City Gate's parking lots. Adding to the confusion, Mayor Gates ordered his driver to turn on his lights and siren, as if that would somehow make thousands of cars and trucks disappear. On a good day the drive to First Presby—as most Chicagoans called the hospital—would take about half an hour. Today it would take twice that long just to move the first mile.

Gates closed his eyes and reflected on how a mere two weeks earlier every local news program showed clips from Granny's hundredth birthday party. Most called her the most beloved woman in the city. Someone would have to answer to him for what happened. Heads would roll. And there was no way the police union would save the job of whomever arrested his grandmother.

Sophie "Granny" Gates was holding court in her hospital room. At least a half-dozen newspaper and radio reporters plus a couple of TV news crews were squeezed into a room not much bigger than her bed. Several more waited in the hall, their microphones and tape recorders held as close to the open door as they could reach to catch the amazing press conference. The top half of Granny's bed was cranked almost straight up so she could see everyone. A powder blue blanket was draped very properly over the century old woman's legs while her forehead was swathed in a large bandage. A tube from an IV hanging next to her bed snaked under the blanket.

This certainly is a pleasant turn of events, Granny thought as she smiled then winked at her police escorts. Both men smiled and winked back at their prisoner. Barely two hours earlier, she had been handcuffed and bleeding, now she was the toast of the hospital.

When they arrived at the Emergency Room, patrolman Walsh grabbed a wheelchair for her. "I've been walking longer than the two of you put together, and I certainly don't need you to push me now," she protested.

Walsh pleaded, "You've had quite the day already. Please let us at least do this for you."

"All right, but only because you're such nice young men."

"Just doing our job, Ma'am." Officer Zelermann said.

"Then stop calling me that. It makes me sound old."

"I'm sorry, Mrs. Gates."

"I told you to call me Granny. It makes me sound younger."

"Yes, ma . . . 'er . . . Granny," Zelermann grinned.

Once inside the officers spoke to the woman in charge of admissions and explained the situation. "I know her cut doesn't look serious. It's not even bleeding anymore. But if you don't admit her, our Lieutenant wants her booked for assaulting him," Zelermann pleaded.

"Her?" The woman said with amazement. "She must be ninety years old."

"Actually she just turned a hundred. She's a nice lady who was in the wrong place. She didn't want us to bring her to the hospital, but if we didn't come here we would have had to take her to the station . . . and, like I said, our Lieutenant wants her behind bars. We just need some time to make a few phone calls so we can straighten this out without embarrassing her any further."

"Hmmm. A senior citizen with a head injury. That could be very serious. Yes, I will admit her. Does she have any identification with her?"

"Yes, and you won't believe who she is."

Reporters began to gather at the hospital within minutes of her arrival. Word spread quickly once Radio News 710 interrupted their broadcast with an "Eyewitness on Chicago" exclusive report that the arrest of the mayor's grandmother for assaulting a police officer had touched off the Irving Park Women's Clinic Riot.

"Granny," the head nurse Amy Kammens, an imposing blonde who still wore the traditional white uniform, said as she walked into the room, "you seem to be quite the celebrity. It looks like reporters from every TV and radio station plus all the newspapers are waiting downstairs to talk to you. Would you like to see them or should I tell them to go away?"

"Go away! Not on your life, Missy. Send up the whole kit and caboodle. I've got a lot I want to get off my mind."

Kammens stood at attention and feigned clicking her heels. "As you wish, Granny. But first I need to get your doctor's permission for you to have visitors. Then I'll pass the paperwork along to my supervisor. I'll be back in a few minutes to give you an idea of when you can expect the hoard."

Downstairs, the hospital administrator set down some ground rules to the assembled media.

"I am Gertrude D'Angelo. Let me start out by saying I am not impressed by your fancy cameras. This is a hospital. We have hundreds of patients and you will not disturb any of them. If you do not follow my rules, I will personally throw you out." She pointed towards the door.

D'Angelo did not look like someone to be trifled with. Her stern face was pasty white, yet she wore no makeup, and her jet black hair was pulled back in a tight bun. She wore a light gray pants suit with a white shirt and a paisley tie and could easily have been mistaken for a man.

"Mrs. Gates' attending physician, Dr. Walczak, will be in attendance but will not answer any questions. There will also be two police officers in her room. They have both requested you direct any questions to their watch commander. I can provide his name if you wish."

D'Angelo lowered her voice an octave. "I will decide who and how many are permitted in the room at any given time. The press conference is being held at Mrs. Gates' prerogative. When either Dr. Walczak or Mrs. Gates says it's over, it is over. There will be no whining. You will quietly file out without disturbing any patients or the operation of this facility. Is that understood?"

Without waiting for an answer she continued, "Good. Then since you do not have any questions, I will return to the serious business of running this hospital. As soon as my assistant, Ms. Falvo-Levanthal," she pointed to a woman wearing an outfit very similar to her own standing off to the side, "receives a call from Mrs. Gates' nurse, she will escort you by elevator to the fifth floor.

"Mrs. Gates is in room 505, which will be the third door on your left. You will walk in an orderly fashion and you will keep your voices down in the corridor so you do not disturb our patients."

The reporters were not used to being talked down to, but none dared complain lest they be barred from going upstairs.

In her room, Granny was itching to get before a camera. The nurses rallied around her, sharing their makeup and doing her hair before the camera crews showed up. One even managed to borrow a ruffled white nightgown for her to wear instead of the faded blue hospital gown that was standard issue whenever someone checked in.

Moments later, the pack of reporters burst from the elevator and destroyed the peace of Granny's room. The first thing they noticed when they entered was the headboard of her bed was flanked by two uniformed police officers standing at attention. None were aware of the irony that Granny's honor guards were actually watching their prisoner.

Dr. Walczak was backed into a corner by the surge. He had to push his way to her bedside. With a thick Polish accent he announced, "Mrs. Gates is now ready to answer your questions."

Several shouted at the same time. "Mrs. Gates . . . "

"Call me Granny, young man," she pointed to the one closest to her, a scruffy looking print reporter who held a mini-cassette recorder in front of her. "That goes for the whole lotta ya. And get that contraption out of my face."

"Yes, 'er, Granny, Dan Wolfe, *Chicago Tribunal*. Are you all right?" he asked.

"I've got a big bump on my forehead, but I've got a thick skull. Didn't even need any stitches." She pretended to tap on her head with her left hand while rapping the knuckles of her right hand on the nightstand. The hollow knocking sound made everyone laugh.

"Granny, Vick Naara, the *Daily Sun*. "How does it feel to be the oldest person ever arrested in Chicago? Maybe in the entire country."

"Maybe on the whole planet," someone else added, making everyone laugh again.

"Well, I might be getting old . . . but I sure don't feel old. All I know is the last time I was arrested it took four men and a pony to do it."

Everyone in the room laughed again.

"Now why'd you go and laugh? I'm not pulling your legs. This isn't the first time I've been arrested. I wasn't always an old lady you know."

The reporters stifled giggles and tried not to look stunned at her revelation, and to a one, shouted a variation of "Granny, were you really arrested before?"

"I just answered that question. Weren't any of you paying attention?"

"Granny, were you convicted? Did you spend time in jail?" Naara asked.

"Shhhh. Shush now. Do you want to hear the story or yourselves yapping? Now all of you have to promise not to say anything to my grandson about this. His grandpa, God rest his soul, always thought it was inappropriate for me to brag to the boy about what a fire-brand I was."

All the reporters smiled as they nodded. Even the cameramen, who were recording every word, nodded in the affirmative.

"Well, it was a long time ago, back before the war. Not the one with Hitler. The big one before that. You know, the war to end all wars. Yep, it was back in 1917, and I was a member of the National Woman's Party. We were suffragists trying to get women the right to vote. The NWP went to Washington, that's Washington D.C. I don't think I've ever been to the other one.

"Well, we tried all sorts of things to get the word out. It seemed as if we were marching in parades and holding rallies almost every day, but President Wilson wouldn't listen. So we began to picket the White House. That would be early in the year when it was still cold. February, as I recall."

Granny's body may have been showing its age, but her mind was still sharp. She knew all the details and loved telling a story. Her audience hung on every word.

"The newspapers called us the 'Silent Sentinels of Liberty' and we wanted to make sure old Woodrow, that was President Wilson's first name you know, couldn't leave home without seeing or hearing us. We used to chant a lot, carried big banners too. I remember one read, 'Mr. President, how long must women wait for liberty?' You young ladies have no idea how much you owe to your grandmothers." She directed her gaze at a female reporter.

Two radio stations and one cable news channel were broadcasting Granny's impromptu press conference live to the city.

"We were out there every day, rain or shine, for months until early April. That's when the U.S. of America started to send doughboys over there to fight the dreaded Hun. That's what we called Germans in those days. Well, some people got mad because we were carrying banners that called the president 'Kaiser Wilson.' The Kaiser was the troublemaker with the spiked helmet who started the war, you know, and lot's a little scuffles broke out almost every day. Some days it seemed like there were fisticuffs going on at every street corner. But I don't remember anyone calling what we did riots back then . . . not like you reporters did today. There were hardly enough of us out there today to play a game of cards, let alone cause a riot. Some bull knocks a spry senior citizen down and all heck breaks loose. And mind you, I said heck because I'm a lady, but I'm thinking a lot stronger. Well, I'm getting off track. Where was I?"

"You were telling us about picketing in front of the White House." Wolfe volunteered.

"Oh yes, thank you. Well the fights were getting more and more common. It got so bad some men even hit the ladies. And the police just stood there and watched without lifting a finger. Not until June 22—I remember that day like it was yesterday—that's when they started to arrest us for obstructing traffic. Can you believe that? There weren't more than a handful of cars in the whole city. Most of the traffic was teamsters driving teams of horses pulling wagons and elegant carriages with beautiful horses. Oops, I wandered again . . . where was I? Oh yes, June 22. At least five hundred women were arrested that day." She held up five fingers. "Five hundred!"

"I can tell you this . . . I didn't go down without a fight . . . took four men and a pony to get me down—it did. Then they picked me up by my arms and legs and carried me off to a horse-drawn paddy wagon. They took us to court and found everyone guilty. Every single last one of us. They gave us a choice. Either pay a $10 fine, or go to jail." Granny gave a defiant glare as she folded her arms across her chest.

"Well I didn't have that kind of moolah—it was a lot of money back then—and I wouldn't have given it to them if I had it. So I got taken to the Occoquan Workhouse in Virginia. That was a horrible place. We had worms in our food and cockroaches in our cells. Some judge finally said all of the arrests were illegal and they let us go a couple of weeks later. And wouldn't you believe it, but President Wilson suddenly came out and said that he supported Women's Suffrage. We finally got the right to vote in 1920. They called it the Susan B. Anthony Amendment, the Nineteenth Amendment."

Everyone was in awe at Granny's memory . . . and her history lesson. One of the cameramen shouted out, "So Granny, are you saying that the mayor has never heard this story."

"Sonny, when you're married to a police sergeant for your whole life, and your son was one of the finest, most honest detectives this city ever had, well, a lady has got to keep her little secrets or the grandbabies will never respect her."

The entire room erupted in laughter.

"All right, this news conference has ended," Ms. Falvo-Rosenthall announced from the hall. "This is a hospital and we have people trying to work. Mrs. Gates has told all of you a wonderful story, but she needs her rest. You've taken up enough of her time and Dr. Walczak has to make his rounds."

"Good-bye, Granny," the reporters said one by one as they filed out of the room.

"Come back anytime." She waved to them. "And remember, not a word of this to my grandson."

The news people were still laughing as they started to make their way down the hall. They had a great story. One which all agreed would be pretty hard to top.

Then the elevator doors opened, and there stood Mayor Gates with his bodyguards.

In an instant reporters and camera crews sprang into action.

"Mr. Mayor, do you have any comment on your grandmother being arrested?" Vick Naara stuck his tape recorder right in his face.

The other reporters swarmed around Gates and peppered him with similar questions. "Mr. Mayor, have you bailed your grandmother out yet?"

"Mr. Mayor, have you hired a lawyer for Granny?"

Gates lost his temper as he pushed his way past the reporters. The next question put him over the edge.

"Mr. Mayor, did you know your grandmother has served time in jail?"

"Who said that?" he demanded. "That's an out and out lie!" His voice was becoming even higher pitched then usual. "My Granny has never been arrested! That sainted woman is a hundred years old. She's the most beloved woman in Chicago. And who gave you permission to bother her?"

Gates tried to stare the reporters down, "I don't know what you heard, but Granny is in this hospital because she fell down and hit her head on the curb. Two of Chicago's finest brought her here. So why don't you do a story about how they helped an injured senior citizen by driving her to the hospital. That's your real story. They did their job, and I'm looking forward to personally thanking them," Gates ranted.

"Mr. Mayor, what about the riot?" A reporter at the back of the crowd yelled out.

"Riot? There was no riot. Every time the police arrest a couple of punks, you people call it a riot. You should stop spreading crazy rumors."

"Mr. Mayor, Bob Nakleggler, Chicago Cable TV. We know for a fact at least one officer was shot. We also know at least two dozen people were arrested and three police cars were fire bombed. If you don't believe me, I can show you video of what happened."

"Mr. Mayor, your grandmother told us she has an arrest record," someone shouted.

"Arrest record!" he declared, "Granny has a great sense of humor . . . and she's getting a little old . . . and you people took advantage of her. You should be ashamed of yourselves. This interview is finished." He turned and stormed down the hall. His bodyguards made sure they were not followed.

Within minutes, all three networks interrupted their regularly scheduled programming to update coverage of the riot. Each included at least a snippet from Granny's hospital room press conference as a teaser to get you to watch their evening news. Archivists on the East Coast were busy digging through old police arrest records from pre-roaring '20s Washington because each station wanted to be the first to show Granny's mug shot . . . from the last time she was arrested.

Today had been Phil's most exciting day in years. He spent half the morning watching a miniature war take place right outside his living room—a regular window on history, he thought—but it was pretty quiet now because Elston Avenue was still blocked to traffic. Phil couldn't understand why since tow trucks had removed the burned out squad cars about an hour earlier. A city crew with brooms then swept everything cleaner than it had been in a long time.

About all that was left were two police officers parked in front of the clinic. And the yellow POLICE LINE tape was still draped across the street, keeping the curious away and forcing locals to use the alley.

Since there was nothing much left to see, Phil went into the kitchen to make a sandwich, but decided to eat it standing in front of the living room windows in case anything else happens. He was glad he did that because his eye was caught by a bright light down at the corner. It was a television news crew and he recognized the big number one, his favorite station, on the cameraman's jacket. He pushed the on button on his TV and, while he waited for it to warm up, thought out loud, "I wonder if that reporter would like to come up here and see what I videotaped today?"

A moment later he picked up his phone and dialed directory assistance. "Operator, I would like the phone number for Channel One News please."

CHAPTER 5

FRED MCBARKER LAY in the dark staring at the ceiling. He had spent the last hour trying to rationalize the morning's events, but could find no logical explanation. He was an engineer used to working with facts, not an artist who dealt with abstracts. His world revolved around analytical thought. If you added two numbers together a million times you would always arrive at the same answer. That was his comfort zone.

There must be something I'm missing. Something must have happened that I didn't see. Something so obvious I'll feel foolish when I figure it out, he thought.

So he ran through the collapse again, concentrating on the seconds before the bright flash in the basement. *Think, Fred, think. What are you missing? Could the compression of the building have caused a gust of wind strong enough to blow us outside?* The more he thought about it the more convinced he became his eyes must have played a trick on him. *I had to have imagined it. I know I was terrified. I sure wasn't thinking straight. Maybe the concussion from the explosion threw us out. And the other thing could have been some weird image I thought I saw in the smoke—like seeing pictures in the clouds. And that flash was bright enough to have made me imagine almost anything.*

That could be what happened. I'm sure that's what happened. I was confused—and scared—and I imagined seeing something in the basement.

A sharp rap at the door startled him. Without waiting for an answer, a man walked in and flipped on the light switch. Fred squinted to make out his face.

"Good afternoon, Mr. McBarker. I'm Dr. Henessey." Fred was relieved to see the doctor looked like a doctor should look—a white lab coat—slightly frayed, a clean shaven face and premature gray hair at his temples—no doubt from solving medical mysteries. And most important, a stethoscope around his neck. "I have your test results." He waved a clipboard with a thick stack of papers on it.

"How are the two men they brought in with me? Clemson and Haynes?"

That's a first. A patient more worried about his friends than himself, the doctor thought. Aloud, he said, "I don't know if you're a religious man, but I'd call it a miracle. There's not as much as a scratch on any of you . . . no burns, no cuts, no bruises nothing. All three of you should be dead or at the very least clinging to life on respirators from all the dust you had to have sucked into your lungs. The tests show your lungs are as pink and clean as a newborn baby's. It was the same with your friends. No doubt at all . . . it is a miracle."

"I don't put much stock in miracles. Maybe it was just dumb luck." Fred opened the curtains and looked out the window. *Oh boy . . . I would get one of those people.*

The doctor was standing right behind him when he turned around.

"Look, it's been years since I've even been to church," he stammered. "Who knows," he shrugged, "maybe my mom took me to enough masses as a kid that the protection sorta carried over."

Dr. Henessey gave him his sternest look. "Well I don't know about that. If I don't attend church every Sunday, I feel off all week. Maybe someone is praying for your safety. Your mother perhaps?"

"My mom passed away last year," he responded in a soft voice.

"I'm sorry to hear that. But I have no doubt in the power of prayer," Dr. Henessey steered the conversation back. "I pray every day for God to watch over my family and friends. And I know they're praying the same for me. It sure looks like He was watching out for you. But then again, who am I to say? After all you're the guy Dorothy dropped the building on."

"Huh? Who's Dorothy?"

"Dorothy . . . the *Wizard of Oz* . . . tornado . . . wicked witch."

"Oh yeah. I guess it'll take a while to get my sense of humor back. If that's the only thing that isn't working right, can I leave?"

"I wish everyone who was brought in by air ambulance was as healthy as you are." The doctor picked up his patient's chart and scanned it. "Well, your blood pressure and heart rate are a little high, but I guess that's to be expected. And there's still some paperwork to complete. Then you're free to leave. Oh, before I forget, one of your nurses said there are several men downstairs in the lobby who want to talk to you."

"Is my wife down there? Her name is Fritzi."

"I don't know, but I'll find out. Your chart says she was called right after they brought you in, but it doesn't say if she arrived. I've been busy making rounds for the last couple of hours and haven't been downstairs. Like I said, one of your nurses told me there were several men in the lobby waiting to talk to you. Actually, she said they were several somber-looking guys in dark suits. I have no idea who they are. Should I send them up?"

"No thanks. The only person I want right now is my wife. Oh, and I do want to see my men before they talk to anyone."

"That should be no problem. They're right down the hall. None of you can leave until we finish processing your paperwork, but I don't see any reason why they have to stay in their room. I'll have someone check to see if they're dressed and then I'll send them down here. You've got the big room." He swung his arms out. "They're sharing a double." He moved his hands close together.

"Thank you. I would appreciate that."

"Oh, and one last thing Mr. McBarker. You can stop me if you think I'm out of line, but do you remember when President Reagan was shot?" He kept talking without pausing for a reply. "After he recovered, Reagan met with Mother Theresa, and do you know what she told him?" Again he did not give him time to answer. "She told him God spared his life for a purpose and that purpose was to stop abortion and save babies lives. The news said the building that fell on you was the biggest abortion mill in Illinois, maybe in the whole country. I think that God is starting to get tired of people ignoring 'Thou Shalt Not Kill' and gave us a sign. Everyone says you should be dead. I think you were spared to do His work.

"And I'm not the only one who thinks so," the doctor continued. "I should warn you your friends are talking like a couple of evangelists in a revival tent. They know it was a miracle the three of you lived. Listen to them. Maybe they'll set your mind on the right path."

"Thank you, but I really don't know them all that well. We have to talk about work. About the collapse. But I promise to think about what you said. Now can I talk to the 'preachers'?"

Dr. Henessey's face was blank. His attempt at humor had failed.

"This is nothing to joke about Mr. McBarker. If you think you were lucky, buy a lottery ticket. But when you listen to your friends you'll change your mind."

Fred dressed as soon as the doctor left the room. He thought it strange that all of his clothing was clean and neatly folded . . . no dirt, rips, or anything. He carefully examined each item. These were the clothes he had on last night. He was also certain they had not been laundered as there were still ink marks on the shirt pocket. Then he remembered he had worn a white jumpsuit over them. Thinking he had the explanation, he reached back into the box and pulled out a second white plastic bag. Inside of it his coveralls were as clean as when he took them out of the car trunk.

He was still staring at them when a sharp knock on the door broke his train of thought.

"Mr. McBarker," a nurse called out. "You have guests. Is it OK for them to come in?"

"Yeah. Come on in." He placed the jumpsuit back in the bag and tossed it in the box.

The two building inspectors were dressed in casual clothes—clean casual clothes—when they walked in.

Even in the light, the two men looked so much alike. Their skin was a deep chestnut color; they were the same height and build and both had closely cropped hair and neat mustaches. They could have been brothers.

Billy . . . blue shirt . . . glasses. He remembered.

"Are both of you guys OK?" he asked.

Philo Clemson raised his hand toward the ceiling and proclaimed, "Praise the Lord God Almighty. They checked us out top to bottom, front to back, inside and out. The doctors said were we were so healthy we could even return to work today."

"Great, then we need to talk about what happened this morning. Grab a seat," McBarker pointed to two chairs by the window."

"We've been talking about that already . . . a lot." Haynes stated.

Fred picked up a pad of paper and a pen off the counter and sat on the edge of the bed. "That's good because we need to write a preliminary report with our observations. I haven't spoken with anyone other than hospital people since we got here, but my guess is they've turned the scene over to OSHA since it was an office building. They might even have called BATF to rule out a bomb." He turned to Haynes. "Billy, I want to match our comments to the photographic record. Give me your camera."

"No can do. An orderly said they have it in security along with my wallet and cellphone. He said I'll get them back when I'm discharged."

"I don't want to wait that long." Fred said, "We can write a preliminary report and revise it later. Any small details we can recall might give them direction and help determine why the building collapsed."

"Uhhh, Fred, is it OK if I call you Fred?" Clemson asked.

"Please do. After what we went through together, I won't stand on formalities."

"Fred, we know what caused the collapse." Philo Clemson stated.

"And we think you do too." Haynes added.

"What do you mean you know what caused the collapse?" there was a touch of panic in McBarker's voice. *Calm down Fred . . . you're in charge. Let them do the talking,* he tried to regain control. Fred had decided, while lying in bed, that he was never going to tell anyone what he thought he saw. *Maybe they saw what made the shadow.* He took a deep breath before he continued. "Well, since you two had the opportunity to compare notes, why don't you bring me up to speed."

"Let me start by clarifying something." Billy said, "When we say we know what caused the collapse, we're not referring to the event which took place before we arrived." Philo nodded in agreement. "But we do know what triggered the final collapse."

The look on Fred's face said they should continue.

"When the loading dock floor began to disintegrate, we were able to see into the basement." Billy paused to gauge his reaction.

Philo was too excited to wait his turn. "And we both agree he was tall enough to touch the ceiling."

"He?" Fred sounded nervous.

"Billy is convinced that he was a seraphim, but I'm not entirely sure." Philo said.

"A what? Did you say a seraphim? A seraphim! That's an angel, isn't it? You think you saw an angel?" The string of questions rattled out of Fred.

"Praise the Lord. Everything happened so fast, but he looked just like the pictures of angels in my Bible. So yes, I believe that is what I saw." Billy responded.

"You believe you saw a giant angel touching the ceiling?" Fred tried to sound shocked.

"Only for an instant. Then he swung his fiery sword and knocked the building down." Billy answered.

Fred's eyes were as big as saucers—that was exactly what he saw—but how could he admit it without sounding as if he was crazy. Besides, he wasn't a religious man. He knew there had to be a logical explanation.

"Well, I don't agree with him," Philo interrupted.

"Good, at least one of you is thinking logically." Fred sounded relieved.

"I am indeed. And that's why I'm certain it had to be Michael the Archangel that we saw. After all, he is always pictured with a flaming sword."

"Fred, did you happen to count how many wings the angel had?" Billy asked.

"Wings!" Fred leapt to his feet. "Angel! Who decided it was an angel? Not me!" Spit flew as he lost control his emotions. "I'm in charge of this investigation, and I'll decide what we saw."

Philo and Billy didn't say a word.

"Me." Fred's voice quivered. "I'm in charge."

Philo stood up. He was the same height as Fred and stared straight into his eyes. "Then please tell me, who or what did we see?" he asked in an even tone.

"I . . . I, er . . . we . . . uh." Fred stammered before turning away.

Philo pressed for an answer. "Who or what did I see swinging a fiery sword?"

Billy got up and walked over to his supervisor. "If it's any comfort, what we saw is mighty hard for me to accept too."

Fred broke away from him and walked to the corner. He started speaking without turning around. "Debris was falling all around us. The air was so thick with dust it was difficult to see. I knew the concrete slab was starting to break apart, but I froze. The floor was collapsing into the basement. I knew I was going to die and I didn't know what to do. Then the glow started—that incredible gold glow. It was so bright it burned through the darkness. And I looked in the hole and saw a man.

"I saw a man in the basement. He had a head. He had a body. He had arms. I saw them." His voice was almost a whisper. "It was a man."

Billy walked behind him and placed his hand on his shoulder, "The Bible describes seraphim as having human forms, with faces, hands, and feet. So yes, Fred, I agree that we saw something that looked like a man, but he had wings."

Philo walked over and placed his hand on Fred's other shoulder. "I also saw his wings."

Fred tried to wiggle free from their grasp. "No!" He covered his ears with his hands.

Billy leaned next to his head and spoke. "Fred, you can't hide from the truth. We know what you saw because we both saw him, and he had wings. Our only argument is how many. Isaiah 6: 2 says, 'Above it stood the seraphims: each had six wings; with twain he covered his face, and with twain he covered his feet, and with twain he did fly.' That's why I'm wondering if you counted how many wings the angel had."

Fred wrestled around and pushed the two men aside. "You're crazy! You're both crazy . . . arguing about wings." He started taking small steps backward, then threw himself face down on the bed. "Wings! You should be more worried about who killed those babies we found!" He covered his head with a pillow.

Billy knelt on the bed on one knee and leaned over him. "Fred, that building was an abortion mill. And those babies were killed long before we found them."

"He's right, Fred." Philo sat on the other side of the bed and spoke to the pillow. "Those dumpsters were full of aborted babies."

Fred clutched the pillow tighter. Billy and Philo resumed their debate.

"Billy, Archangel Michael is the defender of light and goodness. Don't you remember when Pastor Johnston told us in Sunday school how Archangel Michael wiped out the entire Assyrian army in one night. So, who else would God send down to destroy such an evil place?" He smacked his left hand onto the bed for emphasis.

"I'm sorry, brother, you make a powerful argument, but I'm still not convinced. God has legions of angels at His beck and call. It could have been any one of them doing His bidding."

"I'm sorry too, brother," Philo replied, "but my Bible has a portrait of Archangel Michael. He is a warrior with an incredible set of wings. He is wearing full armor, like one of King Arthur's knights, and he has his foot on the throat of a dragon. The angel I saw was wearing battle armor and swinging a flaming sword."

Fred lifted his head enough to murmur, "Dragon! Now you saw a dragon? Both of you are . . ." His voice tailed off as he tucked his back under the pillow.

Philo laid down next to him and again spoke to the pillow. His voice was soft, yet firm. "Fred, most people think the dragon is an allegory—that the dragon represents the devil or evil. Archangel Michael vanquishes evil. The angel we saw destroyed that building with his fiery sword. And that abortion mill certainly was an evil place."

"Angel!" Fred pulled his head free. "I get it!" He rolled over and sat up with a big grin. "You two must have been influenced by the security guard they found in the parking lot, the one that kept saying 'angel' over and over again. You guys were expecting to see an angel because that's what that guard kept repeating."

Billy threw his arms in the air, "Praise the Lord! The security guard saw him too!"

"Amen!" Philo added with equal zeal.

Fred's expression changed when he remembered the guard had been taken away before Billy and Philo arrived, so neither could have seen or heard the man. He tried to explain, "I didn't mean he saw an angel. I just said he kept repeating the word 'angel' over and over again. I don't know if the police have figured out what he meant."

"Fred, what else could it be?" Billy threw his arms up in frustration. "The security guard must have seen the angel too!"

"Can we talk to him?" Philo asked.

"No!" Fred shook his fists in the air. "He's probably in jail by now. Sergeant O'Malley said something about a party and drugs . . ."

Billy and Philo stood up and backed towards the window. Fred sat on the edge of the bed and the three men stared at each other. No one said a word. *Why won't they let it drop!* He thought.

After a couple of minutes, Fred got up and locked himself in the small bathroom. He didn't turn on the light. His mind raced. *I can't take much more of this. Maybe I can call a doctor or something. Tell him I don't feel good. That's not even a lie. I feel like my brain is trying to tear itself out of my skull.* He sat on the toilet. *I wonder where Fritzi is. If she's waiting in the hall, she'll ring me up if she finds out I'm hiding in a bathroom. OK, this is ridiculous. I'm in charge and I'm putting an end to it right now.*

Fred stepped out of the bathroom; Billy and Philo were still leaning against the window ledge. "Look, I don't care what you think you saw, but I'm sure there is an explanation—a logical explanation for it. We're engineers. We know how to analyze a situation and find a rational solution to the problem."

Fred picked up the pad of paper from the floor and threw it on the counter next to the men. "And we are going to resolve this before anyone leaves this room." He pointed at Philo. "You. Write. There's a pen here somewhere. Start with finding the babies. Search and rescue will need to recover their bodies from the clinic's basement."

"Fred," Billy interrupted. "That was no clinic. It was an abattoir . . . a human slaughterhouse." Tears welled up in Billy's eyes. "I can't get that image out of my mind. It looked like a Nazi death camp." He took out a handkerchief and dried his eyes. "I'm sorry. I've never seen a dead body up close except all made up at a funeral parlor. It was the most disgusting thing I've ever seen. I felt so helpless," his voice trailed off.

Philo walked over and placed his arm around the man's shoulders. "I felt the same way brother . . . but, it was too late. They were already dead."

Hmmmmmmph! Fred cleared his throat. "I agree it was sickening . . . and also distracting . . . but we need to get back to what we observed of the building. I know it's hard to think straight when your adrenaline is pumping. That's why what we're doing now is so valuable . . . while it's all fresh in our minds. I've been doing some thinking—logical thinking. And the gold glow in the basement must be the key. There had to be a fire burning. Maybe leaking propane tanks—the kind they use on a forklift. I've seen that happen . . . they can rupture and explode."

"The color was all wrong." Philo challenged him. "LP gas could not have burned hot enough to produce a gold flame."

"Heat!" Billy shouted. "That's it. It couldn't have been a gas explosion or we would have felt heat."

"He's right." Philo said, "And the flashpoint would be something like 1,000 degrees. We would've been incinerated."

"OK, scratch the fire. Let's think electrical. Maybe there was a massive short circuit. The main might have grounded out causing an arc to the steel door."

"Uhhh," Billy said. "Edison cut the power while we were walking to the building."

Fred shot him a dirty look. "A backup generator! Hospitals always have natural gas powered generators in case of a black-out."

"Fred, remember." Billy said. You pointed out there were no emergency lights on anywhere in the building."

"But there could have been one."

"There wasn't a fire and there wasn't a short circuit." Philo threw the notepad down and stood up. "I saw what was in the basement making that glow. It was an angel and the glow radiated around him."

No! No! No! "Are we back to that again!" Fred shouted. "I told you, we are talking facts. If you didn't see a mechanical cause for the glow, keep your opinions to yourself."

Philo muttered under his breath, "I know what I saw."

Fred glared at him. "It was dark. We were scared. Your eyes can play some pretty big tricks on you."

"I know what I saw and I think you're afraid to admit you saw him too."

"I said I saw a man. I'll give you he was a very tall man. You'll see when they find his body. It'll be flattened, but they'll find it."

Philo rolled his eyes and threw his arms up. "I give up." He turned and looked out the window.

Fred picked up the notebook and turned his attention to the other man. "How's this sound. Our report can say we saw a man in the basement but didn't see him escape." He tried to get Billy to take the paper. "That's all it has to say. Nothing more. Just drop it right there. If I'm right, they'll find his body in a few days."

Philo spun around, "And if I'm right?"

Fred took a deep breath. His mouth began to move, but he wasn't speaking.

"Billy, tell him what you saw."

"You're right, Fred. He had a body . . . and arms. And he was so tall his head touched the ceiling." Billy stood up and locked eyes with Fred. "He was wearing flowing white robes . . . and he had armor on—shining armor like a knight wore. And he had wings. I couldn't count how many, but he definitely had wings. And with his right hand he was swinging a sword that trailed fire." Billy made a circle in the air with his arm.

Fred took a step back. Billy matched it.

"Praise the Lord. That's an ang . . . Philo paused to see if Fred would stop him from interrupting. Hearing no objection, he continued, "angel." His face lit up with a smile. "That is exactly what that I saw too. An angel. Only his face glowed so bright I couldn't make out what he looked like."

"You both saw all of that in a split second?" Fred stammered.

"You don't forget when you see one of God's messengers," Billy said.

"Amen," Philo added,

"Amen, brother." Billy replied. "And the angel was standing over the babies—the slaughtered innocents—spreading his wings over them. And he was swinging a sword. And it was glowing with fire." He made another circle in the air.

Philo did the same. "When I close my eyes, I can still see him." He smiled.

"There has to be some other explanation," McBarker said. "I mean . . .

"You saw him, didn't you?" Billy stared directly into his superior's eyes as he asked his question. "I can tell by the look on your face that you saw him too."

"I'm not sure exactly what I saw. I'm not sure what any of us saw."

"So what are you going to put in your official report?" Philo asked.

"I don't know what I'm going to do." He turned and walked to the corner. Billy stopped Philo from following him.

"Give him a moment alone," he whispered.

There is no way I can say the building fell down because a giant angel swung a fiery sword. They'd lock me up. There's got to be something else. Anything.

Fred turned around and held the notepad out. His hands were shaking. "C'mon guys. Let's look at this logically. Assuming there are such creatures, why would God let us see an angel?"

"So you admit that you saw him too?" Billy challenged him.

"I haven't said what I saw. It was dark and things happened pretty fast. All I said was I want a logical answer. So I'll ask you again, why would God let us see an angel?"

Billy responded to his question with one of his own. "Why aren't we dead under a mountain of building debris?

Philo shouted, "Praise the Lord."

Fred's shoulders drooped. "I don't know." His voice faded away. His chin dropped to his chest.

"Do you want to know what I think?" Philo asked. "I think . . . no . . . I know the explosion was caused when St. Michael swung his mighty sword and destroyed that temple of evil. Then he protected us from a thousand tons of concrete."

"Amen, only it was a seraphim," Billy added with a smile.

Fred clutched the pad in his hand. "So how can we write a report if you two can't even agree on what you saw?"

"We know what we saw." Philo said. "We just can't agree on which one."

Fred sighed. "So I can at least write that we can't agree on what we saw before the explosion."

Billy took the notepad out of his hand and flipped it to a blank page. "That's fine with me—after all, you're in charge. But could I just ask one little technical question? Could you please explain how an explosion could lift all three of us up—without injuring or killing us—and carry us to safety in the parking lot?"

"Amen to that," Philo said. "And don't forget, there were concrete and steel debris falling all around us, yet we didn't even get dirty."

"Oh, you noticed that too," Fred shrugged.

"It would be a little hard to not notice that." Philo threw his arms out and spun in a little circle. "These are the same clothes I was wearing. My jumpsuit—my white jumpsuit—looks brand new. It's back in our room, but I can get it if you don't believe me."

"No need," Fred admitted. "Mine is clean too." His voice was little more than a whisper.

"Praise God!" Billy shouted. "His hand has protected us. He delivered us from a certain death."

"And if you don't believe one of God's angels saved us," Philo continued, "would you please explain how we ended up sitting in the parking lot in the middle of a circle of clean asphalt? When the EMTs reached us, they had a hard time walking because of all the debris. Everything else was at least covered with glass shards, but where we were standing—nothing. Not even a layer of dust. Even my shoes are clean. There's not even a scuff on them." He lifted his leg and shook his foot. "Fred, why won't you admit you witnessed a miracle?"

Fred stood speechless. It was almost as if they had read his mind. Their questions were identical to the ones that had been going through his mind from the moment he stood in the parking lot and surveyed the building's total destruction. His complexion grew pale as he looked down at his own clean clothing.

After a long pause he stammered, "I saw someone too . . . just before the explosion. Someone tall. I said I wanted to put that in our report. Is it possible the floor sloped up in the rear and the ceiling sloped down? Couldn't that have given the illusion of extreme height to whomever we saw?" he asked without conviction.

Neither man answered.

"He had to have been at least fifty feet away. And the lighting was bad . . . and we were all excited and repulsed from seeing two dead babies and then hundreds of them spilling at our feet. I'm not ashamed to admit that I was terrified. I thought we were going to die."

"I was scared too," Billy said. "I also thought we were going to die. But I know what I saw."

"I also know what I saw," Philo said. "I saw him as clearly as I am seeing you now. But if you want to put in your report that it was a man, go right ahead. You're the boss. But what will you say when they don't find his body?"

Fred shrugged then swung his head low. "I don't know. I really don't know. I haven't thought that far. It . . . it makes no sense at all. I still can't understand why I, of all people, would be saved by an angel. That's what doesn't make sense to me."

He straightened his back and raised his head. "There, I said it. I can accept God protecting the two of you. You believe in Him. But I haven't given Him a thought in years." Tears flowed down Fred's cheeks as he confessed. "Why me?"

"Why not?" Billy put his hands on his hips. "Maybe Jesus thought you needed to be reminded that you are one of His children and that He loves you."

Philo bowed his head, "All praise, Jesus Christ, King of Kings, and Lord of Lords. His name is above all names."

"Fred, why don't you sit down," Billy leaned over and patted the mattress. "Let me read you something from the Bible that might help ease your mind."

Fred sat on the edge of the bed. His shoulders were hunched and his hands dropped into his lap.

Billy took a small, well-worn, black leather book from his shirt pocket. He opened it almost to the center and had to flip only a page or two to find what he was looking for.

"I'm going to read you part of Psalm 91. Many people find comfort in this Psalm because it reassures them God watches over us and uses His angels to do His bidding."

He stood ramrod straight as he read. "Psalm 91, verses eleven and twelve, 'For He shall give His angels charge over thee, to keep thee in thy ways. They shall bear thee up in [their] hands, lest thou dash thy foot against a stone.' Some newer translations say 'The Lord will command His angels to guard you in all your ways; they will lift you in their hands, so that you will not strike your foot against a stone.'"

He sat down next to Fred. "You were saved for a purpose. There is something God wants you to do."

Fred managed a small smile. "You're the second person who's told me that today."

"Count me as the third." Philo chimed in.

"Praise the Lord. Fred, can we pray with you? We can ask God for guidance and understanding. He allowed us a glimpse of one of His messengers. He saved us from a certain death. We can ask Him what He wants us to do."

"And thank Him," Philo added. "You must never forget to thank Him."

Fred was raised a Catholic, but it had been many years since he had set foot in a church. He couldn't remember much about praying, although he'd been taught for eight years by the good sisters of Our Lady of Perpetual Penance . . . no, that wasn't the right name. That was what the boys called it when they imagined they were being funny. It was Our Lady of Divine Providence. He recalled getting down on his knees to ask God for something material. He could remember being very specific: a red bike. No, make that a candy-apple red, ten-speed Schwinn bicycle with hand brakes. He also remembered praying to pass a test or get a good report card. He could even recall praying to make a sick person well. But he had never thought to thank Him.

His eyes darted from man to man. "I . . . don't . . . know . . . what to say."

Billy smiled at him. "Fred, we'll talk to Jesus together."

CHAPTER 6

THE REVEREND JOHN James Jefferson was a uniquely Chicago institution. Jackie, as he insisted on being called, claimed the title Doctor of Divinity but wouldn't say where he had earned it. The closest he would come was his frequent boast that he had enrolled in an obscure Bible school down in Mississippi to avoid being drafted during the Vietnam War.

Jackie was equally vague about how he had earned a living before he showed up in Chicago. Sometimes he hinted he had been a traveling Southern Baptist minister but no one could find any evidence supporting that claim. In fact, several reporters tried unsuccessfully to find proof that he had ever worked in any capacity for any known religion, let alone as an ordained preacher.

Finally, when Jackie was forced to grudgingly admit he never actually had a pulpit to call his own, he declared himself pastor at large for all Chicagoans who did not belong to a church.

In truth, Jackie was an embarrassment to most men of the cloth. He dressed like a stereotypical pimp, preferring bright pastels that contrasted with his rich ebony complexion. A matching hat and shoes were a must. Jackie also wore so much jewelry that if he ever fell into the water he would sink like a rock. Most of it was cheap costume pieces, but what they lacked in quality he more than made up for in quantity. *Some day*, he often fantasized as he ran his fingers over his many rings, *I'm going to replace all of this with solid gold.*

For several years he hung out on the fringes of the civil rights movement barely earning enough to support his "ministry." Most legitimate community activists avoided him like the plague as his flamboyant outfits and over-the-edge rhetoric tended to redirect attention to him and away from their causes. The tired but oft-told joke in the media was the most dangerous place to stand is between a TV camera and Jackie. In private, however, more than a few would admit they admired his ability to milk 150 percent out of a photo op—plus he was always good for a headline-worthy quote.

It was a very different story among real activists. They resented the way the lion's share of media coverage always seemed to go to Jackie, while the crumbs fell to their causes. This drew the ire of event organizers who soon learned their only chance to get their message out was to keep the Reverend Jefferson out. And the easiest way to do this was to schedule their press conferences on private property where they could control who was granted admission.

Jackie could do little but watch from outside as his income stream dried up almost over night. Desperate, he searched for a new angle. He began to haunt his local library, devouring old newspapers and magazines for an idea. It didn't take him long to find an article in a financial weekly which seemed to offer a way to guarantee an endless income stream for a minimal amount of work. He drew a *shhhh* from the librarian when he laughed out loud as the idea grew in his mind. It seemed almost too easy. There had to be a catch.

Intrigued, he next went on line where he entered a single word: greenmail. He devoured several web pages until he found one that gave a step-by-step account of how a little known minority activist had threatened to organize a consumer boycott against a prominent retailer for perceived racial injustices.

Jackie grinned as he envisioned himself as the lead story on the evening news leading a protest demanding justice. *Jackie Jefferson, defender of the oppressed* had a nice ring, he thought. This would, of course, be followed by a hastily-called meeting with company executives where they would beg him to subdue his outrage in exchange for a significant contribution to his ministry. The idea so excited Jackie that he vaulted the stairs up to the law library to see if his scheme was illegal or just despicable. An hour later he had his answer—despicable, but legal if done correctly.

He walked home that night a happy man, grinning with each step as he formulated "the plan." He pretty much had it all thought through by the time he climbed the stairs to his attic apartment. Ignoring his growling stomach, Jackie jumped straight into bed so he could get an early start in the morning.

He was waiting at the library doors the moment they opened and he spent the entire day reviewing the annual reports of hundreds of local corporations. Jackie was a quick study in the art of greenmail and knew exactly what he was looking for: the right ratio of cash-on-hand to potential racial guilt. A half hour before closing time he struck pay dirt.

He was researching nursing homes and found one owned by a publicly-traded corporation that showed a very healthy income stream as well as ample cash reserves. Make that *very* ample cash reserves. And, judging by its address, he was confident it would have enough sympathetic liberals living there to allow him to pull off the plan.

Having found a golden goose ripe for the plucking, Jackie worked harder that week then the previous fifty-two put together—waking up at the crack of dawn—researching, planning, and scheming. His target audience lived very comfortably in a four-thousand-dollar-a-month, state-of-the-art assisted living center, and he knew it wouldn't be easy to convince a crowd of affluent senior citizens they were actually down trodden. Jackie rehearsed his speech dozens of times in front of a mirror until he perfected his delivery. Now all that was left to do was whip up the emotions and wait for the negotiations to begin.

On Monday morning he showed up on the front lawn of the exclusive north shore retirement home dressed like a peacock in heat with a TV crew from a local cable news outlet in tow. Waving an oversized, gilt-edged Bible and using a bullhorn to amplify his baritone voice, he proclaimed, "I am like a modern day Moses, commanded by the Lord God Almighty to lead you from the bondage and oppression of a system that does not care about anything but your money."

Seeing that he had grabbed the attention of a handful of residents and staff, Jackie continued. "My dear friends, and you are all truly my dear friends, I love each and every one of you and care very much about you. That is why I am here today." A few more seniors wandered over to see what all of the commotion was about. "This is not a retirement home. This is a warehouse of humanity where greedy administrators stack you like firewood until the angel of death comes to harvest your souls."

Jackie felt a pang of guilt but smothered it by imagining he would be hired as a paid consultant, maybe even an honorary board member, showing them the way to right a wrong. But deep down he knew nothing would change. He knew he would never even bother to make a token follow-up visit to his victim, let alone do anything to justify his paycheck. He would sit back and wait for their monthly checks to roll in. He steeled his nerve and continued, "I look out at your faces and what do I see? Verily I say unto thee I see the wisdom which can only be earned through a lifetime of hard work and suffering. And yet they do not give you respect. Do they honor you as wizened elders? No, they treat you like children unable to make decisions for yourselves."

Jackie was on a roll. This was the first warm day of spring and more and more residents walked outside to hear his speech. The staff was also taking quite an interest.

"How many residents of this home sit on its board of directors? I will answer that question. Not one." He intensified his harangue when he noticed a group of men wearing expensive suits standing off to the side. "Is there a reason why that same board of directors could not find even one, not even one, retired executive from amongst the many who reside here whom they deem worthy of having an opinion?"

He turned towards them as he delivered his closing remarks. "I am here to restore dignity to you. I am here to serve you. And I will be here every day until the changes that you deserve, nay, I say the changes that you *demand* have been made. I thank you."

The crowd responded with polite applause then returned to milling about the beautifully landscaped garden, admiring the thousands of tulips that were blooming in every imaginable color.

Jackie had succeeded both in stirring the water and picking out a likely stooge to manipulate—a white-haired man who had the disoriented look of a person suffering from dementia. He winked at his crew then strutted over to speak with the mark.

Several residents noticed the procession and followed them. Jackie paused for a moment for the cameraman to set up the shot, then reached out and vigorously shook the man's hand.

The reporter noticed the name tag plastered across the man's sweater and asked, "Mr. Leighter, would you like to say something for tonight's news?"

"Why sure, I'd be glad to oblige," Leighter replied. "Well, to be honest, I don't remember this young man's name, but I do like what he was saying. I guess we should all thank the good Lord for sending us the Reverend . . . whoever he is."

Amidst a howl of laughter, Jackie's new nickname was born—one the media gleefully seized on and used with feigned reverence.

Within minutes the Reverend was invited inside the administrator's office for some "refreshments." Within two hours the Reverend Jackie Jefferson was the new Spiritual Consultant of the Golden Twilight nursing home earning an annual salary of $12,000. They even hinted at a bonus if he would forget to show up for his promised Sunday services. Not bad for a morning's work.

From that day on, anytime someone with a wisp of gray in his or her hair had a newsworthy problem, the Reverend was sure to swoop down and steal the spotlight away.

With menacing glares, Mayor Gates' bodyguards disbursed the crowd of reporters. Then they ordered the two police officers guarding Granny to step out into the hall with them. They stood in front of the door and made sure the mayor could spend as much time as he wanted with his grandmother. Before leaving, Gates assured her she was not going to jail and said he would leave her police guards in place to make sure the press didn't bother her again.

"Sidney, they were no bother," Granny said. "Heck, I enjoyed the attention. But could you please check on my friends? The nice nurses told me Kaye and Ruth are sharing a room downstairs. You remember them, the twin sisters from across the alley. They still live in the same white frame house with the green roof on Whipple Street."

She paused until he said he remembered them. "The nurses also told me that Sandy, she's the one that used to own a snack shop with her husband Dan down on Ashland Avenue by Division Street, and Dorothy, you went to school with her grandson William, and her sister-in-law Vanessa, I don't know if you've met her," she traced her index finger on the palm of her grandson's hand as though drawing a family tree, "are still in intensive care," Granny rambled on. "Can you please tell them I'm sorry I started all that ruckus?"

He wrapped his arms around her and hugged her tight, "Granny, you didn't start anything. But I promise you, the policeman who did will soon be apologizing to each one of you."

Granny was mortified at the prospect and tried to dissuade him, "Oh Sidney, that's not necessary."

"I'll decide what's necessary. Now you lie down and rest . . . and promise you'll call me if you need anything." He guided her onto the edge of the bed.

"Oh, you've got enough to worry about running the city and all," she protested.

"I'll always have time to worry about you." He leaned over and kissed her on the forehead. "I love you so much, and I felt so helpless when I found out you were injured. You should've called me."

Granny threw her arms up in exasperation, "Oh Sidney, we tried. My how we tried. Those two young policemen who drove me here kept calling your home and your cellphone, but all they got were busy signals."

Gates shrugged. "I'm sorry. I was tied up with the collapse."

"Sidney, those boys aren't in trouble for taking my handcuffs off are they?" She asked. "They were so polite . . . they treated me so nice."

"No. Granny, they did their job the way grandpa or daddy would have. I'll be sure to thank them before I visit your friends. I have to go now. You call me if you need anything. Anything. I promise I'll answer my phone."

The moment the mayor opened the door to leave, Dr. Walczak pushed past him. Gates' bodyguards had kept him waiting in the hall for almost ten minutes and he showed his displeasure by ignoring him. He walked right to Granny, greeted her warmly, then sat on the bed and asked how she felt.

Gates hovered over the doctor, not even trying to conceal his anger at the slight. Walczak pretended not to notice and took his time taking her pulse and temperature. After making a few notes on her chart, he stood up, looked the mayor straight in the eye, and spoke in an authoritarian tone. "Your grandmother is a most amazing woman. I gave her a complete physical. All of her test results came back fine. She does have a small bump on her forehead . . . just a minor contusion . . . very little bleeding. We did a series of x-rays just to be sure, and they confirmed nothing was broken. We put an icepack on to keep the swelling down and gave her something for the pain. Due to your grandmother's age, we would like to keep her overnight for observation—just to be careful."

"Do I have to sign anything?"

"No, she insisted on signing the consent forms herself," Dr. Walczak turned to his patient and smiled.

"Doctor, before you leave. I need to find the women who were brought in here with my grandmother . . . but all that I have are first names."

"If you go to the nurse's station, I'm sure they can give you directions. Granny has made friends with the entire staff."

As the doctor walked away, Gates turned to the two police officers who stood at attention flanking the door. "Thank you so very much for watching over Granny. I know you were under a lot of pressure, but you remembered your pledge to serve and protect. Your actions might be the only thing the department did right today. I will not forget your kindness." They were still standing in proud awe a couple of minutes later when they watched a candy striper escort the Mayor downstairs.

"They're here to see Granny's friends," the young girl, oblivious to who Gates was, said when they arrived at the nurse's station

The Hispanic woman sitting behind the computer monitor said, "Good afternoon, Mister Mayor, they told me you were coming." She turned the screen so he could see it. "You can visit with the Hansen sisters in room 605. They were brought in suffering from pepper spray. Their eyes are still a little swollen and red, but they're off oxygen. I should warn you there are two police officers sitting down the hall waiting to take them to their station for booking as soon as they're released. Their doctor is appalled at how these women have been treated and refuses to release them until they've had a chance to speak to their lawyer."

"And the others?" Gates asked.

"Two of them have asthma and one has emphysema. They're all on oxygen in intensive care, so you can't see them right now. The paramedics identified them for special attention on the ride over because permanent damage or even death could be caused by exposure to irritating gasses. Don't your police know the elderly are always much more vulnerable to the effects of pepper spray?"

Gates stood there looking uncomfortable without replying.

"The fourth lady is recovering from surgery. She suffered a compound fracture of her arm when a police officer fell on top of them. He's in Room 609 with a broken wrist, if you care to visit him. We have two other policemen in 612 who were tear-gassed and there's a couple more downstairs in the ER being stitched up."

She tapped a few keys and the computer screen changed. "Oh, and I almost forgot my favorite. We've got one of your boys in blue in surgery who was shot in the butt. So what happened out there? A war?" She made no attempt to hide her sarcasm.

Gates mumbled a thank you then walked away shaking his head. "I want to know everyone who is responsible for this," he growled as he pushed past his security detail, "and I want to know today."

Both men were punching keys on their cellphones as they tried to keep up with the mayor's determined gait. True to his word, he visited the two neighbors who used to babysit him so many years ago.

He found the Hansen sisters sitting on the end of the bed.

"Sidney," they said in harmony. "What a pleasant surprise."

He knelt down on one knee in front of them. "Ladies, I am so very sorry for what happened today."

"No need to apologize Sidney, this is the most excitement we've had in years," Kaye said with a huge grin. "And besides, Granny was on the television."

"Did you get to see her?" Ruth jumped in.

"No, maybe I'll catch it later."

"No. I didn't mean on television. Did you get to see her in her room?" Ruth explained herself.

"Yes, Ma'am. I just left there, and she's doing great. She has a bump on her head, but otherwise she's doing great. The doctor wants to keep her overnight as a precaution."

"I always knew your grandmother was hardheaded." Ruth's quip made everyone laugh.

"Well I wish I could stay longer but I have to run." He stood up and straightened his tie. "Goodbye, ladies. Call me if you need anything," Gates said as he backed out the door.

"Say hi to your mother for us." Ruth called out.

As soon as Gates closed the door, he turned to his bodyguards and said, "I don't care who you have to call, but none of these ladies is going to be inconvenienced any more than they have already been. Get me the Commander from seventeen on the phone. I want whoever tried to arrest these women waiting for me when we get there. I also want the States Attorney there . . . and enough investigators from the Office of Professional Standards to interview everyone in uniform who was there. I used to be the States Attorney, and I know there is no way any sane person would ever try to bring this collection of little old ladies up on charges."

Jackie sat in his limousine and ran everything through one last time while his crew set up. He was still smarting at that morning's bad luck and wanted to make sure everything went right this time. His attempt to use an elderly resident to crash the press conference was foiled when her grandson spotted them right before they entered the building. The young man's words still rang in his ears, "Grandma, thank God I found you. Mom was worried and sent me to bring you home."

What were the odds we would bump into Estelle's grandson? Just one more minute and we would have been inside.

Even though a police officer was checking identification at the door, the lure of a room full of media was too powerful, so Jackie decided to give it a try anyway.

"Good morning, Officer Czyszczewski, he tried his best to pronounce the name on her uniform. "I am the Reverend Jefferson." He extended his hand, but the policewoman did not shake it. "Several of my flock await me inside."

She stepped in front of him blocking his path. "I'm sorry Reverend Jefferson, but my orders say admission is limited to City Gate residents. You don't live there, you don't get in." She thumped a list of names on a clipboard. "But my lieutenant is right over there," she gestured towards a squad car, "if you want to talk to him about it."

Jackie took a deep breath and bit his lip. "No, I do not wish to impose during this time of trial. I will make other arrangements." He knew from experience his face was well-known among police brass and the last thing he wanted was to have a camera crew film him being turned away.

The building's collapse was only one of the days breaking stories. Having struck out at the press conference, it was only natural a hospital full of senior citizens would be an irresistible lure to Jackie. Especially if the senior citizens had been tear gassed and accused of everything from assaulting a police officer to public mopery.

It was almost noon when Jackie's footsteps echoed off the polished marble floor in First Presbyterian Hospital's reception area. His team of six men, including two carrying large video cameras on their shoulders, followed close behind. A steady stream of people were entering and leaving the building and Jackie singled out a woman struggling with two small children. "Please, allow me to be of assistance," he said as he swooped down to pick up the blanket which her son had dropped. She stammered a nervous thank you when she realized they were being filmed.

Jackie proclaimed as she walked out of the building, "Children truly are a blessing from God." He then returned to the work at hand.

"Excuse me, my good lady," Jackie said to the attractive young woman sitting alone at the hospital's reception desk. "I am quite confident you know who I am." Without allowing time for a response he continued, "However, if you are amongst the very small uninformed segment of our population, please allow me to introduce myself. I am the Reverend Jackie Jefferson. Several members of my senior citizens outreach are patients in your fine facility and they need to have their souls attended to."

The receptionist stared at the man wearing a two-tone purple, perfectly tailored, crushed velvet, pinstriped suit—complete with a Roman collar—with a look of disbelief. "You do know this is a hospital, sir?"

Jackie turned around to face his entourage. Striking a pose, he smirked, pivoted on one foot, and again faced the amazed receptionist holding his favorite prop, an oversized Bible. "Again, I repeat to you, miss, I am the most Reverend Jackie Jefferson. I ask only the hospital extend to me the full privileges and consideration as are due an ordained member of the cloth."

"Oh boy," she rolled her eyes. "Could I please have the names of the patients whom you are here to see?" This was the first time Laurie McKennae had worked the reception desk by herself and she intended to follow the rules to the letter.

"Miss McKennae," he read the name off her badge. "I am very sorry, but I do not have their names with me at this moment. I am here to see those lovely ladies who were pounced upon so viciously by overzealous members of the very group that is sworn to uphold their safety. I am here to pray with those innocent women who were struck down for no reason other than society has no use for anyone whose skin is wrinkled and their backs stooped from a lifetime of hard work. I am here to give spiritual comfort to those silver-haired members of my outreach who are here looking for relief from their undeserved physical pain. God knows their names and He sent me here to tend to their spiritual needs."

"And God didn't tell you their names?" The receptionist asked in amazement.

Jackie caught himself as he almost laughed at her witty response. "Miss McKennae, I mean you neither disparagement nor disrespect, but I do take great umbrage at your lack of recognition of the magnificence of my purpose. I have been personally sent by our Lord and Savior, Jesus Christ." He wished he had taken the time to memorize an appropriate Bible verse or two with which to intimidate her.

"Since you seem to have a great difficulty accommodating my simple request, I must ask, no, I must insist, I be permitted to speak with your supervisor."

"I'll gladly call her right now." She picked up her phone and dialed. It was answered on the second ring.

"Mrs. Prince, this is the receptionist, Laurie McKennae," she sounded anxious. "There's a man in the lobby demanding to see you."

"I am not just any man. You will kindly address me as the most Reverend Jackie Jefferson," his voice boomed out, drawing the attention of everyone in the lobby.

The receptionist turned away and lowered her voice to a whisper, "He says wants to see several patients, but he doesn't know who they are . . . and he has a camera crew and some other people with him. He's making me nervous. He insists on talking to you."

McKennae ended the conversation with, "Thank you so very much," when Mrs. Prince said she would be bringing hospital security with her.

Relieved, she pointed towards a leather sofa. "If you would please have a seat over there, my supervisor will be down in a moment."

Jackie cocked his head and smiled. "I apologize for having troubled you so, young lady. I find fault lies not with your actions but in your being inadequately trained by those who misuse the title of supervisor to recognize me, a highly respected emissary of our Lord. Yes, child, the same Jesus Christ who knows what is in every man's heart and will return at the end of the world to separate the wheat from the chaff," Jackie gave a well practiced sincere smile for the camera, "has sent me here today."

Jackie placed his Bible on the desk and leaned forward with his palms extended. "If you would be so kind as to allow me to place my anointed hands on your head, I will pray that God Almighty will help you find peace, tranquility, and salvation. And I will ask Him to walk with you all the days of your life."

The receptionist looked terrified. She started to roll her chair back to avoid his touch. Seeing this, Jackie stretched his arms further out, but lost his balance. His hands missed their target and landed on her shoulders, then slipped and raked across her chest.

"You will unhand me this moment," she screamed. "You're no man of the cloth. You're a pervert."

The room became quiet. All eyes were on Jackie as he stammered, "I . . . I . . . I mean that I, er . . . it was an accident . . . I was trying to save you."

"No thanks, mister most reverend," her voice raged with sarcasm. "Jesus died on the cross for me and paid for my salvation with His life. So I don't need you to save me because Jesus already did that."

She picked up Jackie's Bible and held it in front of his face. "You should try reading this book; you could learn a lot. Start with John 3:16, 'For God so loved the world, that He gave His only begotten son, that whosoever believeth in Him should not perish, but have eternal life.'"

Jackie stood frozen. His eyes were wide open, and his mouth hung open, but for once he couldn't think of a thing to say. The camera continued to record it all. Time seemed to stand still; no one made a sound. Then, as they say in boxing, he was saved by the bell.

A loud ding came from the elevator bank behind the receptionist's station. Jackie hoped it was Mrs. Prince, and he would be able to extract himself from the pounding he was taking from this young believer. Jackie had never seen a real miracle, but when the elevator doors opened, he knew he had the next best thing.

Mayor Gates stepped from the elevator followed by his bodyguards. Gates was ambushed by the Reverend even before he could take two steps.

"Mayor Gates, I am so genuinely and profoundly saddened to learn that the matriarch of your highly respected family has been viciously assaulted by rogue members of the Chicago Police Department. I have been praying nonstop for her healing. All of my vast congregation has been praying for her nonstop since we learned of her travails."

One of the bodyguards, a burly former linebacker from Notre Dame, sprang into action. He was a step away from tackling Jackie when the mayor noticed the video cameras and shouted, "Stop!"

An audible sigh of relief could be heard as Jackie struggled to regain his composure. "Thank you, Mister Mayor . . . thank you, indeed. All I wanted to tell you is I came here, in person, to this place of healing, to visit with your Granny. Yes, I came here to pray with her and ask the intercession of Jesus Christ, the only Son of God our Father, the same Jesus Christ who raised Lazarus from the dead, returned sight to the blind, healed the lepers, and restored strength to the paralyzed. Mayor Gates, I came here to ask Jesus Christ to remove the pain her frail body must be suffering after her savage beating."

Gates was already in a bad mood, a real bad mood. This was the third time today some clown with a microphone and camera had caught him off guard. "Where are my PR people?" he fumed. His highly paid public relations and media experts were supposed to shield him from such attacks.

"Mr. Mayor, I repeat, I have come here as a man of peace, yet these callous and capricious bureaucrats are denying me the opportunity to minister to your beloved grandmother's spiritual needs." He paused, dramatically sweeping his Bible through the air for full camera effect.

Without a word being spoken, the mayor's bodyguards pushed forward and swept Jackie out of their way as though he was an annoying insect. Two hospital guards, uncertain of what to do, stood off to the side watching in amazement. The look of determination on the bodyguard's faces told the Reverend's posse today was not the day to push their luck. They parted their ranks.

"Did you catch that?" Jackie asked his cameraman. "That thug pushed me." Turning his attention back to the crowd of hospital employees, patients, and visitors who had gathered to watch, he announced, "All of you are eyewitnesses. That man assaulted me."

Most shook their heads and snickered under their breath at the Reverend's antics as they started to return to work, however the hospital security guards, now numbering four, stood shoulder-to-shoulder, blocking entry to the elevators.

"Will I finally be allowed to do the Lord's work or do you want to hear from my lawyer?" Jackie demanded.

"I'll tell you what you're going to do, you pompous ass." Jackie spun around to see who spoke. A woman, not much taller than five feet, stepped out from behind the line of blue uniforms.

"Mrs. Prince!" Laurie shouted.

"When your hands touched my assistant's breasts, you sexually assaulted her and she is pressing charges. So your lawyer had better be a criminal lawyer because everything is on tape . . . yours and the hospital security cameras. You're going to be arrested. That's what you're going to do." She signaled the security officers. "Please hold the assailant. The Chicago Police will be here in a moment to take him into custody."

CHAPTER 7

THE PRESIDENT OF the Council of Women was furious. Her day had begun well before sunrise when she was awakened by a telephone call from a reporter asking her to comment on the disaster that had befallen their world headquarters.

Michelle "Micci" Staylor fumbled for the phone in the dark. "Disaster? What . . . huh? You woke me up." She grabbed the alarm clock. "Do you know what time it is? That's right. It's four frigging thirty in the morning, so if this is a joke, it ain't funny," was about all she could get out before she slammed the phone down so hard she woke up Shannon, her latest "life-partner."

"Who was that? Is everything OK, Micci?"

"It's nothing. Some crank caller. Go back to sleep." Staylor answered in a gruff voice.

Both women closed their eyes and tried to fall back asleep when the phone rang again barely a minute later.

This time it was the C of W's treasurer, June Dannon, on the line. "Micci, bad news. I just got a call from the night manager at Vigilant Security. Something real bad happened."

"Well?" Staylor demanded without emotion.

"He said an airplane crashed into the Women's Pavilion."

"My building! How's my building?" Micci shouted.

"He didn't know. He couldn't reach the security guards and all our cameras are down. All he knew for sure was someone called 911 and said a plane crashed into our building. The emergency operator wanted to know how many people were inside and said fire trucks and ambulances were on their way.

"Where are you now?" Micci asked.

"I'm still in my bedroom. I called as soon as I hung up. So what do you want me to do?"

Micci struggled to rein in her emotions. "Meet me there. It'll take me about fifteen minutes to get there. You're closer than I am, so call me as soon as you get there. And don't talk to anyone."

"OK, I'll see you there."

Staylor was muttering under her breath as she picked a sweatshirt and a pair of faded blue jeans off the top of a pile of laundry on the bedroom floor. All of her concern was for the building at City Gate. She didn't give a thought to how many lives would be lost in an airplane crash. She dressed in the dark, not even bothering to invest the usual ten seconds to run a comb through her short hair. A pair of well-worn work boots completed her outfit.

Staylor cared little about her appearance. It had been many years since she wore makeup, and this morning's outfit differed little from that of a typical workday.

"I'll call you later," she said to the motionless lump under the blanket without checking to see if she was awake. Staylor learned it was an utter waste of time to try and include her arm-candy in handling a problem . . . any problem. She was selected by Micci solely for her nubile body anyway. That was one of her favorite perks as head of the C of W—access to impressionable young women who would do anything to advance the cause.

The twenty-four hour news station she turned the radio dial to was broadcasting live from the building . . . her building. Staylor always thought of it as her building because acquiring it had been her goal from the moment she saw the architect's preliminary sketches. This was a building with prestige—it had the premium location in City Gate and was the first building thousands of drivers would pass on their way into Chicago every morning. Plus, every passenger on every airplane flying in and out of O'Hare would see Council of Women World Headquarters in bright red letters across the roof.

Staylor was devastated when she first laid out her proposal to acquire the building—complete with a lavish power point presentation—to her fellow board members at their annual convention a little over eight years ago. She capped off her talk by rolling out a huge, detailed model of the complex. The centerpiece, however, was a magnificent scale model of the C of W World Headquarters, complete with full interior detail. There were even hundreds of little cars in the parking lot and tiny little people walking up the stairs.

She expected to be praised for her vision. Instead they laughed at her and claimed there was no way they could ever afford such an extravagance. When the votes were counted it was 10-2 against buying the building.

Why couldn't I make them understand the greatest feminist organization deserves the greatest building? She thought as she stormed out of the room after the vote.

Staylor was unwilling to accept defeat and swore to seize control away from the board members who lacked her vision. First, she worked to persuade the stodgy, old women who founded the group almost fifty years earlier—the very ones who fought for so many years in a futile attempt to get the Equal Rights Amendment passed—that they should retire. She was able to convince a couple of them that the time had come for them to enjoy their golden years and turn over the reins to a new generation.

Her next task was a lot more difficult. She had to run off at least three well-qualified, college-educated, professional women who were serving on the board. Staylor often opined those women were the ones who naively thought they had made it to the top on their own. It infuriated her that they reaped the benefits of her hardcore feminist activism and then refused to devote their entire lives to advancing the cause.

Staylor switched her energies to stirring unrest by spreading rumors and gossip through the rank-and-file. Ultimately, four of the targeted women said they were, "fed-up with all of the infighting," and resigned not only from their positions of authority, but from the group as well. *Better off without them*, she thought.

With six openings on the board, it was necessary to hold a special election to fill the vacancies. It wasn't very hard to convince women in their twenties that the time had come for them to assume leadership roles, and Staylor had little trouble lining up a half-dozen like-minded members who were willing to serve.

As the day of the election approached, Micci's minions—as they liked being called—used every dirty trick at their disposal to buy the voting loyalty of the vast number of unhappy housewives, low level office workers, retail clerks, and malcontents who made up the majority of the C of W's membership. These were "Micci's people," the part-time foot soldiers who were so good at mindlessly following orders.

She mobilized them to fight her battle for total control over the destiny and future of the largest organization of feminists in the country. Yes, she thought of this as a war and she would win at all costs. Her goal was simple—to make the C of W the voice of women everywhere in the world. She would control their health care. She would control their reproductive and civil rights. Their bodies would be hers.

With "her people's" intimidating support, Staylor was able to guarantee absolute control of the nominating committee and insure her handpicked fanatical hardliners would face only weak, token opponents. It surprised no one when her slate scored a clean sweep, nor that their first matter of business was electing Michelle Staylor president, making her the uncontested leader of the 125,000 member woman's group.

Later that same day, she signed the multimillion-dollar purchase contract for building eight at City Gate. It would take another two years for the office tower to be ready for occupancy which gave Staylor plenty of time to ratchet up the group's cash flow. The C of W already had a handful of storefront women's clinics that were mainly staffed by volunteers. Most had access to a doctor who was willing to drop in for a couple of hours each week to prescribe birth control pills or give a shot of penicillin, but for the most part they limited their services to giving a free pregnancy test, a short lecture about sexually-transmitted diseases, and a handful of condoms to walk-ins. Their only source of income was a jar on the desk labeled "donations."

Staylor planned to increase their income significantly by charging for these services—while not being very particular about the names or ages of the young girls that sought them—and by providing the ultimate family planning service: abortion-on-demand.

Stepping up recruitment efforts was another cornerstone of her plan—the $120 annual dues quickly added up—and she would see to it that no one could leave a clinic without receiving a large dose of radical feminist rhetoric and literature.

The goal was to make each woman a customer for life. By encouraging promiscuity with multiple partners, they could guarantee a steady stream of unwanted pregnancies . . . and that was where the real money would be made.

Many euphemisms would be used to make abortion-on-demand sound more palatable. First, and most importantly, they would never use the A-word. It would be referred to as "reproductive freedom" or "a woman's right to choice." Performing a "procedure" was about as close to the truth as they were willing to go. Also, the unborn baby would have to be dehumanized. So they developed catch phrases like fetus, products of conception, and cluster of cell tissue. She also planned to make use of a favorite phrase that had a dark double meaning—every pregnancy a wanted pregnancy—because every unwanted pregnancy was money in the bank . . . their bank.

Staylor grew more and more upset that almost all the doctors who were willing to abort babies were men, most often from Third World countries.

She wanted women doctors for women's bodies, but had considerable trouble even keeping female nurses on staff.

What was wrong with these women? Why couldn't they see that we're providing a service for women who don't want the inconvenience of being pregnant?

Almost overnight Staylor succeeded in changing the direction of the C of W from one which sought to help women to one whose goal was to control how women thought . . . and the seemingly endless piles of money needed to finance this quantum leap was being generated by family planning worthy of Adolph Hitler.

And now, after fighting her way through a gawkers' traffic jam, then intimidating her way past a police roadblock, Staylor arrived at the outermost parking lot just in time to see the crowning glory of her rise to power disintegrate into a pile of broken concrete and twisted steel. Everyone standing around her seemed mesmerized as the ground shook and the tower sank gracefully from sight. Some fell to their knees, but most stood there with their mouths hanging open in amazement. Closer to the building, the reactions were more urgent with many screaming in horror. The rumble of the collapse soon drowned out everything else.

For the first time in many years, Staylor almost cried. Then she got mad.

The police officer directing traffic stared in disbelief as she wheeled her SUV around him, shifted into four-wheel drive, and started a crazed sprint towards the smoking hole. Staylor slammed the brakes to the floor and slid to a stop at the edge of the debris field at almost the same time as the emergency crews. She leapt down from her jacked-up Blazer without even turning it off and joined the crowd running towards her former building. Anyone who noticed Staylor assumed she was part of a rescue team and ignored her . . . even when she ran past the three dazed building inspectors. She didn't stop running until she reached the edge of the hole.

They did, however, take notice when she began to scream, "My building! My building! Who did this to you? I swear I will punish whoever did this to you."

"Is she with you?" one of the paramedics asked McBarker.

"No. We're all with me. I mean the two of them are with me . . . all three of us are together. I have no idea who she is."

"Do you know who she is?" he asked his men.

Paramedics had already slipped oxygen masks over the mouths of Haynes and Philo so they shook their heads in the negative.

"Who did this to you? I demand revenge!" Staylor continued screaming.

A team of rescue workers wearing bright orange protective suits and helmets with breathing apparatuses walked over to her. Their leader's voice sounded mechanical when he asked, "Who are you?"

No response.

"Are you OK?" he reached out and placed his gloved hand on her shoulder.

"Don't touch me," Staylor screamed as she jumped back. "And no, I'm not OK. My building has died. No, it's been murdered."

"Uhhhhh. OK . . . Could you please come with us. It's not safe this close. The air is full of concrete dust. Let us take you back and check you out."

"No," she screamed. "I'm not leaving until I know who did this to my building. I demand revenge."

While one team was busy with Staylor, the remaining EMTs were busy preparing the building inspectors for a ride to the hospital. All three men said they felt fine and tried to refuse help, but the paramedics wouldn't take no for an answer. "You've inhaled a lot of dust particles. We might need to vacuum your lungs out," one of them joked.

A doctor was waiting inside the ambulance. "I'm going to do a quick check of your vital signs before we move you. We have orders to prepare you for transport to a hospital by helicopter."

In the background, Staylor's crazed ranting could be heard. "Could she have been inside?" One of the paramedics asked Fred as he slid the stretcher into the waiting ambulance.

"I don't see how. We didn't see anyone get out," he responded.

Staylor assumed a defensive position with her back to the gaping hole. She picked up a three-foot-long piece of metal debris, part of a window frame, and swung it back and forward to keep the rescue workers away.

"We're not here to hurt you. We're here to help you."

"Stay away . . . this is my building. You're trespassing!" she screamed.

"Who are you? Were you inside when it happened?"

"No, you fool. I was in bed sleeping!" She continued screaming hysterically. "Don't you know who I am? This is my building! Why did you let them do this to my building?"

"Ma'am, you're injured. Why don't we walk back to the ambulance, so I can treat you?"

"Don't use sexist terms with me," she screamed. A moment later, she looked down and noticed her hands had been sliced open by shards of glass which were still embedded in the window channel. She let her grip relax and the blood-covered aluminum bar dropped to the ground with a metallic thud.

One of the EMTs walked up to her and attempted to look at her wounds. "You're bleeding. Let's walk back to my rig. I'll clean the wounds and dress them." His partner tried to slip between her and the edge of the hole.

Staylor noticed him and broke free from the paramedic who had taken her arm. "Take your hands off me. I'm not leaving! She swooped down and picked up the bloodied piece of metal and started swinging it again. "Nobody touch me! I have a right to be here . . . it's all of you . . . you're the ones who are trespassing! All of you! Get away from my building!"

The team leader made a radio call for backup. "Chief, we have a woman in street clothes who's starting to lose it. She's injured but refuses treatment and is threatening my men. No sir, we have no idea who she is. The building inspector said she's not with them, and he didn't think she had been inside the building. She appears to be in shock. Could we get a little help in removing her?"

The call went to Deputy District Chief Yaegermann who turned to sixteenth District Police Commander Beeman and said, "Ike, could you spare a couple of men? We've got a situation at the hole. They've got an unidentified woman who refuses to leave."

Beeman turned and pointed to a nearby officer. "O'Malley, take two of your men. Grab masks and go help the paramedics. They have a thrillseeker who isn't being very cooperative. Get her out of there and into an ambulance—in handcuffs if you have to." To no one in particular he added loudly, "And make sure that no one else gets through the line."

"Kent, Williams," O'Malley called out the names of the first two men he recognized. "Grab masks, we've got work to do."

While a paramedic was helping the men pull on gauze surgical masks, another police officer walked over and said, "Sergeant, I heard what the Commander said. We've got someone you might want to talk to. She claims to be with the woman at the hole. She's standing right over there," he gestured towards a group standing by a squad car.

"Bring her here," the O'Malley called out then resumed putting his mask on.

"I'm June Dannen. I'm the treasurer of the Council of Women." He thought it odd that she had both hands shoved in her pants pockets. "That is, that was, our headquarters building. The woman is our president, Micci . . . Michelle Staylor. She gets very emotional about that building. If you let me talk to her, I'm certain she would come with me."

"Whadda we have to lose?" O'Malley responded. "Here." He handed her a package. "There's a lot of junk in the air. You'll need to put this mask on. And watch where you walk. There's broken glass everywhere."

"Micci is a good person. I don't want her to get hurt either," Dannen said.

"Well, hopefully she'll listen to you. If not, we have orders to bring her out."

Within minutes, the group set off on foot towards the hole. A light plume of smoke still hung over the pile of rubble, but was being dissipated by a strong wind. Several news choppers, however, hovered around the hole, and the downdrafts created by their blades caused dust clouds to twist and dance beneath them.

It seemed odd the way the debris so completely filled the foundation hole until it was almost level with the parking lots that surrounded it. No vertical traces of the building could be seen as they walked forward. Only the defiant silhouette of Staylor rose above the rubble.

About two-hundred feet from the hole, they met up with the rescue workers.

"So, did they send you to tune her up?" The paramedic was serious.

"Are you kidding? O'Malley responded. There must be a hundred cameras watching us. No, we'll play this one exactly by the book. This lady says they're friends, so hopefully she can talk her into coming with us."

"If she won't leave, you should at least get her to wear a mask. Her lungs must look like a coal miners'." The paramedic handed him a white plastic bag.

"Thanks. Are you ready?" O'Malley asked Dannen who had a blank look on her face.

She shrugged her shoulders. "It's so hard to believe it's gone. I mean, yesterday I was working on the top floor, and today everything's gone. Why?"

"I have no idea. Maybe someone back there can answer you. My job right now is to keep your friend alive. So can you help her?"

"I should warn you. Micci doesn't like men, especially policemen. Could you stand a few feet behind me when I talk to her?" Dannen asked.

"Whatever it takes to end this." O'Malley replied.

On a normal day, Dannen was as militant as Staylor and held the police in the same contempt. They both harbored grudges against the force for allowing "anti-choicers" to picket with impunity in front of their clinics and even on this very site. The surreal scene of destruction stunned her into complacency and her only goal was to help her mentor.

"If you're ready, let's get going." O'Malley pointed forward. "We'll be about twenty feet behind you. If you need us, all you have to do is gesture like this." He clinched his hand into a fist at his side with the index finger pointing towards the ground, "and we'll be right there."

"I'm sure that won't be necessary." Dannen started walking. After a few steps she called out, "Micci, Micci, I'm coming to talk. OK?"

Staylor continued standing stiff as a board, her hair and clothing covered by a light gray dust. She made no reply.

"Micci, everything will be all right." She continued talking as she walked closer. "We've got insurance. We'll start over and rebuild even bigger and better then before." She paused when she was about twenty-five feet from the friend. "Micci, you're hurt. Why don't you let the doctors bandage your hands?" There was no response.

Dannen took a couple more steps forward then froze when she realized Micci's face was pure white . . . and it was twisted into an expression of terror. She had never before seen her longtime friend express any emotions other than contempt and hate.

Micci should be furious, not afraid, she thought.

She took two more steps forward and noticed Micci was crying. The tears formed rivers of mud down her cheeks.

Dannen clenched both hands into fists. "Micci, are you OK?" she asked.

Still no reply. She took a few more steps until the two women were within ten feet of each other.

"Micci, it's me, June." She opened her hands and swept her arms up as though she was going to embrace her but, before she could take one more step forward, Micci took one back and vanished. She didn't seem to plunge. It was more like she disappeared.

"Micci!" June screamed, "Micci!"

O'Malley and his men covered the twenty feet in a few seconds. Officer Kent grabbed hold of June as she fell to her knees looking for her president.

"Where'd she go? You were right here. Where'd she go?" O'Malley demanded of the stunned woman.

"I . . . I don't know. She was right there. Look, you can still see her footprints." Dannen's hand shook as she pointed at the ground.

O'Malley and Williams walked over to where they last saw Staylor and looked at the pile of debris.

"There's no hole." Williams sounded confused. "What could she have fallen into?"

Dannen screamed out, "Where's Micci?"

"You were with her," O'Malley demanded. "You tell me."

Williams pleaded, "Sarge, this don't make sense. She was standing right here." He pointed at her footprints. "Then she sank into the ground."

"Hang on. I gotta call this in." O'Malley clicked his radio. "Uh, Commander, the intruder appears to have fallen into a hole. No sir, we can't see her . . . we can't even see the hole. I don't know where she fell. It's like the earth opened up and swallowed her."

"It sounds like there's some kind of hidden sink hole. Get out of there right now," Beeman ordered.

O'Malley said, "OK, you heard the boss, let's get out of here. And watch where you're stepping."

"What about Micci?" June plead with the Sergeant. "We can't leave without Micci. "You've got to do something. You've got to save her."

"Sarge, where did she go?"

"Williams, I wish I knew. I wish I knew."

CHAPTER 8

IT HAD BEEN ten long minutes since Fred admitted his life had been saved by an angel and he was having a hard time coming to grips with it.

"Fred, if you had died this morning, do you know for certain you would have gone to heaven?" Billy broke the silence.

McBarker didn't say a word. He sat on the edge of the hospital bed, shrugging his shoulders. "Fred, how would you have answered Jesus Christ when He met you at the gates of heaven and asked why He should let you in?" Billy tried his best to get a response.

"All three of us have been given an incredible gift from God," Philo added. "We should be dead right now, buried under tons of concrete. But we were given a second chance."

McBarker mumbled something as he pulled his hand free and wiped his eyes with his sleeve. Philo walked over to the nightstand and returned with a box of tissues.

"I . . . I saw it," Fred stammered between sobs. "You saw it too. It was real. It all really happened."

Billy and Philo nodded to each other, then wrapped their arms around their supervisor. For several minutes the only sound was his labored breathing interrupted by whimpers.

"Yes, Fred, it really happened," Billy said. "The three of us were allowed to witness the mighty power of our God. I don't know why we were chosen. I'm just a lowly sinner. I know I'm not worthy to watch one of God's messengers doing His bidding."

"Nor I." Philo added.

Billy looked Fred straight in the eyes. "But I do know He allowed us to witness His angel destroying that evil place and that He sheltered us from all harm. Not many people are so blessed."

"But why me?" Fred pleaded. "Why me? Why would He care what happened to me? I didn't even go to church last Christmas."

"Because God loves and cares about you." Philo felt Fred's body start to tremble and tightened his grip. "Fred, God so loved the world that He gave His only begotten Son, that whoever believes in Him shall not perish, but have eternal life. Jesus Christ died on the cross for you. He wants to welcome you at the gates of heaven and say, 'Enter good and faithful servant.'"

"But why did He choose me? I can understand someone like you. Someone who . . ."

Philo didn't let him finish. "Fred, only a foolish man would pretend to understand why God spared our lives. But I am convinced He has some mighty big plans for the rest of our lives."

"Are you familiar with the story of Saul? He was riding on the road to Damascus to persecute Christians when a blinding light from heaven knocked him to the ground. Jesus asked him, 'Saul, Saul, why do you persecute me?' Saul changed his name to Paul and spent the rest of his life preaching Jesus is the Son of God. Fred, if Jesus could choose a man like Saul to carry His 'name before the Gentiles and people of Israel' he could surely choose to save your life."

Fred spoke in a whisper. "But I'm a nobody," then buried his face in his hands.

Billy waited a moment than added, "If God could choose a man who was 'breathing out threats against (His) disciples' surely he could choose you."

The three sat in silence on the bed for another five minutes before Fred spoke again. "I have no idea what I should do."

"We can help you enter into an intimate personal relationship with God," Billy stated with confidence.

"Fred, this is the most important decision you will ever make in your life," Philo added with great zeal. "I know you're still pretty shaken up, but I can't think of a better time to ask. Are you ready to make a commitment to Jesus Christ without reservation?"

A long minute passed before Fred nodded.

Billy stood up, pointed towards heaven, and proclaimed, "Ours is truly an awesome God. We have been saved from a certain death by a miracle. Fred, you know what you saw. You know your earthly life was spared. Are you certain you want eternal life with Jesus?"

He nodded again but this time added, "Yes."

"Praise the Lord," Philo shouted.

"Amen to that, brother," Billy replied. "Fred, I'm an elder at my church. We teach this prayer to lost sheep who want to be welcomed home by the Shepherd."

Fred looked nervous; frightened.

Fred, if you sincerely express your trust in Jesus Christ by praying with us, He will give you eternal life. I ask you now, do you accept Jesus Christ as your Savior?

Fred nodded.

Then pray with me."

Fred followed the men in reciting,

Lord, I have sinned. I am sorry for my sins. With your help I want to turn from my sin. Take control of my life. Lord, I want eternal life. I want an intimate, personal relationship with you. I want to know for certain I will live with you in heaven forever. In Jesus name I pray.

For the next half hour Billy and Philo took turns telling their new brother about Christ's sacrifice. Accepting Jesus dying on the cross for his salvation almost overwhelmed him, and he peppered his teachers with dozens of questions.

"Fred, Philo. I think this would be a good time for each of us to thank God for the gifts which He gave us today. Let's bow our heads."

The warmth of Billy's words gave Fred confidence. *How did he put it? Grace, God's Redemption At Christ's Expense, GRACE. Thank you God for saving my life . . . and thank you for giving me eternal life.* For the first time since they were admitted to the hospital, Fred smiled. A sharp knock on the door brought a sudden end to the tranquility they were sharing. Fred didn't know why, but he felt very peaceful after his first talk with God.

The door swung open and a young Hispanic intern dressed in pale green hospital scrubs entered. Gonzalez was stenciled across her pocket. "Excuse me, gentlemen. Your wives are down the hall at the nurse's station. Should I send them in?"

Fred wished he had more time to prepare to face his wife—he was certain she would think he was nuts when he told her the truth—but there was no way he could selfishly make them wait. He had no idea all three had been awakened by phone calls from a reporter asking them to comment on their husband's deaths.

"Please, send them right in."

"Oh, and Mr. McBarker, there's two guys from the Department of Buildings in the lobby who are real adamant about talking to you as soon as possible. There were also two detectives who wanted to talk to you earlier, but I didn't see them when I went downstairs to get your wives. I hope you're not mad at me, but I blew the building guys off by saying that I would have to check on your status. Then I snuck your wives up in an employee elevator."

Fred laughed, "Mad at you? Are you kidding? No, no. Thank you very much."

Gonzalez gave him a wink and a grin. "Bosses are the same no matter what you do for a living. They don't want to understand your family should always come before work. Your wives are real worried, so I'll give you as much time as I can."

A few seconds later the three women swarmed into the room.

Fritzi McBarker was a classy woman—an executive at a Loop insurance company who never left the house without her clothes and makeup looking perfect. Today she looked drained . . . her skin was pasty, her blue eyes were red and swollen from crying, and her blonde hair was a mess. Fred thought she never looked more beautiful as she leapt into his arms. Billy's and Philo's wives threw their arms around their husbands and started sobbing.

In between tearful kisses, Fritzi kept up a steady patter of affectionate nagging, "You keep telling me how safe your job is . . . you never told me a building could fall on you. TV keeps showing a cloud of smoke after the building collapsed. They said you were dead." Her voice cracked and she had to clear her throat before continuing. "If you had really died I would have killed you."

Fred chuckled at that one.

Mauves Haynes and Margaret Clemson were expressing similar sentiments, but they liberally peppered them with praise and thanks to God for watching over their husbands.

McBarker wanted to work a "thank you, God" into his conversation but wasn't sure he knew when, or how to do it. He was very aware the last time he and Fritzi had been in a church was her mother's funeral—no, there may have been somebody's wedding since then—but he was confident she must have said a slew of "please don't let my husband die" prayers as she drove to the hospital. Thanking God afterwards was something that most likely would not have occurred to her . . . not that Fred had ever done it before. As Fritzi kept repeating how happy she was that Fred was alive, he was struggling to work up the courage to tell her she should thank God for saving him.

He fidgeted and looked nervously at his feet. "Uh, honey. There's, uh, something I have to tell you. You see last night we were saved . . . He was interrupted in mid-sentence when the door flung open and two serious-looking men in suits with police badges hanging around their necks on lanyards burst into the room.

"Which one of you is McBarker?" the older of the pair, a rail-thin bald man with a jet black goatee, demanded.

With his wife's arms still draped around his neck, Fred spun around and stated, "I am."

"The reunion's over. We've been sent to bring you downtown. There's a lot of people who want to get back into their condominiums, and somebody decided nobody goes home until they talk to you."

Fred's mind flashed back to the horrific scene that took place just moments before the building rained down in front of them. He started to wince when he thought about the dead babies, but was filled with peace when he visualized the messenger of God who saved him from a certain death.

"Yes, of course. But what about my men?" Fred asked.

"No one said anything about anyone but you. So they stay." The bearded officer stated.

"Or, they can go," the other man added. "We don't care either way. They're not our problem."

"What about our boss?" Fred asked. "The hospital orderly told me Commissioner Reynold O'Dea sent a team from the Building Department to talk to us. They're waiting for us downstairs right now."

"Then let 'em talk to your friends. We have orders to take you downtown without delay."

"But I just got to see my wife a few seconds ago. Can't I at least have a few minutes with her?" Fred pleaded.

"You are not taking my husband anywhere," Fritzi's emotions poured out. "I have been waiting since before you woke up to talk to my husband so you can tell whoever sent you they will have to wait a little longer."

The younger officer backed off and looked at his partner.

"Sorry, but no can do. We're late already. Tell ya what. 'Cuz I'm a nice guy you got thirty seconds to kiss your wife good-bye. That's it. We've got a car waiting downstairs."

"Can she at least come with so we can talk in the car?" Fred implored.

The bald man was getting irritated. "Nope. You got your kiss, now let's get going." He grabbed Fred's arm and started pulling him towards the door.

"I love you, honey. I'll call as soon as I can. I don't know when I'll be home, but there's so much I want to tell you. I had an unbelievable experience," Fred continued talking as he was led out of the room. "I don't even know where to start. Billy, Philo, before you talk to Rey, tell my wife about grace. She needs to know everything"

Fritzi looked stunned. "Grace?" Her mood changed from concern to anger in a split second. "Grace? Who is Grace? Frederick McBarker, Junior, you are not leaving until you tell me who Grace is." She followed the three men down the hall. Her eyes flared, and voice grew louder and angrier as they walked away. "Fred McBarker, you'll wish you were dead when I'm through with you," she screamed as the elevator doors closed.

CHAPTER 9

PAM ROMENELLI DID what she always did when she was nervous. She said a prayer. The wind kicked up a bit, sweeping her long blonde hair across her forehead. Before she could comb it, her cameraman held up his hand and counted down the seconds by clenching his fingers one at a time.

When Tony made a fist she began speaking. "Thank you, Dick," Pam acknowledged the news anchor introduced her segment. "I'm standing in the middle of Elston Avenue. Normally, at this time of the evening, I would be dodging rush hour traffic as thousands of Chicagoans hurry home from work. Tonight the street is deserted, blocked by police cruisers. Behind me, all is now quiet. Earlier today, however, this major traffic artery was the scene of one of the strangest riots in the history of Chicago." The camera zoomed out to show the street scene.

"The clouds of teargas have dissipated," she went on. "Tow trucks have hauled away the burned-out shells of three Chicago police cars. Over two dozen local residents, including the mayor's grandmother, Granny Gates, have been arrested. Unconfirmed reports place the number taken by ambulances to First Presbyterian Hospital at over twenty. One police officer is said to be undergoing surgery for a bullet wound which eyewitnesses tell me was fired by an overzealous fellow member of the department. Local residents are calling it the Albany Park Riot."

The camera zoomed back in on Pam.

"This young man, who would prefer to remain anonymous, witnessed the entire incident unfold. Sir, would you please tell us what you saw?"

A young Hispanic male, his baseball cap pulled down and the collar of his leather jacket up to hide his face, stood next to the on-the-scene reporter. A small crowd of curious bystanders hovered behind them.

"Yeah, I saw it all," he spoke with heavily-accented street English. It was like this old lady, see, she lives 'round the corner. And, I like, see her all the time walking real slow with this cart thing to help her walk, 'cuz she's like, real old, you know? She was just doing nothin' when this cop grabbed her and cuffed her . . . like, real hard like and he throwed her down on her face. Smack . . . you could hear it where I was hangin," he gestured towards a vacant storefront. "Then these other old ladies, they like, come over and started yelling at the cop to stop. And man, all these other cops, they were just like, hanging around over there not helping that old lady on the ground."

He pointed to where the officers had been standing. "So the cop in charge, he starts yelling 'Arrest everyone.' Then he like, started shooting his gun off, like, at the air, and spraying mace at the old ladies. That's when I split. That cop was like, nuts, and I didn't want him to hassle me none. Man, I thought he might even shoot me 'cuz I saw him bein' nuts whoppin' up on an old lady."

Several spectators began shouting comments about the police, none of which were complimentary.

"Did you see who was throwing rocks and bottles at the police?" Pam asked.

"Whadda you, funny lady? Like I said, I split so I don't know nothing. And I'm like, outta here now." The cameraman followed the youth as he joined a pack of similarly attired men.

"Thank you very much, sir," she called out to him. The camera again zoomed in on the reporter. "His eloquent story is remarkably similar to those told by several other eyewitnesses we spoke with earlier today, all of whom declined to go on camera citing fear of police reprisals. We have confirmed the elderly woman our eyewitness referred to is Granny Gates, the mayor's one-hundred-year-old grandmother. She is a member of a group of retired women that call themselves Albany Parkers for Life who pray on the public sidewalk in front of the woman's clinic you see behind me." The camera panned from her face to the former grocery store. Seeing this, the two police officers standing in front of the door turned away from the camera.

Pam began to walk across the street in front of a row of blue police sawhorses. She stopped when her cameraman signaled he had framed the shot.

"This clinic is run by the Council of Women, and one day a week they provide pregnancy termination services for low-income women. A friend of the women said they distribute pro-life literature and counsel pregnant women every Monday morning. A source within the Chicago Police

Department, who prefers to remain anonymous, confirmed their weekly presence and stated, 'There have been no previous arrests of anti-choice protesters at this clinic.' Our source also confirmed 'a heightened awareness' of the women's activities because of the collapse of the Council of Women's headquarters building at City Gate early this morning. He refused, however, to speculate on whether any of the women, whose average age is over seventy-five years old, were suspected of causing the destruction of the eight-story office tower."

"Pam, thank you for that amazing update. Our traffic reporter was wondering if you have any idea when Elston Avenue will reopen for traffic?"

"Dick, at the moment they are even holding back pedestrians. Let me see if I can get the attention of the policemen standing in front of the clinic."

The reporter turned from the camera and started waving. "Officer, can I ask you a question?"

When the policemen turned around she leaned over the barricade, cupped her hands around her mouth, and shouted. "Officer! It's Pam Romenelli, Channel One News. Could you please tell our viewers when you will open the street so people can drive home from work?"

The camera zoomed in on the backs two blue-jacketed officers who ignored her question.

"Officer!" she screamed, "When will Elston Avenue open?"

Still no response. A couple of people then led the crowd in chanting, "Open Elston . . . Open Elston . . . Open Elston . . ."

Trying to keep a straight face, she looked at the camera and stated, "I'm sorry Dick, but they don't seem able to hear us. Reporting live from the scene of the Albany Park riot, this is Pam Romenelli."

Stifling a giggle, the anchor replied, "Thank you, Pam. We'll check back with you later in the broadcast to see if there are any new developments. After the commercial break, we'll bring you highlights of Granny Gates's hospital room press conference."

Pam's cellphone began vibrating the moment she finished her broadcast. She was glad she remembered to turn the ringer off before she went on the air. Only the station and her parents had this phone number and she was certain it would be her mom calling to tell her how proud she was.

Her cameraman, Tony, eavesdropped on the conversation as he packed their gear. It was their first time working together and he was hoping to find out if she was single.

"Romenelli here. You have what? No way. He asked for me? Give me his name and address. Yes, I can see the building from where we're standing. There's a man standing at the window waving."

"Yes, I'm waving back."

Tony and his soundman Jimmy put down their equipment and watched the exchange.

"No, I don't think we can get there by the front door. Can you ask him to meet us by the alley? Great, tell him we'll be there in a couple of minutes."

Pam turned to her news crew and said, "You're not going to believe this, but the guy I'm waving to—see him up there—claims to have a videotape of the entire riot. And he wants to give it to me."

The Channel One News team quickly packed up their gear and prepared to scoop every other network in the country.

In the city of Chicago, public alleys run parallel to almost every street and offer an alternative for those who would prefer not to be seen. They were the highway of choice for bums, gang bangers, and other ne'er-do-wells who didn't mind the panorama of graffiti covered garages, overflowing garbage cans, and the occasional well-fed rat. Pam, Tony, and Jimmy slipped away from the small crowd and walked around the corner to the alley. As could be expected, when the public had been denied use of the street and sidewalk they moved to the alley. It didn't take long to become clogged as a steady stream of foot traffic competed with slow moving cars trying to squeeze past one another in the narrow bypass.

As soon as they rounded the corner and saw the congestion, they were glad they hadn't tried to bring the station's van.

About halfway down the block a white haired man stepped out from next to a row of garbage carts and waved for them to follow. Phil was waiting in the gangway next to his garage and greeted them with, "Wow, so you're that news lady, here in person. Thanks for coming."

Pam shook his hand. "Good evening, Mr . . . . er."

"Oh please, just call me Phil. Everyone does."

"Then Phil it is. I'm Pam and this is my crew, Tony and Jimmy."

"Let's get inside. Too many strangers around." He pointed towards an open door. "Would you like some coffee? I made a fresh pot."

"No thanks, maybe later. Phil, my producer said you have a videotape of the entire riot."

"Shhhh." He held his finger to his mouth, "We'll talk upstairs."

Jimmy shot Pam a "what a nut" glance, but as soon as Phil secured the door with a two by four across it, he lightened up.

"Yep, I've a tape of the whole shebang. Would you like to see it?" He gave a sly grin. "C'mon upstairs . . . second floor. I've got it hooked up to my Zenith in the front room . . . it's a nineteen incher. It's got a Space Command remote control too."

Phil motioned the trio up the well-worn stairs of the enclosed porch that covered the entire rear of the building. "Go on in. It's open."

The kitchen looked as if they had stepped back in time. There were no cabinets and the appliances—a Roper range and a Hotpoint fridge—were ancient.

"Go ahead and walk on through. Sorry, I didn't have time to clean. I didn't know I'd be having company," Phil motioned towards the sink full of dishes. "Give me a second to lock the door."

The group waited in the dining room for their host to take the lead.

"Phil, your home looks just fine." Pam looked at the faded, sepia-colored wedding picture hanging on the wall above the ornate mahogany buffet. "Are you married?"

The second Pam saw the sad look on his face she regretted asking the question.

"Was . . . for almost forty-five years. My wife passed on almost five years ago. Since then it's just been me." He shrugged his shoulders and sighed. "I've thought about getting a dog for company, but I don't have the patience to housebreak one. Gets a little lonely at times though. Well, enough of that. You didn't come up here to hear me get all melancholy. Let's get settled in the front room and I'll show you what I got. You two have a seat on the sofa. Pam, you can sit in my recliner." Tony noticed a tripod poking out from behind the curtains and made a beeline towards the bay window. He dropped to his knees and examined Phil's one-time, state-of-the-art video camera.

Jimmy eyes almost bugged out when he saw the ancient videotape recorder sitting on top of the equally old console television. He walked over to examine the Sony VideoRover II AV-3450 Portapak. "Uhhh, Phil, this thing looks like it's older than I am. Does it still work?"

"Sure it works." Phil was a bit offended. "Just because it's not all new and fancy like that one you use doesn't mean it doesn't work just fine.

Well at least everything works but the battery—that won't hold a charge any more. But don't worry. I've got the adapter plugged in. I bought her at Polk Brothers back in '75. I got tired of my old Kodak 8 mm movie camera and wanted to videotape our first grandchild. I took it everywhere the next year during the Bicentennial. My wife and I went out East on a vacation. We even went to Washington to see the tall ships. I've still got that tape if you would like to see it."

"No, no thanks," Jimmy said. "Pam, this thing weighs more than some of the super models you've interviewed. Phil, you must have been mighty strong to carry it all over."

Everyone laughed.

Tony joined him and began examining the machine. The reverse lever made a resounding thud and the tape began to rewind. "Is there any chance you still have the manual? I've never seen a tape cartridge like this before . . . it looks like a three-fourths-inch format. I know we don't have anything in the van that can play that tape and I don't know if I can patch this into my equipment to make a copy."

"I'm sure I have the paperwork. I never throw anything away. I'll just be a minute."

"I'll bet Judas taped the Last Supper on this thing," Tony said after he left the room.

"Shhhh. He's coming back." Pam scowled.

"Yep, it was right where it belonged . . . in the drawer next to the sink with all my warranty books. Got the sales receipt too. It cost me $1,650 plus tax." Phil handed Tony the videocorder's owner's instruction manual.

"Uhhh, Pam. This sales brochure says it makes professional quality black-and-white video programs . . . black and white!"

"Of course it's in black and white . . . so's the TV set. But it still shows everything that happened right outside that window." Phil gestured towards it. "Now do you want to watch the pictures of the riot from start to finish, or do you want to want to keep complaining?"

When it rains it pours. At a television station most days can be divided into two categories . . . one big story that monopolizes the entire news portion of the broadcast or a collection of several little stories that are juggled to fit the time available. Pam's producer now had his hands on a videotape containing the final segment of a news triple crown. His station started the day by showing footage of the City Gate building collapse they purchased from an independent producer. By the afternoon news cycle, it was replaced with a five-minute segment of their reporter's coverage of Granny Gates's hospital bed press conference.

Tonight, however, the lead story would be Phil's remarkable video of the riot. They would show the entire ten-minute-long recording. Not only was it much longer than any segment they had run in recent memory, it would be the first black-and-white footage of a current event the network had shown in more than three decades. Pam would introduce the videotape recording and allow Phil's voiceover commentary to enhance the monochromatic viewing experience.

The producer knew he had a sure time-slot winner. The images on the tape were crisp and sharp. The nostalgic lack of color added an honesty reminiscent of the old newsreels to the images. And Phil had a great sense of composition. Most amateurs shook the camera as they swung from left to right while they zoomed in and out. This video was much better. Phil opened with a long establishing shot that showed the entire scene. Then he slowly zoomed in and panned the picketers. The camera next followed Granny Gates from the moment she rounded the corner until she was whisked away in a police car.

Within minutes of receiving it, Channel One began running teaser commercials for Phil's video. The voice over began, "Tonight at 10 P.M., exclusively on Channel One News, your news team will show a ten-minute videotape of the entire Albany Park riot, including the assault of Chicago's most beloved citizen by a high-ranking member of the Chicago Police Department. No other network can bring you this film. Only Channel One news has the video, only Channel One news has an exclusive interview with the man who witnessed and filmed it all. Tonight at ten."

Police Commissioner Finnegan was not in a good mood. His day began with a telephone call alerting him to an airplane crashing into a building at City Gate. Later, while he was waiting to speak at the mayor's press conference, a riot broke out in the seventeenth District. And now, to top it all off, one of his aides interrupted him to say Channel One was promising to show a video of one of his lieutenants roughing up the mayor's grandmother. He opened his desk drawer and took out a bottle of antacid pills. He took two . . . then two more.

CHAPTER 10

THE DEPARTMENT OF Buildings was a featherbed of patronage workers. It was created in response to the Great Chicago Fire of 1871 and, since the city hadn't burned to the ground again, most people assumed they were doing a pretty good job. In reality, it was the place where children of loyal Democratic workers were rewarded with plum jobs that offered high pay for short hours and minimal work. Sure, every few years some crusading newspaper reporter would do an exposé and try to shake things up, usually losing their own job in the process—and under Mayor Harold Washington, the racial makeup of new hires shifted from Irish Catholic to black Baptist. All in all it was a good place from which to retire.

When Reynold O'Dea was appointed commissioner of the department by Mayor Gates, his first official act was to petition the city council for funds to remodel his offices. No-bid contracts were awarded to several well-connected construction companies and a small army of union workers hired. Within days, the number that actually showed up was considerably less. Despite working Saturdays—at time-and-a-half—it took more than two years to complete to job.

The two plainclothes police officers hustled McBarker into the reception area of Commissioner Reynold O'Dea's opulent City Hall suite. The room looked more like an exclusive country club than the outer office of a civil servant. A large fireplace took up much of one wall. The O'Dea coat of arms, replete with crossed swords, hung above it. Rumor claimed the antique marble mantle, which was decorated with a score of carved cherubs, had been liberated from a gold coast mansion shortly before it was demolished.

On the other wall, Rey's portrait hung in a gilded frame, flanked by Chicago's and Ireland's flags. Scale models of a half-dozen skyscrapers, including the John Hancock Center and Sears Tower, stood next to them.

Several hunter green Chippendale wingback chairs were arranged in conversation groups, and at the center of it all, was a very elaborate, carved desk.

"Hello, Jane," Fred said to the receptionist. "They tell me Rey can't wait to see me."

"Good afternoon, Mr. McBarker." The middle-aged brunette reached for the intercom. "I'll let the Commissioner know you've arrived."

A moment later, the door behind her swung open and a well dressed, but slick-looking man with a cigar in his mouth called out from behind his desk, "C'mon in, Fred. Glad you could make it. We've got a lot of people anxious to get back into their condos. You know we need your report so we can give them the go ahead." He chided him.

Fred worked for O'Dea long enough to know he was the consummate political machine hack but expected at least a token expression of relief that three of his employees had cheated death that morning.

O'Dea stood up and gestured towards an open door to his left. "Let's go into my conference room. I just had it remodeled." He boasted. "We've got everything you'll need in there."

Rey dismissed the officers with a curt wave of his hand. "Boys, thanks for driving him down. I won't be needing you any more."

As Fred followed him into the huge room, he took in the elegant, matched-grain black walnut paneling, inlaid hardwood floor, ornately carved trim, and sculpted plaster ceiling. This was his first time there since the room had been gutted and rebuilt from the studs out.

"So what do ya think?" Rey asked. "Did the taxpayers do a great job or what?" Fred had to admit the conference room was as magnificent as any chamber he had ever seen . . . and he had toured more than a few castles in Europe during his last vacation.

Fred responded, "It looks nice, Rey," even though his boss wasn't listening. He was too busy announcing, "Look who I found," to the five men sitting at the far end of the conference table. The piles of boxes, blueprints, and papers were so high the men had to stand up to see who had entered the room. Four of the men wore casual clothes. The fifth stood out because he wore a dark gray suit and tie. He spoke first, "Frederick?" The gray haired man seemed surprised. "Frederick!"

"Hello Professor Rosa."

Rey put his hand on Fred's back and urged him forward. "I see you know everyone here. Someone bring him up to speed. And since you don't need me, I'll be at lunch. I'll be back in an hour. Call me if you know anything sooner." He started walking towards the door. Just before he left he turned and said, "Oh, and remember, priority one is getting the condo owners back into their own beds tonight."

Fred's top assistant John Garand said with a big smile, "Hey, Fred, glad to see you're not buried at the bottom of that hole. I'd feel real guilty getting a promotion that way."

"Only John would break a whole building just to get a promotion," Mitch "Blaster" Arnold, a controlled demolitions expert joked, drawing laughter from everyone.

"Aw c'mon, guys, we all would have gotten promotions . . . and a day off with pay for the funeral." Garand's response caused an even bigger roar.

"It's nice to see who my friends are." Fred put his hand on his heart and feigned being hurt.

Garand deadpanned, "Don't worry, we would have sent flowers . . . pressed flowers."

Fred groaned at the pun.

"I hate to interrupt the fun," Joe Petraski, a structural engineer said, "but Rey only gave us one hour to come up with a plausible reason why a brand new, eight-story office building, in the words of my two-year-old son, fall down-go boom, and that it's not going to happen again."

"Fall-go-go-boom? Does your son work for search and rescue?" Fred asked, "Because that's exactly how they described the collapse this morning."

"I think it was the big yellow bird's phrase of the week," Joe replied referring to a popular public television character, "but it sure describes what happened."

"Since when does Rey go to lunch this late in the afternoon?" Fred asked, feigning amazement. "Was he actually working at noon?"

Garand asked, "Since when does Rey only take an hour for lunch?" Everyone in the room laughed. "I could go on like this all afternoon, but we've got a lot do," Garand waved his arms over the piles of paper before him. "I guess we should start by filling you in on what's been going on while you were lounging around a cushy hospital room getting a sponge bath."

He dug through the pile and came up with a stack of photographs of the complex. "Rey wants us to determine if the residential buildings are in danger of collapsing from some common design flaw. I tried to explain we would first have to learn the cause of eight's initial structural failure before we could determine what caused its ultimate destruction. He told me—and I'm not making this up—he didn't care about finding out why some office building fell down because it wasn't going to go anywhere. He only wanted me to tell him the other buildings weren't going to fall down. He must have said at least six times he was receiving a lot of pressure from upstairs to certify the residential buildings are safe and that was all we should concern ourselves with."

Fred sat down, moved a slew of coffee cups and half-eaten donuts out of the way, and spread the pictures on the table,

"Unbelievable." Michael Rosa sat down next to him and said, "I've been a structural engineer for almost forty years. I've taught at Wright City College for over twenty of those years. Frederick, you were one of my students. Be honest with me. Is this man serious?"

Fred looked the gray haired man straight in the eye and said, "Professor Rosa, knowing Rey, I'm afraid he is."

"How can that be? I've never seen or heard of a building like this collapsing anywhere in the world. We might have to dig the entire structure piece by piece out of the hole and maybe—and I'm saying maybe—we might learn why it collapsed. And your boss wants to let people move back in tonight. The man is mad."

"That's our Rey." Garand made a circling motion with his finger next to his head.

"Mad or not," McBarker said, "I know Rey and he'll be expecting some kind of an answer when he comes back. C'mon John. Get serious. So what exactly do we know for a fact?"

"OK boss. Here's everything we've got. As you probably determined from your initial inspection, the building was not struck by an outside force, i.e. an airplane or a truck bomb. Also the exterior of the building did not show any evidence of an internal explosion. There was no visible blast hole—no twisted metal consistent with an explosion. We've got some great video taken from a police helicopter. I could bring it up on one of the laptops, but I have to show you Rey's toy." He punched a button on a remote control and the paneling opened to reveal a huge television built into the wall. He pushed another button, and it turned on.

"How'd you like to watch the Cubs game on that baby?" Mitch asked.

"There's at least one more just like it. The paneling behind us also slides open. Garand pointed towards the other end of the room. "There's a fully stocked bar hiding down there."

"I wonder what that cost the taxpayers?" Mitch wondered out loud.

Before anyone could answer, scenes of the building eerily glowing from dozens of spotlights filling the screen. The image kept getting larger as the helicopter approached the scene.

Garand continued. "You're in the picture in a moment . . . when they start sweeping the walls top to bottom. There you are."

"There's some great shots of all four walls. All of the windows are broken out, but we're speculating that was caused by pressure from the compression. The prints say the building topped out at 110 feet, not counting the HVAC and elevator equipment on the roof. Coming up you can see some detail of the interior of the upper floors. Now we're switching to another view. This was shot by someone on the ground with a telephoto lens. I spoke with the guy and he said he tried to get some interior shots of the first floor but there appeared to be walls behind all of the windows. Here's a better view." Fred got up and walked closer to the television. He ran his hands over the screen.

"See how there's some kind of obstruction right behind them." Garand continued his narration. "Now here's a strange thing. It looks as if there were vertical bars, or something, behind the windows. They don't look like part of the window frames, and we're not sure exactly what their purpose was."

He paused the video on a close-up of the bars inside the horizontal window mullions. Fred traced the bars with his fingers.

"There were burglar bars and privacy walls behind all of the first floor windows," McBarker said. "That place looked as secure as a federal penitentiary. It even had steel security doors."

Professor Rosa pounded his fist on the table and exclaimed, "There is no way the fire department would permit someone to seal up all the windows and doors on an office building. It would be a death trap."

Nix Seidler, a structural engineer who inspected the project several times during construction shrugged his shoulders and said, "Fred, we haven't been back inside since they got their Certificate of Occupancy after the build out was completed. They must have added those features without bothering to get permits."

Professor Rosa pointed to the television and demanded. "Who is responsible for this . . . this travesty?

Nix started digging through a pile of papers. He held one up. "We tracked down the building's only tenant . . . some kind of women's group or something. We know who their custodian is—a Jenna Ricco-Melenke—but she wasn't very cooperative over the phone. Rey wasn't too happy with that and made a call to have the boys in blue uniforms invite her to join us. He told the receptionist to let us know when they get here."

Garand resumed speaking, "Fred, if you don't mind, while we're waiting for her, I'd like go back to the copter shots. There's something I really want you to see coming up." Without waiting for an answer he said, "Mitch, hit play."

A picture of buildings seven and eight filled the screen. The one in the background was much shorter than the other.

"As near as we can tell, the building's been reduced to about sixty-five to seventy feet tall. Now here comes a really interesting overhead shot. It's high enough to capture the entire building . . . he must of hung out the door to shoot this straight down. See how all four walls are bowed out by the same distance. We estimate it to be as much as a nine- or ten-foot deflection from the original square footprint."

Garand picked up the remote control and joined Fred next to the screen. "Next he's going to zoom in on the wall. Look at the detail on the columns. Every single one has the same bend. The rebar did an amazing job holding it together for as long as it did. Now here comes the most puzzling shot of all." The view of the roof kept getting larger and more detailed as the cameraman zoomed in.

"We almost didn't notice this at first because of the shadows from the flood lights on the ground, but watch as the camera angle changes." Garand hit the pause key to freeze the picture.

Everything on the roof was flattened. The air conditioning units, satellite dishes, cellphone antennas, and elevator equipment was crushed flat.

Garand pointed out each feature. "It was almost as if something unbelievably heavy was placed on top of the building, then removed."

"When I first saw the building, I thought it looked as if someone had sat on it," Fred stated.

"Great," Garand joked, "Did you happen to see which way the Green Giant went?"

No one laughed.

Mitch Arnold spoke for the first time. "Fred, this problem is even more complicated than it seems. We have two separate and distinct incidents here—the first caused the damage that we are now looking at—the great weight placed on the building as it were. The latter event triggered the progressive collapse. I can't even begin to speculate on what caused the initial compression, but I can speak with a little bit of authority on what brought this building down."

He grabbed a legal pad and began sketching the skeleton of a building.

"Before the city hired me," Mitch continued, "I worked for over a decade doing controlled demolitions. I mainly dropped bridges, but I also imploded my share of five- to ten-story buildings. The key to dropping a structure of this mass into its own footprint is to simultaneously destroy the integrity of the core columns. A couple of seconds later, all of the perimeter columns are cut with controlled explosions. Gravity takes over and the entire mass is pulled swiftly and neatly to earth. There is no other way this building would pancake as it did."

"Fred, Blaster knows what he's talking about. I've seen some of his work. He's good." Joe complimented him.

"Well, something had to start the progressive collapse," Garand stated, "but we're getting a little ahead of ourselves. We should concentrate first on what caused the building to compress." He pointed to the television. "If that didn't happen, would the building have collapsed?"

"Frederick, you were at the ground level," Professor Rosa said. "You were always a keen observer. Did you notice anything that might give us a direction to start from?"

"The pictures!" Fred exclaimed. "Billy's pictures. There should be a series of photos of the inside of the building. They would be the last ones that Billy took before it collapsed. They should answer everything."

"Has anyone downloaded pictures from Haynes' camera?" Garand called out.

"Not me," Joe Petraski yelled back from across the room.

"Me neither," Mick Seidler answered.

"Nope." Mitch Arnold shook his head.

"So what's on these pictures?" Garand asked.

"You'll see as soon as you give me the camera."

"Fine. Who's got the camera?"

"Rey said it was in one of those boxes when I got here. But I haven't had a chance to look for it." Nix pointed towards a large stack in the corner of the room. "Am I the only one who's curious? C'mon, someone, find the camera."

"We're on it." Nix pointed to the pile farthest from him. "Mitch, you take that pile and I'll look through these." He spun his chair around and lifted the lid off a box.

"Can you at least give me a hint what we're going to see?"

Fred sounded agitated. "No, if it's not in the pictures, I'm not going to say anything more. That's final."

"But, Fred, if it will help the investigation," Garand was puzzled by his secrecy.

"John, I said no and I mean no."

"But you said they could explain everything," Garand pleaded.

"Don't push it." Fred poked him in the chest with his index finger. "Billy, Philo, and I talked in my hospital room about what should be on those pictures. But it wouldn't be right for me to discuss what we think unless the pictures confirm it."

"OK, OK. Don't go all postal on me." Garand backed up and held his hands up as if blocking an attack. "I'll look for the camera."

"John, I'm sorry. I . . ."

"No problem Fred. You've had one heck of a day. Why don't you take a break until we find it? Grab a cup of coffee."

"It's just that when we were together I was so certain of what we saw. But the more time goes by it seems so . . . so . . . John, I couldn't describe it well enough to make you believe me. I have a hard enough time believing it myself. I guess that's why I want to see the pictures so bad."

"Wow, those must be some pictures."

"They will change your life." Everyone in the room was listening. "I will say one thing for certain. The clinic, that's what was on the first floor—a woman's clinic, was actually an arbortuary. There were dumpsters full of mutilated babies . . . hundreds of tiny bodies. It was so sickening . . . so shocking. That will be in Billy's pictures."

"Fred, I'm sorry. That must have been awful." Garand put his hand on Fred's shoulder.

"I can still see their broken bodies . . . looked like dolls. Perfect little dolls. But they were all dead."

Rosa gasped. "Frederick, how could that be?"

"I don't know, Professor . . . never imagined anything could be so horrific. It was like the pictures from Nazi death camps, only worse. Much worse." His voice grew soft.

"Frederick, I don't care what Mr. O'Dea says. Get out of here and go home. Or go see a doctor or your priest. You need to talk to someone."

"No, I've got to do this. But John, one more thing. We agreed someone was in there with us."

"Did he make it out?" Garand was shocked to hear of a casualty.

"Not as far as we could tell. But that's all I'm saying until we look at the pictures."

"Whoa, like we didn't have a big enough mystery already," Mitch commented from behind a pile of boxes.

Garand stared at Blaster. "More work, less talk." He turned back and continued, "Fred, I'm going to call the team at the site and let them know what to expect. I don't know when they'll begin pulling the rubble out of the hole, but they might speed it up if they know there's a man's body at the bottom."

"I didn't say it was a man," Fred said with great emotion. "I don't . . . it looked . . . Just tell them they will find aborted baby bodies—hundreds of them. I'm not sure what else." He looked drained as he slumped in his chair.

While Garand was talking the phone, Fred sprang up and shouted, "Wait a second! Did anyone talk to the security guards they found in the parking lot? They might have seen it too."

"They were still in the hospital when I checked about an hour ago," Joe Petraski said. "One is totally out of it. They said they'll call if there are any changes. The other guy gave a statement. They e-mailed it over a while back. Let me find it." He started typing on a laptop. "Here it is."

He spun the computer around, so Fred could read the guard's statement:

> I was sitting at the front desk watching the security monitors. The pictures change automatically every ten seconds. Everything was real quiet. There was nothing going on anywhere. The parking lot was empty. The last picture I saw was the parking lot. I could see my car where I left it. Then I was sitting outside. Honest to God, I never got out of my chair. I don't know how I got outside. They locked us in every night for our protection. They told us there was somebody that didn't like them and that was why we had to be locked in. Then I saw the building starting to fall down. I don't know nothing else.

"He lets them lock him in every night," Joe commented. "Sounds like a great minimum wage job. So how did he get outside?"

Fred answered, "All of the doors were locked when we got there and the only way out was through a hole in the back wall. What about the other guard? Did he say anything?"

"Nope," Joe replied. "They said he was incoherent when the EMTs brought him in. He was already under sedation when they tried to talk to him. I'll call and see if there's been any change."

"So that leaves the pictures," Fred said.

"Yeah, but we haven't found the camera yet," Mitch said. "We've still got at least three dozen more boxes to go through. It looks like they dumped everything the developer had into boxes and schlepped 'em in here. Do you want me to keep looking?"

"Yes. Keep looking." Garand said.

"Fred, this might help," Joe interjected. The engineer unrolled a large blueprint on the table. The casual observer would never guess Petraski was one of the most brilliant structural engineers on the City's payroll based on his scruffy appearance—ripped blue jeans, a Grateful Dead T-shirt, and a pony tail. It had also been a couple of days since the fifty-year-old man had shaved. "Professor Rosa and I have spent most of our time confirming the four residential buildings have nothing in common with the office towers . . . other than identical exteriors."

"Joe's right . . . assuming they followed the blueprints," Nix Seidler added.

"Which is a pretty big assumption considering one of their buildings collapsed," Mitch stated. "And I've demolished my share of buildings which weren't built according to plans."

"Fred, this doesn't leave this room," Joe added. "But we're more than a little concerned. Professor Rosa and I were getting a lot of pressure from Rey to give the all clear on the residential towers before everyone else got here. I hope you're not gonna let him rush you."

"Not a chance," Fred said. "I don't care if they have to sleep in hotels for a week. Nobody is moving back in until I'm satisfied the buildings are safe."

"That's a relief," Joe said, breathing an exaggerated sigh. "We were uncomfortable because they were built before either of us was hired by the city. We've never even been in them."

"But we do have inspectors crawling all over them," Nix added. "They have confirmed the residential buildings have steel skeletons . . . no slip form concrete there."

"That's what the prints and permits showed, but we didn't want to take a chance," Joe unrolled another set of blueprints. The four men huddled over the large drawings as he pointed out specific details.

"Until you got here, Rey kept popping in every ten minutes or so to tell us that he's getting a lot of pressure from the mayor to let his friends go home," Garand looked at his watch. "It's been almost fifteen minutes. I'm surprised he hasn't called you yet."

Fred sighed and shook his head at the responsibility that had been dumped in his lap.

"And we're still more than a little concerned that the contractor—a huge Democratic contributor and personal friend of 'Hiz Honor'—might have cut a few corners and built them a little cheaper than the plans indicate," Joe added.

Nix thumbed through a yellow legal pad. "Everything we're hearing from our people says they followed code on the condominium towers. They found a few minor violations but nothing of any consequence. They checked them top to bottom." He found the page he was looking for and handed it to Fred. "We had them go through every unit looking for stress cracks and signs of settlement. Nothing other than a few routine nail pops. Same from the elevator, electrical, and plumbing inspectors. We even had a guy riding up and down on a window washer's rig. You name it, we checked it. About the only thing we didn't do was x-ray the steel. Everything came back with a clean bill of health."

"What about the commercial buildings?" Fred asked.

"We haven't had a chance to look at them," Joe replied, "They're cast-in-place concrete, just like the one that collapsed. They were built using a 'flying' form around a concrete core . . . a whole different ballgame than the condos. Our priority up to this point has been the residential towers."

"Fred, I hate to dump this on you," Garand pushed a sheet of paper in front of him, "but Rey wasn't any too happy when he couldn't intimidate us into signing off on the all-clear. Now you're the senior man here, so it's your call whether or not all of those rich people get to sleep on their designer sheets tonight."

"There were no irregularities at all in any of the reports?" Fred asked.

"Minor violations . . . some flashing installed incorrectly, missing caulk around a few windows, things like that." Nix responded.

"Would you guys sign off on this?" Fred asked.

"You're the man making the big bucks," Garand replied.

"Thanks. Can I pass the buck down to any of you guys?"

"Sorry boss," Garand said. "You're the senior man after Rey so the final decision is on you."

"Have any of the inspectors returned?"

"Nope," Garand responded. "They're all still on site. I told them to re-inspect everything. They've finished two buildings and they're about halfway through the others. Give me a moment, and I can pull up the preliminary reports on my computer." He sat down and started typing.

"It's not that I don't trust you . . . but since it will be my name on the bottom line . . ." Fred stammered.

"And your neck if any of them fall down tonight," Garand added.

"Oh, for the days when I was inspecting porches," Fred added with a sigh.

"I understand completely," Joe said. "I wouldn't want that responsibility."

"Lucky me. While I'm reading these reports, can someone please see if there are any videos of the building collapsing." Garand slid his laptop computer over to Fred.

Mitch grinned, "Do we have videos of the collapse? We've got all the network feeds . . . we've got three from the fire and police departments, plus we've got the helicopter footage. That one doesn't show too much below the top couple of floors because of the dust plume. Which would you like to see? I can just run through them in order if you'd like."

"It doesn't matter," Fred replied. "Yeah, run them all, please. I want to watch it collapse. I'm having a real hard time when I think how close I came to dying this morning. It really distorts your perspective. Makes you rethink your priorities. Maybe watching it go down will help me sort things out."

Fred watched the building crumble from several different angles. To no one in particular he began to speak, "We talked a lot at the hospital about what we saw and I guess I was wondering if any cameras caught anything. You don't have any with close-ups of the back of the building do you?"

"You saw everything we have," Mitch replied, "which isn't to say other tapes won't turn up later. There were a lot of cameras out there when it went down. I'll make a couple of calls and see if there's anything new."

"Thanks, and speaking of cameras, let me know as soon as you find Billy's. That should have some great detail shots of the first floor just before the collapse."

"Only four more boxes to go," Nix replied.

Fred swiveled the chair around to face the table. He opened the laptop computer and began to read the dozens of reports that were being filed. "Do we have a printer hooked up? I want hard copies of some of these."

"Can do . . . give me a second to get some paper from Jane," Mitch replied.

A couple of minutes later he returned with a ream of copy paper and said, "As soon as I fill the paper tray the printer will be ready to go."

"Fred, I found Billy's camera." Nix was standing at the other end of the table, holding a camera in the air. "But there's a problem. When I hooked up it up to download the pictures, I received an error message. Someone removed the memory card."

CHAPTER 11

IT WAS ALMOST 4:30 and the Hansen sisters were growing more bored by the minute. They had been brought in handcuffs to First Presbyterian over seven hours earlier and were being held captive in a hospital room.

Ruth and Kaye interrupted their prayers to watch coverage of the riot on the mid-day news, but the afternoon talk shows made staring out the window an attractive alternative. Neither, however, wanted to turn the TV off as they kept interrupting with follow-up stories and they were hoping to hear how their friends were doing.

So they turned the volume down and stood side by side praying while watching cars enter and leave the hospital's parking lot. There wasn't much else they could do as the police officer standing outside their door refused to let them leave the room.

It had been a very long day for the seventy-five-year-old identical twins. They had been up since before dawn, and their forced hospital stay was violating the routine which they followed every Monday since retiring.

They attended six o'clock mass, sitting in the same pew—the fourth one down, on the priest's right, facing the Virgin Mary's altar. Then they walked a half-mile to the abortion mill where they counseled and prayed the rosary until ten-thirty.

Lunch at the Morning Star Café was next followed by a quick stop at Pancho's Super Mercado. Their selection of fresh meats reminded the sisters of a time long ago when the neighborhood had a corner butcher shop and dinner was only hours removed from being slaughtered at the Union Stockyards on Chicago's southwest side.

They took turns cooking and ate at five sharp while watching the news. After washing the dishes together—they used their good china and crystal every day and washed it by hand—they read their Bibles, sitting side-by-side, in the parlor until seven-thirty when they turned in. When it was hot and humid—muggy the weatherman called it—they stayed up an hour later and sat on the wooden swing their father had hung on the front porch when they were young girls. They didn't know most of the people walking by, but acknowledged each with a wave and friendly hello.

When the days grew shorter and the temperature colder, they ventured outside less often. As children of the depression, neither wanted to waste electricity, and they soon found themselves doing almost everything together to limit the number of light bulbs burning.

But today they were prisoners in a colorless hospital room that was brighter than outside at high noon. So they prayed and waited. Every few minutes Ruth would think a question out loud, such as, "Do you think they are going to keep us here all night?" or "What are we going to wear to bed if they don't let us go home tonight?" Kaye answered each question with a shrug.

It seemed like forever since a doctor—both agreed he looked mighty young—came by and said there was no need for them to remain hospitalized. "But," Dr. Galloway continued, "the policeman standing outside the door," he pointed towards a balding officer with a beer belly, "said you were being held in protective custody pending charges. If I discharge you, he'll take you to the station in handcuffs. And I'm not about to let that happen."

Galloway flipped through their charts looking for a next of kin. "Isn't there someone you could call? Maybe a lawyer? I know they release people all the time after posting a small cash bond or even on their personal recognizance."

"We wouldn't know whom to call." Ruth shrugged in frustration. "From what we hear, all of our friends seem to be in the same predicament."

"Could you please check on them and let us know how they are doing?" Kaye asked. "Maybe one of them has an idea whom we should call. I can give you their names."

"I'm sorry, ladies, I'm a little busy right now making rounds, but I promise I'll have someone look in on your friends a little later." The doctor gave them a reassuring smile before he walked out.

A nurse finally came about an hour later and updated them on the condition of their friends. She wasn't able to see the four in intensive care but their charts said they all were stable. She did speak with Granny Gates, however, who said they shouldn't worry because her grandson was on his way over and would know what to do. So they settled back, closed their eyes, and prayed for their friends while they waited.

Mayor Gates broke their silent meditation when he came by to deliver Granny's greetings and see how they were doing. As he was leaving, he promised they would be going home that afternoon. But first, he had to make a few phone calls to find the right people to get everything straightened out.

"Such a nice young man," they agreed after he left.

That had been several hours ago and the sisters were growing restless. It had been over an hour since they finished eating their nutritionally balanced dinners. They were a far cry from the home-cooked dinners the sisters were used to and consisted of a small patty of bland, ground meat mixed with lots of oatmeal, a dollop of instant mashed potatoes—all without gravy, salt, or pepper mind you—a pile of soggy, over-steamed string beans, and a cup of green gelatin for desert. The young lady who served them said in broken English that she couldn't bring coffee without doctor's orders.

Ruth asked for a Bible, but wasn't sure if she understood.

After an hour of standing, their legs grew tired, so they sat on the edges of their beds—they wouldn't think of messing up the blankets by laying on them.

Ruth turned the volume up and scrolled through the limited selection of channels—they did not have cable—stopping when she saw the Channel One promo for Phil's exclusive video at ten o'clock. "What a shame it will be on so late. Do you think they will play it again tomorrow?" she asked.

"You were there. Haven't you seen enough already?" Kaye snapped. Ruth looked stunned.

"I'm sorry. It's just that I'm so tired and scared and . . ." Kaye began to sob.

Ruth wrapped her arms around her, "There, there, I understand. I'm scared too. But Sidney said we would be going home tonight, and I trust him. Now dry your tears." She handed her sister a lace hanky.

"I trust him too. But every time I look at that television I get so angry. We weren't doing anything wrong and now seven of us are in the hospital. Why? Why?" Kaye's voice quivered.

"I'm sure we'll find out in good time . . . so let's turn that chatterbox off and . . ."

Even though it was wide open, Officer James Kent knocked on the door and asked permission to enter. He was a different officer than had been out there earlier. He was a handsome young man with neat dark brown hair and a gregarious smile.

"Certainly, young man. Please come in and have a seat," Ruth answered with more than a touch of sarcasm in her voice. "You must be exhausted from guarding two dangerous criminals."

"No thanks, ladies . . . but I do have good news. I received a call from my commander. You're free to go," Kent announced.

"Free to go where?" Kaye asked.

"Anywhere you ladies want. You're no longer under arrest. The States Attorney reviewed the incident, and you're not being charged. You can leave right now. Oh, and I was instructed to drive you ladies wherever you would like to go."

"What about Granny? Can she go home too? What about our friends? Are they all right? Are they being released too?" Ruth fired off her questions without giving the officer a chance to respond. "And who is paying for all of this?"

"I'm sorry but . . ." Kent stammered.

"And when are we getting an apology from the madman who assaulted us?" The white haired woman stood toe-to-toe with the policeman, their faces only inches apart.

"All they told me was . . . He tried to complete his sentence.

Ruth cut him off. "Let me get this straight, young man. We were peacefully praying when that madman attacked our dear friend. After he threw Granny to the ground and handcuffed her—she is a hundred years old, you know—he sprayed us with teargas and started shooting his gun." Kent tried backing up, but the feisty woman matched him step-for-step. "Then we were dragged down here—in handcuffs—and the States Attorney says he's not charging us!" She raised her voice with such passion a nurse came running into the room. "What about the madman who caused all of the trouble? Has he been arrested?"

"Mrs. Hansen, are you all right?" The nurse shouted as she entered.

"My sister is a little excited. This policeman says we can go home," Kaye responded.

"I thought I heard an argument. Is this man bothering you?" Officer Kent looked sheepishly at the floor when the nurse pointed at him. "I don't care if you are a policeman. You cannot come in here and harass these women. I want you out of this room this instant," Nurse Ryun barked.

"No, he can stay," Ruth said. "But we won't be staying much longer. He said he would drive us home."

"Your doctor signed your releases hours ago. He's the only reason you couldn't leave." She again pointed at the officer.

Kent was going to explain he just gotten there but thought the better of it when Nurse Ryun glared at him.

"Don't be so hard on the boy. He's just doing his job," Kaye interceded.

"Well I'm ready to leave this instant, but before we go can you tell us anything new about our friends?" Ruth leared at the officer. "Are they going home too?"

Nurse Ryun planted her hands on her hips, squared her jaw, and gave Kent a "this is all your fault" look.

"They're not on this floor, so I'll have to check at the desk. It'll only take a moment." The nurse scowled at the officer "Are you're sure you're going to be all right?"

Kaye smiled, "Don't worry. I don't think my sister is going to hurt him."

Ryun shook her head and muttered, "This is gonna be a long night," as she walked out of the room.

Kent looked at Kaye and asked, "Can I help you ladies pack your things?"

"Young man, instead of driving us home, can you drive us to an attorney?" Kaye asked with a curious edge to her voice.

"Yes, Ma'am." He beamed. "I'll drive you anywhere you wanna go. What's his address?"

"I . . . I don't know." She shrugged and turned to her sister with a blank look on her face. "Do you know any attorneys?"

Ruth looked indignant. "Why would I know any attorneys? But wait, Sidney is an attorney," she nodded for emphasis.

"Oh, don't be silly. He's the mayor" Kaye said.

"But I'm sure he has lots of friends who are attorneys." Ruth gave a sly grin.

"What are you thinking?" Kaye raised an eyebrow.

"Shhhh. Not in front of him," Ruth gestured at Officer Kent. "Young man, could we please have a few minutes alone?"

He snapped to attention. "Certainly, ladies. I'll wait down the hall. Take as long as you want."

The officer walked towards the lounge, hoping not to be noticed as he passed the nurses station.

A woman's voice bellowed from behind a computer monitor. "Officer. Officer."

Kent froze when Ryun stood up. "Yes, you. Come here now." She pointed at him, then at the floor in front of her.

"Yes ma'am," he stammered as he walked over.

"I hope you are proud of the way those women have been treated. How dare you keep them as prisoners all day long."

"Mrs. Ryun," he said, looking at her name badge. "I wasn't . . ."

"It is Miss. Miss Ryun or Nurse Ryun."

"Nurse Ryun, I'm sorry, but I just got here. My shift didn't even start until a half-hour ago. My orders are to drive the ladies home . . . or anywhere they want to go. Honest, I just got here." Officer Kent pleaded.

Ryun looked embarrassed. "Oh. I'm so sorry, I didn't know. I just got here myself and heard quite the earful at the shift change. Did you know they've been held prisoner in that room all day? They said the cop, I guess it was the other cop, was a real jerk. He wouldn't even let them visit their friends who are also prisoners in this hospital. That's why I was so short with you." She tilted her head down and looked over her glasses with sad puppy dog eyes.

"No problem." He laughed and shot her his best, show-off-all-the-teeth smile, "You didn't know. Heck, I don't know very much about what's going on either. I was at City Gate all night. When I finally got off, I went straight home, took a shower, and hopped in bed." Kent added with an exaggerated yawn.

"Were you there when it collapsed?"

"Yes, ma'am. It was the most unbelievable thing I've ever seen. I was across the parking lot, but I could feel the ground shake and the roaring whoosh of wind." He leaned back on one leg and pantomimed the being blown back. "It was incredibly powerful . . . but it wasn't like any explosion I've ever heard." Kent held his hands up as if he was going to cover his ears. "It sounded more like a banshee screaming. And I hope I never hear anything like it again."

"It must have been horrible." Ryun's concern was genuine.

"Yes, Ma'am, it was. He gave her an impish grin and snapped his fingers. "Then I got eight hours to go home, wash the dust off, and catch a few Zs. The desk sergeant sent me straight here the second I walked in. My orders were to relieve the officer on duty and send him back to the station house."

The look on Ryun's face said I want to hear more.

He winked and continued. "I've got to tell you, things were really hopping. There were reporters and camera crews all over the place. Someone said the Mayor and States Attorney were there in person. I heard a rumor that at least a dozen investigators from OPS, that's the Office of Professional Standards, were taking statements." He punctuated his sentences with smiles. She returned each one.

"So I turned on a news channel on my way to find out what was going on. I caught the tail end of a story about a riot in Albany Park." He shook his head, "From what they said, it sure doesn't sound like the department's finest hour. And honest, I didn't know who was in the room until I got a call on my cellphone right after I got here telling me to give those ladies the VIP treatment. That's when I put it all together."

"I'm sorry I jumped to conclusions. Can you forgive me?" Ryun wrapped her hands around his. He was surprised how soft they felt and blushed. "Apology accepted."

For the second time today, James Kent felt as if he was being knocked off his feet. They stared at each other without saying a word. Both liked what they saw. Much too soon, a call bell went off.

"That's room 355, the Hansen sisters." He tried to keep her hands from slipping away. "I guess they're ready for their ride home," Nurse Ryun said.

"Oh, yeah. The Hansen sisters." Kent was disappointed, but tried not to sound awkward. "They mentioned going to see an attorney. It's pretty late, and I don't know if they'll find any still open. But that doesn't matter." He shrugged. "My orders are to be their chauffeur. Anywhere they want to go for as long as they want to go. Oh, and one last thing. Sarge told me in no uncertain terms to keep them away from reporters. So, now you know everything I know."

"Keep them away from reporters," she repeated. "Interesting."

He shot her a boyish grin. "Nurse Ryun. What are you thinking?"

She cocked her head and smiled back. "You know, Officer Kent, when I arrived I noticed a Channel Four news van parked by the Emergency Room entrance."

"I saw it too."

"I'm guessing, but I'll bet there's a news crew in that van."

"I think I know what you're thinking, but I couldn't do that, Nurse Ryun. I have my orders."

She grabbed his hands again and said in a vampish Scarlet O'Hara voice, "Why Officer Kent, I didn't ask you to do a thing." She batted her eyes. "And call me Sally. Besides, all I was doing was thinking out loud." She squeezed his hands.

"Nurse, 'er Sally, I 'er . . . " He struggled to compose a sentence.

"I'm thinking their story deserves to be told. So what if, by some amazing coincidence, a reporter and a cameraman just happened to be standing by the back door as the Hansen sisters were leaving . . ."

"Noooo," Kent sighed. "My car is parked out back by the Emergency Room entrance."

"I prefer to think of it as divine providence." She bowed her head as if in prayer. "Now as I was thinking . . . all patients being discharged are brought downstairs in a wheelchair by a nurse. What if you," she pushed their hands into his chest, "being a true gentleman, went to get your car so these frail women didn't have to walk across the dark parking lot? Of course, the nurse would have to wait at the curb with her patients. And what if a news crew just happened to walk over and just happened to recognize them and just happened to have their cameras with . . ."

He rolled his eyes, "And I just happened to get busted down to crossing guard."

She slowly shook her head from side to side. "Oooooh, I don't think you have to worry about that. These ladies were arrested with the Mayor's grandmother. After all the indignities they've suffered, I don't think your boss would dare say a word."

"So, do I want to know how the people in the van would know who is being discharged? And when?"

She pushed him back, but didn't let go of his hands. "Me thinks the less you know, Officer Kent, the better." After a long silent pause she pulled her hands away and chided him, "All you have to do is go forth and gallantly fetch your chariot whilst I wait with the fair damsels in distress."

He couldn't say why, but he couldn't say no. "I surrender." He threw his arms in the air. "Since we're co-conspirators you might as well call me Jimmy . . . and perchance, are you a frustrated theater major?"

"No, but I will enjoy being on the news tonight. Now, if you'll excuse me, I have to run downstairs for a few minutes . . . something medical I've got to attend to. And don't leave until I get back."

"Yes, sir," he barked with feigned sincerity.

The Channel Four news crew had packing up their equipment and were preparing for a quiet drive back to their studio. They had missed every major story of the day. Their run of bad luck started when they were stuck in a traffic jam a mile away from City Gate when it collapsed. Next, they missed the Albany Park riot. And finally, they arrived at First Presby five minutes after the Reverend Jackie Jefferson was led away in handcuffs.

At all three scenes, the best they could do was a shot after the facts—and those were not exactly what their producer wanted to see.

"Excuse me," Nurse Ryun said as she knocked on the van's door. "I was wondering if you could help me."

The driver, who was also the news reporter, thought she had a flat tire and almost blew her off. But, noticing how attractive she was, he answered, "Anything for a beautiful lady." This elicited hoots and catcalls from the two men in the back of the truck. "What can I do to be of service?" he asked in his deepest voice as he stepped out.

"I don't know if you're aware, but seven of the women arrested for pick-eting this morning are being held under police guard in this hospital."

He seemed confused. "Yeah, so. They won't let us see 'em."

"Two of the women, the Hansen sisters, are being discharged. They will be leaving through the Emergency Room doors in a few minutes," she gestured behind her.

"You don't say."

She looked around to make sure no one was listening. "And they will have a police guard who has been instructed to protect them from the press."

"That sounds like a problem."

"Not really. I happen to know police officer will leave the women under the protection of a nurse while he goes to get his vehicle. And I also know this same nurse has no instructions to keep these ladies from being interviewed."

"By any chance do you know when all of these things will happen?"

"If I were you I would be ready in about ten minutes . . ." She turned and started walking away. "And remember, you never saw me before."

"Saw who?" He swung his head from side to side. "Who said that?"

"Boys, unpack the gear . . . I think we got us an exclusive."

CHAPTER 12

JACKIE COULD NOT remember when he had ever been so mad. No, he was beyond mad, he was livid. No, he was furious. Furious. That would have to do until he could think of a ten-dollar word that would better express his growing outrage. He mumbled out loud as he paced in the windowless room. "I will sue them for false imprisonment . . . then I will sue the hospital. They will pay for this," he vowed.

Jackie rubbed his wrists, still sore from being handcuffed behind his back like a common criminal. He pounded on the door for the hundredth time and yelled out, "I know my rights. I demand to speak with my lawyers."

It had been over four hours since a police officer led him into the room and said, "Wait here while your paperwork is processed." To make time go even slower, a large clock on the wall just out of reach marked the passing of every second with a loud tick. Jackie spun around when he heard the door start to open.

A huge man with skin as black as coal commanded from out in the hallway, "Jefferson. Grab your stuff. They're waiting for you downstairs." He was dressed all in black and it was hard to tell in the dim light where his uniform ended and his skin began.

Jackie picked up his suit coat, "It is about time. When my lawyers are finished with you, I will own this building. I want the name of the inconsiderate lout who abandoned me . . . then I want the name of . . ."

His escort cut him short. "Walk," he ordered, pointing down the hall with his nightstick.

Jackie continued his rant as they went down the corridor.

"Downstairs." The man's voice was mechanical.

Their footsteps echoed on the metal stairs until they reached the building's musty basement. A single bulb hanging from the ceiling barely gave off enough light to see his guard.

"That way," he again pointed the way with the slender club. This corridor was so narrow Jackie's arms brushed against the walls; they were damp. He worried about ruining his suit, but was more nervous about the murmur of voices which grew louder with each step.

"Don't move," the guard ordered when they reached a door with only a small window in it. He pressed several buttons on a key pad then announced into a speaker, "Jefferson, John James Jefferson."

I don't like the smell of this, Jackie thought as the door opened and a dank odor reached his nostrils.

Thirty seconds later he was screaming at the top of his lungs, "I demand to see my lawyers," as the steel door slammed shut. The stink of urine, sweat, and stale cigarette smoke engulfed him.

The Reverend was by far the best dressed man in the cell and that drew the attention of his fellow detainees. Most assumed he was either a pimp or a gay drug dealer. Several laughed at the new arrival. A couple made crude comments.

He turned . . . his eyes darted around. Two of the walls were floor to ceiling steel bars. The others were filthy concrete with graffiti scratched into them.

There were at least twenty prisoners in a cell built to hold half as many. Most had a hard, urban, street look that did not invite a prolonged stare. The largest group was Hispanic gang-bangers who had been arrested at the Albany Park riot. They were not in a good mood. "What you lookin' at, boy?" a punk who couldn't have been more than sixteen demanded.

"Nothing. Sorry." He backed away as the teenager hurled insults at him in Spanish.

"Watch where you going." Someone jostled him. Another threw a shoulder into him. Jackie stumbled but didn't fall. A cold shiver ran down his spine; the hair on his neck stood up. *This is not looking good.* He took a deep breath and tried to steady his nerves. Mistake. The stench made his nostrils flare and he felt queasy. Jackie looked for a place to sit down.

He noticed a couple of middle-aged Puerto Rican men in the corner holding onto the bars, coughing and wheezing. They had been tear gassed and their shirts were covered in vomit. He spotted an open bench in the other corner and tried to walk to it without touching anyone.

When he got to the corner, a wave of nausea swept over him because that's where the toilet was. It was broken and overflowed with human waste. Bile roared up and burned his throat. Jackie doubled over and gagged on the hot acid. Tears of pain streamed down his face as he fought not to throw up.

His cellmates didn't want to get puked on and moved away. He staggered to the worn wooden bench that ran the width of the back wall and collapsed on it.

"Where are my attorneys?" Jackie fumed under his breath. "Where are my people?"

"Yo. I's Zippy." A shirtless black man with tattoos all over his chest towered over him.

"Please sir, I am sick." He clutched his stomach.

"Don't dis me. I say you is Reverend JJ. I know it's you right away 'cuz my gramma watch you all the time on TV.

Jackie looked up. "I am he."

"Yo Willie . . . Skank. I told you I know who he be," Zippy called out to a couple of black youths who were standing behind him.

"My gramma, she sends you money too."

"Tell her I said thank you." *Where are my attorneys?*

"That's good 'cuz now you owe me. So pray them jail doors swing open like they did for that apostle guy you talk about."

Jackie tried to ignore the youth which only drew more attention to him. He shifted his gaze down to the stained concrete floor. *I will fire every last one of those overpaid ambulance chasers.*

Zippy kicked his foot. "C'mon, preacher man. I hear you knows God personally," the youth taunted.

Jackie debated standing up and giving a rousing jailhouse speech worthy of Martin Luther King, Jr. but was so nauseous and distracted by rage and fear he could not perform before this most captive of audiences.

"Please, leave me alone," he responded in a soft voice.

"What's the matter?" A black youth with a large, fresh scar across his face roared. "We not good enough for you to pray for? Or do you only work when people are paying you the long green?"

By the shoes lined up in front of him, Jackie could see at least five men were lording over him. Their backs formed a wall which hid Jackie from any guards that might look into the cell.

"He axed you a question, preacher man," Skank demanded. "Don't yo mama teach you it be bad manners not to answer?"

"I still want him to make me a miracle," Zippy demanded, "C'mon, Reverend JJ, pray me down a big ol' angel to swing that door open like I heard you talk about on TV."

"Lay off him," a large, mean looking, black man demanded.

"You stay outta this," Willie held his hand in front of the large man's face. "We ain't hurtin' him . . . we's funnin' with him."

"Well you should show some respect for a man of the cloth," the man continued, "like I am. Reverend Jefferson, I must apologize for my cellmates."

Jackie looked up and smiled at his defender.

"In fact, Reverend, I respect you so much I tried to pass a collection plate, but the guards took all our wallets . . . and the collection plate too. Can I give you an IOU?" He patted his pants pockets. "Aw man, they took that too." He grinned from ear to ear because he had duped Jackie into believing he had been sincere.

The pack tightened their circle around the frightened man. Even though he had had a couple of minor scrapes with the law this was the first time Jackie had ever been behind bars. *Jesus*, he thought, *I am in big trouble. Please help me.* It was his first sincere prayer in years.

"Jefferson. Jefferson" The guard standing at the cell's door called out.

"I am here," he called out from behind the wall of men.

"C'mon, get your butt in gear. They want to talk to you upstairs," the guard ordered.

A couple of older white men—veterans of the station house lockup—howled and wished him insincere encouragement. "Say your prayers, preacher man. You may be goin' upstairs, but you're goin' down."

"I hope you brought a toothbrush," the second added.

"I had my prayer answered," he replied to the men who had no idea what he was talking about.

"Excuse me, Officer. Might I inquire who, or what, do I have to look forward to upstairs?"

A howl of laughter erupted from the cell, followed by mocking taunts. "My good man, pray tell what fate awaits my sorry butt."

"Officer, might I inquire as to what wine will be served with dinner?"

"Shut up in there," the guard shouted, "or I'll turn the hose on the whole lot of ya. C'mon Jefferson, you'll find out when ya get there. You gonna walk right or do I gotta cuff ya?"

Jackie bristled, "Sir, I pose no threat to you. Do not you know who I am?"

"Ooooh, ooooh, I know. You're number 03204070555," one of his former cellmates yelled out causing the group to again explode in laughter.

Jackie hung his head. "Lead on, sir. I will follow."

"Not on your life. You walk in front of me." The guard pointed down the hallway. "Now go down to that door and wait 'till we get buzzed out."

Jackie looked broken as he shuffled, a far cry from the defiant firebrand he played almost every night on the news. Without the guard saying a word, the door buzzed open. Jackie looked up and saw a camera trained on them. He straightened his hunched shoulders and a twinkle appeared in his eye. It might be only a closed circuit monitor but Jackie was on the air.

Hoping against hope a real TV crew would be waiting outside the door, Jackie feigned a smile and began to compose in his mind a condemnation of the unjust penal system. But that was not to be. All that awaited them was another long, dimly lit hallway with a staircase at the end of it.

Maybe the press awaits me upstairs.

"Keep walking. Go up to the next floor."

Jackie was going to point out the stairs only went up—and for only one floor at that—but did not want to risk antagonizing his escort in such a secluded place.

He stopped when he reached a closed door with a small window in it.

"Knock twice. And do it like ya mean it . . . That's a steel door and ya want 'em to hear it."

A moment later the door swung open, and the guard nudged him into a brightly lit room. The air tasted clean. Jackie squinted from the brightness as he scanned the large office for a friendly face. Instead, he saw only row after row of steel file cabinets and dark gray, metal desks piled high with mountains of paper. Stacks of white cardboard boxes labeled "EVIDENCE" were everywhere.

Most of the desks they passed were empty but a couple near the front had people working at them. They ignored him.

"Over there," the guard said. "The room in the corner. They're waiting in there."

"My lawyers?" Jackie was hopeful.

"Don't know. Don't care. As soon as they sign my sheet, you're their problem." He nudged him down an aisle in the middle of the room.

Jackie tucked his shirt in as they walked—they had taken his belt away when he was booked and it kept coming out. He looked at the suit coat's soiled sleeves. *This jacket is ruined.*

Two uniformed police officers were seated at the table in the interrogation room while a third, a man in a cheap-looking sport coat with a gold badge hanging from his belt, stood just inside the door. "Any problems?" he asked.

"Nah, a model prisoner," the guard said as Detective George Kritt signed his clipboard.

"Take a seat, Jefferson." Kritt ordered. One of the officers gestured towards a straight backed wooden chair next to him.

"Excuse me, gentlemen, but I do not see my attorneys." Jackie announced, "I know my Constitutional rights and I demand my attorneys be present."

"Sit down and shut up," the detective barked. "You've got exactly one chance to keep from spending the night in the cell. Are you going to talk or listen?" Kritt towered over him. His face was red.

"Listen. Listen!" Jackie yelped as he dropped into the chair.

"Good. Now, the young lady you sexually assaulted is willing to drop all charges on one condition."

"But I did not assault . . ." Jackie stammered.

"Don't you understand shut up?" the detective asked.

"But, I did not . . ." *Let me explain!*

"Jefferson, one more word, and the deal is off," Kritt screamed, spit flying from his mouth.

"But . . ." *I can explain!*

"You don't get it, do you?" The detective's voice filled the room, "I thought you were smarter than that but I guess I was wrong. Get him out of here."

Jackie was terrified when the officer sitting next to him stood up and unsnapped the leather strap that secured his revolver. Out of the corner of his eye he saw the second policeman tapping his palm with his night stick. "I am sorry," he whimpered. *This can not be happening!*

"Too late, Jefferson."

"Please, sir. I give you my word." *I can not go back in that cage!*

"OK, Jefferson, because I'm a nice guy I'll give you one last chance," Kritt smirked. "And I'll make it so blunt even you will understand. We have three different videotapes showing what you did so don't even think about lying. You sexually assaulted a seventeen-year-old girl. A minor. You will be a registered sex offender the rest of your life."

No! No! No!

"I tried to talk your victim and her parents out of this, but she wants to show you what Christianity is really about. So, are you going to argue or do you want to hear your last chance?"

"No, sir. I mean, yes, sir. I mean I will be quiet," Jackie tried to sound humble.

"Good. As I was saying, the young lady you sexually assaulted is willing to drop all charges if you make a public apology. Oh, and you have to go to church with her family next Sunday. This is Sergeant Harnett, he's a CAPS officer," the detective pointed to the white haired officer standing by the window. He was older but looked to be in great physical shape. And there was a cockiness in the way he tapped his hat with his billy club that demanded respect.

"Do you know want to hear the details?" Kritt asked.

Jackie nodded. *Do I have any alternatives?*

Harnett sat down next to him and began speaking. "The cornerstone of the CAPS program—which I'm sure you know stands for Chicago's Alternative Policing Strategy—is to encourage local 'problem-solving' by police and residents. What you did today is a lot more serious than the usual problems we get involved in, stuff like petty theft, graffiti, and vandalism. The States Attorney and I spoke with the young lady and worked out the following offer."

Harnett picked a well-worn leather briefcase off the floor and placed it on the table next to his baton. He removed a thick manila folder and thumbed through until he found what he was looking for. He slid a sheet of paper in front of Jefferson.

"First, you will make a full apology in a venue of our choosing. Your apology will be as public as your assault . . . that means TV and press coverage. And I have to approve the text of your statement. If you deviate from it, the deal is off. And there will be no question and answer session afterwards."

Kritt stood behind Jackie, reading over his shoulder.

"Second, you will accompany the victim and her family to their church for services next Sunday. She specified you wear conservative clothing and not call attention to yourself. Also, no lawyers or press. Just you. And I'll be in the pew behind you in case you don't show proper respect in the Lord's house. After the service you may join them as their guest for brunch or you are free to go."

"Can I speak to my lawyer?" Jackie asked hesitantly. "I never enter into a contractual arrangement without his valuable input and guidance." *I know my rights! They must allow me to speak with my attorney!!*

"In a word, no. This deal expires in one minute." The Sergeant tapped his watch with the billy club. "Of course, if you don't sign it, you do have the right to have legal counsel present during your arraignment and interrogation."

"It looks as though you gentlemen have me over the proverbial barrel. By chance do either of you know to which denomination the young lady belongs?"

Kritt laughed. "You better hope she's not a fire and brimstone fundamentalist."

"Sir, I'll have you know I am an ordained Southern Baptist minister . . . my credentials are impeccable."

Harnett tapped the sheet with his stick. "Jefferson, save the showboating for someone who cares. If we have a deal, sign on the bottom line. And don't forget to fill in your contact information so I know where to reach you. I'll be in touch to arrange the press conference. It looks like Wednesday afternoon, but I have to firm that up. The young lady and her family want to be present and we're working around their schedules. You can get the details on the church service at that time."

Jackie spent about five minutes reading and re-reading the single page before he asked for a pen and signed two copies of the agreement with a great flourish. "Am I now a free man?"

"Almost. I have to fill out a couple of forms. Then I'll take you downstairs to get your personal property back." Kritt answered.

"May I please use your telephone to arrange transportation home?" Jackie asked.

The detective slid an ancient phone in front of him. "Local calls only. I'll be at my desk. Bring him over when he's finished, and I'll escort him to the property cage. Figure it'll take me about five minutes to push the papers . . . ten if there's fresh coffee."

"You're the boss. I'll wait with him," Sergeant Harnett said. He turned to the officer who was sitting silently across from him and said, "Thanks, Dave, I won't need you any longer. Could you let 'em know downstairs the prisoner is being released?"

Again Jackie chose to not say anything. The time for that would come, but this was not it. He lifted the receiver and started to punch in a phone number.

"You have to dial nine for an outside line," Harnett said.

"Thank you." *Why did you not tell me that before I dialed?*

The phone was answered on the first ring. "Jefferson residence."

Mrs. White, this is the Reverend Jefferson. Please put Samuel on the phone." He turned away from the CAPS officer and began to speak quietly but forcefully. He shielded the phone with his hand.

"Where are you? Why are you not here? Where is everyone? Where are my attorneys? Jackie slammed his hand on the table. "Unacceptable!"

Harnett interrupted. "Everything all right?"

He took a deep breath, held it for a moment, then exhaled. He took a second deep breath before answering, "Yes, thank you."

"Samuel, enough excuses. We will talk about this later. I want you to bring my car. No, drive your car. I do not want anyone to recognize me."

Hartnett watched with amusement as Jefferson spoke through clenched teeth. *That mans gonna pop a vein,* he thought

"Where am I? I am at the police station!" His voice grew louder. "Where do you think I am! Did not anyone follow me here?"

Jefferson's hands trembled. His voice quivered.

"I do not believe this. I am in jail and everyone went home for the night! Hold on, I will get the address. Sergeant, could you please tell me where I am."

"I thought you knew. You're at a police station," he replied with a sly grin.

Jackie took a moment to reign in his emotions before speaking. "Allow me to rephrase that. Could you please tell me which of Chicago's many fine police stations I am at, so I might take my leave and allow you to return to protecting the innocent through your diligent pursuit of crime?"

"*Touché.* You're at the Seventeenth District, 4461 North Pulaski Road."

Jackie cocked an eyebrow at Harnett. *The first helpful answer I have heard today.*

"Did you hear that? Good. It should take you about ten minutes to drive here. Pick me up something to eat. I have not eaten all day. And do not park. I will be watching for you."

Jackie hung up the phone and turned to see a patrolman standing in the doorway holding a computer printout that was at least three feet long.

"Am I glad I caught you before you were released. Mr. Jefferson, you might want to make yourself comfortable. You won't be going anywhere for a while. You now belong to the City of Chicago Bureau of Traffic Enforcement."

"But we have a deal. I signed the agreement," Jackie shouted, waving the sheet of paper in front of the officer.

Harnett replied, "I don't think this has anything to do with why I'm here."

Detective Kritt heard the commotion coming from "his" interrogation room and walked over to see what was going on.

Jackie stammered, "T-tell him. Tell him we have a signed deal."

Kritt shrugged. "I don't know anything about this. Officer?"

Officer Stan Numowski was working overtime and looked it. He collar was unbuttoned and he sported a five o' clock shadow. There were sweat stains under both arms.

"Detective, Mr. Jefferson, I'll be glad to explain. Mr. Jefferson, we've been processing the large number of people arrested in this morning's riot. We're not used to this volume on a weekday so things fell a little behind. We've been running fingerprints and rap sheets as fast as we can—we even had some senior citizens that were being held at the hospital—but procedure says we have to process 'em in the order they're brought in. I hope you understand we can't sacrifice accuracy for speed. So, when we were finally able to run you we came up with this."

He held up the computer printout. "It appears you've neglected to pay a few parking tickets. Thirty-five to be exact. Then there's a ticket for an expired city sticker . . . another for running a toll booth. No, make that two . . . there's at least four for parking in a disabled parking space . . . and even one for a code # 09-76-220 (b) Non-reflective tint beyond 6" of the top of the windshield during operation."

Numowski got very condescending. "Uhhh, oh, it looks like you missed a court appearance for driving without proof of insurance. And here's your biggest problem . . . a skipped appearance for an accident you had a couple of years ago. It looks like the judge suspended your license. I'm still waiting to see if there's an outstanding warrant for your arrest."

Sergeant Harnett said, "I hope whoever you called has a bag of money with him because you're not going anywhere until you square this up."

Detective Kritt slapped a clipboard thick with papers. "My paperwork's all done. So you're on your own with this one."

Jackie's shoulders slumped. He shook his head and asked, "Could I please make another phone call?"

"Help yourself. I would suggest you call your attorney. And you might have him bring a change of underwear. I think all the traffic court judges have gone home for the night," Harnett responded as he and Kritt walked out of the room. "I'll be waiting right outside when you're done."

"You should have thanked God when He answered your prayer in the holding cell," a voice whispered from behind him.

"Who the . . ." Jackie said as he spun around to see who was speaking to him. His words were cut short when he saw no one was there. Now, on top of everything else, he was hearing voices. *Will this day ever end?* Jackie thought.

CHAPTER 13

CITY HALL HAD pretty much cleared out before the massive clock in the lobby chimed its fifth note. Tonight, however, every light in Suite 900 still burned bright. Outside the block-long granite building, a score of reporters waited for a statement from the Commissioner. Security had been so tight that none had gotten close enough to read the new brass plaque, "City of Chicago Department of Buildings, Where Building a Better Chicago Begins," that greeted visitors to the ninth floor. Sheriff's Deputies escorted them outside when they locked down the building for the night.

So they hung out on the sidewalk, shot the breeze, and watched their deadlines pass.

Upstairs, the conference room table was piled so high with boxes and papers that the telephone rang several times before anyone could find it

"Got it," Fred shouted as he pulled the phone out from under a large blueprint. "McBarker here," he said into the receiver.

The voice on the other end of the phone screamed so loud everyone in the room recognized it as their supervisor, Reynold O'Dea. "Are you watching TV?" he bellowed.

Fred's voice was a mixture of surprise and anger. "Watching TV? What? Are you kidding?" Everyone stopped working to eavesdrop. "Rey, we've been going over prints and specs and inspection reports nonstop since you left. We haven't even stopped to grab something to eat. So when would we have time to watch TV?"

O'Dea ignored the question. "Turn on Channel Three News right now," he ordered.

Fred covered the mouthpiece with his hand and called out, "Somebody turn on the TV. Channel three."

The other men started digging through the clutter for the remote control. Garand called out, "Who had it last?" as piles of paper were patted down for the missing remote.

"Found it!" Petraski called out as he pushed a button. In an instant the sixty-inch screen was filled with Phil's black-and-white video of the riot.

"Oh my gosh. That was shot today," Garand said as he watched a police car explode in flames.

"Three. Rey said turn on channel three." Fred shouted the moment he noticed the glowing red number one in the lower corner of the screen.

The stark, monochromatic images were replaced with a full-color picture of a woman in great discomfort with cartoonish flames surrounding her back side. Channel three was well-known as Chicago's rogue station—more like a supermarket tabloid than a serious news source—and they were always pushing the limits of good taste with their programming choices. They were also well-known as the channel that would report anything for ratings . . . and this was sweeps week.

"Uhhh, Rey, it's a commercial for hemorrhoid cream," Fred said.

A stream of obscenities exploded from the phone followed by "After the commercial! After the commercial! They said they would have the exclusive story after the commercial!"

"What exclusive story?" Fred fired back.

"What story! You know what story! How City Hall is covering up the reason City Gate fell down. That's what story!" O'Dea screamed.

Fred started to respond, "Rey, I don't know what you're talking . . . but was cut off by O'Dea yelling, "Well?"

"Well what?" Fred asked, "Now there's a commercial for pickup trucks."

"Who did you talk to?" O'Dea demanded.

"Come on, Rey. You know me better than that. I don't talk to reporters . . . period. That's not my job. Besides, I've been here busting my butt trying to get the mayor's friends back into their expensive condominiums. Those were your orders. That's all everyone's been doing for the last six hours."

"Well, you must have talked to somebody about the collapse," he thundered.

"When? I was brought straight here by two cops. I didn't even talk to them. You can ask them if you don't believe me," Fred shot back. "And who said I said anything?"

"I don't know who said what, but somebody shot their mouth off." O'Dea challenged him, "I want to know what's going on right now . . . and I want to know it before anyone else does. So you tell everyone there they had better not talk to anyone but me. Whoever that TV guy talked to had better not be from my department or they're fired. I don't care who they think they know, they're out."

McBarker gritted his teeth. One hand clenched the phone while the other fist swung wildly in the air. "Rey, I've been torn from my wife's arms at the hospital—practically at gunpoint—dragged downtown, and locked up in your office. I've been up since well before dawn and had a building almost fall on my head. I am too tired to play games. Now I have no idea what the reporter is going to say, so I will call you back after I watch it."

Fred considered for just the briefest moment telling O'Dea about his hospital room meeting with Billy and Philo, but knew this wasn't the right time. *I sure hope neither of them spoke to that reporter.*

"You do that," O'Dea slammed the phone down.

Just then the commercial ended, and the wanton face of news anchor Alexandria Wright-Snydler appeared with a video of the collapsing building running behind her. The words, "The secret city hall doesn't want you to know" scrolled across the bottom of the screen.

"Shhhhh." Fred held his hand in the air. "This is it." Everyone gravitated towards the monitor.

"Good evening, Chicago," the anchor shook her trademark black hair and struck a come-hither pose before continuing.

"Tonight Channel Three News is proud to bring you an exclusive behind-the-scenes exposé on the collapse of Building Eight at City Gate. While most of Chicago was nestled in their warm beds, a modern, state-of-the-art office tower crumbled into dust for what the fire department termed 'no apparent reason.' The Mayor and the City of Chicago's Department of Buildings have refused our repeated requests for an explanation."

Well that takes us off the hook, Fred thought.

"Instead, the Mayor's spokesman issued a terse, one-sentence official statement that reads, 'It would be premature to speculate on the reason for this unprecedented occurrence.' While the City of Chicago may claim on the record they are unwilling to speculate we have conducted an exclusive interview that reveals for the very first time supernatural forces are being seriously considered."

Everyone in the room stared at the screen in rapt attention. An aerial shot of the entire complex next filled the screen . . . the camera panned from building to building until it slowly zoomed in on the debris-filled hole.

Professor Rossa broke the silence by asking, "Frederick. Are we considering supernatural forces?"

"Shhhh," McBarker hissed, holding his index finger to his mouth for emphasis.

"And later in this broadcast we will bring you the exclusive story our competition is afraid to bring you. But first, we're going live to late-breaking news from the Englewood neighborhood on Chicago's southwest side where an infant girl in a stroller was slaughtered in a senseless drive-by shooting. George, take it away . . ."

The picture changed to a man who was dressed too good for the neighborhood. The camera followed him as he walking down the sidewalk. He passing several boarded up buildings then stopped at an impromptu shrine on the blood-splattered sidewalk. Several stuffed animals sat in front of a row of jars filled with cut flowers while a dozen small tongues of fire danced on a ring of candles surrounding them.

"Good evening, Chicago. I am standing at the intersection of Seventy-fifth Street and Wolcott Avenue, the site of the horrific slaughter of an innocent young girl. A little over sixty minutes ago, six-month-old Shaniqua Taylor was alive and sleeping in her stroller. Now she lies cold and dead on a marble slab in the Cook County Morgue. Shaniqua's grandmother was pushing her home after attending a church service when two shots rang out . . ."

Fred threw his arms up in frustration.

"I guess it's true . . . if you bleed, you lead," Nix Seidler observed.

"I hope Rey has an ambulance close by. He's gonna have a grabber," Garand mimicked a man having a heart attack.

"All I know is, I'm not answering the phone," Nix stated.

"Maybe you should, kid," Garand joked. "I learned four new words the last time he called."

"OK, guys, back to work," Fred said, "Maybe if we have some answers when Rey calls, we can all go home to our wives."

Blaster sighed, "Aw c'mon, boss, don't be a slave driver. We've been at this all day. Isn't there some law that says you have to give us a break?"

Fred knew Mitch was right. Everyone was getting tired. "Good point. I want everyone back here in fifteen minutes."

Joe Petraski put down an armful of blueprints and said, "Hey, Fred, I know Rey wants you to watch Channel Three News, but this fancy TV has picture-in-a-picture. I can shrink channel three into the corner and flip to the sports channel to catch the score from the Cubs game. The moment their exclusive comes on I'll switch right back."

"Since when are you a baseball fan?" Garand teased, knowing his friend lived and died with the Cubs.

"Would you believe I had a pair of beautiful box seats right down the third base line, five rows up from the dugout," Joe said with an edge to his voice. "My parents bought 'em from a scalper for my birthday present. I was taking a personal day off today when they sent a car to get me at my house. My wife ended up calling our son in sick at high school and took him in my place."

"Bummer." Garand commented.

"No kidding. The first time an office building collapses and it has to happen on the day I've got tickets to see the Cubs play the Cards."

"I hope they're more considerate when they schedule the next disaster," Garand joked.

Fred said, "Go ahead and turn it on, but be ready to switch back the second the City Gate story comes on."

As his men filed out of the room, Fred leaned back in his chair and closed his eyes, contemplating what he would tell his boss. *Of course I have to tell Rey the whole truth . . . but how will I make him believe me without the pictures?* Fred tried calling Philo and Billy earlier but was surprised and disappointed to hear the distinctive ringing of their cellphones coming from underneath the table. Whichever lackey brought Billy's camera from the hospital—minus the memory card—also included their cellphones in the cardboard box.

As soon as I get out of here I'll track down their home phone numbers. I really need to talk to them. I've got a million questions to ask them starting with what's the best way to tell Rey an angel with a flaming sword knocked City Gate down? Man, I sure hope they didn't talk to that reporter. But how else would they know about the supernatural cause of the collapse?

Fred's mind raced a mile a minute and he was having trouble staying focused. *God wouldn't show us a miracle then let us sink, would He?* Fred tried to reassure himself. *No, I'm sure God wouldn't do that. Would He?*

He felt like screaming out loud, but remembered, *the last thing Billy said was I shouldn't hesitate to ask for God's help. But how? If only they were here to tell me how to do it right.* Then, the truth dawned on Fred . . . the answer wasn't in them but in Him.

"Joe, you'll have to excuse me," he said to Petraski, "I'll just be in Rey's office for a moment . . . I need to talk to Someone. Come and get me the moment they show anything."

"Fred, before you leave," Mitch called out. "Can we order pizza? We're starved."

"Yeah . . . that sounds great. You'll have to call the guard downstairs to let you know when the delivery guy gets here."

Fred closed the door behind him and settled into one of the overstuffed leather chairs in the reception area inside of his boss' office. He closed his eyes and started praying, "Hi, God. I know I don't have a right to ask for any favors, but I have a problem. This morning you saved my life and the lives of two of my men. Thanks again. You also let us see something I can't understand, but I know it was a miracle. I guess what I want to ask is if anyone gets fired for what that TV announcer is going to say, let it be me."

His meditation was disturbed by a shout of, "Hey Fred . . . They're showing it!"

CHAPTER 14

THAT EVENING'S TEN o'clock news was more exciting than any in recent memory. From the network's point of view, the collapse of Tower Eight, coupled with the Albany Park riot, couldn't have come at a more opportune time. This was sweeps week, when a rating company determined, through mysterious and secret methods, how many people watch each television channel. Those numbers then determine how much each station can charge for their commercials. Every network pulled out all the stops for sweeps week, and tonight it seemed like every channel had an exclusive. It was a news junkey's dream.

Pam Romenelli was nervous. Tonight would be the first time she sat at the anchor desk with Channel One's trademark hologram rotating behind her. Prior to today, her career consisted of videotaped reports from the field covering minor local news, human interest stories, and filler that, as often as not, never made it on the air. Tonight, however, her story would open the news—and it would be part of the network feed as well. In a few hours, her face would be on millions of television sets all across America. The one thought that kept running through her head was, *Through the grace of God, I was at the right place at the right time.*

She recognized it was only through Providence that an incredible string of events unfolded. First, every other Channel One news crew was committed elsewhere—mainly covering stories related to the City Gate collapse—when word of the Albany Park riot reached the station. Next, Pam's team just "happened" to be a few blocks away covering a Boy Scout membership drive Mayor Gates was promoting as a way to get kids off the street and out of gangs.

Her interview of eyewitnesses to the melee was the first time she appeared live and unedited on television—and management was impressed by what they saw. Now, because a local busybody just "happened" to recognize her from some video snippet and insisted he would talk to no one else, Mr. and Mrs. Vincent Romenelli's oldest daughter was getting her big break.

What were the odds the man who videotaped the riot would be an articulate and distinguished looking gentleman? *Pretty good when you place your trust in the Lord.* Pam thought.

It wasn't difficult to talk Phil into appearing on the air. What took time was helping him pick something "good enough" to wear on TV. They looked over everything hanging in his closet before settling on one of his Sunday-best suits—a dark gray, wool, double-breasted one. A starched white shirt, dark red silk tie, and a spit-shined pair of wing-tip shoes completed his outfit, all of which he had purchased in the '70s at Robert Hall, a Chicago clothing institution that used to be a few miles away in the Six Corners neighborhood.

Phil looked over his selection and had to admit that, with a clean shave and a little trim, he would look pretty dapper. "It'll just take a minute to get spiffed up and changed."

Pam said, "No time for that here, Phil. We have a dressing room waiting for you at the studio."

"Can I shave before we go?" He ran his fingers over the stubble on his chin.

Pam answered, "They'll do that for you in makeup."

"Makeup? I have to wear makeup?"

"Don't worry, Phil, everyone on TV wears a little to take the shine off their nose."

He rubbed his nose with his handkerchief and asked, "Could I at least call my brother before we leave? I want to make sure he sees me. I probably shouldn't say this, but he watches Channel Four because he thinks that white-haired news guy of yours is a commie pinko."

Pam stifled a giggle because she knew everyone in the newsroom agreed their head anchor, Peter Trofeld, was to the left of Joseph Stalin in his political views. "Don't worry, Phil," she said. "When we get in the van, I'll give you my cellphone and you can call everyone you know."

While they were discussing his wardrobe, the technicians confirmed the station did not have any equipment capable of playing Phil's videotape. Their boss was certain, however, they could patch the ancient VideoRover II into their system. After they packed everything up, including the instruction manual, they amused themselves by watching a black-and-white rerun of Leave it to Beaver on the black-and-white TV.

"Why did they call this the good old days?" Tony shrugged .

"OK, boys, nostalgia time is over," Pam emerged carrying a garment bag. "We're ready to roll. The police barricades are still out in front, so we'll leave the way we came."

No one paid any attention as the four joined the steady stream of people walking down the alley, and they soon climbed into their van for the short ride to the downtown studio. Phil ran out of people to call before they had gone a couple of miles, so Pam prepared him for his appearance. "I'll open by introducing you. What would you like to be called? Phil Nollo or Philip Nollo?"

"You'd better just make it Phil. Nobody's called me Philip since I was a boy. Well, my wife used to call me Philip when she was mad at me. Yep, make it Phil—but I guess you could call me Phil Nollo at least once so everybody knows it's really me."

Pam smiled. "You got it, Phil. This is going to be fun. After I introduce you, I'll ask a couple of general questions about the neighborhood—something about how you watch the ladies pray in front of the clinic every Monday and why you videotaped them today. Then I'll announce we're going to run your video and explain why it's in black and white."

The driver jumped in with, "I'll bet the switchboard gets at least a dozen phone calls asking why it's not in color."

"That's a sucker bet if I ever heard one," Jimmy said. "They'll get at least that many from your relatives."

"Excuse us," Pam glared at the two young men "We are trying to work. Now where were we? Oh yes, I'll explain the video is supposed to be in black and white so they shouldn't try to adjust their sets. Then I'll ask you to narrate it. Based on what I described to the Vice President of News, the station has committed to showing the entire tape. There are several long stretches where it gets a little quiet—we'll review them with you before you go on the air—and you can describe what you saw."

"Will they use cue cards?" Phil asked.

"We don't use cards any more . . . we have a teleprompter. But no, my boss wants you to tell the story in your own words."

Phil took a deep breath, "What if I get nervous?"

"Don't worry, Phil. I'll be right next to you. And when the videotape starts you won't even be on camera. We'll be talking just like we are now."

Once they got out of the neighborhood, traffic opened up, and they were soon accelerating down an expressway on-ramp. Ten minutes later, they were met in the parking lot as if delivering a load of gold. A lot of people smelled an award for their coverage of the riot and wanted to make sure Phil and his videotape arrived safe and sound. TV ratings are a cutthroat business. It wouldn't be the first time a rival network tried to hijack an eyewitness.

Two uniformed security guards, each wearing a gun in a holster, hustled the two technicians and their prize through a windowless metal door while two other guards opened the van's doors for Pam and Phil.

A well-dressed man swung opened a frosted glass door marked "PRIVATE" and beckoned them. "Good evening, Mr. Nollo, Miss Romenelli. My name is Charles Jacobsen. Please come with me."

Pam had never been in this portion of the building. The floors had plush carpeting and the walls were covered with portraits of network executives. This was a far cry from the linoleum and painted concrete block walls she was used to.

"Good evening, Ms. Romenelli. Good evening, Mr. Nollo," the receptionist said as she buzzed them in.

"Romenelli? A young intern standing off to the side asked. All of the interns wore identical outfits, khaki pants and a dark blue polo shirt with a big number one on the pocket. They also wore running shoes because they usually were on such tight schedules they had to run everywhere.

"That's me," Pam smiled and waved to her.

"I'm Carly. Please follow me to wardrobe."

"And I'll take Mr. Nollo," Jacobsen said.

"Pam?" Phil hesitated.

"Don't worry Phil. You're in good hands. I'll see you on the set." Pam called out as she walked away from him.

"Your dressing room is right around the next corner," Carly said. "Bernice is waiting for you." Pam craned her neck to peek into every office they passed.

"Here we are." She swung the door open to a room overflowing with racks of clothes. A plump woman sat on the edge of the dressing table with her arms folded. The stub of a cigarette hung from the corner of her mouth.

"Call me when you're done." Carly beat a hasty retreat.

"Take off your blouse," the woman ordered the moment the intern closed the door.

"But we just met." Pam was nervous and attempted a humorous reply.

She rolled her eyes. "Oh great, a comedian. Gee whiz! And I thought you wanted to be a big shot news anchor." Years of smoking two packs a day had given Bernice a raspy voice and she made a wheezing noise when she breathed. "Now strip to the waist."

"Why? What's wrong with what I'm wearing?" Pam pleaded.

"Honey, you're going national tonight and off the rack from your local discount store don't cut it. Don't worry." She kept talking while rummaging through a rack of jackets. "By the time we're done with you, you'll look better than the night the quarterback took you to the prom." She sized Pam up. "You look about a size eight."

"I'm a seven, actually." She struck a pose. "And he was the field goal kicker."

Bernice shook her head. "Whatever. Remember, you're borrowing these clothes, so don't get anything on them. This jacket costs more than you make in a month." She draped an elegant silk blazer across her arm. "I'd tell you who designed it, but my mouth don't pronounce them French names. You'll be wearing an opaque white blouse with a camisole under it. We'll also provide accent jewelry to complete the outfit."

"Do I have time to take a shower? I think I still smell a little from teargas."

"Is that what stinks? I thought you bought the super economy size of perfume where you buy your shoes." She looked down at Pam's mud-stained cross trainers.

"I'm sorry we got off on the wrong foot," Pam tried to make a pun, "but I'm so nervous."

"No problem, sweetie, apology accepted. But remember one thing, no matter how big you get, I'm one of the little people who has danced on the grave of every hotshot talking head they ran through their grinder. I've been here almost twenty years and I stopped counting how many have come and gone."

She leaned forward and motioned for Pam to come closer. "They don't know it upstairs, but we have a pool down here on how long the new talent will last . . . it costs ten bucks a square. If you survive tonight I might even bet you'll last six months."

Pam felt awkward but managed a smile. "Thank you. I'll do my best to help you win."

Bernice chuckled, "You do and I'll buy lunch. The shower is through there." She pointed between two racks of clothes. "By the time they get your hair and makeup finished, I'll have this jacket taken in so it'll be a perfect fit. You'll be sitting behind the desk so you can wear your own skirt and street shoes. Nobody will see them anyway."

"What? No Cinderella slippers?" Pam teased in a friendly way.

"Sure, princess." She pantomimed a crown with her spread fingers. "I'll have Rocco measure your head for a diamond tiara while he's at it," she shot back. "Now get moving. If I'm going to win that bet we've got a lot to do to make you look good enough for prime time. Oh, and don't tell anyone I told you about the pool. They might think I was trying to swing the odds in my favor."

"No problem. Besides, I'm looking forward to you buying me lunch," Pam said.

"Right. And I'll even let you supersize it. Now get going."

Carly was waiting with a robe when Pam stepped out of the shower. "No time to waste," she said. She made a sweeping motion towards the door. "They're waiting for you in makeup." Pam followed her across the hall into a brightly lit room where several women descended on her the moment she sat down. "You're live in ten minutes. Who said you could wash your hair?" one of the stylists demanded. "If we had an hour we could . . ." The roar of two hair dryers drowned out the rest of her sentence.

Pam tried to remain calm as two makeup women jostled for space with the hair stylists. An intern, a young man with a buzz cut and a wisp of a beard, shoved a sheet of paper in her face.

"I'm here to prep you for the interview. Here are the questions they want you to ask. Read it quickly. There are seven more pages."

"What about Phil?" Pam tried to look at him, but the stylists held her head firm.

"I already gave a copy to the old guy to read over."

"Is he nervous?" Pam asked.

"Don't know. He didn't stopped eating the free food long enough to ask him. You wouldn't think a skinny little guy like him could pack away so much. You'd better hope he doesn't get nervous and throw it all up on the air."

Oh great, as if I didn't have enough to worry about, Pam thought as she skimmed over the page. "Will I be able to rehearse with him before we go on the air?"

He looked at his watch. "Don't see how, you're on in eight minutes. But if you get a move on you might have enough time to ask Trofeld for his autograph. He always carries some 8 by 10 glossies for his fans."

What the heck did Phil tell him? Pam wondered as she thumbed through the script.

"Well, that's about as good as we can get her," someone commented. "You've got about sixty seconds to get dressed."

Pam barely finished buttoning her blouse when a woman wearing a large headset burst into the room. "Aren't you finished?" she demanded. "You're on in five minutes." She grabbed the blazer off the hanger and helped her slide it on. "Let's get a move on. The news waits for no one."

The news waits for no one. Pam tried not to giggle at the cliché as she followed the woman into the studio. "Over there." She pointed at the anchor's desk. "First seat on the left."

The moment Pam sat down, she was swarmed by people touching up the just-applied makeup and wiring a tiny microphone under her blazer. "Testing . . . one . . . two . . . three."

"Four minutes," someone announced in a loud voice. Pam took a deep breath, closed her eyes, and did what she always did when she was nervous. *Father, I ask you to calm my fears and place the right words in my mouth. Use me today to bring glory to Your name.*

She then recited the Twenty-third Psalm in a soft whisper, "The Lord is my shepherd . . ." By the third line she realized she was no longer nervous. "Surely goodness and mercy shall follow me all the days of my life: and I will dwell in the house of the LORD forever."

Pam opened her eyes as she finished. Tranquility filled her as she said, "Amen."

The soundman startled her back to reality when he added his amen to hers. His voice seemed to boom out of the tiny earpiece someone had hidden behind her perfectly layered blonde hair . . . almost like a voice from heaven. He saw her startled reaction and said, "I'm sorry, I was doing a final sound level check. I saw your lips moving and thought there was a problem because your voice was so quiet. I didn't mean to eavesdrop but that's my favorite psalm too. Everyone should say it whenever they're anxious to remind themselves they have nothing to worry about. We are always in His hands."

She squinted through the bright lights to see whom her cheerleader was, but could not make him out in the booth. "Hello, Pam, my name's Mike. You're gonna do great," he said.

"I've never sat in an anchor's chair before . . . all the lights . . ."

"Don't worry, Pam. You're never alone when you put your life in Christ's hands."

"Amen to that, brother. And thank you . . . thank you."

From the darkness, a woman emerged leading Phil towards the seat next to her. *He sure cleaned up nice,* she thought.

Pam faked a swoon, "Phil, I almost didn't recognize you. You look so handsome."

He made a gesture as if tipping a hat. "Thank you ma'am. That's mighty kind. But I feel a little silly wearing makeup. Pam, they even added something to my hair to cover up some of the gray. But, what the heck, I guess I do look good enough to be buried."

Pam giggled. "You look fantastic. Are you ready?"

"As ready as I'll ever be. If I start running off at the mouth kick me in the shins . . . my wife used to do that when she wanted to stop me from telling some long-winded story."

"Phil, you're going to do great. All you have to do is talk with me like we did at your apartment."

"One minute," an anonymous voice called out.

Pam shifted her gaze straight at the camera with the red light on. With less than sixty seconds until they were live, Pam was calmer than she had ever been in her life. Tonight would be the first time one of her stories was the lead for the ten o'clock news . . . and Pam knew she would be back behind this desk. Ten seconds before going live from coast-to-coast, Pam draped her gold cross outside of her blouse.

Channel Three's "On The Spot News" milked their "exclusive" interview for everything it was worth, running a teaser promo during each commercial break. Finally, after spending almost fifteen minutes interviewing every conceivable person about a drive-by shooting—none of whom had actually seen it happen—they promised to run the "story the mayor doesn't want you to hear" when they returned from the commercial break.

The station's goal was to keep the viewers tuned in as long as possible. Management recognized they lost most of their viewers to other channels because their weather forecasting skills and sports coverage were the weakest in the market. So to keep their viewers from changing channels, they hyped their lead story to a fever pitch, but always seemed to insert at least one late breaking story and a string of commercials before running what everyone had tuned in to see.

Tonight was no different. It was almost 10:20 before Alexandria Wright-Snydler, finally delivered on their promises.

"Tonight, Channel Three is privileged to bring you an exclusive interview that will tell in stunning detail the real cause of this morning's collapse at City Gate." A videotape of the building collapsing played behind her. "Mayor Gates and the City of Chicago refuse to release any details about the reason for this catastrophe . . . a catastrophe that has made hundreds of condominium owners and businesses who have offices in other buildings in the complex very upset and nervous. What if the building had collapsed in the middle of the afternoon, when it was swarming with office workers? How high would the death count have been?

"The mayor's office recently issued a statement claiming top priority was being given to returning people to their homes. They expect all residents to be allowed back into their units by noon tomorrow. But how can the City of Chicago be certain these glass towers, that look so identical to Gate Eight, will not also crumble into dust?" An aerial shot of the complex bolstered her contention that all of the buildings looked identical. It was obviously file footage as eight buildings glistened in the morning sun. "On the Spot News reporter Greg Ford has an exclusive interview on the secret of Gate Eight's collapse . . . the secret Mayor Gates doesn't want you to know."

The picture changed to a well-dressed middle-aged man sitting in a swivel chair in front of a white wall. Seated next to him was another man whose face was obscured by a computer-generated opaque circle. The station's technicians assured him they would protect his identity by pixilating his face. There was nothing in the room to give a hint about where it had been filmed.

"Thank you, Alexandria, and good evening, Chicago. The two questions on everyone's minds tonight are why did a modern office building collapse and how can we be certain it won't happen again? But this is not the first time that City Hall has refused to answer questions about City Gate.

"From the very day this development was first proposed, almost a decade ago, it has attracted controversy like a flame attracts moths. In order to build the City Gate complex, over one-hundred homeowners had their properties condemned and seized by the City through eminent domain, which is the taking of private property by the government for the public good."

Time-lapse photographs of the complex under construction filled the screen and, in a matter of seconds, viewers watched a whirl of activity transform the vacant site into eight buildings towering over the landscape.

The reporter continued speaking as the video ran. "There are more than one-hundred families who would like to know how the public good was served by building a monument to Mayor Gates' ego."

The scene switched to a room full of men in tuxedoes watching the mayor unveil a large model of the complex. "There are still dozens of unanswered questions about Mayor Sidney Gates' ties to August and Damien, the politically connected, clout-rich, developer of City Gate." He made sure he pronounced *city* to sound like *Sidney*.

"Questions have also been raised about the well-documented fact that every major contractor involved in constructing the eight-building complex made a significant campaign contribution to the mayor in the weeks leading up to last year's historic landslide victory. Alas, no answers have been offered.

"But tonight, On the Spot News has the answer to at least one question. Why did Gate Eight collapse? Seated next to me is a man whose identity must be kept a secret to protect his job . . . maybe even his life. That is why we have mechanically altered his appearance and his voice."

When the man spoke it sounded like something from a 1950s science fiction robot.

"Mister X. Please tell us your story."

"Well, like I told you, I was waiting for an elevator . . . sorry I can't say where. There were five other people waiting to go down with me and they were talking up a storm . . . actually two of them—the guys—they were doing all the talking and the women, they were just listening. I want you to know I wasn't trying to rubberneck, but they were talking so loud I could hear every word even if I didn't want to. At first I tried to ignore them—I got my own problems you know—but I started paying a lot of attention when I realized what they were talking about."

"Without disclosing anything that could reveal your identity, could you please tell our viewers exactly what took place during the elevator ride?"

"Sure. I got in with them and the doors slid shut. They never stopped talking about that building collapse. Only you know they were talking like they were right there when it happened. I mean, they knew all sorts of little details like the building had burglar bars like a jail does. What really got my attention was when one guy said they went inside and found the dead babies."

"Dead babies?" Ford feigned surprise.

"Yep. They both said there were dumpsters full of bloody, dead babies."

"Did either man have any idea where these dead babies came from?"

"Yep. They said there was a clinic in the building. Only one guy said it wasn't really a clinic, but an abortion mill. But I guess they didn't know that at first and got pretty upset about that."

"What else did they say?" Ford continued.

"The two of them started talking real solemn—like they were in church you know—then they said they saw an angel. Both of them said it at the same time."

"An angel?" His voice raised an octave.

"Yep. That's what both of the guys said."

"And did the angel have a name?"

"They argued a little about that, and the one guy used some name I never heard before and don't remember. But the other guy was sure he was named Michael."

"Michael?"

"Yep. But not just any Michael. He thought he was Michael the ark angel." He pronounced it as if it were two words.

"The famous Archangel Michael from the Bible?" Ford asked.

"I don't know. I guess so, but they didn't really say."

"And what did they say Archangel Michael was doing?"

"They both got real excited and started talking at the same time. But it was real weird because it seemed like they were saying the same thing."

"Please tell our viewers what the two men were saying."

"They said he was huge. I mean he touched the ceiling like he was holding it up. Oh yeah, they also said he was glowing and he had wings and he—I mean the angel, not the guys that is—he swung a flaming sword that knocked the whole building down."

"Amazing. So you're saying the two unidentified men witnessed an angel sent from heaven to destroy an abortion clinic."

"Smite. They said God sent him to smite it. And they kept calling it a mill, not a clinic."

"Did they say what happened to the angel after he smote the building?"

"Smite . . . they said smite. I think that means wreck it. I guess the angel went back to heaven." He shrugged, then added, "Oh, and one of the guys also said he had pictures of the angel knocking the building down."

"Did he show the other people the pictures?"

"Well, I don't know because he didn't say that until they were getting out of the elevator in the lobby. I thought it would look funny if I followed them, so I didn't hear any more."

"Thank you very much for sharing your experience with our viewers."

The camera zoomed in on the anchor as he delivered his closing summary, "So there you have it, Chicago. An eyewitness account," the newsman took liberty with the truth to make it more dramatic, "of how God sent an Archangel down from heaven to smite an abortion mill. Rest assured, Channel Three news is sparing no expense in tracking these two men down and acquiring photographs of an Archangel at work. Until then, thank you for watching, and good night."

Channel Four led off with their own well-hyped "exclusive interview." Standing in front of an ambulance parked outside the Emergency Room, field reporter Wesley Schafner introduced the seventy-five-year-old sisters. "Good evening Chicago. With me this evening are two survivors of the Albany Park riot, Kaye and Ruth Hansen." Both smiled and nodded politely.

"They were released from First Presbyterian Hospital only minutes ago after being treated for injuries suffered in a skirmish with the Chicago Police Department." The camera zoomed out to include Nurse Ryun standing next to the women. She maintained a dignified posture.

"I was fortunate enough to catch them before their police escort arrived to drive them home."

"But the Hansen sisters want to share much more than the story of a police melee. Their Channel Four exclusive will answer the question which all Chicagoans are asking."

"Ladies, I have been told you know the real reason the Council of Women headquarters building collapsed early this morning."

Answering in a tandem only twins could achieve, Kaye and Ruth stated. "God responded to our imprecatory prayers and smote that most evil place into dust."

Even a veteran newsman like Schafner was caught off guard by the bluntness and confidence of their answer. He wished he had been allowed a few minutes to prep them before the camera rolled, but Nurse Ryun was very specific: "You have exactly two minutes. Two, not three. Then they're leaving in a police cruiser."

Schafner recognized few viewers would care little about the story of two little old ladies who had been tear gassed. He needed an angle. He racked his brain and decided to take a chance by running with a rumor he overheard one orderly telling another—that for some unknown reason these elderly women knew why a modern office building fell down. Instead, they sounded as if they were losing their grasp on reality . . . maybe he had the wrong women?

How many ancient sets of twins could be getting released from the hospital this evening? He wished he had taken a safer route, but he didn't have the time to start over. Besides, a bizarre story from a couple of nuts, beat returning to the station empty-handed any day.

During the long pause that followed, the cameraman zoomed in on the sisters. The parking lot's sodium vapor lights cast a pink glow that was not very kind to their wrinkled faces. Even worse, their white hair blended into the ambulance.

Schafner thought quickly and decided to have some fun with the ladies. "Smote? That's I word I haven't heard since Sunday school . . . it's so Old

Testament," he said with more than a hint of sarcasm in his voice. "How do you know for a fact God returned to Earth to smote an office building?"

Ruth was older by almost ten minutes and her "kid" sister deferred speaking first to her. "Every day we say at least one rosary and pray to Our Lady of Guadeloupe to end the slaughter of pre-born babies."

"It's not only us," Kaye added. "There are tens of thousands praying every day for God to end the slaughter of the innocents . . . Catholics, Protestants, Jews, all coming together to pray to our Creator for that common purpose. We appealed to the court of divine justice to either bring the abortion providers to repentance or to justice. This morning He answered."

"Last night we had the same dream." Ruth said. "An angelic messenger of the Lord appeared to us and said, 'Fear not. He who knows what is in every heart and every mind has heard your plea and will answer your prayer.' Then we watched Archangel Michael swing his mighty sword and smite the obscene building into dust." They sliced their right arms through the air.

Schafner was befuddled. "Uhhh."

"And, young man, in case you were wondering, smote is the past tense of smite. I said smite because we saw it happen."

"We both woke up and checked the alarm clock," Kaye punctuated the words by tapping her index finger across her palm. "It was exactly 4:14 A.M."

"So we dropped to our knees," Kaye went on, "and said a prayer of thanksgiving to God for showing us His miracle."

"Then we went back to sleep because we had to be at the Albany Park abortion mill to rescue babies at eight," Ruth finished.

"I was hoping that God would have destroyed that evil place too. Until then, we'll keep praying." Kaye said.

"Be patient, Sister." Ruth squeezed her hand. "All things come to she who waits."

"You're not trying to tell me that you're praying for another building to be destroyed, are you?" Schafner asked.

"Do you attend church, young man?" Ruth asked.

"I'm not the one who receives visions."

"Maybe if you started praying and going to church you would," Ruth said.

Nurse Ryan held her hand in front of the camera. "I'm sorry, the interview is over. Their ride is here."

The reporter lowered his voice, "Well, that's all the time we have. Thank you for appearing on camera with us." The cameraman zoomed in on the reporter. "This is Wesley Schafner reporting from First Presbyterian Hospital." *I'll be lucky to still have a job.*

Channel Six, "Your News Source," definitely had the weakest hand at that night's card game. The best they could come up with was Ms. Carrie Randall, Council of Women's executive vice president. The contrast between their news anchor, Arlene Dailey—a former Miss Illinois—and the rather masculine Ms. Carrie, as she demanded she be called, could not have been more dramatic. Dailey was dressed like a professional and perfectly coiffured. Ms. Carrie had a mullet haircut and wore a flannel shirt over a black T-shirt and a denim vest.

Although she looked like a caricature of an Amazon lumberjack, she declined the station's offers to help her get ready for live TV. "I don't need no makeup," she insisted.

The interview began with Dailey asking Ms. Carrie if the Council of Women had an official statement on the collapse of their world headquarters.

"You bet your *beep* we've got a statement . . . it was a conspiracy . . . a *beep* conspiracy."

"Ms. Carrie, we're live—so if you could please watch your language."

"What! What the *beep* did I say?" She glared at the anchor. "Fine, I'll mind my Ps and Qs. So what do you wanna know?"

"You said it was a conspiracy," Dailey said. "Could you please tell our viewers why you believe this and whom you believe is involved?"

For the next minute and thirty seconds, Ms. Carrie rambled on with a bizarre tale of intrigue and collusion so far-reaching that no sober person would ever believe it.

Channel Eight took advantage of Building Eight's collapse by having one of their interns work out a graphic that incorporated their logo onto a wall with "City Gate Eight" carved into it

Their reporter was one of the lucky ones who got into Granny Gates' room with a tape recorder and, after an introduction by anchor Sherman Robinson, ran the interview in its entirety. They put together an incredible photograph montage of the Women's Suffrage movement that ran during her monologue, including a photo of an elegantly dressed woman whom they identified as "Bitzy" Gates, better known to all of Chicago as Granny Gates.

Faded sepia and black-and-white images documented their march on the nation's capitol with newspaper front pages interspersed to carry the storyline. They had hoped to find another "Silent Sentinel of Liberty" to interview but had to fall back on some grainy file footage from either the late 1930s or early 1940s. The technicians cleaned up the audio as well as they could, but the cracks and pops were a perfect compliment to the vintage look of the film that had snippets of a half-dozen interviews with women who had been arrested with Granny back in the teens.

Most local stations considered ten thirty to be the end of the news day—their early-morning shows wouldn't begin until seven o'clock—unless they picked up the East Coast network feed at six—and started shutting their studios down for the night. Only tonight was a special evening.

The interview hadn't even ended when Channel Four's automated switchboard lit up like a Christmas tree. Hundreds of callers wanted to tell Wesley Schafner they had the same dream as the Hansen sisters. "You have reached Channel Four news. If you have a news tip, please press four now. If you know the three-digit code for the party to whom you wish to speak, please enter it now. If you would like to hear a company directory, please press one now. Or you can stay on the line for the next available operator." Most pressed four.

The only person answering the phone was a nineteen-year-old intern expecting a call from his girlfriend. Instead, he was besieged with testimonies from viewers who wanted to share their tale of last night's vision. Each one insisted he listen to their entire story.

With no one else answering the phone, most callers moved on to option one and entered the first three letters of the anchor's last name; S—C—H. Within an hour, Schafner's mailbox was filled to overflowing with testimonies from dream eyewitnesses. His box would have filled much sooner, but the station only had twelve incoming lines.

It was much the same at Channel Three, where callers wanted to confirm every word Greg Ford's guest said because they saw it happen in their sleep. Being a small channel with a limited budget, they shut down for the night the minute the news ended and switched to a network feed for nine-and-a-half hours of sitcom re-runs. Since the station did not believe in paying overtime, the four-man news team ignored the blinking lights on the desk phones. Besides, their boss and all of their friends and families had their cell phone numbers if they needed to get through. It would certainly be a very interesting morning when the switchboard opened Tuesday morning at nine.

CHAPTER 15

THE BROADCAST BOOTH was almost dark. Only the amber glow of dozens of small lights on the console provided any illumination. Roger Hogue preferred it that way because his listeners were creatures of the night. A thick pane of glass separated Hogue from his producer, Allen. The small studio was soundproof and he worked alone. Always alone.

Most late night radio personalities kept the door to the control booth open, but Hogue demanded it not only be closed, but locked. He also insisted Allen use no more lights than absolutely necessary to stay on the air so as not to spoil the mood.

It took the young man a long time to get used to working with the quirky host, but it was his first job in radio and he didn't want to make waves. Someday he wanted to be behind the microphone.

"Ten seconds." Allen warned over the intercom that the commercial break was coming to an end. Roger swallowed a gulp of coffee and punched one of the glowing buttons.

"George from Des Plaines, you're our next caller on AM 770, WCHI, the Voice of Chicago."

The man's voice was hoarse. "Thanks for taking my call, Roger. I wanted to say I also watched the news and saw the two old ladies who claimed they saw an Archangel wrecking the City Gate building in a dream."

"That's tonight's topic. So what do you think? A vision from God or a couple of nuts?"

"Well, it's always bothered me the way these psychics wait until after something happens to claim they predicted it. I remember back when I was a kid and Kennedy got shot. It seemed like a couple of weeks later all of these people popped up claiming they'd had visions telling them all about it before it happened. I mean, if they really knew it was going to happen, why didn't they warn him?"

"Are you saying these pro-life activists should have warned the baby killers that an archangel was going to rain down some Old Testament vengeance on their abortion mill? Come on, George, that was the answer to their prayers. And they never claimed to be psychics."

"Well, they could have tried to stop him."

"George, get serious. Even if they wanted to, how could two little-old-ladies stop a twenty-foot-high Archangel from swinging his fiery sword?"

"I don't know exactly. Maybe they could have at least called the police to evacuate the building or something."

"Hel-lo, George. Didn't you hear? The archangel evacuated the building. He threw the security guards out on their butts. There was no one was inside when the walls came a-tumbling down."

Roger Hogue was the uncontested king of late-night talk radio. His quick wit and less-than-subtle sarcasm made him an instant favorite of night owls throughout Chicagoland. He was also very proud to be a Christian, pro-life, conservative who believed God specified marriage was to be between one man and one woman. Period. He lived for nights like this one, where most of the callers were so filled with emotion they ignored all of the facts.

"Well, I still don't think it's right for them to pray for something bad to happen. Just think about how many people are going to lose their jobs."

"George, George, wake up, George. You're looking at it all wrong—you should be thinking of how many babies won't be killed there tomorrow. I really don't care how many abortionists have to wait in line at the unemployment office because of this.

"Let's move right along to the next caller. Agnes from Highland Park, you're on the air."

Every radio host with a call-in format was deluged with listeners who had an opinion on the day's most controversial topics: the Hansen sisters' claim to have witnessed in their sleep an angel smiting the C of W head-quarters and the mystery man who claimed to have overheard an elevator conversation where two men said they saw the archangel firsthand.

"Hello, Mr. Hogue." She had a soft voice with a touch of southern twang.

"Call me Roger."

"Oh yes. Well, uh, hello, Roger. I also saw the man with the blurry face on television and was wondering if the men he saw are the same men they keep showing in the video of the building collapsing?"

"Agnes, one of our earlier callers hung the title 'ear-witness to the eyewitness' on the blurry man. Popular opinion is he overheard two of the building inspectors from the video talking about what happened. It will be interesting to hear what city hall has to say about this in the morning. So, what do you think? An archangel or mass hysteria?"

"I was raised Catholic, and I seem to recall the nuns telling us to never pray for something bad to happen to someone or else God will make it happen to you. So I guess those Hansen sisters had better watch out."

"Agnes, Agnes, Agnes. Didn't the good sisters teach you an imprecatory prayer can be said for a righteous cause? Can you think of anything more righteous than saving the lives of innocent babies?" Hogue paused for a moment to give her time to think up an answer.

"Then I guess I'm not entirely clear on what they were doing. Didn't they pray for God to kill the abortionists?" Agnes asked.

"You must have just tuned in. We had several men of the cloth on earlier who explained what they were doing. Hang on, I took some notes." He turned the brightness knob on computer up just enough to read the screen.

"Ah, here they are. Pastor Busch, he's a Lutheran pastor, Missouri synod, quoted the Great Reformer Martin Luther, 'We should pray that our enemies be converted and become our friends, and if not, that their doings and designing be bound to fail and have no success and that their persons perish rather than the Gospel and the Kingdom of Christ.' Does that clear up what they were doing?"

"Well I'm still not comfortable with praying for bad things to happen. And I don't believe there's anything in the Bible that says it's permitted."

"Agnes, do you go to church? Agnes? Agnes? Well it looks like Agnes didn't want to answer my question. But just in case you're still listening, Agnes, go check out the Book of Psalms. Start with Psalm 35. Some call it one of the war psalms. King David wrote it when he was surrounded by so many enemies he knew he didn't have an earthly chance of winning. He asked God to 'fight against those who fight against me . . . ' and ' . . . let them be as chaff before the wind: and let the angel of the Lord chase them. Let their way be dark and slippery: and let the angel of the Lord persecute them.' This is not a prayer of vengeance, but rather a prayer of dependence. This is truly a prayer said by those who have no power—in this world.

"And it sure sounds like what the pro-lifers were doing at City Gate. They were powerless against this multimillion-dollar baby-killing machine. And never forget, the prayer warriors followed the admonition of Romans 12:10, 'Do not take revenge, my friends, but leave room for God's wrath, for it is written: It is mine to avenge; I will repay, says the Lord.' They did not make the building collapse. An archangel of the Lord did.

"I see all of our phone lines are blinking, so I had better take another call. Carol on the south side of Chicago, you're on the air."

"Roger, this may sound like I'm making this up, but I had the same dream as the Hansen sisters." The woman's voice quivered.

"Do tell. Do tell."

"It's strange because I never can remember my dreams, but this one was so vivid it woke me up. Was I ever relieved to find I was still in my own bed. And, yes, I also saw the Archangel. He was huge and swinging a flaming sword. And I could hear the most beautiful chorus of voices singing praises to God. They grew louder and more beautiful as the building was crumbling and somehow I knew this was a heavenly choir of the hundreds of dead babies that were lying at the angel's feet."

"Wow. I just got goosebumps. The ear witness spoke of dead babies . . . and we've had two other callers who had the same dream, but you're the first person to mention a choir of the innocents. Did you see them too?"

"Yes, I saw them pouring put of huge metal containers."

"The garbage dumpsters?"

"I guess that's what they were. Oh, Roger, it was horrible—they were all bloody—some of them were torn apart. But then a brilliant gold light flooded the room, and I knew he was there to bring them home."

"Now my goosebumps have goosebumps."

"Then I found myself outside, looking down on the building; watching it collapse into dust. It disturbed me so much I couldn't fall back asleep. I laid there praying. Later, when I finally got out of bed and turned on one of the early-morning news shows, I saw a replay of the building collapsing. I knew that was the building I had seen in my dream. You're the first person I have told about this."

"Thank you for sharing that with us, Carol. OK, Chicago, this is the first we've heard of someone hearing as well as seeing mutilated murdered babies in their dream. Did anyone else out there hear the choir? Listeners? Let's go next to Nick in Oak Park. You're on the Voice of Chicago."

"Am I on the air?" The young man's voice echoed.

"Nick, you're on a ten second delay so you're going to have to turn your radio off."

"Is that better?"

"Yep. So Nick, did they have a vision from God or are they a bunch of nuts?"

"I don't want to crack wise on old people, but my grandma, she is always telling us about stuff she says she saw that didn't happen. Like you know how it is. When people get that old they get a little confused. So I was thinking that maybe they heard that ear witness guy on TV earlier, and they just think that is what they saw."

"Nick, how old are you?" Roger asked.

"Me? I'm twenty."

"How old is your grandmother?"

"I'm not sure, but she's real old. I guess she's gotta be at least eighty."

"Does she live with you or in a nursing home?'

"My parents finished the basement for her. She's got a little apartment down there."

"Does she go grocery shopping and cook her own food?"

"Sometimes she eats upstairs with us but, yeah, usually."

"Can she drive a car?"

"Yeah. But she only goes out during the daytime when traffic is light."

"Sounds like a lady who knows her own limitations. What does your grandmother do besides drive a car and cook."

"She volunteers down at the school teaching little kids stuff."

"So let's see. Your grandmother is able to teach children, go shopping, cook, and drive a car. Nick, do you have a job?"

"Nah, things are bad out there, and no body wants to hire me."

"Have you thought about volunteering with your grandmother?"

"Nick? Nick? Hmmm, what a surprise. Nick has vanished into the night. That means we have one open line.

"Diana in Lake Villa, thanks for calling in. My producer says you're a member of cow."

A deep, gruff, vaguely female voice answered. "We demand to be addressed as the Council of Women or the C of W. You only expose your ignorance and prejudices by pronouncing the name of our organization incorrectly."

"OK, I'll go there. So, Diana, what's the C of W's position on the Lord God Almighty smiting your building?" he goaded her.

"That's Ms. Rhinelander. You will address me as Ms. Rhinelander. And we take great umbrage at any insinuation that some fictional male supreme being had anything to do with what was obviously an act of urban terrorism against women's rights."

"You say *we*. What exactly is your position in the group—your title—because you speak like you are you more than just a member? Are you an official spokesman?"

"I am the vice president and secretary of the C of W's Intolerance Initiative. And spokesman is a sexist term. The correct title is spokesperson. It is gender neutral."

"And you say the C of W believes this was an act of urban terrorism. Do you have any ideas who might have destroyed the building or how?"

"We know for a fact that this attack was in direct violation of the FACE law."

"The FACE law?"

"Oh, I assumed you would be familiar with the Freedom of Access to Clinic Entrances Act of 1994, which states, and I quote, 'Whoever intentionally damages or destroys the property of a facility, or attempts to do so, because such facility provides reproductive health services shall be subject to the penalties provided in subsection (b) and the civil remedies provided in subsection (c).' Shall I read these penalties to you?"

"No need to, Ms. Rhinelander, I'm very familiar with them. But it seems you choose to forget that the FACE law also covers anyone who damages or destroys the property of a place of worship," Hogue said.

"That is none of my affair—we are concerned solely with the terrorist attack on our world headquarters."

"So are you saying the police should try to arrest the archangel that smote your building with a fiery sword?"

"Archangel!" she screamed. "Only insane people see archangels! There is no such a thing as an angel! We demand the police arrest those Hansen sisters."

"But they were in bed when it happened."

"That doesn't matter. It was a conspiracy and they're part of it. They obviously know more that they are telling anyone. We want, no, we *demand*, the police sit them down and force them to talk. If they sweat them, they'll tell who the ringleaders are."

"Sweat them! They're seventy-five years old!"

"I don't care how old they are," Rhinelander shot back. "Since when is there an age limit for terrorists? We know those women are healthy enough to harass our clinic workers, every week, rain or snow. Nothing stops them. We have pictures of them from our security cameras, harassing the girls we are trying to help. Those two have been at our Albany Park women's clinic every week for over ten years, and, if they're healthy enough to do that, they're healthy enough to blow up our office building!" she ranted.

"OK, Ms. Rhinelander, let's change the subject just a little bit. What is the C of W's official position on the reports that two city building inspectors not only saw an angel destroying your building, but took pictures of it happening?'

"Lies! All lies! Isn't it obvious, they're all part of the conspiracy? We demand the police also arrest them."

"Are you aware this station received a phone call from an orderly who said one of your security guards is telling everyone at the hospital he also saw an Archangel smiting your building?"

"We demand they arrest him too!" She was talking so loud and fast it was becoming hard to make out what she was saying. "He was inside the building. He must have let the terrorists inside to plant bombs. And stop saying 'smite'! I demand you stop using that word! Our beloved building was destroyed by an organized terrorist conspiracy."

"Do you have any proof of that?"

"Yes, I do. Our president, Michelle Staylor, was kidnapped by the police as part of the conspiracy. They didn't want her to talk. They didn't want her to tell the truth."

"But the police say she committed suicide by jumping into the debris pit."

"Micci would never do that. She is the smartest woman in the world . . .

Roger let her ramble. "She is a god to thousands of women worldwide. Can't you see the police are part of the conspiracy?"

"But I saw a videotape of her disappearing into the hole. It's been on the news all day. The only person close to her was one of your C of W buddies."

"Then why won't the police let me talk to June? What are they afraid of? No, they won't let anyone talk to her. She was there when Micci was kidnapped. She knows what really happened. The police claim she's heavily sedated because she was traumatized by what happened to Micci. But I know they're lying. The real truth is she was a witness to the police kidnapping Micci and they are silencing her."

"But the videotape."

"They obviously made a fake tape. They're all in on it!" Even though Rhinelander sounded like she was losing it, Hogue wanted to keep her on the line as long as he could. He knew this was the type of caller that made his show number one. "First they blew up our building, then they kidnapped our leader!"

"But all of the experts agree that there wasn't an explosion. Why do you believe there was one?" Roger asked.

"There had to be an explosion! Why else would our world headquarters collapse? Didn't you hear your own news? They let everyone in the condominiums go back home. If the buildings weren't safe they wouldn't let them go home would they? That proves it was a bomb."

"The statement from the Department of Buildings said the four residential buildings were inspected top to bottom and found to be structurally safe.

They also said even though the buildings appeared identical, the residential towers had steel skeletons while the office towers had cast-in-place concrete support systems."

"Lies, lies, and more lies. They know those buildings won't collapse because they know our world headquarters was destroyed by terrorists."

"Do you have any proof that there was a bomb?"

"Nothing else could have destroyed the building so thoroughly."

"God could easily have brought the building down. After all, He destroyed Sodom and Gomorrah."

"Those are children's fables. Only weak people believe them."

"So you don't believe in God, but you do believe there is a massive conspiracy which includes collusion between the Chicago Police Department, the Chicago Department of Buildings, your security guards, all of the television networks, a whole bunch of structural engineers, and two little old ladies to cover up the real reason why your building is now a pile of broken concrete and your president is missing."

"Yes."

"Yes! That's all you have to say is yes?"

"Why not? You accurately summed up the official position of the Council of Women. You seem to forget, we are the victims."

"Ms. Rhinelander, we're running long and I have to take a commercial break. I wish I could devote an entire program to you, but my call screener tells me that we have dozens of listeners on hold who want to comment on your allegations. Since you're going to be the subject of the next segment, would you like thirty seconds to add anything to what you've already shared with us?"

"Yes, I would." She cleared her throat. "You can mock me if you want, but I will be vindicated. There is a conspiracy to destroy the Council of Women—to deprive women of their constitutionally guaranteed right to choice. You will never again force us to be second class citizens—you will never silence us. We will get our revenge on the people who did this! We know who you are! We will . . ."

"OK, that's about enough. This is my microphone, and you're not going to use it to threaten anyone. So, Chicago, what do you think? Are there thousands of people involved in a massive cover-up, or did God finally get tired of the ravings of the mad cows and send down an angel to smite them? We'll be back after a word from our sponsors."

The red light in front of Hogue went off, signaling the start of the commercial break. Roger checked the log and knew he had three minutes and fifteen seconds before he was back on the air. He took his headphones off, leaned back in his chair, and shouted, "I love this job."

More than one radio at the First Presbyterian Hospital was tuned to an all-night talk show and the most popular one with the nursing staff featured a relative newcomer, James King, host of "While Chicago Sleeps" on Radio News 710. The fact that King's wife, Marie, was a delivery-room nurse at the hospital might have had something to do with it.

On a typical Monday night, the number of callers started to drop off after 2 A.M. as listeners turned in for the night. James would often call Marie to find out how many new Chicagoans there were.

Tonight's topic, "Was it morally wrong to pray for an angel to destroy an abortion clinic," seemed to strike a nerve with the audience. Every line was blinking with a caller eager to share his or her opinion—and quite a few were more than a couple of degrees off dead center in their logic.

"Well, I certainly hope the women who owned that clinic file a lawsuit against whatever church sent that angel to destroy it." The tone of the caller's voice changed as she went further down the path.

"This is America and that was private property."

"Are you serious?" Hogue said. "What makes you think a church sent the angel? What if God sent the angel in answer to thousands of people's prayers? Do you think they can sue God? Hello . . . hello . . . are you still there? I guess she doesn't have all the answers. Let's move on to our next caller."

The man sounded either a lot tired or a little drunk. "I wanna start by saying I'm not really a religious type person you know. I mean I went to Catholic school back in the '70s, you know, with nuns in habits and all that. And I went not just to grade school but to an all-boys Catholic high school with monks and priests, so I know a little bit about angels. But I don't need that formal church type stuff—they're always asking for money you know. One thing I remember the nuns always telling us that if we got God mad enough, He would send angels down to kick our butts. I mean I thought that was just some old nun trying to scare a buncha dumb kids, but I mean it looks like she musta like knew some things. You know like maybe she had some kinda inside line on that stuff."

"So, caller, it sounds as if you think God sent the angel down to do some old-fashioned smiting."

"Yeah, that's what I said. It was just like them old nuns said He would."

"So, do you think God is playing fair by sending a warrior angel with a flaming sword down to punish evildoers?" King asked the caller.

"Man, if He does that there's gonna be a whole lotta people in deep trouble."

"Thanks for sharing that. Next caller, you're live on While Chicago Sleeps."

"Good evening, Mr. King. I find your topic of great interest because I believe what happened this morning was the opening act of God expressing His displeasure with this country. Ever since June 25, 1962, when the United States Supreme Court struck down school prayer, this country has been turning away from its Creator. Did you know the Supreme Court banned reading the Bible in school a year later? And people wonder why God is angry."

"Caller, you're making some great points," he interrupted, "but you're getting off topic. Is it morally wrong to pray for God to destroy an abortion clinic?"

"I took a philosophy course in college where we debated for an entire semester if it would have been wrong for someone to have killed Adolph Hitler in 1935, saving millions of lives by preventing World War II."

"So you're saying that would have been good?"

"No, what I'm saying is all that was destroyed was a building. The angel came in the middle of the night. He didn't come at high noon when the building would have been filled with hundreds of people. Even the security guards were protected from harm—you must make the distinction between people and bricks. So how could it be morally wrong to pray for God to destroy an unoccupied building? That sounds like a pretty compassionate way to stop someone from killing babies, if you ask me. I'll hang up and listen for your response."

"That's an interesting way to spin it. Chicago, what do you think?"

Unlike many callers, the next woman was prepared and had her facts down pat. "Good evening, Mr. King. I'm calling because praying for God to strike down evil is not only morally right but it's straight from the Bible. Remember, these people are not asking God to destroy their personal enemies because that would be wrong. They are asking God to destroy His enemies, God's enemies. Abortionists who flaunt His commandment 'Thou shalt not kill' are certainly no friend of our Father. Are you familiar with Psalm 58?"

"Not from memory," King responded.

"Then if you would permit me, verses six to ten. 'Break the teeth in their mouths, O God; tear out O Lord, the fangs of the lions! Let them vanish like water that flows away; when they draw the bow, let their arrows be blunted. Like a slug melting away as it moves along, like a stillborn child, may they not see the sun. Before your pots can feel the heat of the thorns—whether they be green or dry—the wicked will be swept away. The righteous will be glad when they are avenged, when they bathe their feet in the blood of the wicked.'"

"Wow. Vanish like water that flows away. That sure sounds like what happened to the president of the C of W."

"Oh, but there is more, much more. In Psalm 55, King David says, 'Let death take my enemies by surprise; let them go down alive to the grave.' That's what we all saw happen on the news."

"That's a mighty powerful prayer. I'm glad the angel's on our side. We're going to continue this topic when we return from our break. I'm James King, and you're listening to While Chicago Sleeps."

Roger Hogue finished his fourth cup of coffee. "Welcome back, Chicago. So what do you think, listeners? Is there a massive conspiracy to cover up a building collapse? And who do you thing is behind it? Let's kick off this segment with Rita way out in Lake in the Hills. Rita, you're on AM 770, WCHI, the Voice of Chicago—and you've got a tough act to follow."

"Good evening, Roger. I called before you had that odd woman because I wanted to tell you I also had a dream about an archangel."

"Dreams about angels were tonight's topic. We've moved on to Ms. Rhinelander from the C of W."

"But Roger, you might want to hear this. I just woke up from my dream."

"You mean tonight?"

"Yes, I went to bed early this evening—around eight o'clock. I wasn't feeling very well and laid down to rest. The next thing I knew I was watching a huge angel with a glowing face."

"What did he look like?"

"He was dressed in armor like a knight—but he had wings too. That's how I knew he was an archangel."

"Was it the warrior angel Michael?"

"Yes, I'm certain of that."

"And what was Archangel Michael doing tonight?"

"He was standing on the roof of a building."

"Are you saying you saw a rerun of the destruction of the eight-story building?"

"No, this was different. This was a short building. I think it was only one story tall. It was a brick building with almost no windows . . . and there was barbed wire all around it."

"Was he holding a sword?"

"Was he ever! It was huge and flaming, and he was swinging it in the air. Fire trailed behind it as he traced a figure eight above his head. Then he brought it down and there was an explosion of light when he connected with the wall right above the entrance. The entire building crumbled as he sliced into it. Each time the explosion of light was so intense, so bright, I was momentarily blinded. When it was all over and the building was a pile of rubble, he looked at me and smiled. Only I didn't actually see his face—but I know he smiled."

"Did you hear the choir of the innocents singing?" Roger asked.

"No, not singing. But I could hear trumpets or some kind of horns. I don't know what they were playing—I've never heard anything like it before—they were so beautiful."

"Do you have any idea where this took place?"

"No, not exactly. But I did see a CTA bus parked down the block so it must be somewhere in Chicago. And that's about it. The first thing I did, well actually the second, because the first thing I did was to say a prayer thanking God for showing me His awesome power, was to call you. It's funny because I don't listen to the radio very much, and I've never called in before."

"Well, Rita, thank you for your call. Could I ask you hold on for a minute? I want my screener to get your phone number off the air, so we can follow up if this comes to pass."

"Thank you for allowing me on. And, Roger, it's not if, but when."

"Well, Chicago, there you have it. An actual prediction before it happened. That should make George from Des Plaines happy. Any Chicago police officers on patrol tonight please call in on 312-555-0770 if you see any abortion mills being destroyed by Archangel Michael. My call screener will put you right through."

And on and on into the long night the callers came and went.

CHAPTER 16

MONDAY ENDED A lot more boring than it began—at least for most Chicagoans. For Lieutenant Frank Warren, the chiming of the clock at midnight meant only one thing . . . four more hours until the bartender announced, "Last round." He had invested twenty dollars trying to forget the indignities of the day and his drink of choice was the traditional blue-collar boilermaker.

Frank drew the attention of his fellow bar patrons because he drank the way his grandfather taught him. You dropped a shot of whiskey, glass and all, into a stein of beer and chugged it before any could "boil" over. Most observers had never seen a man drink like that, let alone one dressed in a police uniform. Frank's demeanor told the curious it would not be a good idea to try engaging him in conversation.

He reached into his pocket for another twenty to lie on the bar, but instead pulled out a receipt for his badge and gun. He crumbled it up and shoved it back into his pocket.

"Calling it a night, Frank?"

Eddie had been a bartender since returning from Vietnam and still looked like a Marine recruiting poster even if his buzz cut had turned gray. He was a pretty good judge of when to cut a man off and hoped his longtime friend would take the hint.

Frank shook his head no and fished around until he found several wadded-up bills. He counted at least fifty dollars and wondered if that would be enough to make his brain stop thinking. He dropped the money on the bar, tapped his empty glass, and nodded.

Eddie scooped up the empty and wiped the counter off. "Yes, sir. Another one coming right up."

Despite four boilermakers, the afternoon's events were still too fresh in Frank's memory. He could not believe that after over thirty years of service he had been suspended indefinitely from the department. He could still hear his lifelong "friend" Sidney Gates screaming his demand for Warren's immediate dismissal. His only hint of a smile came when he recalled how the mayor's hand-picked chief administrator of the Office of Professional Standards, Hector Alledo, argued back just as vocally that the mayor did not have the authority to fire any police officer. *Man did he get in Sid's face.*

It looked to everyone in the room as if the mayor was going to have a stroke, or at least burst one of the veins throbbing in his temples when Alledo told him the suspension would be with full pay pending an investigation by OPS *I've never seen a man's face turn so red . . . and the way his body was trembling.*

He was almost disappointed Alledo hadn't reminded Sid that the Police Board would have to hold a full hearing before the matter could be resolved and any punishment doled out. *That probably woulda killed him,* he pictured the mayor flopping on the floor, his hands clutching his chest, as he had a massive grabber.

The more he drank, the more Warren became convinced nothing that happened was his fault—he was just following orders. His watch commander announced at roll call, "No one is going to picket in front of the clinic today," then told him to handle it. *That's all he said, "Handle it."* *If only that troublemaker hadn't been there with that camera it would be my word against some old lady—well, a bunch of old ladies. And why did it have to be Granny?* he thought as he tried to get the bartenders attention for another refill.

My Uncle's Place was a throwback to the old days when all Chicago neighborhoods had corner taverns that catered to local clientele. Many were ethnic in nature with names like O'Leary's Tap or Herr Schlimmer's *Bier Stube.* Others had cute names that reflected the owner's personality. The rumor was some long-gone owner with a sense of humor came up with the name, so his friends could tell their wives they were going to stop by my uncle's place instead of the local beer joint.

In the fifty-some years he had been going to the tavern, starting when he wasn't tall enough to see above the massive oak bar, Frank had seen the clientele change as Irish, Italian, and Germans fled to the suburbs and a new wave of immigrants, mainly Polish and Mexicans, moved into the neighborhood. Even though the bar had changed hands at least twice, the only visible differences were it now sported a neon *cervesa fria* sign in the window and a new giant-sized Cubs schedule hung above the juke box—that still held a half dozen Sinatra records. That and the yellowing hand-printed "No Checks Cashed" sign taped to the register was now in English and Spanish.

Regulars knew Uncle's was a great shot'n-a-beer place to have a quick, cheap drink on their way home from work. It was a million miles removed from the sports saloons and yuppie drinking emporiums that seemed to be springing up overnight as the neighborhood was getting gentrified. And the bartenders knew when to leave a man alone with his problems.

"One more, LT?" Eddie asked using Marine slang for lieutenant.

Before leaving First Presby the Hansen sisters decided to have Officer Kent drive them straight home. They agreed there would be plenty of time in the morning to call Sidney. Besides, with Granny still in the hospital, they didn't want to be pests.

Kent pulled up by the emergency room entrance in his 1988 Monte Carlo SS—burgundy with smoked glass t-tops and the optional leather interior. Its 350 V-8 engine made a low rumble. Nurse Ryun rolled her eyes when she saw it was a two-door coupe.

"I'm sorry there's not more room. I slid the passenger seat as far forward as possible. It's the only car I have."

"No need to apologize," Kaye patted him on the shoulder. "I'll take the back seat. I am the younger sister after all."

It took a couple of minutes for her to squeeze in, but soon they were ready to go.

"All buckled up ladies?" Kent asked before he shifted into drive.

"Of course, we are," Ruth answered. "You may now drive us home."

However, after giving the chauffeur their address, Ruth smiled to her sister then asked, "Excuse me, young man. Did you say you would drive us anywhere we wanted to go?"

"Yes, Ma'am. I'll be glad to take you anywhere."

"If it's not an imposition, could we please stop at the supermarket? We didn't have a chance to shop earlier."

"Why, that's a wonderful idea," Kaye said. "But I was wondering if we could first stop at the Morning Star Cafe. I was so upset I couldn't eat a bite of the food they served at the hospital."

"Ladies, it would be my pleasure, but only if you let me treat."

"It's a deal," Ruth answered for both of them.

The restaurant was typical of a thousand corner snack shops across the city—a counter ran the length of the room and a half-dozen linoleum-covered tables lined the wall by the windows. Breakfast was served twenty-four hours a day, seven days a week.

The owner, Gus, greeted the sisters with outstretched arms, "So how are my two best girls tonight?" He gave each a hug and a kiss on the cheek. "So what's this, you got a new boyfriend?" He gestured at Officer Kent.

Kaye blushed.

"He is our personal driver for the evening," Ruth said with pride.

"You take good care of my girls or I'll give you one of these," Gus made a fist.

"Yes sir."

Dinner was very enjoyable, with the Hansen sisters taking turns telling stories about the "good old days." Both of the ladies ordered the special of the day—meat loaf with home-style gravy—that included soup and desert. At first Kent said he wasn't hungry and only ordered a cup of coffee, but Ruth insisted he eat. "You really must eat something. You're so thin."

"The food here is excellent," her sister chimed in. "Almost as good as ours."

"Yes, Ma'am." He handed Gus his menu. "Make that three specials."

Ruth was finishing her last scoop of tapioca when she noticed her sister trying to stifle a yawn.

"James, we have had such an enjoyable visit, but it's getting late. My sister and I have lunch here every Monday. Please promise you will join us again soon."

"It will be our treat," Kaye added.

"I'm on evenings this month, but I promise I will when the shifts change. Here's my business card. I wrote my cell phone number on the back. If you ever need anything—a ride somewhere, anything—call and I'll be there. Now, ladies, we have a date with the grocery store. Let me settle up with the cashier, and we'll be on our way."

The Hansen sisters strutted with pride as they were escorted by Officer James Kent while they shopped for groceries. He insisted on pushing their shopping cart down the isles of the Super Mercado. As they approached the checkout, Juanita, the cashier, made a mental note to ask the ladies why they never told her they had such a handsome grandson.

The Reverend Jackie Jefferson was home . . . but he was far from calm. His housekeeper had met him at the door with his slippers and a half-filled brandy snifter. He managed to say "Thank you, Mrs. White," as he seized the glass before storming into his first-floor office.

A minute later, Jefferson's driver and his lawyers crept into the turn-of-the-century gothic mansion. All three men looked relieved that their boss was nowhere in sight.

"Where's he at?" Samuel whispered to Mrs. White.

She gestured towards the closed double doors beyond the parlor. "I don't believe the Reverend wants to speak with anyone at the moment. Why don't you boys follow me to the kitchen, and I'll whip you up something to eat."

As Jackie sat in his leather recliner with the lights off, he reviewed the day's events and how his highly-paid staff had let him down every step of the way.

He had been silent as they walked from the police station to Samuel's car—a brand new, black-on-black, Cadillac Coupe de Ville, but opened up with both barrels before the car pulled away from the curb. "Why, may I ask, did you not pay your parking tickets?" he demanded of the driver. "Not just one ticket . . . not ten tickets . . . not twenty . . . not twenty-five! Not even thirty! You received *thirty-five* tickets with my car—my car—and you forgot to mention a single one of them! Why Samuel? All you had to do was hand them to my accountant and he would have paid them. Did you think they would just go away? If you were not my brother-in-law, I would fire you on the spot! The only smart thing you ever did was sweet talk my baby sister into marrying you."

"And you?" he said, turning to confront his lawyers. Two middle-aged black men, wearing almost identical charcoal gray, silk suits, cowered in the backseat. "In the name of everything that is sacred, where were you while I was incarcerated?"

Jackie swung his arm out and pointed a finger inches from the face of the man sitting behind him. The lawyer leaned back as far as he could. "Did you think I would enjoy spending the day in jail?"

The man did not answer.

He then challenged the other. "And where exactly were you while I was locked in a jail cell with common criminals? I came close to being beaten, maybe even killed by them."

He also did not answer.

The lawyers knew the Reverend well enough to know he was truly mad—not his TV camera righteous indignation mad, but real, sincerely mad—and they knew better than to try to explain they had been meeting with the district attorney trying to arrange his release. So they sat in silence as they listened to the tongue lashing.

"How much am I overpaying the two of you?" Jackie was trembling when he turned around on the leather seat.

Later, when he calmed down, they would explain the police station only had a holding cell and he would have been transferred to the courthouse at Western and Belmont Avenues to appear before a judge . . . and that's where they had been.

Neither man was a criminal attorney familiar with ways to shortcut the process. Instead, they waited in line with a score of others as the clerks worked through the backup caused by the morning's riot. They posted his bail the moment his case was called.

The silence lasted for less than a minute. Jackie bolted upright and directed his anger back at his driver. "For your information, if you ever receive a ticket for anything—I do not care why or what for—you will personally pay it that very day or you are fired! Look at this," he yelled, waving a sheet of paper in the man's face. "Do you know what this is? Well, I will tell you what it is. It is a list of Department of Revenue Payment Processing and Hearing Facilities . . . there is one located at 2550 West Addison Street. There is one at 800 North Kedzie Avenue. There is one at 2006 East 95th Street, and yet another at 400 West Superior Street.

"And last, but not least, there is even one at City Hall. You could have driven to any of these any Monday through Saturday and paid your tickets . . . but no." Jackie crumbled the sheet of paper in his fist and dropped it in the man's lap.

"Instead, I had to have some metermaid lecture me on how you were mailed a 'notice of determination' twenty-one days after you received each ticket. Then you were mailed a notice of 'final determination' twenty-one days after that. You must have received at least a hundred notices from the City of Chicago, yet you never mentioned a single one."

Jackie was so close Samuel could feel his breath on his face. "Why not? Can you answer me one that one simple question?"

When the driver did not answer, Jackie leaned even closer.

"Why did you not come to me? Why! Why did you not tell me? No answer . . . I thought you would be man enough to say something. Anything. Well?" Jackie was so mad he was spewing forth words without any thought of peppering his sentences with the ten-dollar words for which he was so famous. This was hangin'-out-back-in-the-'hood Jackie speaking.

"Now look at this!" He thrust a packet of papers in front of the driver's face. "You were ticketed for parking in a disabled parking space five times. Five times at $150 each violation—but that's the fine if you pay them on time. The fine for every single ticket on these pages has doubled because you ignored them. So let's see $1,500 for page one. $1,500! And that's just for the first page." He let the sheet fall, shuffled through the remaining papers, then shoved another in front of him. "Now let us look at page two. You were ticketed eight times for parking within a hundred feet of a fire hydrant. Eight times! Those tickets cost $100 each. That's $800. Eight hundred dollars!

"No wait, make that $200 each which makes it another $1,600. You even managed to get a ticket for parking in violation of a Wrigley Field bus permit zone."

Samuel had to keep shifting his head to see the road.

"Look at this—two more pages of parking tickets—make that unpaid parking tickets. Would you like to guess how much these four pages of tickets adds up to?" He held another sheet in front of his driver.

"Come on, Samuel, take a guess."

No response.

"Then I will tell you. All totaled you cost me over $6,000 in parking tickets and to top it off, my drivers license is suspended! And it never occurred to you to mention to me that you have been collecting parking tickets by the pound!" Jackie was breathing hard, like an asthmatic fighting for air. Sweat poured down his face. "Well, what do you have to say for yourself?"

The driver's shoulders hunched down and he kept his eyes straight ahead. Not a sound escaped his lips. Jackie suddenly swung around to face the two lawyers again. "And what took the two of you so long to pay these tickets? Three hours! Three long hours of my life! What could possibly have taken you three hours to pay some parking tickets? Three hours. You are so lucky that detective let me wait at his desk instead of throwing me back in the jail cell. I want you to send a letter to his supervisor thanking him for his compassion."

The two attorneys were both veterans of many a courtroom battle, but neither was ever more relieved than when the car pulled up in front of Jackie's graystone mansion.

Fred McBarker's mind and body were numb. His day began almost twenty hours earlier when Gate Eight, as they were now calling it, collapsed at his feet. He had also seen Archangel Michael in action and been introduced to the Lord on a very personal basis.

Any one of these events would have been enough to make him want to crawl inside himself and reflect on how his life would forever change, but first he had to sign off on the report certifying City Gate's four residential buildings were structurally sound. This would allow over four-thousand residents to return to their condominiums—and all of their lives were his responsibility.

Why couldn't this wait until morning? he wondered. Not that Fred was looking forward to morning. That was when he had a nine o'clock meeting scheduled with Reynold.

He could still hear him screaming on the phone, "Is that man crazy or what? Giant armor plated angels with swords wrecking the city! He must be crazy! How could they put that garbage on TV? I'm calling our lawyers to demand a retraction . . . and I want that reporter fired. Then I'll sue them—every last lying one of them. I'll sue them for every dollar they've got. That's what I'm going to do. Flaming angels running amuck!"

Rey continued to ramble, "Why would a giant angel want to wreck a building? If he wanted to do some good, he should wreck that TV station. That's what he should do—with everyone in it—starting with the lowlife weasel who interviewed that crazy man. I want someone to find out who that man is, so we can sue him for making us look bad . . . or causing a public panic or something. The lawyers will know what to do. Fred, I want you in my office tomorrow morning at nine sharp. We're going on the attack!"

"Do you mean Wednesday?" Fred asked.

"No, tomorrow . . . Tuesday!" he screamed back.

"Sorry, Rey, it's after midnight so that makes today Tuesday."

"You know what I mean!" he screamed.

"But Rey . . . I need to talk to you before . . ."

Reynold cut him off in mid-sentence. "Tomorrow. 9:00 A.M. sharp. We'll talk then. And wear a good suit. There'll be TV cameras there," he said just before he hung up.

"Rey, no. We've got to talk now." But it was no use . . . the connection was broken. Fred tried to call Rey back, but his call was answered by voice mail. Fred looked at his watch. It was 12:12 A.M.

If I leave right now, I might be able to get six hours of sleep. He thought for a moment and decided not to call home because he was afraid he would wake up his wife. Little did he suspect Fritzi was still awake and sitting in their living room with Billy and Mauve Haynes and Philo and Margaret Clemson, praying for him.

Sergeant John O'Malley couldn't sleep even though he had been awake more than twenty-four hours. As he tossed and turned in bed, his mind fixated on the woman who vanished right in front of his eyes. John had seen a few magicians on stage, but they were always many feet away and the audience's attention was inevitably distracted by their scantily clad assistants. This was different. This woman was standing barely twenty feet away. It was broad daylight. There was no smoke or mirrors, not even an *abracadabra*, but she disappeared nonetheless. She was there one second, then she wasn't.

John recalled yelling for his men to stand back as he ran to the edge of the debris-filled hole. "Get this woman out of here," he shouted as he passed Dannen. The more he thought about it the more he realized how foolish he had been. The ground was covered with a layer of small rubble several inches thick, and he had no idea what might be hidden beneath it. He expected to see a body—hopefully still alive—lying at the bottom of some kind of a gaping chasm, but was stunned when he realized there was no hole at all. The entire foundation looked as if it was filled to the top with a mosaic of broken concrete.

Every time he closed his eyes, he could see Dannen's face, tears running down her cheeks as she screamed, "Micci! You've got to save Micci!"

Where could she have gone? Convinced he was overlooking some small detail, he replayed the bizarre incident in his mind for the twentieth time. *Maybe there was some kind of sinkhole or something.*

But he always got hung up when he recalled gazing at the debris-filled hole and seeing nothing but twisted steel and broken concrete. *Where could she have gone?* Hoping to find peace, he tried remembering it all the way through to the end. He closed his eyes and forced himself to concentrate on what had happened next.

"Get out of here," O'Malley remembered yelling back. "Be careful where you step. Try to follow our footprints. That should be safe."

His radio cracked to life. "O'Malley. This is Commander Beeman. What's going on? Where's the trespasser?"

"Uhhh, Sir. I don't know. She just vanished."

"You mean she fell into the hole?"

"Uhhh. No, Sir. There's no hole. I can't see anywhere she could have fallen into. I mean there is no hole anywhere. And there's no body—living or dead. Something really weird is going on," O'Malley stammered.

"Then get out of there right now."

"Yes, Sir!" he replied without hesitation.

O'Malley turned and retraced his footsteps—which was easy because they stood out in the thick layer of dust—until he was at least twenty feet away. Then he picked up the pace and didn't stop running until he caught up to his men standing next to an ambulance. They were holding Dannen's arms while a couple of paramedics tried to calm her down.

"No!" she screamed. "I have to go back. I have to save Micci!" She struggled to escape. "Micci, I'm coming! I'll save you!" Her legs kicked wildly as she fought to break free. She was sobbing so hard she couldn't be understood. She kept on yelling.

"She's hysterical. I'm going to sedate her. Hold her still," the medic with the needle said. Within seconds she hung limp between the two policemen.

"You take her legs." The other paramedic directed O'Malley. "Let's get her on this gurney."

As soon as they finished loading her into the ambulance, O'Malley turned and found himself face-to-face with Commander Beeman.

"O'Malley! The trespasser. Where'd she go?" He demanded.

Where'd she go? O'Malley kept repeating those words in his mind as he lay in his bed staring at the ceiling. *Where did she go?*

Muhammad Ali Hammudiluh sat at his kitchen table clutching the help-wanted ads. He had been thinking about changing professions ever since the nightmares began. He was terrified the horrible vision from which he had awakened would come true if he didn't change jobs.

The lack of sleep had taken its toll, and the once handsome man looked much older than his forty years. The circles under his blood shot eyes were as black as his unkempt hair and his face was covered with a motley growth. His skin had lost the dark amber color so typical of Pakistani men. It was now a pasty white.

Dr. Hammudiluh's hand trembled as he sipped his third cup of strong coffee. He was trying desperately to stay awake as long as he could because he was more afraid than ever of falling back asleep. In his other hand, he toyed with a small yellow prescription bottle of uppers that he had brought home from the clinic. He briefly considered taking the entire bottle before gulping two pills in a desperate attempt to postpone seeing another of the dreams that had haunted him every night for more than two months.

His nightmares had begun with a child's voice crying out, "Why? Why did you kill me?" He had awakened his wife when he had sprung up from the bed and demanded to know who was harassing him.

"Return to sleep, my husband," she assured him with a kiss on his forehead. "You have had a bad dream. See, there is nobody in our bedroom except you and me."

But the moment he fell back asleep the soft voice returned to ask, "Why? Why did you kill me?" Hammudiluh spent the next two hours lying in bed staring at the ceiling.

That evening, he was very tired and went to bed an hour earlier than usual to catch up on some shuteye. He was sleeping so soundly, he didn't even notice his wife when she slipped under the blanket next to him. But a little after three, the voice returned and again asked, "Why? Why did you kill me?"

He jumped out of bed and grabbed a flashlight from the nightstand, determined to find whoever was playing this cruel trick on him. He searched the house from top to bottom until the first rays of the sunrise streamed through the windows. Frustrated, he took a cold shower, then dressed. Dr. Hammudiluh had twelve procedures scheduled and, at $250 each, his employer would not appreciate it if he missed work because he was tired.

He was so busy at the clinic he forgot all about the phantom voice. That changed when he closed his eyes and tried to take a quick nap in the lounge. "Why? Why did your kill me?"

Hammudiluh bolted out of the chair. "Who said that!" He demanded. No one answered.

His eyes darted around the room trying to find where his tormentor was hiding. Except for a small kitchenette area, the walls were lined with boxes of medical supplies. The rest of the day he eyed his co-workers with suspicion. *I will find the perpetrator and I will extract my revenge,* he vowed.

The clinic was short of physicians so Hammudiluh had to stay until they closed at five. Rush hour traffic on the Edens Expressway was heavier than usual and he yawned all the way home. He skipped dinner and, even though he was fatigued, took a couple of sleeping pills and was able to get a decent night's sleep. The next night, however, the voice returned to haunt him. Only now it was joined by another. Together they asked, "Why? Why did you kill us?"

More furious than frightened, he went to the bathroom and took three sleeping pills; but the duet returned anyway to chant in harmony the same question over and over, all night long, "Why did you kill us?"

The following night he took two sleeping pills after dinner and four more before crawling into bed in a futile effort to silence the voices.

Though exhausted, Dr. Hammudiluh didn't even try going to bed the next night. Instead, he sat in front of his computer and looked for an answer on the Internet. After a couple of hours, the words on the screen started to blur and his chin dropped to his chest as sleep overtook him. Moments later he was jarred awake by a whisper of, "Why? Why did you kill us?"

Everyone in his household was awakened as he roared with rage, "Leave me alone! I did not kill anyone!" His wife and children found him curled up on the floor under the desk sobbing. "There is no one here but us," she reassured him as she wrapped her arms around his trembling body. "Please tell me, my husband, who are you yelling at with such emotion? And why do they accuse you of murder?"

He opened his mouth, but no words came out. *How can I tell the mother of our children that I no longer deliver babies, but earn my paycheck by killing them?* He spent the rest of the night whimpering in his wife's embrace as she tried to comfort him.

That long night was finally interrupted by the alarm clock an hour before the sun came up. The clinic opened at six in the morning so women could "take care of their problem" without missing work or school. As junior man, he was scheduled for the early shift.

Though his wife urged him to stay home, Dr. Hammudiluh was determined to go to work. He ignored the breakfast his wife laid out and stared at the cup of strong coffee. *Maybe Dr. Patel can help me. But I must be very careful how I approach him so he does not think I have lost control of my mind.*

Though a relatively young man, he had dark circles under his sunken eyes and was yawning constantly when he arrived at the clinic. His colleague immediately noticed, and, after they talked in private about his problem, offered some samples of a new prescription sleeping aid. "Do not give it another worry. What you are going through is perfectly normal. It is nothing but stress caused by those religious fanatics outside. Their chanting upsets everyone in the clinic, but you will soon learn to ignore them," Dr. Jayent Patel assured him."

"But first, what you must have is a good night's sleep to clear up your head." The older physician took out a key and unlocked a drawer in his desk. He laid a handful of brightly colored small cardboard boxes on the desk.

"A friend at the hospital gave me these samples. He said the drug rep said not to take these unless you want to sleep for eight hours because they're strong enough to knock a horse out cold," Patel warned him.

Sleep for eight hours. Praise Allah. But are they strong enough to silence the demons in my head? Hammudiluh wondered.

Every evening after that, he took two of the pills right after dinner and was out cold within a half-hour. Unfortunately for his wife, while he slept, he frequently bolted upright in bed and swung his arms swung wildly in the air as he screamed curses at his invisible tormentors. In the morning he claimed to remember nothing. Soon she was sleeping in their daughter's room.

"It is not good that I am forced to flee from our marital bed," his wife told him after a week of sharing their eight-year-old's princess bed. "And it is also not good for our children to hear their father screaming like a banshee. I love you, my husband, but if you are unable to bring yourself to peace, I fear I must return with our children to my mother's house." A week later they packed up and left for an extended visit with *ammamma*.

Over the course of the next few weeks, the voices not only became louder and increased in number, but he could now clearly see the bloodied faces of the dismembered babies who were chanting, "Why? Why did you kill us?" He abandoned his bed and tried instead his recliner with the volume on the television turned way up and every light in the room on, determined to collapse from exhaustion. This too proved to be only a temporary solution.

Hammudiluh tried taking double the recommended dosage, but still found himself waking up in the middle of the night, covered in cold sweat. He kept two tablets on his nightstand for when he woke up, but was unable to find little more than a few hours of relief. Even worse, though, was the sliver of a memory that stuck with him long after he had given up any hope of sleep—a memory of being unable to wake up as thousands of bloody faces surrounded him chanting.

Sleep deprivation will drive even the strongest of men to desperation. That night he took six sleeping pills and washed them down with a large glass of whiskey. It was the Muslim's first taste of alcohol and it burned going down.

Thus the stage was set for his worst nightmare ever. One in which a huge winged-warrior swinging a flaming sword swooped down from heaven to destroy the clinic where he worked. Hammudiluh "awoke" to find himself standing in the center of a large room while debris rained down all around him. At his feet, hundreds of dead babies—what he used to call with great contempt "fetuses"—were pouring from dumpsters. The abortionist tried to turn away as he recognized his work, but they surrounded him.

Somehow he knew these were his aborted babies and was awestruck as he watched their tiny bodies mend in front of his eyes . . . their arms and legs reattaching to the torso. Once whole, they began to sing a haunting song that grew louder with each passing second. Just when he thought his ears would rupture from the volume, an explosion of golden light as bright and intense as the sun filled the room, rendering the abortionist unconscious.

When Hammudiluh awoke the room was lit with a flickering red glow and he could taste blood in his mouth. He slowly stood up, then turned around, hoping to see he was still in his family room. Instead, he was confronted by a giant warrior looking straight down at him.

The winged angel swung a fiery sword around the doctor. Flames shot from its tip and engulfed his entire body. He felt the searing heat consuming him and smelled the sickening odor of burning flesh. Wave after wave of pain ripped through him. He looked down and watched the skin melt off his body, puddling around his feet. Flames licked his face. When he tried to shield his eyes with his hands, he saw his fingers burning like candles. The pain grew even more intense and seemed to last for an eternity, yet he could not scream . . . he no longer had a mouth.

The only sound was the babies rhythmic chanting, "Why? Why did you kill us?'" His hands were reduced to blackened stumps, yet his outstretched arms continued to burn furiously like two crazed torches as pieces of blackened flesh flaked off revealing his skeleton. Individual bones crumbled into powder from the intense heat.

The last thing he saw before his eyes exploded was the warrior angel bend down and spread his wings around the babies, protecting them, gathering them up. Then the angel destroyed the building with one mighty swing of his sword.

He awoke sobbing hysterically. His heart was pounding and his entire body convulsed uncontrollably. He had vomited and soiled himself. But there was no one in his expensive suburban estate to comfort him—two weeks earlier, when he admitted the truth about his job, his wife swore never again to return. Now he curled up on the floor in a fetal position, too terrified to open his eyes, let alone move.

Hours passed before he realized the television was blaring away and the screen was filled with images of City Gate Building Eight crumbling into dust. The sight of his nightmare being fulfilled caused a terror so intense that it seemed intent on ripping his very soul from his chest to engulf him. He again blacked out.

When he came to, he was disoriented and had lost all track of time. The room was silent but wisps of smoke and the distinctive smell of burned flesh hung in the air. Thirsty, he dragged himself to the kitchen where he was surprised to find the help-wanted section of the newspaper still lying on the table. He dropped into a chair and began to read. The pages were captioned "HEALTH CARE OPPORTUNITIES" and ad after ad promised "great jobs" for registered nurses, including one which offered a $2,500 sign-on bonus. He was not discouraged that there were no positions seeking an OB Gyn, but wondered, *Would anyone hire a doctor who had been killing a dozen babies a day for the last year?* It mattered not. He had made up his mind he would never again show up for work at a C of W clinic. No, he would call them and quit . . . and he would give no notice. He didn't know where he would go from here, or what he would do, but he vowed that he had killed his last baby. A great weight seemed to be lifted and, as he continued to scan the newspaper, he even dared wonder if his wife would come back if he returned to practicing medicine. With that decision made, Dr. Hammudiluh didn't even sense when he slipped into his first restful sleep in months.

Granny Gates enjoyed being treated like a celebrity by the hospital staff. Doctors and nurses kept popping in, "Just for a moment," to check on her, but each ended up staying for an extended visit. Pretty soon there were five people in her room talking and laughing as if they had known her for years. They were amazed by her energy and her unshakable outlook on life. When a young orderly yawned out loud she chided him for not getting enough sleep.

Everyone turned to stare at him. He blushed and asked, "Well what about you, Granny? You said you've been awake since before sunrise."

"Don't give me any of your hooey young man. You sound like my grandson, always telling me to sit down and take it easy. Let me tell you some good advice. God has let me walk this earth for over a century, but I don't think He'll leave me here for another hundred. So I'm going to pack all of the living I can into whatever days He sees fit to give me until He calls me home. And all of you should do the same.

Everyone enjoyed her ability to cut through the bull. When one of the nurses asked the secret to a long life, she didn't hesitate to answer, "All you have to do is not be home when the angel of death comes knocking on your door."

Everyone laughed at that one.

"Granny, I can't believe how time has gotten away from us. It's five after midnight. I'm afraid we all have to do our rounds," the head nurse thumped her fingers on a clipboard. "I'll check in on you in about an hour. If you're still awake I'll buy you a cup of coffee."

"I sure could go for a cup of java. Heavy on the cream and two sugars if you please."

"You've got it." Her smile disappeared when she saw no one was getting up to leave. She clapped her hands. "Now the rest of you, back to work."

"Wait!" Granny held up her arm. "Don't any of you forget what I told you. Read your Bible every day. It has the answers to all of your problems in it. Go to church every Sunday. And say your prayers. That way, when your time comes, you'll know you're going up and you won't have to worry about going the other way."

"Yes, Granny," they all said as they filed from the room. One of the nurses, however, paused to tuck her in and kiss her on the forehead as she wished her a good night.

"I'll see you in the morning," she said.

"I'll be here. And I sure hope breakfast is better than what they called dinner."

Alderman Whyte unplugged his phone before crawling into bed. He was tempted to wake his wife so they could talk but thought the better of it. He hoped the antacid tablets he took would stop his stomach from churning long enough for him to get some quality sleep. Today seemed like the longest day of his life with an endless stream of whiners demanding he do something immediately . . . and threatening not to vote for him if he didn't perform. Funny, only a day ago, the thought of getting out of politics would have scared him, but now, lying in bed, all he could think about was retiring. He was eligible for a full pension, complete with no-cost medical coverage. *I wonder if Doris would like to move down to Florida . . . or maybe even Hawaii*, he thought.

Over at Northwest Memorial Hospital the C of W's treasurer, June Dannen, was sound asleep from the sedatives. The only sign of life in the dark hospital room was the steady beep of her monitor. Her chart was prominently marked, "Contact psychiatric immediately when patient awakens." No one working the nightshift knew who Dannen was or why she was a patient, but they all hoped she didn't wake up until the day-shift replacements arrived.

Pam Romenelli was too excited to sleep. Her interview with Phil had gone even better than she could have hoped. Phil sure wasn't camera shy and really composed himself well on the air. He gave such a colorful running commentary that many staffers thought he was a retired sportscaster. After it was over, everyone in the studio told her how great she did, including a man who walked over and identified himself as the station manager. He then asked her to come to his office tomorrow at nine o'clock to talk about her future. Even though her parents went to bed after twice watching the interview with her, Pam rewound the videotape to watch it just one more time. While she was waiting, she resumed thanking God for giving her this marvelous opportunity.

It was a little past midnight when Mayor Gates got home. He had long ago lost his tie and suit coat and the collar of his shirt was unbuttoned. *It's about time.*

Gates was relieved to see all of the lights were off. *Thank God, they're sleeping.* He dismissed his bodyguard with a curt wave of his hand and tried to open the door without making any noise. But the moment he stepped inside, his wife threw on the lights and demanded, "Sidney Reginald Gates, how could you let that man do that to Granny?"

Karen Gates stepped out of the shadows wearing a ratty old bathrobe. Her hair, which was always looked perfect, was a wild mess.

Gates was caught off guard and stammered, "Oh, hi, Honey, I . . . "

She never gave him a chance to finish. "Don't oh 'Hi, Honey' me. Your mother is upstairs crying her eyes out in our bed." She poked her finger into his chest. "She is so upset I had to call the doctor to prescribe a tranquilizer."

Gates took a big step back. "You don't understa . . ."

"Don't give me your 'I don't understand' song and dance. I'm not some doey-eyed reporter you can sweet talk." She kept pressing forward until her husband was backed into a corner. "So tell me, mister big shot politician, was the lieutenant that assaulted Granny the same Frank Warren who has sat down at our dinner table more times than I can count?"

I'm gonna kill that SOB Mayor Gates thought.

Before going to sleep, thousands of pro-lifers throughout Chicagoland prayed, "Thank you, Father, for sending your angel to destroy that abortion mill."

CHAPTER 17

THERE WAS ALMOST no traffic on Elston Avenue, which wasn't unusual for a quarter past four on a Tuesday morning. And the few cars on the street were driven with great determination. Many of their drivers would fail a sobriety test, but even the stone cold sober ones exceeded the speed limit.

The hour after the bars closed was always a dangerous time to be on the road as most drivers challenged the yellow lights and the drunks often ignored the red ones. Ambulance crews working the graveyard shift called them "ghost drivers" because they appeared out of nowhere, often with a crash. Some early-morning drivers made a habit of covering the brake and being prepared to stop at green lights—just in case.

It was still a little early for commercial trucks to be on the road, however, the first wave of package vans delivering newspapers were leaving the printing plants north of downtown. They dispersed across the city on the diagonal roads that radiated out from downtown, Milwaukee, Elston, Clark, Lincoln, Ogden, and Grand—all of which followed old Indian trails. Other than these angled thoroughfares, which most drivers used as "short cuts" across the city, Chicago was laid out on a grid system with north/south and east/west arterial streets spaced one mile apart. The short cuts intersected with all of these through streets and the result often was three heavily-traveled streets coming together—a traffic strangler Chicagoans called a "six-corners."

The sky was still pitch black and the city's three-hour-long morning "rush hour" wouldn't begin until sunrise. Until then, the most frequently seen vehicles were street sweepers, garbage trucks, and a slow procession of CTA Owl Service buses that were mostly devoid of passengers. They were joined by a steady stream of patrol cars watching for the worst of the late-night revelers.

Most of the buildings along these busy streets had a store on the first floor with an apartment or two above them. In years gone by, the shopkeeper lived upstairs, but now, more often than not, they were rented to people on limited incomes. Most inner-city residents had grown accustomed to the routine noises of life, including the frequent screaming of police, ambulance, and fire truck sirens. Those on commercial streets also learned to ignore the idling motors of delivery trucks and the never-ending blare of car horns. They even learned to ignore the bone-jarring rumble caused by semi-trailers hitting large potholes. However, the horrific roar of a brick building crumbling into dust does have a way of waking even the soundest sleeper from his or her deep slumber. More than a few people would later swear they were knocked out of bed by an unearthly roar of trumpets moments before they heard the walls come crashing down.

Even after all these years, Nick couldn't get used to being up this early. His constant yawning earned him the nickname of Sleepy, which, he had to admit, was a heck of a lot better than some of the handles hung on his co-workers.

The day after he dropped out of high school, Nick began working for the *Tribunal* loading endless bundles of newspapers and, much to his mother's dismay, made a career out of it. He was a hard worker who never missed a day on the dock. This was rather unusual for a manual laborer and impressed his supervisor. Within twelve months, he became an assistant dock foreman at the paper. Two years later, he had his supervisor's job. Nick did a great job, but hated when he had to discipline one of his old friends—he wanted to be one of the guys, not some middle management flunky.

Claiming he was fed up with the endless paperwork that came with the job and, against everyone's advice, Nick decided to try his hand on a vending machine route. Most bus stops have a newspaper rack or two chained to a streetlight, and his new job was to keep the *Tribunal*'s filled three times a day. On his final visit he would open the coin box and collect the money.

Since territories were assigned on seniority, Nick was given a route that meandered through some of Chicago's more exciting neighborhoods. Things went well for the first year, but then he ran into a string of bad luck. He was robbed three times in the next six months. The last almost cost him his life when a crackhead became enraged that all the money Nick had was a sack full of quarters and shot him twice. As he lay on the sidewalk in a puddle of blood, the attacker pointed his gun directly at Sleepy's face and pulled the trigger. *Click*. The gun misfired.

After two months in the hospital, and almost a year of therapy to regain the use of his right leg, he showed up at the newspaper, walking with a limp, and asked for his old job back. "Nick, great to see you," his old boss pumped his hand. Alvin "Big Al" Houghman was a lifer at the paper. He may have only been a little over five feet tall, with a beer gut that hung over his belt, but he ruled the loading dock. His philosophy was simple, do your job, don't screw up, and don't bother me with your problems. Nick was one of very few kids who hit it off with him.

"So whadda wanna come back here for? I thought you was entitled to full disability." He shifted a soggy cigar butt in his mouth as he talked.

You never tried to live on what this paper considers full disability pay, Nick thought, but said nothing.

"Well, it's your call," Al motioned him closer and spoke just above a whisper, "but between you, me, and the wall, you ain't the first guy to get rolled on that route. If you get yourself a good shyster lawyer, you could sue this paper for a ton of money. You'd be set for life. I mean, why in the world would you want to come back here to bust your hump when you could hit the lawsuit lottery?"

"Big Al, I couldn't do that. The paper's been great to me, and everyone tried to warn me before I took that route. Hey, I got a little careless and didn't pay enough attention to who was hanging around. So how's that the paper's fault? I want to put that behind me and earn an honest living again."

And the last thing I want is to open things back up and have some accountant look too closely at my books and figure out I was skimming from them, he added to himself.

"You know," he went on, "the paper's been real great paying my doctor bills and all that hospital stuff, but I'm going nuts hanging around the house watching soap operas all day long. My therapist said my leg was about as rehabilitated as it was going to get and it was OK for me to go back to work. So how about it? He says I can do just about anything but play short stop on the paper's softball team . . . well at least not until next summer." That drew a hearty laugh.

Nick cracked a toothy smile, "Besides, I kinda miss hanging out with you guys." What he didn't mention was his wife, tired of playing nurse to a cripple, left him and he was now living in his retired parents' basement with his three-year-old son. He thought. *If I'm bringing home a regular paycheck again, mom will have to stop bugging me about money and going to go church with her.*

Al wiped his right hand off on his ink-stained shop apron and slapped Nick on the back. "Sleepy, you must be nuts, but I'd love to have ya back. You always was the best worker on the dock. Let me talk to the guys in personnel and see what I can do."

To show their appreciation for not being sued, the *Tribunal* gave Nick a job as a driver delivering bundles of newspapers to commercial accounts. Even better, he had an assistant in back who would help load the truck then haul the bundles of seventy-five newspapers—fifty on Sunday because of all of the glossy sales inserts—into the stores.

The only downside was, after sleeping in for so long, Nick more than lived up to his old nickname. On his first morning back, he couldn't stop yawning as he renewed old friendships. They were glad to have Sleepy back. That was four years ago, but he still yawned a daily hello to the other drivers.

This Tuesday morning was no different. All Nick could think about as they pulled away from the paper's loading dock was the jelly donut and cup of coffee that would be waiting for him at their second stop.

His first delivery was only about five minutes away in a neighborhood where factories were being converted into loft condominiums. As usual, there were no open parking spaces in front of the convenience store, so he put his four-way flashers on and blocked the curb lane of Elston Avenue while Hector "Little Man" Hernandez carried two bundles of papers inside. Nick offered to help, but the skinny youth was trying to prove himself—so he closed his eyes and tried to grab a couple minutes of sleep.

Seconds later he was jarred awake by the loudest trumpet blast he ever heard. He spun around in his seat expecting to see one of his friends hiding in back playing a practical joke on him. But there was nothing there but thousands of newspapers stacked neatly in rows. *He must be outside*, Nick thought as he slid the door open. His foot barely touched the street when the second ear-piercing roar of trumpets knocked him back into his truck.

The City of Chicago Bureau of Sanitation was responsible for collecting garbage in the alleys behind houses and small apartment buildings. Theirs was a relatively comfortable job with the three-man crews receiving union wages, full medical benefits, and paid vacations.

Commercial buildings, including restaurants and bars, had to contract with private firms to empty their large dumpsters and garbage containers. Most of the independent waste haulers used specialized trucks with huge hydraulic lifts on the front . . . but only one person to do everything. In order to maximize use of these expensive trucks, the company employed a graveyard shift of part timers to handle daily pickups right after the fast food joints closed. Their shift usually began at midnight and ended when they returned to the transfer station with a full truck.

Johnny had an inner-city route that included several of the hot new nightspots that were springing up in the suddenly hip neighborhood. His shift began at four in the morning—the latest city regulations permitted a bar to be open. He hated the hours, but kept working there because they were a good fit with his college schedule . . . even if the pay wasn't the greatest.

His supervisor reminded him every night to keep it quiet as a good part of his route had apartment buildings mixed in with the stores and bars, but it was hard not to make noise when you were emptying a two-cubic yard container chock full of beer bottles.

Tonight, however, the sound of smashing glass was drowned out by something a hundred times louder. *Wanna bet I get blamed for that too*, he thought as the first trumpet fanfare erupted.

Quentin Morgan always felt unique. Growing up, he often wondered if he was the only black child in America named Quentin. His mother had been a huge fan of the 1960s supernatural soap opera *Dark Shadows* and named him after one of the vampires.

Now that he was an adult, it wasn't his name that set him apart from his fellow workers. No, Q, as he insisted on being called, was one of a very small group of Chicago Transit Authority bus drivers who didn't mind working the midnight shift in the city's high-crime neighborhoods. Thanks to pre-paid fare cards he no longer had to carry cash, but that didn't mean some gang banger wouldn't try to rob him anyway. Most backed off rather quickly when they realized the man in the gray uniform was six-foot, seven inches tall and 280 pounds of pure muscle. More than one ended up wishing he had tried to rob a liquor store instead.

Q enjoyed talking with people and found the most interesting ones were out in the hours before the sun came up. On an average night at least one lonely soul would take the handicapped seat closest to the driver. It wasn't unusual to pick up a talker and have him ride to the end of the line and back again. Q always steered the conversation around to religion. "Have you accepted our Lord Jesus Christ as your personal Savior?" he would ask.

A couple riders became regulars and he looked forward to having lively conversations with them. Tonight, however, his bus was empty, and he took advantage of it by singing hymns of praise at the top of his lungs. Q had picked up some overtime driving a peaceful #80 Irving Park Road route from Lake Shore Drive out to the western edge of the city. It had been a long time since he had driven this route and he looked forward to the change of scenery.

The run began in an urban valley created by some of the most expensive high-rise condominium buildings on the northside of the city and headed west, passing a mix of small storefront boutiques and two flats. At Ashland Avenue, the road widened to four lanes with massive concrete planters down the median. These were part of Sid Gates' plan to beautify the city. Most automobile drivers resented them because they were so tall they blocked their view. Q was high enough in his bus that they presented no problem.

With almost no traffic or riders to slow him down, he was making great time on his third eastbound run of the night. He frequently checked his watch to make sure he wasn't running ahead of schedule because the CTA had spotters watching to make sure a rider didn't miss their bus because the driver was early at their stop. He was exactly on schedule which meant he would have about a minute to run into the donut store at Elston Avenue and grab a cup of coffee and muffin to go.

Q eased the lumbering vehicle next to the curb and pushed the button for the emergency flashers. As he was getting out of the bus, the sky in front of him lit up with a bright gold flash. He braced himself expecting to hear an explosion, but instead heard music—beautiful music.

Q grabbed the two-way radio and called central dispatch, "This is a number eighty headed eastbound at Elston Avenue. I want to report an incident taking place about one block south on Elston Avenue. I think a building is on fire."

"Driver, turn down your radio."

"Dispatch, that's not a radio. It's outside the bus."

"Driver, please repeat."

"Dispatch, I do not see any emergency vehicles. Should I check it out?"

"That's a negative #80. We'll relay your call to the fire department. Do you copy? I repeat, resume your run #80. Do you copy?" The reply was barely audible above the music.

"Dispatcher, something real strange is happening down there. It looks like a building is glowing bright gold. There's something else though . . .

in the sky. I can't make it out from here, though. I can barely hear you over the trumpet music. I'm going to step outside to get a better look."

"Number eighty driver, I repeat, resume your run. We have forwarded your call to the 911 dispatcher. They will handle it. Do you copy? Driver, do you copy?" The dispatcher shouted. Q didn't answer because he had dropped to his knees on the sidewalk when he saw what towered over the one-story building.

"This is Roger Hogue and you're listening to the Voice of Chicago on AM 770, WCHI. Herb in Norridge, thanks for waiting so long. My screener says you have some experience with police brutality."

Talk radio was still debating the events of the day and the callers were almost unanimous in their condemnation of the police.

"Yeah. It's like '68 all over again," the caller referred to the "Days of Rage" riots at Chicago's 1968 Democratic National Convention. "I got my head busted open by some cop because I was protesting the Vietnam War. But now they don't care who they beat down. I mean, if the mayor's own grandma can get beaten by the cops, is anyone safe?"

"The police claim they responded with a show of force because they were worried about having another Paul Hill. You might recall he's the man who murdered a Florida abortionist and his bodyguard in a shotgun ambush. After the destruction of the biggest women's health clinic in Illinois, police brass said they wanted to make a strong statement against violence at reproductive centers."

Herb made a sarcastic laugh. "Yeah, they made a statement all right. They beat up a bunch of blue-haired, little old ladies wearing support stockings and praying the rosary. They had some lawyer on the news saying he's going to sue the city for millions of dollars for violating those people's constitutional rights. And you know who's gonna pay that bill? We are—that's who. Every single taxpayer living in Chicago is gonna hafta pay higher taxes because of them out-of-control cops."

Hogue cut in, "You must be referring to the slick-looking lawyer who held a press conference in front of City Hall this afternoon. I have his press release right here. He accuses the police of using illegal tactics like herding and sweeping innocent bystanders along with the protesters. He states at least thirty-two individuals were arrested without probable cause and in violation of their First Amendment rights to free speech and peaceful assembly. He also says he knows of at least ten innocent bystanders who are still hospitalized. I have something else here from our news department."

The microphone picked up the sound of Hogue tearing through a pile of papers. "It's in this pile somewhere. Here it is. 'Neither the City of Chicago nor the Chicago Police Department will respond to any specific allegations until our lawyers have an opportunity to review the lawsuit.' Typical bureaucratic mumbo jumbo."

Hogue crumpled the paper close to the microphone. "I don't know about official statements, but during the newsbreak we played an interview of some top cop who said the officers acted within the law and was confident they would be exonerated."

"Roger, I heard a rumor the cop who was doing all the shooting has been fired."

"Herb, we've heard a lot of unconfirmed scuttlebutt, including one caller earlier tonight who claimed an officer was shot where the sun don't shine by a brother in blue. One thing is for certain, the involvement of Granny Gates changed this from a routine charge of police overreacting, to a front-page story across the country. And that took a lot of doing, considering all of the other strange things that took place today. Thanks for the call."

Hogue switched to his serious voice, "Chicago, there are nights when I'm digging deep for a topic that will keep you awake, but tonight has been nothing less than incredible. We led off with a warrior angel destroying the headquarters of a national women's rights group, moved on to the earth opening up and swallowing their CEO, and now we're discussing the police assault of 'Chicago's most beloved citizen.'

"And after the commercial break we'll change the subject to the arrest of Chicago's most colorful man of the cloth. That gives us about ten minutes, so let's take the next call. Greg from Albany Park, you're on the air. How close are you to the scene of the riot?"

"Thanks for taking my call, Roger. My name is Greg and I live on Drake, about a half-block south of Elston. I could hit it with a rock from my front room."

"Were you at home when it happened?"

"Yeah, but I was sleeping. I work second shift and missed the whole thing."

"Greg, you're going to have to turn down the music. It sounds like a brass band is marching by."

"I don't know who it is, but it's outside. I'm on the back porch right now. There must be someone down the alley with a radio really cranked up. My apartment is on the third floor, but all the porch windows are wide open catchin' the lake breeze. Hang on a second, and I'll go to the front room. There, that's quieter. Whoa, that's weird."

"What's weird, Greg?"

"It's that woman's clinic where the riot was. It's like all lit up. I mean they always got the parking lot lights on, but it's brighter right now than anything I've ever seen before. It's almost like it's glowing, but not just the building. The sky is like . . . well glowing. It's got a gold color, not pink like the street lights."

"Are the police still there?"

"They were there when I drove by on my way home. But it's way too bright to see if they're still there now."

"Does it look like the building is on fire?"

"No. I don't think so. It don't look like no fire I ever saw. Like I said, everything's glowing real bright gold."

"Are there any fire trucks on the scene?"

"Man, like I said, it's so bright I can barely make anything out."

"Is there any smoke visible?"

"Not that I can see but, oh my God. Oh my God. I must be imagining that . . . it can't be. Please God please, don't let him kill me," he whimpered.

"Greg, what do you see? Greg, what's going on? Greg! Are you still there? Greg!"

Most tavern owners have a great relationship with the police in their precinct. Every year they sponsor their eighteen-inch softball team, buy each player a jersey with the bar's name on the back, and spring for a free round after each game. If the team wins the championship, the trophy is presented to the tavern where it is proudly displayed on a shelf behind the bar along with the other dust-covered mementos of winning teams the bar had subsidized over the years.

In return, the bar received an impressive level of personalized service from their beat cop. Another benefit is that they are given a "secret" phone number answered by the desk sergeant. This was an unofficial phone line that bypassed the switchboard, very useful indeed when discretion was needed. The Chicago Police Department recorded all incoming telephone calls and sometimes it was prudent to not have a record exist . . . such as when a bartender called the station house to say their lieutenant had drunk seven boilermakers and was preparing to drive home.

"Hill speaking." The man sounded somber.

Whichever officer answered the phone was always John Hill. He would either pass along the message or handle the problem without wasting time filling out a lot of forms.

Tonight's Hill thanked the barkeep for calling and added, "I'll have someone there in a few minutes. Don't let the LT know anyone's coming though. He might not want to stick around."

Hill scanned his duty roster to see who was available. "Kent, I hear you like playing cab driver. I've got a special assignment for you. Do you know where My Uncle's Place is?"

"Sure, everyone does. It's over on Elston, a couple blocks north of Addison."

"Good. LT Warren is there and he needs a ride home . . . only he doesn't know he needs a ride. He's had a real bad day, and I don't blame him one bit for tying one on, but that's neither here nor there. He shouldn't be driving tonight. You played ball with him, right?"

"Yeah, Sarge, last two seasons."

"Good. I need you to drop in and convince him he should let you drive him home. Here's his address," he offered the officer a slip of paper.

"Don't need it. I've driven him home after a game."

"Even better. Take your own car. I want you to keep it real low key. You got a windbreaker you can wear over your uniform?"

"Sure, Sarge, a Cubs one."

"A Cubs jacket . . . just what a depressed man needs to see." He shook his head. "And, Kent, he doesn't need a friend to talk to. He just needs a safe ride home."

"Yes, Sir."

Kent had his car radio tuned to a news-talk station and punched the button for a classic rock station when he heard the riot was still their topic of discussion. It took him only two songs to drive from the station, and he was soon parking right in front of the bar. A moment later he entered the dimly lit building. The bar was pretty deserted even for a weeknight. Just a handful of regulars nursing beers while Sinatra belted out, "This is my kind of town" on the jukebox.

Kent spotted Warren sitting off in the corner. "Hey, Eddie," Kent called out as he walked towards him.

The bartender stopped wiping the bar off, acknowledged him with a nod, then walked down to the far end of the bar to give them privacy.

Kent sat down on the stool next to Warren. "Hey, LT. How ya doing?"

The lieutenant moved closer and squinted his eyes. "Kent? Wan somethin' ta drink?"

"Sorry, but I can't." He held his hand up. "I'm still on duty."

"If ya don't wanna drink with me go 'way." Warren waved his arm towards the door.

"OK, I'll have a ginger ale."

"Ginger ale. Whadever. Eddie," he yelled out to the bartender, "get my frien' ginger ale." He turned and grabbed Kent by the jacket and demanded, "S'why you here?"

"I was in the neighborhood and just popped in."

"Bull!" He let go and slammed his hands on the bar. "Who called ya?"

"LT, you've got a lot of friends who are worried about you."

He pushed the young officer away. "I got no friends. Nobody cares 'bout me. Nobody cares they're railroadin' me."

"Frank, that's not true. All of your men are with you. They're closing here soon. How about we stop somewhere for a bite to eat."

"Go home." Warren emptied his drink.

"OK. I'll drive you home."

"No! Eddie!" He waved the empty glass in the air. "Eddie!" The bartender ignored him.

"C'mon Frank. It's time to go home."

"No. You go home. I stays here."

"No can do. Eddie called last round. Let's go get a donut and a cup of coffee. I'll treat."

He slammed the empty glass to the bar. "Whadever."

The bartender shook his head no when Kent took out his wallet and offered to square up the tab. "We're cool," Eddie said.

Warren grabbed Kent's arm and pulled himself up. "Let me hit the john 'fore we leave."

"I'll wait out here, Frank."

As soon as Warren stumbled into the bathroom, Eddie asked, "I heard what happened. Is he going to be all right?"

Kent shrugged. "I don't know a lot of the details. I haven't spent more than a couple of minutes in the station today. Most of what I know I heard on the radio."

"Do you need a hand getting him into your car?"

"Don't think so. I'm parked right in front so it shouldn't be a problem."

Eddie cracked a smile, "Keep his window open, if you know what I mean."

"Thanks."

"C'mon Cubby, I wanna jelly donut," Warren said as he shuffled towards the door.

"Right behind you, Frank."

One of the other patrons held the door open. "Need a hand?"

"No thanks, we're good."

Warren grabbed his head as the cool night air hit him. "Ooooooh," he moaned.

"Almost there, Frank."

"Dat your car?" he asked when Kent opened the passenger side door.

"Yep. I sold the Buick and picked this up last year."

He buried his face in his hands. "Shuddup and drive."

Kent buckled himself in and was going to offer to help Warren with his seatbelt but thought the better of it. He pulled a U-turn and drove northwest on Elston until they caught a red light. As they waited for the light to change, he noticed Warren appeared to be asleep.

Kent was wondering if he should skip the donuts and drive his friend straight home when an incredibly bright flash illuminated the night sky. It appeared to be about three blocks in front of them and was so intense he assumed it was an explosion. Kent still had a red light, so he made sure there was no traffic coming before he hit the gas. He pulled his cell phone out of his pocket and punched in 911 as he drove. He switched the cell phone to his left hand and held the steering wheel with his knees as he turned the radio down.

That's odd, he thought. *Who would be playing a trumpet so loud this late at night?*

Kent's question was answered a second later. Awestruck, he slammed the brakes so hard the car nosed down, and Warren slammed into the dashboard.

Kaye knocked twice then entered the pitch-black bedroom. "Sister, are you asleep?"

"No," Ruth turned on the light on the nightstand next to her bed. "I've been expecting you."

"He came back."

"I know. I saw him." Ruth was smiling.

Kaye sat on the bed next to her twin and hugged her. "I knew he would come back. I knew God would answer our prayers to destroy that evil place."

CHAPTER 18

FRED FELT LIKE his head had just hit the pillow when his cell phone rang. "McBarker," he managed to mumble.

"I'm sorry to wake you, Mr. McBarker. This is Jacobsen with the Chicago Emergency Communications Center. We have you down as the person to call in case of an emergency."

"Huh. What are you talking about? What emergency?"

"Sir, we had a building collapse."

"Building collapse! That was yesterday! Who is this?" he demanded.

"My name is Jacobsen, Byron Jacobsen." The young man's voice cracked. "I'm a dispatcher at CECC. My supervisor told me to call you. And yes, Sir, there's been another building collapse."

Fred took a deep breath. "Is this a joke?"

"No, Sir, I'm sure it's not. We confirmed it with the fire department Battalion Chief. He said he had two companies on the scene and it is definitely a building collapse. Would you like to speak with my supervisor to verify this is a legit call?"

"No, I believe you. Almost no one has this number. But isn't there anyone else you can call?" Fred pleaded.

"I'm sorry, Mr. McBarker. He said you're the only one on the list."

"What time is it?"

"A couple of minutes shy of four-thirty."

"When did the collapse occur?"

"We received several phone calls between 4:15 and 4:20."

Fred found the pad of paper and pen that he kept next to the bed. "Give me the address."

"3800 block of North Elston Avenue. I'm sorry, but I don't have an exact number."

"Are there any fatalities?"

"I'm sorry, but I don't know. We dispatched four ambulances along with the fire trucks, but haven't received any updates."

"What type of building was it?"

"I'm sorry, but I don't have that information either. I can try and track down someone who's there and have them call you with the details."

"Yeah, please do that. It'll take me about twenty minutes to get dressed and drive there."

"I'm sorry I don't know anything else. And I'm sorry I had to wake you."

Fred shrugged. "It's not your fault. You're doing your job."

"Honey, who's on the phone?" Fritzi asked.

"You're not going to believe this, but there's been another building collapse."

"Another one! Can't someone else handle it? You just got into bed. This is crazy," she rambled. "They woke you up in the middle of the night last night too. There has to be someone else they can call."

"Who? I'm First Deputy," Fred answered.

"What about your boss. Let him take a turn."

"Rey! Now that's funny. It would have to be his own house falling down to get him out of bed before sunrise."

"Well it's not fair. After all that happened to you yesterday. You almost got killed."

"Yeah, but I got to see an angel." Fred smirked.

Fritzi threw his pillow at him, "Keep that up and you'll be seeing him again—real soon." She laughed, "Do you at least have time for me to make you a cup of coffee?"

"Stay in bed, honey, I'll get it."

"Fredrick McBarker, Junior, the very least I can do is brew you a cup of coffee. Otherwise I might feel guilty when I go back to sleep in our nice, warm bed, snuggling with our puppy dogs under a king-sized down comforter."

"I would hate to be responsible for your tossing and turning while I'm out in the cold, cruel night solving the engineering problems of the world. If it will give you a clear conscience, brew away. But you'd better make it strong, I've got a feeling it's going to be another long day." He rubbed his hand over the stubble on his chin. "I guess I should shave."

While he was getting ready in the bathroom, Fritzi called out from the kitchen, "Fred, do you think the archangel did this too?"

"St. Michael? I don't know what to think. I don't even know what collapsed or even what to expect when I get there. For all I know it could just be a routine fire. The kid who called didn't have any details."

"Well, you be careful. I don't want to turn on TV and see another building falling down on top of you."

"Yes, dear," he answered as he wrapped his arms around her from behind.

"I'm not joking. I'm too young to become a widow."

"Fritzi, don't be afraid. If the angel is there, we know he's not going to hurt me. It's funny though, a little over twenty-four hours ago, I would have said anyone who claimed to have seen an angel—let alone a warrior angel destroying an abortion clinic—was crazy. But I saw it myself. I know it happened. I know the angel is real. And it's not only the angel. So much has happened and I've seen and heard so many absolutely amazing things that I'm more curious than scared. This may be hard to believe but I'm not even worried about facing Rey. I know I'll probably get fired when I tell him what I saw, but I'm not afraid. I am ready to tell the truth."

"Maybe he'll cancel his press conference."

Fred broke up laughing. "Ray, cancel a chance to be on TV! Rest assured, if there's even a single reporter with a camera, Rey will be center stage." He pantomimed his boss holding his arms up and welcoming a crowd like a South American dictator.

Fritzi threw her arms around him, "Fred McBarker, you are crazy. But I'll still love you when you're unemployed.

"And I will always love you."

They embraced each other in silence until Fred said, "I have to get going."

"Should I make you a sandwich or something?"

He kissed her on the forehead. "No, I never eat this early. I don't even think my stomach's awake yet. I'll pick up something before I have to go downtown."

"Do you think this building was another abortion clinic?"

"I don't know. Billy and Philo said they have at least a half-dozen in the city and even more in the suburbs. I didn't think to ask for their locations."

"Well, if you do see the angel, can ask him to smite one out in DuPage County next time so you can catch up on your sleep." Fritzi added with a smile.

"Smite. All those years of college and graduate school and I never used that word once and suddenly it seems the only appropriate word to describe what I saw."

Fritzi stayed in the kitchen while Fred finished getting dressed.

"Your coffee is ready. Should I pour you a cup or fill a thermos?"

"Thermos. Good idea. I can drink it while I drive. Now go back to sleep." He pointed towards their bedroom. "I'll call when I have an idea of what's going on."

"And you drive careful. There's a lot of nuts out this time of the morning."

"Yes, dear," he teased. "Who'd a thought I'd be saying this, but don't forget to say a prayer for me. I'll need a lot of help if Rey puts me in front of a room full of reporters before I have a chance to talk to him in private."

"Trust me, I already started."

Fred and Fritzi lived with their miniature dachshunds, Corby and Peanut, in Sauganash, an exclusive neighborhood at the northwest edge of the city. It was named in honor of the leader of the Potawatomi Indians who settled the area in the early 1800s and the streets were named after Native American warriors. Their English Tudor style house was far too large for only two people, but they loved the neighborhood—even though people always gave them a strange look when they said they lived on Minnehaha Avenue.

Fred's car was parked at the curb. As he walked to it, he looked up and down the tree-lined street and wondered if he would still be able to afford living there if he lost his well-paying city job. Changing careers at his age made him more than a little uneasy and he laughed out loud when remembered the last private sector job he had was frying burgers at McDonald's while in high school. He wondered what career opportunities would be available if Rey fired him, but he kept coming back to something Billy had told him: "Place your trust in the Lord and you'll never walk alone again."

This early in the morning, the drive in on the Edens Expressway took about half as long as Fred expected. He arrived before receiving the promised phone update. As he got closer, he noticed Elston Avenue was blocked by police cars, so he pulled up behind a stopped CTA bus on Irving Park Road.

A uniformed police officer walked over, knocked on the passenger window, and said, "You can't stop there. You have to keep it moving."

Fred pulled his ID card out of his jacket pocket, "McBarker, Department of Buildings. Could you please tell me where I should park and direct me to whomever is in charge?"

The officer nodded. "Sure thing. Pull around this bus and I'll move my squad. You can park anywhere you find an open space. They've got a command center set up about two blocks down. It's in front of what is left of the building."

"Have you seen it?" McBarker asked.

"Yeah, I drove by on my way down here to block this intersection. Not much more than a pile of broken concrete."

"Thank you."

The officer spun around. "Oh, and don't forget to hang your ID around your neck. They're treating this as a crime scene."

"Crime scene? Why? Were there fatalities?"

The officer shrugged. "Don't know, but the coroner drove through about ten minutes ago."

"Thanks, you've been helpful."

McBarker drove his sedan past a number of parked cars before he came to an open spot. After easing the car in, he opened the trunk and debated on taking out a jumpsuit, but decided to take only a clipboard and his camera. *I sure wish I knew what happened to the card from Billy's camera*, he thought as he slammed the lid down.

When Fred reached the edge of the cluster of activity, he recognized one of the policemen, a black-haired man with an impressive mustache, from the night before. Fred walled over to him and said, "Excuse me, officer . . . "

The cop tapped his name tag. "Wheeler. Hey, I remember you. You're one of the guys the building fell on. Well, you don't have to worry about nothing tonight. This sucker is flat as a pancake." He slammed his fist into his palm as he repeated, "Flat as a pancake."

"What collapsed? I mean, what kind of building was it?"

"Some woman's clinic. Somebody said it used to be a grocery store."

"Was anyone inside?"

"There were two phone-company guys working in there, but they got out a couple of steps ahead of the collapse. You want to hear something really funny? They were wiring this building up so that woman's group from yesterday could move their HQ here. Talk about a streak of bad luck." Wheeler laughed.

"Oh yeah, since you're the building guy, you might find this interesting. I overheard one of them talking a mile a minute about how they heard real loud music playing, just before the building started to shake and sway. He said when the ceiling tiles started to fall down they dropped everything and took off running. They barely got out before it crashed down." The policeman slammed his fist into his palm again for emphasis.

He went on, "That phone guy also said he thought there was some kind of an explosion or at least a fire on the roof because it was so incredibly bright they had huge shadows running ahead of them."

"I'd like to talk to them. Do you know where they are now?" Fred asked.

"Last I saw, the paramedics were checking them out. Over there," he gestured towards a pair of ambulances parked next to each other. "That was about fifteen minutes ago, so I'm not sure if they're still there. But they must still be alive because none of the meat wagons have left."

Fred shook the officer's hand. "Thanks, you've been a big help."

"Glad to be of assistance." Wheeler tapped a finger against his hat.

Fred decided to look at what was left of the building before he spoke with anyone else. He walked the half-block until he reached the yellow POLICE LINE—DO NOT CROSS tape draped across the sidewalk and shook his head when he saw how thorough the destruction was. He hoped the remains of the building would give some direction to his interview with the phone installers, but that vanished when he saw the building was compressed into a layer of masonry and concrete about one-foot tall.

This had to be the work of the angel. The officer said they ran for their lives when the collapse started. I wonder if either turned around to see the great destroyer at work. Fred knelt down, touched the concrete, and said a silent prayer.

Time to get to work. He took his camera out of its case and started taking pictures of the general scene. The area was well lit but Fred used the flash anyway. The mosaic of shattered concrete on the top of the pile puzzled him. Why would an old grocery store have a three-inch thick concrete roof? Could this building have collapsed on its own from the weight of this load? No, that would be too big of a coincidence.

He stepped over the yellow tape and began to shoot a series of close-ups of the edge of the pile. Dropping to his knees, Fred took out a pocketknife and started probing the exposed layers with its blade. The bricks, or what was left of them, caught his eye.

A deep voice bellowed from behind him. "Excuse me. Can I help you?" It demanded.

Fred turned and was blinded by someone shining an intense flashlight at his face.

"McBarker, Department of Buildings. I'm here to investigate this collapse," he held up the lanyard holding his photo ID.

"You might want to talk to Commander Washington first. He's in charge here. He doesn't want anyone touching anything until the detectives have first crack at it," the officer said.

"Why detectives? I was told there were no fatalities."

"I didn't ask. I just do what they tell me. I'll warn you though, the Commander's not in a very good mood, so you really should get his permission before you touch anything."

"Officer, I'm the First Deputy of the Chicago Department of Buildings. Unless a felony has been committed, I'm in charge of this building, or at least what's left of it."

"Look buddy, I'm just a traffic cop. I don't know you, but I do know who gives me my orders. Couldn't you please talk to the Commander first? He's the man in the custom tailored uniform with the gold oak leaf on the collars. You would be doing me a big favor because I would hate to have to shoot you." He winked. "Nah, I'm kidding about shooting you . . . way too much paperwork. But someday I would like to get a promotion, and you'd make me look real good if we walked over together."

Fred winked back. "Since you put it that way, how can I refuse? Lead on."

The two men walked across the street to the command van. *What the heck is going on here?* Fred thought when he noticed a SWAT team standing around their black truck. After he spoke with the two men standing in front of the van's large door, the officer motioned for Fred to follow him inside.

The inside looked like the bridge of a destroyer . . . the wall was lined with dozens of flashing lights and TV monitors. The counter was cluttered with computers and telephones. Two long-haired men wearing T-shirts and blue jeans huddled over a printout. Off to the side, Fred could see a grayhaired police officer sitting behind a desk and almost laughed when he saw the officer wasn't kidding about the gold leaves.

"Commander Washington, excuse me, sir. This gentleman is from the City of Chicago. He says he's a building inspector."

"Actually, I'm First Deputy McBarker, Department of Buildings. I was called by CECC."

"McBarker, have a seat. Officer, you're dismissed. I suppose you're wondering what's going on here. Well, let me lay it out for you. The administration believes this collapse is part of a conspiracy to intimidate a legal business enterprise. I don't know if you are aware the same woman's organization that owned this building also owned the City Gate building.

"They were moving what was left of their offices into this building when it too was destroyed. And they do not believe it was a coincidence. Add in the riot that took place on this very street yesterday and you can understand their concerns. That is why the department is considering this a crime scene." Washington stood up and leaned over the desk. "I intend to do everything in my power to arrest those responsible."

Is this guy for real? Fred thought.

Washington looked down at him. "Understand?"

Fred stood up and stared right back. The two men were little more than a foot apart. The two technicians stopped working and watched the power struggle. The standoff ended when a cute female police officer walked in and announced, "Coffee's here."

"McBarker, I will let you stay as an observer, but you will not return to the building unescorted, and you will not touch anything." He made a fist then slowly extended his index finger in Fred's face. Any questions?"

McBarker didn't back up an inch. "Commander, I'm curious. Since you're treating this as a crime scene, what do *you* suspect caused this collapse?"

Washington was caught off guard by the question. It took him a moment to answer. "Well," he stammered. "Based on preliminary statements from eyewitnesses, there was an explosion."

"An explosion?" McBarker asked.

"Yes, we have numerous reports of a blinding flash right before the building collapsed. And I think you will find this is consistent with what transpired yesterday at City Gate."

"Sorry to give you the bad news, Commander, but I was one of the inspectors inside that building when it collapsed. I am also the person who certified the four residential towers were structurally sound, and it's my name on the paper that let hundreds of people move back into their condos. So I know a little more about what happened there than you do. And even from my brief inspection, I can guarantee this collapse was not caused by either an explosion or a fire.

"Therefore, I am putting you on notice that pursuant the National Construction Safety Team Act the investigation of major building failures is the responsibility of the National Institute of Standards and Technology. They will be on site at City Gate later this morning and, since the Chicago Police Department believes they are related, I will request NIST assign investigators to this structural failure as well. So, unless you believe there are victims to be rescued or bodies buried in the rubble to be recovered, you will assign officers to preserve and protect all evidence at the disaster site until either a field investigation can be conducted to establish the likely cause of the building failure or they release the site to your control.

"Now I would like to speak with the eyewitnesses." Fred surprised even himself with the forceful way he responded to the officer formerly in charge.

Washington's face turned red as his hands clutched the edge of the table. It looked as though he was going to lose control, "Give him what he wants," he growled to no one in particular. "But this ain't over. Not by a long shot"

CHAPTER 19

FRED MCBARKER WASN'T the only person whose Tuesday wake-up had a dollop of *déja vu* heaped on top of it. There was a soft knock on the door before it opened with a creak.

"Mr. Mayor? Mayor Gates? It's Officer Gammon." He squinted to see into the dark bedroom. "I'm sorry to wake you so early, but we've got another situation."

"Huh? What's going on? Why . . . did . . . you . . . wake . . . me?" He emphasized every word.

"Sir, another Council of Women's clinic has been destroyed."

"What?" Gates demanded as he sprang up in his bed. "You've got to be kidding. Are you sure?"

Although this officer wasn't working the previous night, his shift had been briefed on what transpired by the men they'd relieved. He had also been warned not to disturb the mayor unless it was an emergency that couldn't wait until at least thirty minutes past the crack of dawn.

"I'm sorry, sir, but it's true. I confirmed the information with the CECC dispatcher before I even thought about waking you," he stammered. "He said the first fire units on the scene reported the building had been destroyed by an explosion. I told him to call me as soon as he learns more details."

"Where? Was anyone killed? Is anything else under attack?"

"The Council of Women was moving their headquarters into one of their clinics on the northwest side—an old A&P grocery store on Elston Avenue just south of Irving. There were several construction workers inside, but they think everyone escaped. And this is the only incident CECC is aware of."

"Unbelievable. This is simply unbelievable. When will this nightmare end?" Gates demanded.

"Mr. Mayor, should I ready your limousine?"

"Yes, yes. I am the mayor. I've got to go." He dismissed Gammon with a wave of his hand. "Go put on a pot of coffee. And make it strong, Lucky."

Gates was yawning when he walked downstairs and found his bodyguard sitting in the kitchen talking on a cell phone. The officer covered the mouthpiece and said, "The coffee will be ready in a minute, Sir."

"Who are you talking to?"

"I'm on hold for the battalion chief in charge. His assistant said there were several eyewitnesses including two police officers, and I'm trying to get more details."

"Police officers? What officers? Were they on duty? We didn't have any guards at the clinic, did we?" Gates stammered.

"I don't know, Sir, but I will find out."

"Do that," Gates commanded. "So what else do you know for a fact?"

"Officers have secured the scene and are establishing a two-block perimeter around it."

"Tell them to make it at least three blocks. I don't want any camera crews close enough to get a picture of it."

"Yes, sir."

"Anything else?"

"CECC called Commander Washington about ten minutes ago. He's on his way down to take charge. I told them to have him call you as soon as he arrives."

"Washington," Gates made a thumbs up. "Max is a good man. He's old school."

"Yes, Sir."

"Before we leave, I want you to disconnect the phone. The last thing I want is a repeat of yesterday morning when everyone and their brother who ever made a campaign contribution bothered my wife."

"No problem. I can turn the ringer off so the phone can still be used for outgoing calls."

"You're absolutely sure this is on the level?"

"Yes, Sir. I shut the ringer off on my phone all the time when I'm sleeping."

"Not the phone," he growled. "Are you sure this isn't just some run-of-the-mill fire in an old building where the roof collapsed?"

"Yes, Sir. I wouldn't have awakened you if I wasn't 100 percent certain."

"Fine. Then let's get going."

Gates' usual driver had called in sick which left their detail a man short. It also left them without an experienced limo driver. In typical police fashion, that job fell by default to the low man on the seniority totem pole, twenty-five year old Erick McCafferty who joined the elite unit only two weeks earlier. The patrolman had caught Gates' eye when he received a commendation for disarming three crackheads robbing a downtown bank.

Driving a stretched, bulletproof, Lincoln Continental took a lot of practice, and this would only be McCafferty's second time behind the wheel of the big car. The novice driver was too busy adjusting the mirrors to notice Gates standing beside the open passenger-side door.

"Excuse me, Lucky. Is there a reason you're unable to perform your duties?" he asked.

The driver was about to say, "If you don't like the way I'm doing it, do it yourself," when he realized it was Gates speaking and not his partner teasing him. He made an audible gasp before stammering, "Yes, Sir. I'm sorry, Sir, but I'm new." He kept talking as he stumbled out of the car. "I don't usually drive . . ."

Gates cut him off in mid-sentence. "Where is my usual driver?" he demanded.

"I'm sorry, Sir, but he called in sick," McCafferty said as he ran around the car to hold open the already open door. "I don't know why they didn't replace him, but it's just Officer Gammon and me tonight."

"Great. How do they expect me to do my job if they don't provide qualified staff?"

Neither man responded to Gates' insult as they took their places in the front seat of the car. Both knew any cop who aroused the mayor's displeasure soon found themselves walking a beat on the west side.

Gates said, "And don't bother me until we get there," before closing the privacy partition behind them.

"What should I do if Commander Washington calls?" McCafferty asked the older officer.

"You better hope he doesn't," Gammon shook his head.

After that exchange, they drove in silence into the city. They had been warned during their briefing not to listen to the radio.

The weight and length of the armor-plated limo made it a lot more difficult to handle than the compact Chevy McCafferty was used to. At least twice they heard Gates expressing his displeasure when McCafferty took a curve too fast.

When they arrived at the police blockade, the officer directing traffic recognized the city flags on the fenders and moved the blue sawhorse barricades so they could proceed. The driver navigated around several fire trucks and emergency vehicles until he was within fifty feet of the command trailer.

"We're here, Sir," he announced on the intercom.

Commander Washington also recognized the car and walked outside to greet the Mayor. He was a bear of a man with snow-white hair and a ready smile. As Gates approached, he thrust his hand out.

"Sidney, what the heck are you doing up so early? There's nothing here that couldn't have waited 'til later. About all I've got right now is a pile of bricks and a truckload more questions than answers."

Gates turned to his bodyguards and glared at them. "Nothing that couldn't have waited until later! You will answer for this later. Stay with my car. Polish it or something," he barked. "Do you think you can do that without screwing up?"

Both stood at attention and ignored his latest insult.

Washington gestured towards the command van. "C'mon, Sid, let's go inside and talk. There's too many big ears out here."

When the door closed, both bodyguards stood down and expressed their colorful opinions of their boss.

From the outside, the white and powder blue command van looked like an ordinary luxury motor home. The only outward signs that it was anything different were a five-point gold star painted on the door and a satellite dish on the roof.

The inside, however, was another story. The rig was divided into two areas. The front half was crammed full of workstations, computers, telephones, and TV monitors. A couple of young men in light blue shirts turned and nodded as the men entered.

"Anything new?" Washington asked.

"No, Sir." Both replied.

"Let me know the moment anything changes." He motioned for Gates to follow him, "Back here." In the rear was a private office with oak paneled walls and custom built-in cabinetry. "Have a seat," He pointed towards a pair of expensive leather chairs arranged around a small table.

"Sid, I'll level with you. I don't know what to make of this," Washington started, "I've got a flattened building and two of my men swear they saw a giant angel with a flaming sword on the roof just before it went down. Warren was off duty and admits he had been out drinking all night. Even though the man sounded sober as a judge, he stunk like a brewery, so I discounted what he had to say.

"But then I spoke with Kent and his story jibed to a T. I've known him since he was a rookie—that was well over five years ago. He was on duty and didn't have a drop to drink. Sid, he's as solid as any cop on the force. If he says he saw something, he saw it.

"So I went back to Warren and pumped him for details, but I couldn't shake his story. They both swear they saw an intense light coming down from the sky . . . then this giant angel, wearing a suit of armor no less, appeared swinging a flaming sword in the air. Their descriptions of the angel were identical, wings and everything.

"After he landed on the roof, trumpets started blaring from the sky followed by a blinding explosion. The more questions I asked, the more detailed their descriptions became. At that point I wasn't sure what to do, and I figured you wouldn't want them around when the reporters showed up, so I sent both of them downtown to talk to the suits." He shrugged.

"Good thinking." Gates nodded.

Washington leaned forward and motioned for Gates to do the same. "Now comes the strange part. I also have a CTA bus driver, a garbage man, and a newspaper delivery guy who swear they saw the same thing. So I shipped all of 'em downtown. Sid, I've been on the force since I came home from 'Nam and I've never heard anything like this. They tell me 911 got at least half-a-dozen calls from locals who also swear they saw the avenging angel in action."

Washington got up and started pacing back and forward. "I may not go to church every Sunday, but I've heard enough sermons on God's wrath to admit I get more than a little bit nervous when people start seeing things like this. It reminds me of the stories the nuns used to tell in elementary school to scare us." He clasped his hands together.

"And you want to hear something else really weird?" He went on. "A couple of my men told me they saw a story on the late news that claimed an angel was seen at the City Gate building moments before it collapsed. I know for a fact a woman called into the talk radio program I had on in my office, and she predicted this collapse almost down to the minute. I know because I heard it . . . and I heard it more than an hour before it happened. I sent someone down to the station to see if we can get an ID on her.

"Then, to top it all off, I've got some pain-in-the-butt building inspector running around who had the nerve to tell me he's in charge and is bringing in the Feds. I've got half a SWAT team following him around because I have no idea what he's going to find. Give me the word, and he's outta here."

Gates wrinkled his forehead, "What's his name?"

"McDonalds or something like that. Do you know him?" Washington picked up an empty coffee cup and fidgeted with it.

"I'm not sure." Gates answered. "Why don't you have him brought by, so we can find out what he thinks?"

Washington crushed the Styrofoam cup and threw it towards a waste-basket. "Sid, level with me. Do you have any idea what is going on?"

"Max, it's the city's official position that City Gate was a terrorist incident. This attack appears to follow the same pattern. I don't know who's targeting women's clinics, but we will find out and nail them."

Gates stood up. "And there never was any angel. I don't care what anyone says. This is the work of human terrorists, cowards who attack in the middle of the night." He started speaking faster. "These people are a danger to everyone in this city. And they're a menace that doesn't care who they drag down with them." He made fists with both hands and trembled as he shook them. "I almost lose it when I think about how they tricked my very own grandmother into joining their pickets."

"How's Granny doing?"

Gates relaxed his fists and grinned from ear to ear. "Feisty as ever. She wanted to go home yesterday, but the doctors insisted she spend the night in the hospital. Man, that interview she gave is sure going to come back to haunt me at election time. My sweet, little old grandmother had a record all these years, and I never suspected for a moment." He shook his head and sighed.

"Coffee should be ready." Washington said. "Still take it black?"

Gates froze in his tracks. "Wait a minute. You said a cop named Warren saw the collapse. It wasn't Frank Warren, was it?"

Washington nodded. "Yeah, that Warren."

Gates spun around and flailed the air with his fists. "That SOB! He's everywhere. He's the guy who screwed up yesterday. I personally suspended him! All he was supposed to do was break up the picket. All he had to do was chase them off, not wage war on a bunch of retired women . . . and on TV to boot!"

Washington made a stop motion with his hands. "Sid, I've been wonder-ing about that. I was sleeping when everything happened and I couldn't believe it when I caught the story on the news."

"So why did we hassle them yesterday?" He cocked his head and turned his hands palms up. "They've been out here for years and we've always left them alone. What changed? You don't think they had anything to do with this, do you?" Washington asked.

"This doesn't leave this room. Capeesh?" Gates had been using that expression ever since he heard it in a gangster movie as a kid. "I've been getting a lot of pressure from the clinic owners to make them go away. You're right. We ignored them for years. To tell the truth, everyone considered them only a minor annoyance. They would jiggle their rosary beads and pass out a few flyers, then go home for another week. Sure, every now and then a patrol car would park across the street to remind them we were keeping an eye on things, but there was never any reason to get any more involved." As the Mayor began speaking faster, his voice became higher pitched.

"That seems to have changed. I don't know." He threw his hands in the air. "They must be getting a lot more effective because all I keep hearing is how they're hurting the bottom line. Every time a woman is scared off, the clinic loses hundreds of dollars. So, naturally, they blame me for allowing their perfectly legal clinics to be harassed—which doesn't exactly make them receptive when they receive my fundraising letters . . . and these are some very significant campaign contributors they're messing with."

"Money!" Washington asked in amazement. "Yesterday was for money?"

"No, it wasn't for money." Gates' face grew redder. "It's way bigger than that. This is about power, about who will control the destiny of my city. I don't know if you know it but they've been registering voters at their clinics. Lots of Democratic voters. If you don't believe me you can go check the records. They control a formidable voting block. So far they've been loyal to the party, but that can change overnight." Bluish red veins were throbbing in his temples and his words began to run together.

"So that's why we broke up that demonstration. To preserve the peace and tranquility of my city." Gates poked himself several times in the chest with his index finger.

Washington's mouth dropped open. "You're letting those people make public policy decisions for you?"

"Max, you really don't get it, do you?" Gates thrust his arms out as if he was going to shake the much larger officer. Washington stood his ground.

"Then I'll explain it. If they can swing three or four city council seats away from us in the next election, we'll all be in trouble. They've been hinting really strong at just that. I don't want a repeat of the council wars of the 70s," Gates referred to the two-year period when the city council was evenly split twenty-five machine votes versus twenty-five reformers and Chicago politics ground to a halt.

"I've even heard rumors they're considering running as many as seven candidates for alderman next November," he went on. "You do the numbers, Max. If they win in five precincts they become the powerbrokers from hell." He held up five fingers then slashed his index finger across his throat.

"If all it takes to keep them happy is to stop a bunch of anarchist troublemakers from harassing them, so be it." Gates slammed his hand on the counter.

Washington crushed another Styrofoam cup. "Anarchist troublemakers? Like Granny and her friends?"

"My grandmother and her friends were duped. They're too trusting and someone took advantage of them." Gates ground his teeth. "And I intend to find out who."

"But all they were doing is praying," Washington tried to rally to the pro-lifers' defense.

Gates slammed his fist onto the counter upsetting his cup of coffee. "No, they were duped into subverting authority and now look, terrorists have destroyed another clinic. I am not going to stand around and let terrorists destroy my city one building at a time. I mean, what if a hospital is their next target?"

Washington grabbed a handful of napkins and threw them on the sea of coffee before it could stain his cream-colored carpet.

Gates entire body became animated as he kept talking. Sweat poured down his forehead and he loosened his collar. "They've been stepping up the pressure for the last few months for me to stop those pickets." He made slashing motions with his hands.

"I know, I know, what you're going to say." Gates threw his hands up. "The Corporate Council keeps telling me the same thing. They have the legal right to assemble peacefully and all that Constitutional hooey, but everything changed when the tower was destroyed. Just before it fell, I got a call from Micci Staylor—she was the president of the C of W you know—demanding protection at their clinics. A few minutes later the earth opened up and swallowed her whole. And that could only be the work of very sophisticated terrorists."

Gates grabbed the officer by his shoulders. He let go a second later and took a large step back. "This is a vast criminal conspiracy, Max."

Washington's eyes were wide and his mouth hung open as he listened to Sid babble on. A chill went down his spine. "You can't honestly . . . "

Gates didn't give him a chance to complete the question. "No one could blame us for shutting the protesters down. The only problem was Warren lacked the finesse to do the job discretely. So, of course he got suspended. I would have fired him on the spot if that union lackey hadn't butted in." He wrung his hands.

"You've got to trust me on this one. There's lots more going on that I can't even tell an old friend like you. But I've got my reasons. And I promise that was the last picket this city is ever going to see in front of a clinic."

The moment Gates paused to pour himself a glass of water, Washington roared back. "An old friend? Sid, we grew up with Frank. You used to go steady with his sister. I would have thought that made him an old friend too."

Gates swallowed hard and threw the empty cup on the floor. "Don't you see, he screwed everything up. I'm protecting my city from terrorists." Gates poked himself in the chest. "My city!"

Washington exhaled and shook his head. "Sid, I'm not some punk reporter you've trying to intimidate. You're the mayor. You do whatever you think is right. You don't have to rationalize anything to me. I'm just a cop trying to solve a puzzle."

Gates wasn't sure if he should get mad or be relieved that Washington wasn't stepping up to defend his fellow officer. He decided to change the subject. "Solve a puzzle." He lightened the tone of his voice. "Hey, that's good. So why don't you get that building inspector in here? Let's hear what theories he has. And see if he can make the pieces fit."

Gates laughed at his lame joke while Washington turned away and spoke into his radio.

"OK, they'll bring McBarker—that's the building inspector's name—right over.

"Can I have a cup of coffee while I wait?"

Washington glanced at the mess on the counter. "Only if you promise not to get it all over my office."

Gates laughed. "Do you have anything to eat with it? A bagel or something? My stomach's not used to getting up this early."

"I'll send someone to the donut joint down the block," Washington said, then relayed the mayor's request on his radio.

"Either a sun-dried tomato or an onion bagel. And tell them heavy on the cream cheese. With chives if they've got it."

A couple of minutes later, there was a sharp knock on the door.

"That's either breakfast or the puzzle solver," Gates again laughed alone at his wit.

Washington put his hat on and straightened his tie. "Enter."

Fred McBarker stuck his head inside.

"Excuse me, Commander. You sent for me?"

Washington motioned him forward. "McBarker, c'mon in. Have you met Mayor Gates?"

"Hey, I know you. You were there yesterday." Gates said.

"Yes, Sir."

"So why did it fall down?" Gates demanded.

"May I?" McBarker didn't wait for an answer but laid his clipboard on the table. He took a camera out of his pocket and scrolled through the pictures. "This is very preliminary. However, I could find no visible signs of an explosion." He saw Gates was ready to argue with him." McBarker held up his index finger. "Before you say anything, let me show you something. This may have looked like a hundred other former grocery stores you see all over the city, but it had a very unusual modification which I'll assume was done for security." McBarker turned the camera for Gates to see. He clicked the button and advanced a few frames.

"At some time after it was constructed, someone added a three-inch thick layer of concrete on top of the conventional wooden truss roof." Washington leaned over to look at the pictures.

"The concrete cap was a low-grade mix, and it wasn't steel reinforced, so it cracked into several hundred pieces when it collapsed. But it fell as a single unit and none of the pieces are out of place. See." He scrolled through several more frames.

Gates stared at the images. "It looks like a jigsaw puzzle."

McBarker continued, "Yes it does. But if there had been an explosion, a section of the roof would be missing with debris scattered all around it." Instead even the sidewalk next to the building was clean."

Washington took the camera and looked closer. "I didn't notice that when I looked earlier."

Gates took the camera back. "So what are you telling me?"

"Quite simply, it appears the building wasn't destroyed by an explosion but collapsed straight down onto itself."

Washington tried to frame his question in such a way as to see if McBarker knew more than he was telling them. "But why this morning? I mean, that building has been a woman's clinic since before I was assigned to this precinct, so I can only assume the concrete had been up there for years. Why now? Could something else have contributed to the collapse?"

"I was told they were remodeling the building. Maybe the contractor somehow compromised the roof structure." Fred paused. *Yeah, like I'm going to tell you an archangel stomped his foot and destroyed this evil place.* He continued out loud, "I'm sorry, but determining the exact cause will take weeks, maybe months."

"But what about the explosion everyone saw?" Gates asked.

Fred shook his head. "The only thing I can say for certain at this time is that there are no visible signs on the roof of either an explosion or a fire."

Washington cocked his head. "Are you saying this building might have fallen down from the weight of the concrete? And the timing might be just an incredible coincidence?"

"All I'm saying is it's too early to state definitively what started the collapse. It will take a detailed investigation of the remains to either confirm or rule out any cause."

Gates jumped in. "But what about the eyewitnesses? They saw an explosion."

McBarker shrugged. "Well, Mr. Mayor, when I attempted to speak with them they were nowhere to be found. Rumor is they were driven away in a police cruiser." He tried not to snicker when he asked Washington, "Commander, perhaps you could help me find them?"

CHAPTER 20

THE 4200 BLOCK of North Meade Avenue was lined with rows of identical brick bungalows. It was 5 A.M. and the windows in all but one were dark.

Billy Haynes' wife, Mauves, held his hand while Philo and Margaret Clemson sat facing them on the couch, also holding hands. Even though they had been up all night praying, singing hymns of praise, and reading the Bible, the Holy Spirit swelled within them and swept away any thought of sleep from their minds.

"Pastor Robertson, it's Billy. Billy Haynes. I'm sorry to wake you so early, but we need your help."

"Billy, is it your mother?" his voice was deep and solemn.

"No, Sir, Mom's fine. The whole family is fine."

"Praise the Lord. Then what can I do for you, Son?"

"If you don't mind, Pastor, I'll put you on the speakerphone, so everyone can hear you."

"Certainly. Who is with you so early on this beautiful morning?" His voice sounded warm and inviting as it resonated through the living room.

"Good morning, Pastor, it's Mauves. We're so very sorry about waking you, but we waited as long as we could to call. Oh, and the Clemsons are with us."

Both called out greetings.

"Good morning, my children. So what is the reason for this august gathering?"

"Pastor, I'm sure you saw the collapse of the City Gate building on television," Billy began. "Philo and I were there when it happened."

213

"Then we owe the Lord many thanks and praises for protecting you from harm."

"Pastor, you don't understand. We've been thanking God all night because we were inside the building when it fell down."

Philo Clemson jumped in. "There was no way we could have gotten out of there alive."

"Tell him about the angel!" Mauves couldn't contain her excitement.

The men spent the next half-hour telling their spiritual leader all of the miraculous things they had witnessed, ending with the story of their new brother in Christ.

"So what does it all mean?" Margaret asked.

Pastor Robertson began, "I find it most interesting these events took place at City Gate. Many years ago, as a divinity student, I was privileged to visit Jerusalem. I entered the city through Damascus Gate, the northernmost of the eight gates into the Old City. It is a beautiful passage with high, ironclad doors that used to be closed every night to keep out marauders. Most people do not realize the Old City of Jerusalem still has many gates dating back to biblical times through which you can walk. Nehemiah 3, which was written over 400 years before the birth of our Savior, gives a detailed account of who rebuilt the city gates by name as well as the walls between them."

Mauves and Margaret thumbed through their Bibles until they found the correct book. They then shared them with their husbands.

"But I digress. For hundreds of years before the time of Christ, the city gate was the center of everything. It was a meeting place where venders sold exotic goods from all over the known world. It was also where the law and proclamations were read to the public and justice was administered by the elders. In Amos 5:10 we learn, 'They hate the one who convicts (the guilty) at the city gate and despise the one who speaks with integrity.' That is because there are several references in the Old Testament to prophets delivering admonitions and messages from God at the city gates.

"I think you will be very interested in what Isaiah 45:2-3 has to say about city gates."

Pastor Robertson waited until the sound of turning pages stopped. When he resumed speaking, his voice had dropped a couple of octaves. "The Lord says, 'I will go before you and will level the mountains.'" He paused after each sentence for emphasis. "'I will break down gates of bronze and cut through bars of iron. I will give you the treasures of darkness, riches stored in secret places, so that you may know that I am the LORD, the God of Israel, who summons you by name.'"

Mauves began to sob and clung to her husband.

"'Your mountains were made of concrete. And their metal doors—the modern equivalent of gates of bronze—were broken down, their bars of iron cut through.'" His voice grew much deeper. "My children, Psalm 139 tells us who the riches stored in a secret place are. Billy, Philo, God has spared you for a purpose. I believe He wants you to dedicate your lives to saving His most defenseless creations—His unborn children. Our true riches."

Many people throughout the Midwest relied on the weathermen at Radio News 710 to tell them what to wear that day. Chicago's location in the center of the country allowed their signal to boom across the Great Plains, out to the Mississippi River, and across the Great Lake to western Michigan. On a good day, when the atmosphere cooperated, their broadcast could even be picked up throughout the Upper Peninsula.

Radio News 710's morning show had the most listeners in the country making it the venue of choice for savvy public relations people trying to get their word out. They were also a part of the Emergency Broadcast System which warned of severe weather hazards, including tornadoes. That drew in legions of new listeners whenever dark clouds menaced the horizon.

Closer to home, hundreds of thousands of commuters throughout the six-county Chicago area listened, hoping to learn of a way around the day's inevitable gridlock, bottleneck, accident, or traffic-stopping calamity. Today, an even larger number of drivers sitting in bumper-to-bumper traffic tuned their radio to the station hoping to find an alternative route to work.

Lloyd Belton's smooth voice sounded the same whether the traffic was sailing along or shut down. Today was no exception. " . . . and the in-bound Ike has normal delays. It'll take you every bit of forty-five minutes to get to the Circle Interchange from Mannheim Road. That about wraps it up for area expressways and the tollway system, so let's hand it up to Robert Lambert, reporting live in Radio News 710's traffic copter, hovering above the scene of yet another building collapse on the city's northwest side."

Compared to Belton's comforting midwestern twang, Lambert's voice sounded tinny and mechanical. "Thank you, Lloyd, and good morning, Chicago. For the second day in a row we're high in the sky looking down at police cars blocking the same major traffic artery. In pre-dawn darkness the fire department responded to reports of an explosion in a one-story commercial building in the 3800 block of North Elston Avenue. The first call was logged in at 4:20 A.M. and came from a CTA bus driver who reported seeing a blinding flash of light. This was followed by a flurry of calls from local residents who claimed they had been knocked out of bed by an earth-shaking explosion.

"A Chicago police officer arrived on the scene moments later and confirmed the location as the Irving Park Women's Clinic. This same clinic was the focus of yesterday's riot where more than three-dozen people—including the mayor's grandmother—were arrested. That might explain why the initial dispatch was upgraded to a 2-11 alarm. However, the first units on the scene reported the building had collapsed to the foundation.

"There has been no word on injuries, but from what we can see, it would seem unlikely for anyone inside to have survived.

"We are monitoring emergency radio frequencies but have not heard any significant radio chatter in over ten minutes. This could mean the fire department has switched to using secure cell phones, a practice that is becoming more common to discuss something they don't want to go out over the air. At this moment we have no idea what that could be.

"From my vantage point, there doesn't seem to be a lot of activity going on right now. A couple of fire trucks left a few minutes ago, but it doesn't look like Elston Avenue will reopen anytime soon. We'll keep you posted if anything changes."

Belton's smooth voice returned. "Thank you, Robert. Well northwest-siders, it looks like you can expect an even slower than usual commute this morning. Our suggestion is you switch to public transportation as both Metra and CTA report all trains are running on schedule. But if you insist on driving, leave yourself plenty of extra time as the Kennedy is a parking lot all the way downtown. With traffic being detoured, both Addison and Irving Park are also bumper-to-bumper as drivers slow down to gawk at the police activity. You might try Western Avenue, but that's also slow going in both directions. Hopefully they will have things straightened out in time for tonight's rush hour.

"Repeating, Elston Avenue is closed to all traffic between Addison and Irving Park. Drivers should seek alternative routes or do the smart thing and park your car and hop a blue-line train to the Loop."

He paused for a soft hum, then continued. "Well that tone says its 6:15 which means its time to pay some bills. I'll be back in a couple of minutes, so don't go anywhere."

During the commercial break, the Morning Drive radio personality checked with his producer, Marie Willingham, a frazzled-looking woman with a headset on, for the order of the next segment.

Willingham dug through a slew of papers on her desk until she found the schedule. "Morrow is ready to go at the building collapse, so we'll lead with her. We'll open with the usual 'breaking news' intro then interview some guy from the neighborhood who says he got knocked out of bed by the explosion. She's trying a get a fireman or a cop lined up too. That should take us to 6:24, maybe 6:25 max. You can take calls until we break for network news at 6:30."

"Should I limit it to the explosion or throw it wide open?" Belton asked.

"Let's stick to what happened at the clinic this morning. They were getting some pretty wild calls last night, and I want to keep things a little tighter. We'll try to screen the calls as much as we can to firsthand accounts, but it seems like every conspiracy nut has a theory on the City Gate collapse. When word gets out about another clinic getting flattened, it ought to really shake 'em out of the trees."

"I caught a few of the calls as I was getting dressed. So, is there any comment from the city about the angel with an attitude?" Lloyd was half serious.

Willingham laughed. "Yeah, right. About the closest they came to mentioning anything about the collapse was when they issued a short statement allowing the condo dwellers to go home late yesterday evening. I haven't heard anything about the office towers, but there's talk of a building department press conference this morning. Of course, we'll go live if it happens. I'll have someone check and let you know if we can pin down a time."

She waved her arm to catch an intern's attention and shouted, "Gotta run," as she sprinted out of the broadcast booth.

When the commercials ended, Belton resumed, "Welcome back to Radio News 710 where you hear every breaking story as it evolves. We're following a developing story at the Irving Park Woman's Clinic on North Elston Avenue. Let's go live to Jillian Morrow at the scene of this morning's explosion for an update."

"Thank you, Lloyd. I'm standing a little over three blocks away from what is left of the Irving Park Woman's Clinic. This is as close as the Chicago Police Department will permit anyone to approach. I have spoken off the record with several firefighters who said an explosion collapsed the building to the foundation before they arrived.

"I was able to confirm two construction workers fled the building moments before the collapse. Both refused medical assistance and speculation is they are in police custody being questioned about any role they may have had in the explosion."

Belton interrupted. "Jillian, we can hear a lot of yelling in the background. What is the mood of the crowd?"

"They're not very happy, Lloyd. Approximately two-hundred people were evacuated from their homes and apartments because of a possibility the explosion was caused by a natural gas leak. Some of the people I am standing with are barefoot and wearing pajamas. The fire department distributed blankets, but there is nowhere for them to sit down or get something to eat. Other than this, the city has pretty much left them to fend for themselves. This is in stark contrast to yesterday morning when the city provided luxury hotel rooms for displaced City Gate condo dwellers. Several people have . . . "

A loud roar drowned her out in mid-sentence.

"Jillian, we lost you for a second."

"Sorry, Lloyd. The yelling you heard was in response to an announcement someone made on a bullhorn advising residents that they would not be allowed to return to their homes until at least nine o'clock, which is over two-and-a-half hours from now.

"The second roar you heard came when he repeated what he said in Spanish. Wait, he's making another announcement right now. I don't know if you can hear him, but he's saying the electric service has been cut to the area while emergency crews check for natural gas leaks."

"Jillian, who made the announcement?"

"He didn't say and I couldn't see who he was. He was standing behind a row of squad cars almost a block away."

"Jillian, this just came in. The city issued a statement saying their preliminary investigation has determined the explosion appears to have been caused by remodeling work which was being performed without a permit."

"That would be good news. There's a rumor running through the crowd that the clinic was destroyed by a warrior angel sent down from heaven because God is displeased."

Lloyd added with a chuckle, "The city's statement should put an end to that."

"That remains to be seen. Of greater immediate concern to area residents is a rumor that several eyewitnesses were whisked off by the police."

"Have you been able to authenticate this?" Lloyd asked.

"No, but we have been able to visually confirm that Mayor Gates' limousine is at the scene. A couple of bystanders told me earlier that police officers said the mayor has personally taken control. If this is true, it would be a most unusual development."

Jillian used this as her opening to swing into serious reporter mode. She knew this may turn out to be have been nothing more that a routine contractor screw up, but she had dreams of having her own show, a serious talk show, and for the moment, she owned the microphone.

"However, no one I spoke with could, or would, comment on the unprecedented news blackout which the police have clamped down on what they describe as a 'routine explosion.' They also refuse to tell us why we can't get any closer to the scene of the collapse. From where I'm standing, I can see dozens of police, fire, and rescue personnel milling about, drinking coffee and smoking cigarettes. They don't appear to be concerned about a gas leak. Does the city know more then they are telling us?"

She let the question hang in the air for a count of five before continuing.

"I have spoken with several displaced area residents in an attempt to shed some light on what happened in the pre-dawn darkness. All but one declined my invitation to appear on the air, often citing the disappearing eyewitness rumors. One, however, has agreed to tell his story."

Morrow made her voice sound ominous. "I am with Mr. Jose Rodriguez who lives a little over a block from the scene of today's disaster. Mr. Rodriguez, could you please tell us what you saw and heard last night?"

The Hispanic man's accent and grammar marked him as someone who learned English on the streets of Chicago. "Sure, I was sound asleep when I got woke up by some real loud music. I thought it was that punk upstairs cranking his stereo up, so I banged on the ceiling and yelled for him to lower it. Then I remembered they got evicted out last week, so I go to my window to see who is playing a horn outside."

"A horn? Do you mean a musical instrument?" Jillian asked.

"Yeah, I guess so. 'Cuz it weren't no car horn. It was like a trumpet, I think, playing the music. But it was real loud."

"Did you recognize the melody?"

"Melody? No, lady, it was like the same thing a bunch of times in a row, you know, not no song. So then I looked out the window and saw this real bright thing through the trees."

"What did this bright thing look like?"

"It was like real weird, and right away I knew it wasn't gonna be good. So I closed the window and drapes because I was afraid I was gonna see something I could never unsee, and I got back in bed. Then, like a second later, *boom*! I mean the boom was so big it knocked me outta bed."

"Do you have any idea what you saw before you closed the curtains?"

"Not real for sure. Like I said, it wasn't bothering me and I really didn't wanna to see no more of it."

"Were you afraid of it?"

"Heck, yeah. Look, lady, that whole building got all smashed down. Was I scared? Yeah, I got scared. I don't know what that thing was, but it was real big, and I don't think it was real happy. You wanna know if I was scared? You think about it. It was big enough to do that. You'd be real scared if you saw it too."

"So you did see it," Jillian stated.

"I saw too much more than I ever woulda wanted to. I mean, I was hoping it was a dream until the big boom came. That's when I got real scared because I knew it was for real."

"Can you describe for my listeners what you saw that scared you so?"

"Yeah, but I gotta get going. It was real big and glowing brighter than anything I ever saw. I was looking through them trees with all them leaves, so I didn't see a whole lot of his bottom but a bunch of him was taller than the trees. He looked like a real big shiny guy—like he was on fire, but I didn't see no flames. Then he turned around and I saw he had like wings on his back. That's when I knew I didn't wanna see no more. No how, no way. So I got into bed. Then *boom!*" He paused. "Now look, lady, I gotta get going to work. I gotta take the bus on acounta they won't let me get my car outta the garage and I'm gonna be real late."

"Thank you, Mr. Rodriguez, for that amazing firsthand account of the destruction of the Irving Park Woman's Clinic," she called out as he hurried towards the bus stop.

"Well, Lloyd, his account is eerily similar to the calls we received last night on The Voice of Chicago." Jillian referred to several listeners who called in to their 10:00 P.M. to 2:00 A.M. show claiming they'd had premonitions of a giant avenging angel. "One can only wonder what City Hall will have to say after they hear it."

Lloyd was caught off guard by her interview and tried to steer his show back on track. "Jillian, that's quite the tall tale." He snickered. "On a more serious note, the station has received several calls from area residents trying to confirm a rumor the police will reopen Elston Avenue at nine. Has anyone given you any indication if this is true or when they might open up for traffic?"

"Let's see what I can find out. Officer, officer," she called out to a traffic cop standing inside the barricades. "Jillian Morrow, Radio News 710. When will Elston Avenue reopen?"

The officer shrugged his shoulders and shouted back, "Your guess is as good as mine."

"Sorry, Chicago, but it doesn't look like Elston Avenue will be . . ."

A loud roar drowned out the rest of her sentence.

"Jillian, I'm having trouble hearing you over the shouting. More bad news?"

"Lloyd, there's a growing crowd of people who are pretty angry with the police because they not only blocked Elston Avenue, but also the side streets that intersect with it. I'm starting to see a lot of pushing against the police barricade and shouting for officers to at least let them get their cars out of their garages so they can drive to work. I hope we don't have a repeat of yesterday's violence."

"Jillian, keep us posted on developments and we'll break into our regular program if anything changes . . . and stay safe."

"Thank you, Lloyd, reporting live from . . ."

"Excuse me. May I speak on the radio?" The tone of the man's voice made his question seem more like an order. Jillian was startled to look up and see a man dressed in an old-fashioned monk's robe towering over her. He had seemingly appeared out of nowhere, his face hidden beneath the cowl-like hood. Jillian's technician shrugged as if to say it was her call.

"Can we talk about it when I'm not on the air?" she asked.

"No, I don't have much time. I need to speak now."

"Uhhh, Lloyd, I have a very persistent gentleman who would like to speak. I don't know what he wants to say. Maybe it's about getting to his car. Do we have time?"

"Yeah, but I'll keep my finger on the kill button," her producer responded into her earpiece referring to the button that every radio station employed in case someone said something slanderous or used one of the forbidden words.

"Sir, may I have your name please?"

Taking the microphone from her hand, he responded, "Joel 2:28. 'And it shall come to pass afterward, that I will pour out my spirit upon all flesh; and your sons and daughters shall prophesy, your old men shall dream dreams, your young men shall see visions.'" He handed the mike back to the surprised reporter, turned, and walked away.

"Wait, Joel. Come back here. What do you mean? Whose sons and daughters?" she shouted to no avail because he had disappeared into the crowd as quickly as he had appeared.

"Sounds like you picked a winner," her producer said to her. "Just sign off and we'll kick it back to Lloyd. Oh, and Joel wasn't his name. He was quoting a book of the Bible."

Without skipping a beat, the reporter closed her live broadcast with, "Well, Lloyd, it looks like I just spoke with a biblical prophet who wanted to let our listeners know that our callers from last night can expect to dream more dreams tonight. This has been Jillian Morrow reporting live from the scene of the collapse of the Irving Park Women's Clinic."

"Thank you, Jillian, for your report." Lloyd Benton said. "We invite our listeners to keep their radio tuned to Radio News 710 all day for up-to-the-minute traffic reports as well as continuing coverage of today's building collapse. I have just been handed a note from my producer advising we will have a guest speaker in the ten o'clock hour giving his analysis on this recent phenomena of everyday people having dreams in which they claim to have watched one of the buildings collapse. So stay tuned if you want to learn if these buildings were destroyed by an avenging angel running amuck or if this was just an incredible coincidence."

Having completed her assignment, Jillian was helping her technician pack up when her cell phone rang. "Jilly, I want you to stick around there," her producer said. "This story is playing out way too strange and I have a feeling something big is bound to happen."

"Sure, no problem. Do you have a time in mind for my next report or do you want to keep it loose, and I'll keep you posted if something starts to happen?"

"That's a good idea."

Few things attract television cameras like a building crumbling into dust, and this morning was no exception. Most of the crews were tired from covering the City Gate collapse, but dutifully sought out a piece of turf where they could film without showing the competition. All were grumbling about how far away they had to stay from the now-vacant lot and settled for filling their background with a collage of fire trucks and police cars. The early reports were rather brief because they had so few facts, and they directed most of their attention to the traffic problems this would cause. That all changed when the six o'clock mass at Our Lady of Guadeloupe Catholic Church let out.

A group of neighborhood women walked from church and began to gather at the inner line of sawhorse barricades. Since the street was closed to traffic a block back at the intersection, they spread out across it from sidewalk to sidewalk. When all were assembled, the Hansen sisters passed out prayer cards to the crowd and, with their voices blended as one, led the group in prayer, "Saint Michael, the archangel, defend us in battle. Be our protection against the wickedness and snares of the devil. May God rebuke him, we humbly pray; and do thou, O Prince of the heavenly host, by the power of God, cast into hell Satan and all evil spirits, who prowl about the world seeking the ruin of souls."

Several *amens* were shouted by a crowd watching the women.

Ruth Hansen held her Bible high and shouted, "The Lord God Almighty sent His Archangel Michael to destroy this evil place."

Another *amen* roared out, this time coming in unison from the line of prayers which had quickly grown to over three dozen.

Kaye Hansen spoke next. "We know from Psalm 145 that the Lord is slow to anger and of great mercy. For over thirty years our heavenly Father, the author of all life, has watched as tens of millions of His children have been slaughtered in abortion mills. We now stand as witness to His righteous anger and to thank Him for showing mercy by smiting two abortion mills in the darkness of night instead of during the day when they would be swarming with those doing evil's bidding."

"Jack, are you getting this?" one of the TV reporters asked his technician.

"Shhhh. I haven't shut the recorder off since we got here."

It was a most incredible sight. By seven-thirty at least 300 people were worshipping in the street with more arriving every minute. Believers of every Christian denomination were flocking together to join in praising God. The newly arrived spoke excitedly of what they had seen in their dreams and were a little disappointed to learn everyone there had shared their vision. That feeling vanished as they joined with their brothers and sisters in Christ in the spontaneous ecumenical celebration.

It was almost eight when April Packard arrived at the scene. With Michelle Staylor still missing and June Dannon in the hospital "for observation," Packard became the acting leader of the Council of Women. Her first official act was to receive a phone call from the police department telling her, "There has been an incident."

At first she thought it was a dream. Not a pleasant dream, but rather some strange nightmare where she was reliving the previous morning's interruption. She remembered how Micci called her while she was driving to City Gate and shouted, "Our building has been attacked!"

But today was much different. The voice on the phone was a policeman's who, after establishing her identity, asked a series of questions. "How many people were inside your clinic on Elston Avenue? What was the nature of the construction work? Was any excavating taking place as part of the remodeling?"

"Why are you asking me these questions? I demand to know what happened," she railed on the caller. "Well!"

"I'm sorry to inform you, Ma'am, but there has been an explosion at your building. Two construction workers escaped but we need to know if there were anymore inside."

"Another terrorist attack!" she screamed. "Why didn't you prevent this? We were promised extra protection by that worthless mayor of yours. Have they arrested anyone yet?"

"I'm sorry, Ma'am, but I . . ."

She didn't let him finish. "Don't call me *Ma'am*. You will refer to me as Ms. Packard."

"I'm sorry, Ms. Packard, but . . ."

She cut him off again. "How badly damaged is our building? And if you don't know, then with whom, exactly, do I have to speak to get some answers?"

"I'm sorry, but I don't have any details. I can find out and let you know, but first the fire department needs some information."

"You had better find out. And no, I don't know what the contractor was doing. I hired them to install a switchboard and extra telephones. I don't care how many people they had working because they guaranteed the job would be completed by nine this morning."

Packard threw her arms in the air and screamed. It took her a minute to compose herself enough to speak again. "Do you understand why I really don't care? Then let me tell you. In case you're not aware, you let terrorists blow up our world headquarters yesterday morning. We were supposed to move what was left of our offices to the clinic today." She screamed again. "Where are we going to go now? Your incompetence has allowed terrorists to attack two of our buildings in two days. And you think I should care about some telephone installer!"

She took a deep breath. "So there, you have my answer. Now answer my questions. What took you so long to call? Has anyone been arrested? What are the police doing to protect our other clinics?" She paused and waited for an answer which never came. "Well?"

"I'm sorry, but I don't know." The officer stammered. "I can have someone call you back or you can drive out to the scene. I'm sure they can answer all of your questions. Would you like me to send a car for you?"

"No! Do you think I'm helpless? I can drive so don't give me any cop attitude. But first I want your name because I'm not very impressed with the way you people do your job." As soon as the officer finished spelling his name, she slammed the phone down.

Traffic was miserable and Packard had to park on a side street over half a mile from the clinic. As she approached on foot, she noticed a crowd of well over one-hundred people kneeling across Elston Avenue in prayer. The sidewalks were crowded with clusters of people wearing an eclectic collection of blankets.

Kaye and Ruth began, "Our Father, who art in heaven."

Packard recognized the two elderly women leading the prayer. She had seen them at many prayer vigils in front of the C of W's clinics through the years. They stuck in her memory because they were so identical in appearance and dress she thought she was seeing double the first time she saw them. *That must have been almost twenty years ago when I was new with the council,* she thought.

When the first pro-lifers began to hold prayer vigils in front of the abortion clinics, the employees confronted them and tried to intimidate and harass them into leaving. Gradually, as the laws regulating sidewalk protests were clarified by the high courts, they learned to ignore them. That was unless they perceived any violation of the law, no matter how slight. Then they jumped on the phone to the police and demanded action.

Packard knew there was nothing she could do legally to stop the group from praying this far from the clinic, but she gave it a shot anyway. She walked up to the first policeman she saw and asked, "Officer, why are you allowing these people to gather in the street without a permit?"

"Lady, this street has been closed down by order of the Chicago Fire Department. Can't you see the row of squad cars blocking it?" he gestured to his right, then to his left. "No way nobody's going to drive down it until they give the all clear. Until then, feel free to walk on the street without fear of traffic, compliments of the Chicago Police Department."

"In that case, I demand to see whomever is in charge. I represent the owners of the building that had the explosion."

The officer nodded then spoke into a microphone clipped onto his collar, "Sarge, McMichaels here. I was just approached by a woman who says she owns the clinic building. She wants to see whoever is in charge. No, sir, I didn't get her name."

Packard overheard him and handed her business card to the officer.

"Thank you. Packard, April Packard. She's the Council of Women's Vice-President and Secretary of the C of W Intolerance Initiative. OK, Sarge, I'll keep her here with me."

"He said you should wait here. He's sending someone down to get you."

"Thank you. Do you know if they have arrested the terrorists who destroyed our buildings?" She tried to stare down the officer

"Sorry, but I really don't know. I'm from traffic, and I've been standing here for two hours letting emergency vehicles in and out. Mostly out, for the last half hour, so things must be winding down. You'll have to speak with the detectives to find that out."

"Thank you. Like every policeman I've spoken with today, you've been less than helpful."

While they waited, Packard and the officer watched a steady stream of people walk by to join the prayer vigil where people were now standing two and three deep.

Stepping in front of a young woman pushing a baby in a stroller, Packard asked, "Excuse me. How did you learn of this protest?"

"Protest? What protest? We're not here to protest. We're here to give thanks to the Lord God Almighty for destroying this evil place."

"Thanks? You prayed for a terrorist attack?" Packard threw her hands in the air.

"Terrorist attack! Who told you that? Last night our Heavenly Father allowed me to watch as His servant, Archangel Michael, fifty-feet tall and clad in the indestructible armor of truth and righteousness, swung his flaming sword to destroy this temple of murder. I could even hear the trumpets of heaven announcing that he had come to do our Father's bidding."

Packard pointed right in the woman's face. "You were here? You saw this happen? You heard trumpets?" She shook her head and roared, "What are you, nuts?"

The woman smiled at her. "No, I'm not nuts. I'm one of the luckiest people in the world because God allowed me to watch it all happen in a vision. It was as though I was looking down from above, and I knew there were hundreds of other people watching even though I couldn't see them. I can still hear the choirs of heaven singing His praises."

The woman's eyes opened wide and a joyful smile covered her face. "I don't know why He chose me, but I will be forever grateful and shout His majesty to everyone I meet. Now if you will excuse me, I need to join my brothers and sisters in praising His glory."

Packard rolled her eyes as she watch the woman being embraced by her fellow prayer warriors.

"I could have told you she would say that," Officer McMichaels said. "You can tell who is coming here to pray. Their faces are radiant. See, here comes another," he gestured towards a middle-aged man walking towards them. "That man has been touched by the Holy Spirit. See how his face glows."

Packard turned to look at the glowing man, then spun around to tell the officer to keep his opinions to himself. She did a complete circle before she realized he was gone, but at the same instant became aware of the hymn being sung by the women at the barricade.

"I hear the mighty thunder, Thy pow'r throughout the universe displayed. Then sings my soul, My Saviour God, to Thee, How great Thou art! How great Thou art."

I know this song. She closed her eyes and drifted back to her childhood, sitting in Sunday school as Pastor Johanssen taught them an old Swedish folk tune. She had tears in her eyes when she remembered being in the children's choir when they stood in front of the church and attempted to sing a verse in Swedish at the pastor's funeral.

Her tears flowed as she remembered how her classmates sang it at her father's funeral and a mere six months later at her mother's.

"What joy shall fill my heart! Then I shall bow in humble adoration and there proclaim . . . "

April's sadness was replaced when a wave of serenity swept over her. She no longer felt in a hurry to speak to the police.

In a voice so quiet as not to be heard by anyone, she mouthed the words, "My God, how great Thou art!"

She took a handkerchief from her purse and began to dry her eyes. *I'll just stand here a while and observe*, she thought as the song ended with its magnificent refrain:

"How great Thou art! How great thou art!"

When Dr. Muhammad Ali Hammudiluh called to quit, the answering service intercepted his call and told him there were troubles with the new phone system. The operator refused to accept his resignation and suggested he tell them in person at the clinic.

They don't pay me enough to deliver that message, the operator thought.

Even though he had had only a few hours of sleep, the former abortionist felt rested and at peace. As he dressed, all he could remember of last night's dream was a tiny baby holding his arms wide and saying thank you.

Hammudiluh had no idea what he was going to do after he quit, but there was no way he would change his mind. Because of the traffic jam, he decided to park his car when he was over two miles from the clinic. The walk felt good because his mind was racing in so many different directions it had been almost impossible to concentrate on driving.

As he got closer, he started to see an incredible amount of activity ahead, including several police cars. *Oh no, not another riot, I hope no one recognizes me,* he thought. He kept walking, hoping to be ignored by the crowd, but soon found himself engulfed by a group who all seemed to know him. Their smiles beamed at him, and he felt at ease.

"We have been praying for you," a young woman said as she embraced him.

He was surprised and confused, but not frightened, when several men threw their arms around him and welcomed him as their friend. "Doctor, you made the right choice," a young woman said. "We will always remember you in our prayers," said another.

A tranquility swept over him—a peace that he had never known before in his life, and he readily accepted their invitation to pray with them. He held hands with strangers who called him their brother and listened intently to their prayers of thanksgiving. They closed their prayer with, "Jesus forgives and saves."

Then a well-dressed man stepped in front of him, shook his hand, and said, "Today is the first day of the rest of your life as a doctor." As the man walked away, Hammudiluh looked down and found he was holding a business card from the director of personnel at one of Chicago's most prestigious hospitals. "Call me tomorrow for your new career," was written across it.

As the group seemed to melt into the crowd, the former abortionist stood in awe. Tears of joy streamed down his cheeks. Then he did something he had never done in his life. He threw himself face down on the ground and thanked Jesus Christ for saving him.

Two men were walking through the crowd holding up large hand-drawn pictures of Archangel Michael destroying the abortuary while others held their rosaries aloft. The prayers were so loud that few noticed when an old school bus pulled up alongside the police cars blocking traffic—but everyone took note when the eighty-member strong Divine Justice of our Lord Missionary Baptist choir stepped off the bus and began singing. Their flowing white and gold robes made them look like a vision of heaven.

CHAPTER 21

GRANNY GATES HAD been dressed since well before sunrise. In fact, she was wide awake since about four when she had a dream so vivid she thought she had died and gone to heaven. When it ended, she determined she was still alive by slapping her wrinkled cheek. She sighed, closed her eyes, and tried to recapture that incredible place where her century-old body was free of all aches and pains.

Her arms swept through the air in front of her as she remembered how it felt to float through the sky, the wind caressing her hair as block after block of the city passed beneath her. The only sound she could hear was a multitude of heavenly host praising God in song. All too soon, she came to a stop above the women's clinic where she picketed every week.

Granny could sense hundreds of people were with her—people she knew—listening to the choruses of heaven singing God's praises as they watched Archangel Michael, glowing brighter than the sun and clad head to toe in shiny armor, descend from the clouds. He landed on the abortion mill's roof and towered over the surrounding buildings as the peal of hundreds of unseen horns announced his arrival.

The trumpet fanfares grew louder and louder as the warrior unsheathed his flaming sword and held it in the air. Gold-colored lightning leapt from its tip and flashed towards the sky. Everything became silent when Michael spread his majestic wings. He paused for a moment, looked straight at the elderly woman and smiled. It was the most peaceful and serene smile she had ever seen. Tears streamed down Granny's face as she thanked God for allowing her to be a witness to His greatness. Then the archangel swung his mighty blade in the air twice—flames trailing behind it—before he closed his eyes and bowed his head in prayer. The last thing she could remember was the eruption of light and the awesome sound of the explosion as he destroyed the building with a single blow of his fiery sword. It still echoed in her ears as she lay in her bed in the hospital room.

Granny had no doubt that what she witnessed was real as she thanked our Father for allowing her to be a spectator to His awesome power. When she finished her morning prayers, she put in her hearing aids, made up her bed, folded the nightgown she had borrowed, and sat in the dark talking with God while she waited for the nurse to tell her she was being discharged.

At least a couple of hours had passed and she could hear an increase in activity outside in the hall, but still no one came. She opened the curtains on the window, first a crack, then all the way and flooded the room with sunlight. The clock on the wall said it was a few minutes after seven, so she pushed her call button.

When a nurse's aide arrived, Granny informed her, "I'm leaving now. There is somewhere I must go. Would you please call my grandson to pick me up?"

"I'm sorry, but I don't have the authority to discharge a patient. You'll have to wait until the doctors make their rounds at nine," the young woman responded in a gentle, but firm, voice.

Granny replied every bit as forcefully, "You don't understand. There is somewhere I must be right now and I'm late enough already."

"I'm sure you are," her tone was condescending. "I'll put a note on your chart telling the doctor to visit you first. If everything checks out, you'll be home in time for lunch," the young woman walked out of her room, closing the door behind her.

Even though she did not want to be a pest, Granny continued pushing the call button hoping someone else would come to check on her.

"Is everything all right in here?" The nurse demanded as she walked into the room.

Granny folded her hands and smiled. *Good, a real nurse. Not some kid who's still wet behind the ears. She'll be able to help.* "Please, I must leave now. There's somewhere very important I must go. Your service has been the cat's meow, and I feel about as good as an old lady has a right to feel, but I really must leave right now. I can't wait until noon. Could you please find it in your heart and do whatever you have to do so I can leave now?"

The nurse shook her head. "I'm sorry, Mrs. Gates. We have procedures to follow, paperwork to fill out. You don't want me to get in trouble, do you?"

Granny slapped her hands on her knees. "Don't patronize me, young lady. I know my rights, and I'm leaving." Without giving the nurse an opportunity to respond, she got up, took hold of her walker, and started to move towards the door.

"And where do you think you're going?" An orderly stepped in front of the doorway, blocking her exit. The man was well over six-feet tall and his shoulders seemed to touch both sides of the doorframe.

Where'd that roadblock come from? Granny had no idea the nurse had him waiting in the hall outside of her room.

"I'm sorry, Mrs. Gates." The nurse took her arm and led her back to the bed. "Why don't you make yourself comfortable?" She patted the mattress. "Your doctor will be here in a couple of hours. He'll give you a quick check up and sign you out."

"Applesauce!"

"Applesauce? Are you hungry?" the nurse asked.

"No! Didn't your grandparents teach you anything? It means horse feathers only I'm too much the lady to use such a strong word. And call me Granny. Everyone calls me Granny. Mrs. Gates is my daughter-in-law—the mayor's mother."

"I'm sorry but . . . . "

Granny didn't give her a chance to finish. "Don't *but* me, missy. I agreed to stay the night, and the sun's been making hay since a quarter of six. So I'm leaving now, and you can't stop me." She started walking towards the door.

The nurse threw her hands up and pleaded, "Mrs . . . . I mean, Granny, you have to give us a couple more hours. Two hours and I promise I'll have a doctor here. If he gives the OK, I will personally help you check out. You have my word."

Granny looked her straight in the eye. "Couldn't you please talk to my grandson?" Her voice trembled on the verge of tears.

"I'm sorry, but I'm too busy to argue. There's a telephone on the night-stand. Feel free to call anyone you want, but you're not being discharged until the doctor sees you. Press nine for an outside line and wait for the dial tone. Now if you'll excuse me, I have other patients to attend to," the nurse said as she turned and walked out of the room.

"She is a very good nurse." The orderly stepped into the room and closed the door. "I must assume she is very tired from working the all-night shift. The hospital is understaffed. But please do not worry. I am here to keep you company. Would you like me to show you the telephone?" He pointed at the nightstand.

Granny shook her head. "Finally, someone in this hospital who wants to help. Kiddo, I know where the phone is, but those buttons are so dang small I couldn't read them without my cheaters. "

"Cheaters?" the orderly asked.

"Specs. You know, reading glasses. Someday I pray you'll get old enough to need a pair too. I want you to call my grandson because he can pull some strings and spring me. Here's the number." She handed him a wrinkled business card.

"The mayor? You want me to place a telephone call to the mayor of the City of Chicago?"

"Yep, he's my grandson," she said with pride.

"I have never before spoken with any mayor."

"Don't get too excited just yet. He'll probably have that highfalutin' assistant of his answer."

"It is ringing," he handed her the phone.

"This is Granny. Let me talk to Sidney. Yes, I know he's a busy man but they won't let me leave the hospital. Yes, but . . . Well, if he's in a meeting, why don't you come and get me? Don't hang up on me . . . I want to speak to my grandson right now!"

The orderly could only hear half of the conversation but could tell it wasn't going as smoothly as the elderly woman wished. She slammed the phone on the night stand. "What a bunch of baloney. That man—if I was twenty years younger he would need a high colonic to get my boot outta his—can you believe he put me on hold or whatever that thing they do to make you tired of waiting and hang up is called."

"I am very sorry. Would you like me to call someone else for you?"

"Who? My grandson said he would pick me up. No, I'll just hang onto this phone until that mope gets back on so I can give him a piece of my mind. But I am dying for a cup of coffee. Could you be a sweetie and bring me a cup? Boston."

"Boston?" The orderly was puzzled.

"You're not from around here, are you?"

"No, Granny. I am from a small country in eastern Europe that has a very long name. I moved to Chicago after President Reagan destroyed the evil empire," he grinned from ear to ear, "and now I am an American."

"So you used to be a Rooskie, eh?"

"Yes, but now I am 100 percent Yankee Doodle Dandy. You know, I love baseball, mother's apple pie, and the Chicago Cubbies."

"Well I wouldn't brag too much about being a Cubs fan, but I have to admit you speak English real good."

"Very well."

"Well what?" she asked.

"You speak English very well."

"Well I'd better. I was born here and lived in the US of A all my life. Heck, I've been speaking it since before your parents were a gleam in the czar's eye."

"I am very sorry to have corrected you, but the word you wanted to use is 'well'. You see good is an adverb . . ."

"Adverb! I don't need an English lesson. In Chicago we speak real good. And so do you. Hardly an accent at all."

"Thank you very much. I was an English teacher in the old country." He changed the subject. "So what is Boston coffee? Is it similar to espresso?"

"Espresso! That's overpriced sludge." Granny sighed. "You know I really wanted to set that wisenheimer's ears on fire." She hung up the phone. "But all this talk about coffee has got me thirsty. Why don't you rustle us up a wheelchair so we can go for a roll down to the cafeteria. My treat. And on the way I'll teach you all about talking like you were born here."

"I would appreciate that very much Granny. The wheelchairs are stored at the far end of the hall. If you would please wait here, I will return with one without delay."

"I'm not going anywhere without you," she said with a sly smile.

A couple of minutes later the orderly rolled a wheelchair into the room. "We must be very careful when we leave. I do not think that nurse would appreciate it if I helped you gallivant around."

"Gallivant. I'm impressed." She took his arm as he helped her into the chair. "Now let's skedaddle before the iron maiden catches us. You push, and I'll keep my good eye peeled for her."

"Good eye peeled?" he asked.

"Sonny, at my age you're lucky to have a good anything. I'll explain the rest when the coast is clear."

"Ah, I know that expression from watching old gangster movies," he turned the chair to allow her easy access.

"Mick-hail-o-vits?" she said tentatively when she got a good look at his name tag.

"Granny, you pronounced my name perfectly. Are you certain you are not from the motherland?"

"Sonny, I don't even like vodka," she said drawing a laugh.

"Please, you are now my friend. Call me Misha."

"Well Misha, we're burning sun, so let's shake a leg."

"It is starting to shake. Now don't forget your purse and sweater. It might be a little cool downstairs," he said as he turned the chair and rolled it out of the room. "I will carry your walker in case you want to go for a stroll through the hospital's gardens. The roses are very beautiful this time of the year."

The corridor was deserted as most of the staff was finishing paperwork from the night before. Most of the doors were closed and they rolled to the elevator bank without being seen. A *bing* rang out to signal the arrival of the elevator. The doors slid open revealing a couple of well-dressed men standing in the middle of the oversized car.

"Excuse me, gentlemen, I have a patient. Would you please press Lobby." Misha said as the men moved to the sides so he could roll her in. Granny didn't recognize either man, but chose to remain silent lest she accidentally say something that could interfere with her escape plan.

The doors opened to a three-story glass atrium, complete with a stone floor, waterfall, and a reflecting pond flanked by dozens of trees and bushes.

Looks like a Tarzan movie. Granny thought.

"The coffee shop is right by the front door," he said as he rolled her through the lobby. "If you are agreeable, we can sit outside on the terrace while we drink our Boston coffees."

"That sounds peachy." She leaned forward to get a better look. "My, my. It sure looks beautiful out there."

Granny smiled when she saw the terrace was surrounded with row after row of rose bushes. "I love red roses. My late husband used to stop at a florist and buy me one every Friday."

He winked at her. "When no one is looking, I shall pick one for you."

Granny blushed, then giggled. "Is it warm outside? The windows in my room don't open up."

"Granny, it is a perfect day for you to be outdoors. Now, if you would be so kind as to explain to this young lady what we will be drinking."

"Sure thing. Sweetie, we would like two coffees—light sugar and real heavy on the cream. You do have real cream don't you. I can't stand that powdered junk."

"That is it?"

"Yep, it's that simple."

"But why do they call it Boston."

"I don't rightly know. And if I once did, I forgot."

"Oh Granny, you make me laugh. Please, allow me to pay."

"Nothin' doing, Misha. I said it was my treat, and I'm paying." She rummaged around in her purse and took out her wallet.

"Yes, Ma'am. Thank you very much. If I could impose on you to hold the tray until we are outside I would appreciate it greatly."

He pushed her chair through the automatic doors and stopped next to one of the wrought iron tables. "It is very peaceful out here this early in the morning. This is good place to sit and relax and watch people coming and going. If you look over there," he gestured down the circular driveway that ran in front of the hospital's elaborate glass facade, "you will see where the taxi cabs park after they drop off their fares. They will wait there until someone flags them down for a ride to somewhere important."

Granny noted that four large sedans with the word TAXI written across their doors were idling curbside.

"It can become very difficult to get a taxi cab when the nightshift ends at eight," he paused to take a sip of coffee. "This Boston coffee is very good. As I was saying, at the moment, the day-shift workers are arriving and the nightshift is trying to finish their work before going home. Everyone is in such a hurry they are too busy to even notice us. But later, it is very different. The tables will be filled with patients waiting for their test results and families waiting to hear from a doctor or the lab. The day goes very slowly for them, but many use the time to pray. You can easily spot those who are praying, just as those with whom God has shared a glimpse of His awesome power can recognize each other," he smiled at her.

Misha looked at his watch. "Granny, I hope you will not think me rude, but I must ask you to please excuse me while I attend to a personal matter inside. I will not be long, perhaps five minutes."

"Take your time." Granny patted him on the hand.

"I hope you will not grow bored sitting out here all alone."

"Don't you worry about me. I'll enjoy people watching until you come back. Now skedaddle."

The moment the automatic doors closed behind him Granny was up. She grabbed her walker and began moving with great determination toward the driveway. "Taxi!" she shouted while waving her handkerchief to draw their attention.

I remember when all I had to do was hike the hem of my skirt and flash a little flesh to get a cab. Those hacks woulda been fighting to give me a ride. I sure had great gams, she thought as she made her way towards the closest cab in the line.

CHAPTER 22

THE MORNING'S SUN flooded the Haynes' living room. Billy and Philo sat on the sofa with their backs to the windows. Both were sound asleep. Margaret and Mauves were in the kitchen drinking coffee—strong black coffee. All four were exhausted from the long night.

The ringing of the phone broke the home's silence. Billy jumped up and answered it before the second ring, "Haynes here."

"Mr. Haynes, thank goodness you answered." He recognized the young woman's voice as O'Dea's receptionist. "I've been trying to reach you for over an hour. Why haven't you answered your cell phone?"

"I'm sorry Jane, but they took it at the hospital and I never got it back." He yawned. "Besides, Rey told me to take a couple of days off." Billy noticed Philo was awake and motioned for him to move closer so he could hear the conversation. "But I take it you're not calling to see how I'm doing."

"I'm sorry. I should have asked first. Are you good enough to come downtown?"

"That depends on why you want me to come downtown," Billy raised an eyebrow. Philo shrugged back.

"Mr. Haynes, I hate to say this, but there's a situation developing, and the commissioner wants you and Mr. Clemson down here right away. But if you're not fully recuperated from yesterday's trauma, . . . " she left him an easy out.

"Whoa. Situation! What kind of situation?"

Philo leaned in close to hear her response.

"I'm sorry, but I really don't know. You know how secretive the boss can be. He's got a press conference scheduled for nine and Mr. McBarker is supposed to speak about the City Gate collapse." She lowered her voice to a whisper. "You might want to turn on the news before you tell me if

236

you feel good enough to drive downtown. I think it has something to do with the situation."

Five minutes later, four more Christians were on their way to the Irving Park Women's Clinic.

Fred McBarker kept checking his watch. It was almost seven-thirty. O'Dea had commanded him to be at City Hall for a nine o'clock press conference. He knew even on a good day the drive down would take every bit of a half-hour. *If I leave in about ten minutes that should give me plenty of time to speak with Rey before it begins.*

Even though there were still many hours of work ahead of him, he stopped inspecting the flattened rubble and began to organize his scribbled notes into something resembling a field report. He also previewed the hundred-plus digital images he had stored in his camera, jotting down notes on which were the best shots.

Man, I wish I had a chance to talk to some of the witnesses. Even though Commander Washington had told his men on the scene to cooperate, it seemed as if everyone who had seen what happened was downtown at police headquarters.

I'll have to send someone over there to pick up copies of the interviews. If I still have a job after I tell Rey what I saw yesterday.

Fred noticed he was being watched by two men in cheap suits as he walked over to tell Washington he was leaving. *Must be detectives. I wish I had someone here to keep an eye on this. Well, there's not much they can do to screw up a flattened building.*

Even though the door to Washington's office was open, Fred knocked and waited to be invited in. He noticed the officer and mayor were watching a local news program.

"Enter."

"Commander, thank you very much for your cooperation. I'm leaving for now, but there will be other inspectors by later."

Gates stood up and challenged him, "Well. Why did it fall down?"

"I'm sorry, but I couldn't determine a cause. The building will have to be excavated layer by layer to see if there are any clues buried in the rubble."

"And the explosion everyone heard?" Gates drew out the word everyone.

"That might have been the sound of the building collapsing. The roof must have made quite a bang when it slammed onto the concrete slab. I'm going to have my office send someone to interview the eyewitnesses. I'm hoping one of them might have seen something that can give me direction. Well, I have to be getting downtown for a meeting with my boss, so thanks again for your help."

McBarker turned to leave, but froze in mid-step when the Divine Justice of our Lord Missionary Baptist Choir burst forth in song, "Amazing grace, how sweet the sound . . . " This was no somber funeral dirge, but rather a joyful gospel version that made everyone spin around in the direction of the singing.

"What's going on?" Washington pushed past Fred and shouted. "Who the . . . make them turn that radio off."

Several officers, as well as the detectives who were tailing Fred, were standing outside the command center listening to the mighty chorus. A couple sang along with them. Washington bellowed, "Shut them down! Right now! They're interfering with a police investigation."

The choir was on the second verse before anyone moved. One of the uniformed policemen began speaking into a portable radio, "This is Walton. The Commander wants you to shut down whoever is playing the music." He had to repeat himself several times to be heard above the singing. "What do you mean it's not a radio! Huh. Well. Huh. I'll get right back to you."

"Sir, that's not a radio. It's a choir," the officer reported.

"A what?" Washington demanded.

"A choir. Like in church."

"What is a church choir doing serenading us?"

"I don't know. I didn't ask."

"Well ask!" Washington was not impressed by what he was hearing. "I want to know why they are singing here."

The officer started to shout the question into his radio as the closing lines of the hymn, " . . . was blind, but now I see," were sung.

"Sir, they stopped. Do you still want me to ask why they were singing?"

"Yes. I gave you an order! Do it now!"

Before Officer Walton could relay the question, he was distracted by a roar coming from the south, out of sight behind him. The opening staccato of snare drums echoed off the two- and three-story tall buildings like a rolling peal of thunder. Windows rattled as the thunders spoke seven times, each louder than the one before. The sticks struck the drumheads with such precision they sounded as one, and their roar reverberated until the air trembled. Leaves fell from trees as birds took flight in terror. The rumble grew more formidable by the minute until it was felt by every witness. Then it stopped. But only for a moment.

It was followed by a crisp trumpet blast. The number of horns grew as their wail layered upon itself, growing louder and louder as their pitch grew higher and more intense. Many covered their ears as the banshee-like scream became painful. Then all became silent.

"What the . . . !" Washington screamed.

"Didn't those phone guys say they heard trumpets just before it fell down?" A uniformed officer asked aloud. A dozen pairs of apprehensive eyes started scanning building facades in case they too started to collapse. Then the drums resumed their haunting, rhythmic beat. They were joined by a compliment from a score of bass drums from the north.

"Someone find out what's going on." Washington clenched his fists and threw his arms in the air. "Who is making that noise?" He dropped his right arm and pointed at Walton. "Now!"

The officer fumbled for his radio. "This is Patrolman Walton calling whoever is in charge of the southern perimeter. The Commander wants to know what is going on over there?" Washington stared at him while he waited for a reply.

"Sergeant Grezalona here." Walton stuck a finger in his ear to block out the drums.

"Could you please repeat that. How many? Over a hundred?"

"What? Over a hundred what?" the Commander barked at the officer.

"And there's more getting off a bus. How many?" He covered the mouthpiece. "Sir, three school buses are unloading people in choir robes at the roadblock on Addison. And that was a drum and bugle corps we just heard . . . at least fifty kids. They got off a bus and started playing."

Washington pulled the officer's hand towards his mouth and shouted into his radio. "Are you saying fifty kids made that racket!" He didn't wait for an answer. "I want to know why they are here."

"Did you hear that?" Walton shouted above the steady drumbeat.

"Find out who is in charge and have them brought here now!" Washington fumed.

Walton shouted the commander's order as loud as he could. Then he repeated it.

"Sir, he said it looks like the St. Patrick's Day parade down there, but no one's in charge. They're just showing up."

"They're obviously marshaling somewhere. The bus drivers must know what's going on. Ask one of them!" Washington turned and threw his arms in the air. He let out a loud sigh and yelled, "Am I the only one who knows how to question suspects?"

Walton interrupted his rant. "Sir, I think you should hear this. I'm speaking with Sergeant Dolan. He's in charge at the northern barricade. Sergeant, could you please repeat that?" He handed his radio to his superior.

"I said there must be at least three hundred people dressed in church robes—robes of every color you can imagine—and there's more coming every minute."

"Dolan, Commander Washington here. Where are they coming from?"

"Commander, they're getting off church buses. I can see a couple more unloading about a block down. Something's going on. The kids with the drums and bugles are moving off the street to let the choir through. They're lining up on the sidewalk like an honor guard."

The steady patter of drums could be heard in the background. Spit flew as Washington yelled into the radio. "Find out who's in charge and bring them to me."

"Yes sir," Dolan replied. He turned to two officers standing next to him and said, "Jenkins. White. Grab whoever's in charge and bring 'em over here."

Both men started scanning the crowd.

"Sir, the choir is now marching down the middle of the street towards the barricades."

The drumbeat began to pick up in tempo and volume.

"They're being followed by kids in school uniforms. I think they're from a Catholic grammar school . . . maybe ten, twelve years old. There must be a hundred of them."

Washington took a deep breath then asked, "Dolan, how many men do we have on the line?"

"Six, seven counting me."

"Good. In about one minute I want you to give the order to disburse. The last thing I want is another riot. I have about twelve men with me and I'll . . . "

Gates tapped Washington on the shoulder. The commander spun around. He hadn't seen him walk over. "Max, I don't want a repeat of yesterday's fiasco."

The commander stared at the Mayor. "Sid, I'm handling this."

With a flourish, the drums grew silent.

"Hey," Gates smirked, "the racket stopped. Maybe they're going to leave."

"Walton." Gates handed him the radio. "Find out what's going on."

Before the officer could ask the question, it was answered by over five hundred voices singing "Battle Hymn of the Republic." They were joined by a similar number of singers at the opposite end of the roadblock.

It was dark and Pam lay in bed praying. She had a 9:00 A.M. appointment with the Station Manager to discuss her future as a broadcaster, and she was talking with God, thanking Him for the incredible opportunity. When her phone rang at six-thirty she was already putting the finishing touches on her makeup.

"Romenelli here."

A young male voice responded. "Sorry to wake you Miss Romenelli. This is Lenny Kregel from news. They need you to do a remote ASAP."

"Where? I have to be at the station at nine." Pam froze.

"Don't know nothing about that. All they told me was you're supposed to go to the clinic where the riot was . . . only now it's blown up."

"Blown up?" She stammered, "What do you mean blown up?"

"Don't know. But I'm supposed to warn you the whole neighborhood is shut down by the police, so you can't get any closer than three blocks away. Your crew said they'd pick you up where you had lunch yesterday. Oh, and you're supposed to call your buddy Phil and see if you can get into his apartment to film what's going on."

"How am I going to get to his apartment if there's a police blockade? And what about my appointment?"

"I'm sorry, all they told me to do was to call and give you that message. I'm just a go-fer down here. I really don't know nothing else."

"Thanks, Lenny." Pam choked back a tear. "Can you tell them I'll be there in about fifteen minutes."

"Sure thing, Miss Romenelli. And I'm real sorry to wake you up so early."

"No problem," she sighed. "I was already awake."

Pam sighed again. She had laid out her nicest dress to wear to the interview and knew it would be overkill for a remote, especially if she might have to sneak past police barricades to get the shot they wanted. She was reluctant to call Phil and wake him up so early after his big night but figured he would most likely be awake from all the commotion.

"Phil, good morning. This is Pam, the reporter from yesterday. I'm sorry to wake you so early, but I need a favor."

He chuckled, "I was wondering how long it would take you to call. C'mon down. The coffee's fresh, and I've got the best seat in the house."

"Thanks, Phil, but there's a problem. The station said the police aren't letting anyone get any closer than three blocks away."

"That's an inconvenience, not a problem. Make sure you're wearing loose pants and a good pair of climbing shoes. You'll have to hop a fence or two, but I know a nice little shortcut that'll get you here. Your station is showing a picture from a helicopter, so I can see where they've got the squad cars. If you have someone drop you off on the shoulder of the expressway by where the bridge used to be, you can scurry up the hill and slip into the alley without being seen. Tell them not to dilly dally. They should drop you off and drive away."

Phil opened the curtains a crack. "I can see a lot of cop cars driving around, so stay off the streets. That alley doesn't go through to Elston, so they're probably ignoring it. It deadends at a big apartment building about a half-block from my place. It's got a big metal gate next to the garage. It looks real secure, but they never lock it.

"Next you'll have to shimmy over a couple chain link fences until you are across the alley from my place. They can't see you in the gangway, so call me before you get there. I'll let you know if anyone's poking around. I already unlocked my gate and back door, so let yourself in and come on up."

Pam closed her eyes and smiled. "Thanks, Phil. You're amazing."

"Glad to help. Now get going, I've got one heck of a story to tell you."

"Thanks again. I'll see you in about a half-hour."

Pam went back to her closet and selected a comfortable pants suit to wear. *Maybe I can bring the dress in a garment bag,* she thought for a moment then laughed at the thought of getting caught climbing a fence because of it. Besides, she knew she would have to help her cameraman Tony with his gear since the third member of their team would be driving the getaway van.

The police and firefighters were standing in small clusters as they listened to the joyous refrain, "Glory, glory, hal-le-lu-lah! His truth is marching on," when Pam began broadcasting from Phil's living room.

"Good morning, Chicago. This is Pam Romenelli reporting live from the remains of the Irving Park Women's Clinic. This same clinic was the focus of yesterday's riot in which the mayor's grandmother, Granny Gates, was among the dozens arrested. Today it lies in ruins, destroyed by an explosion early this morning"

The opening shot had Pam standing in front of the picture window with the rubble-strewn vacant lot behind her. Next the camera swept down the street from an open window, pausing on the dozens of parked squad cars and fire department vehicles before zooming in on the emergency personnel and police officers. His lens was good enough that he could focus on individual faces.

"What is even more amazing, however, is what you hear in the background." She paused to allow the music to completely take over.

"As He died to make men holy, let us die to make men free, while God is marching on."

Without realizing it, Pam began to sing the chorus out loud. Tony tried not to be obvious as he backed up to include her in his shot.

Phil's voice boomed from off camera. "I don't know who's doing the singing, but I feel like I'm hearing a sliver of heaven."

Pam smiled at Phil and responded, "Actually what we are hearing is one of the most incredible, spontaneous gatherings of church choirs this city has ever seen. I have been told more than a thousand people have joined together in song and more are arriving by the minute." Pam's producer had briefed her with what little they knew before she went on the air.

The camera again shifted to a shot down Elston Avenue. Viewers were quick to note several officers pointing their way.

"We can't see the choirs from our vantage point, but from the looks on the faces of the police officers below, they know they are witnessing something wondrous."

The street was quiet as the choir ended with a magnificent, "Amen."

The camera's view again shifted to Pam with the remains of the former abortuary behind her. "Police officials appear to have been caught off guard by this unprecedented public outpouring of faith and worship."

"Pssst, Pam," Phil said loud enough to be picked up on the mike, "I think they know we're up here. And they don't look any too happy."

The camera swung away much quicker than you would expect a professional to move it. Coupled with the quick zoom-in, the effect was that of someone trying out his first camera. When the camera movement stopped, the screen was filled with the red face of Mayor Gates. There was little question he was furious as he pointed up towards the cameraman. Tony's waving back to him only made for a better close-up as he began to—as Granny liked to call it—"pitch a conniption fit." Incredibly, all of the background noise ceased long enough for the microphone to pick up Gates's screaming, "Stop that man! I want him off the air!"

"Oh boy," Pam said as the knocking on the downstairs door became banging. "It looks like we're going to have company."

"Now don't you worry," Phil sounded confident. "That's a steel security door down there. The sales guy that sold it to me said it was guaranteed to keep home invaders away for an hour. It's got a lifetime warranty."

The camera zoomed out to show the SWAT team running in formation towards the building.

Pam tried to remain professional, but was getting nervous. "Uhhhh, Phil, you might want to get out of here. I don't think that door will stop the ramrod they're carrying."

"This is my house and I'm staying put."

Pam turned back to the camera, "We're going to keep broadcasting as long as we can. I don't . . . " Pam stopped in mid-sentence as a loud crashing sound was followed by the pounding of combat boots as the officers stomped up the stairs. The apartment's front door bowed in as the first shoulder slammed into it.

"The Chicago police are storming this building to prevent us from broadcasting pictures of Mayor Gates live from the scene of this morning's . . . "

Pam stopped again in mid-sentence as the door tore from its frame and slammed to the ground with a resounding crash. Tony spun around to follow the action. Within seconds, a dozen heavily armed tactical officers, clad head to toe in black, burst in.

"This is still America, isn't it?" Phil challenged the leader. "Just who the heck do you think you are smashing my door down like a bunch of jack-booted Nazi storm troopers?"

"You are ordered to cease and desist all activities and immediately evacuate this building by order of . . . "

"Hitler? Is that who gave you your orders?" Phil stood toe-to-toe with him. "I fought a war against fascists like you. Go ahead, shoot me, but I'm not leaving my home."

The leader made a hand gesture and two of his men engulfed the elderly man and started to hustle him out of the room before he could react. He then pointed at Tony. "You! I want that camera off right now!"

"Let go of me!" Phil's voice trailed off as he was dragged down the staircase.

"How dare you do that to him! This is his home. And what about me? Are you going to do that to a woman?" She pointed her finger at his bulletproof vest. "Which of you is brave enough to shred the First Amendment?"

Noticing all eyes were focused on the reporter, the cameraman casually lowered the video unit until it was at waist level. He hoped they would think he complied and stopped transmitting.

The leader made another hand gesture and two more men lunged forward, attempting to grab Pam. She jumped backward just far enough for the men to miss and fall on top of each other at her feet. Before she could react, two other men blindsided her, knocking her on top of the two who were trying to get back up. Arms and legs were flying everywhere as she started to kick and scream.

"Subdue her!" the leader screamed

"Police brutality!" she screamed back as they cuffed her wrists behind her back. Pam's last words as they dragged her to her feet, her blouse pulled out of her pants and her hair looking like she had just lost a fight with four cops were, "This is Pam Romenelli, Channel One news, reporting live from the latest incident of police brutality." She was still squirming as an officer lifted her off her feet and carried her out the door.

At that instant everyone seemed to realize the camera's red light was still on. Two of the men in black advanced on Tony shouting, "Turn that off now!"

He backed up as far as he could against the open window. "OK, I'll turn it off." He was about to comply when he noticed four news helicopters hovering to the east, their arrival hidden by the morning sun.

They reminded Tony of his youth back in Vietnam when the Hueys would come in hot and low over the rice paddies. He was happy to see them in the '60s, and he was happy to see them now because he knew each would have a camera trained on the front of the building . . . and he was in that shot.

At that same instant, the combined southeast and northwest blockade choirs launched into a stirring rendition of "Onward, Christian Soldiers."

Tony used the distraction to leap out the second floor window. He landed hard, almost at the feet of the Mayor and Commander Washington. "Well hello, Mr. Mayor, any comment on the latest charges of police brutality?" was all he could say before he was slammed to the ground.

Though knocked a little out of focus when it hit the pavement, the camera captured the struggle as he was shackled and dragged away.

Before the police threw him into the backseat of a squad roll, he made a point of flashing his best smile for the quartet of hovering video brethren.

CHAPTER 23

JACKIE JEFFERSON LAY curled up in the darkness. Except for a sliver of light between the heavy curtains, the room was black. His breathing was labored and his body twitched. He was asleep, but not at rest. A sharp rap tore his mind back from what little peace he had found.

"Unky Jackie. Unky Jackie. I's sorry I gotta gets you up, but you ain't gonna believe what be happenin'." The young man couldn't contain his excitement as he knocked again on the solid oak door. Jefferson covered his ears and tried to ignore the determined attempt to wake him up.

After a moment's pause, the intruder began knocking even harder and called out, "Unky Jackie, you gotta gets up."

Leon's uniform on an average day consisted of a faded flannel shirt, a pair of khakis, a baseball cap, and a well worn pair of running shoes. Today he was dressed as though for church. His hair was combed and his face shaved. The crisp collar of a white shirt peeked above the soft blue sweater his uncle had given him last Christmas. A pair of dark blue pants and a spit-shined pair of wingtips completed the ensemble.

"C'mon, Unky Jackie. You gotta gets up right now."

"Go away, Leon. I do not wish to be disturbed." He sounded groggy. Jefferson was not used to drinking. The large snifter of brandy he consumed before falling asleep on the leather couch in his office caused his head to pound. Sensing the young man would not leave him be, he asked, "Leon, what time is it?"

"'Bout seven fifteen."

"After all that transpired yesterday could you not at least have had the decency to allow me to sleep?"

"I's real sorry but this be real important or I wouldn't be bother'n you."

Jackie sighed, "I suppose you are not going to allow me to fall back asleep. The door is not locked. Please come in."

Leon bounded into the room.

"So what, pray tell, can be so important this early in the morning? And why are you all dressed up?"

"I gots the news on the TV and they says they started singin' gospel and shoutin' Amens all 'bout the angel," he blurted out.

"Speak slower, Leon. I do not understand why you woke me to tell me this."

"I was watchin' TV for the sports man to says how the Cubs done."

"Leon, I repeat. Why did you wake me? And why are the church bells pealing?"

The young man snickered. "Bells a'pealin'? You're funnin' with me, Uncle Jackie. Bells not a'pealin'; a banana's a'pealin.'

Hiring his sister's eighteen-year-old son as an assistant had been one of the few selfless acts Jefferson had ever done. The young man was an energetic worker, but was, to put it kindly, a little slow. Every morning his mother would drop him off on her way to work and pick him up after dinner. The staff grew to love the adult-child and patiently worked with him, teaching him how to master domestic chores. He became quite the helper in the kitchen and loved crinkle cutting potatoes for french fries so much they had them at least three times a week.

From there he worked his way up to being Jackie's valet, or *valley* as he called it. Then one Friday night, about two years ago, his mother failed to show up. His staff tried calling her cell phone, but it was no longer in service. It was the same with her home phone number. Jackie drove to her apartment, but no one answered the doorbell.

Fearing the worse, the police were called. Using the landlord's passkey, they discovered she had abandoned her son, leaving behind a vacant apartment and a note reading, "I've gone west to start a new life. Please take good care of my boy."

That night Jackie gave the young man his own room in the mansion.

Leon thrived with his extended family. But he did miss his mommy. Jackie had a hard time holding his tongue whenever he asked when she was coming back and always tried to say something positive about the boy's mother such as, "I'm sure your mother will call when she achieves her dreams."

The reality was, he had grown extremely protective of his nephew and knew he would never let that irresponsible woman take him away from his home. No, Leon was his responsibility now, and this was his home.

However, the two never appeared together in public because Jackie was determined to shield him from the prying eyes of the press who might, in an attempt to hurt his ministry, try to embarrass Jackie at the young man's expense.

"Leon," his voice was firm, "do you know why the church bells are ringing?"

"Yes'ir."

Knowing how literal his nephew could be, he rephrased the question to "Leon, why are the church bells ringing?"

"They's must be accounta the angel."

"Leon, I do not understand. What do you mean they are ringing on account of the angel?" Jackie never stopped trying to correct the youth's grammar and speech. Despite his best efforts, however, he continued to slur his words

"The one they's singin' gospel about. I tied to tell ya, I saw'd him too. He was real big, and he be all on fire, and he swung this real big ol' sword. I means the sword be on fire, nots the angel. And he looked right at me and he smiled. Unky Jackie, that angel he smiled at me. Then he maked a bad store blow'd up. *Kaboom.* He really wailed on that store with that sword a' his." He swung his arms as though chopping something with an invisible sword.

"You saw this on television?"

"No, sir, I saw's it happenin'."

"Leon, you were home in bed all night."

"I knows I was. But I saw's it happenin'. And now it be on TV. You believes me, don'ts you?"

"Yes, Leon. But I believe you had a dream."

"Uhh-uhh. I sawed it all for real. C'mon, Unky Jackie. Yous gotta believes me. C'mon, you watch the man on TV. He'll tell you all 'bout the angel."

It is not like Leon to make stories up. Jackie thought.

"Please, Unky Jackie," he cocked his head to the side and smiled. "Please."

The young man was so adamant that Jackie relented, "Leon, if you would please bring me a cup of coffee, I would be happy to watch television with you."

"I got's the TV set on. The real big one in the front room. You go sit in your favorite chair, and I be right back with you's coffee. I'm gonna ax Mrs. White if any cookies be made."

"Thank you, Leon, that would be fine. But first, I need to freshen up and change. I will be along in about five minutes."

"OK, Unky Jackie."

As he walked up the stairs to his room, he couldn't help but be curious about what had the young man so worked up. *What could church bells ringing, choirs singing gospel, and angels with flaming swords possibly have in common?* Then he realized he was so wrapped up trying to make sense of the strange story he had forgotten all about his headache.

"Unky Jackie, hurry up. They's showin' it." Leon's voice echoed up the staircase.

"I will be down in a minute, Leon." he said as he finished washing a bit of shaving cream off of his face.

"Listen to 'em singin'. They's shown so many choirs I can'st even count 'em." Everything else he said was drowned out when he turned the sound up.

"Leon. Leon. I am here." Jackie shouted. "It is no longer necessary for the television to be that loud."

"Yes'ir. I wanted you's to hears it upstairs." He grinned as he turned the volume down with the remote.

The young man sat at one end of the beige suede couch with his feet tucked under him. Jackie had tried to teach him how to sit properly, with his feet flat on the floor, but finally gave up. *All the things I have to do today . . .* he thought as he sat down next to his nephew.

"Looky, that newsman is gonna talk!" he bounced up and down on the couch.

The screen was filled with a close-up of a dark-haired man. He had a heavy look on his handsome face. "Good morning Chicago, I'm Dennis McKnight." As he spoke, the camera zoomed out to show the mass of people gathered behind him.

"We are at the scene of one of the most remarkable, impromptu chorale events this city has ever witnessed. There appears to be a lull in the singing, so I'll try to bring you up to date on this morning's remarkable events.

"In the pre-dawn darkness, a construction accident touched off a natural gas explosion which destroyed a one-story building on Elston Avenue. The Chicago Police Department evacuated the neighborhood pending arrival of gas company repair crews. Two of their gray trucks arrived over an hour ago and we can see several workers standing next to them. They do not, however, appear to be doing anything other than enjoying the rousing renditions of gospel favorites."

The camera zoomed in on McKnight. He paused for a moment, smiled, then continued. "For the last hour, two groups have been assembling to sing religious hymns in the safety areas the police set up. Many are dressed in flowing robes of every color of the rainbow. The choirs have grown to well over a thousand people each and we have been treated to some of the most inspired music this side of the Promised Land.

"I'm going to take advantage of this break in the singing to see if I can find out who organized this festival. Sir, excuse me," he said to an elderly white-haired man standing a couple of feet away. "Could I ask you a few questions on the air?" McKnight had singled the man out because of his distinctive black and gold robe.

"Certainly, my son, I would be honored."

"If we could start with your name and what church you are affiliated with."

"I am Dr. Lucius Mays II, senior pastor of the Church of Our Risen Lord and Savior in the Pullman community on Chicago's southeast side."

"Dr. Mays, I'll make it simple. What's going on here?'

"What's going on here!" He laughed as he repeated the question. "You really don't know, do you?"

"No, Sir, I don't. But that also goes for the Chicago Police Department, the Mayor's Office of Special Events, and everyone else from the city with whom we've spoken."

"Son, we are witnessing the awesome power of our God. He has answered our prayers and we are here to say thank you."

"Prayers? You prayed for a gas leak?" The reporter had a cocky tone to his question.

Mays turned from the camera and looked the reporter straight in the eye. "Son, do you attend church regularly?"

"Church? What does attending church have to do with anything?" McKnight sounded puzzled.

The tone of Mays' voice dropped and its volume and inflection increased. "It has everything to do with everything," he thundered. "You were created by God for one reason and one reason alone: to give honor to Him. Every day is a gift from Him, everything you own is on loan from Him."

The reporter wasn't sure how to respond and hoped the choirs would start singing again so he could get away from this man.

"I know what you're thinking." Mays moved closer to the reporter until they were almost touching. The pastor was a good six-inches taller than him. "You're thinking, *Someday, when I'm an old man, I'll cut a deal with God.* You'll go to church every once in a while and drop a few dollars in the collection plate and think you have bought eternal salvation. But you are wrong, very wrong." McKnight stepped back until he bumped into someone.

"What do you think each and every person you see standing here has in common?" Dr. Mays didn't give the reporter a chance to respond. "I'll tell you. Every last one has a personal relationship with Jesus Christ. They have accepted Him as their Redeemer and Savior. Are you familiar with the verse, 'For God so loved the world that He gave His only begotten Son, that whosoever believeth in Him shall not perish, but have everlasting life'?" It's not just words, Son. It is the truth. It is His truth."

The reporter stood limp, the color drained from his face.

"Now aren't you glad the hand of the Lord led you to me this fine morning?"

He made no sound as Dr. Mays took the microphone from his hand then climbed into the bed of an abandoned pickup truck. He surveyed the crowd from his advantage.

"So you want to know what's going on here? Everyone here can tell you what's going on but, since you asked me, I would be honored to tell you." The camera zoomed in on him as he held his arms up, his palms open to the crowd.

"What is going on here is 'Our Father, who art in heaven' has given us a sign." Mays pointed to the heavens and bowed his head. Then he smiled before continuing. "He sent an angel down from heaven to destroy this evil place just as surely as He destroyed Sodom and Gomorrah."

The crowd began to circle around the pastor and punctuated his sentences with shouts of *Amen*.

"An angel of the Lord, no less than Archangel Michael himself, was sent to destroy this depraved malignancy." Mays again pointed towards the sky and spoke with practiced cadence. "He was sent from heaven clothed in the armor of righteousness with hundreds of battle trumpets announcing his arrival. He was sent to destroy this temple of wickedness because God has commanded, 'Thou shalt not kill.'" He pointed toward where the women's clinic had been. "He was sent to cleanse our city of this unholy building where innocent young women, each with a child of God growing in her womb, went to see men who had the audacity to call themselves doctors—and in truth they too were pregnant, only they were pregnant with evil."

Mays eyes glowed white-hot against his coffee-colored skin. They did not blink as he stared into the camera.

A chorus of "amens" broke forth.

"Unky Jackie. See, he be talkin' 'bout the angel I saw."

"Shhhh. That man has a gift." This was perhaps the ultimate compliment the flamboyant reverend could pay a fellow man of the cloth.

"Unspeakable horrors took place in that building. Eternal souls were ravaged by debauchery as God's children were murdered . . . torn limb from limb and the pieces flushed down the drain." Mays held up a Bible. "In Proverbs 24: 11-12 we were commanded, 'Rescue those being unjustly dragged to their deaths. Do not stand back and watch them die. Do not try to disclaim responsibility by saying you did not know, for the Lord who made all hearts made yours, and He knows you knew, and He will reward all according to our deeds.'"

"*Amen!*"

"He knows you knew. He knows you knew!" Mays pointed right at the camera. "He knows you knew." He paused for several seconds. "And if those words don't send a shiver down your spine, you are a foolish person indeed." He paused again. When he resumed, his voice was softer; he looked smaller, almost fragile. "We are commanded to rescue those being unjustly dragged to their deaths . . . and whose life could be more just than an unborn baby? Yet we failed to act. We allowed politicians to pass laws allowing women to murder their babies on a whim. Every day, I repeat, every day, hundreds if not thousands of babies are murdered in abortion mills, yet we did nothing. We failed our Father, so He had to send a warrior to destroy this wicked place."

"*Amen,*" the crowd shouted.

"No, this is not just a destroyed building." He turned back to McKnight. "No, this is a sign from heaven above that we must repent of our sinful ways or risk the wrath of God Almighty. Everyone who can hear the sound of my voice is a sinner. Everyone must repent or incur the wrath of God."

"*Amen!*" the crowd shouted with vigor.

Mays voice again boomed out; he thrust his right arm in the air and his eyes flared as he roared, "We have sinned against our Creator, and He has given us a sign. We must change our sinful ways . . . not tomorrow, not next week, but today." He pounded on his Bible. "Right this instant. We must stop murdering one out of every four babies . . . one out of every four. Look around." He swung his arms over the crowd. "Abortionists would have gladly have killed every fourth person you see."

"*Amen!*" The roar was almost deafening.

"And these murderers don't care about the color of the baby's skin. They don't care who their parents are or what their nationality is. No, they are monsters who kill for money. And their road to hell will be paved with bloodstained greenbacks, credit card receipts, and cancelled checks." Tears filled Mays' eyes and he hung his head.

"*Amen!*" Their affirmation echoed off the buildings.

Mays held up his hand for silence. It shook as he cried. The crowd watched in silence . . . the only sound was sobbing.

He sucked in a deep breath, then exhaled. He wiped the tears away with a handkerchief and straightened his back. He looked to heaven, then nodded his head. His lips were quivering when he spoke. "Make no mistake about it. There is great evil in this world. But thanks to Archangel Michael, the devil will have to find a new building where his minions can do their evil deeds."

"*Amen!*" the crowd thundered.

His voice grew louder. "God ordered this blasphemy to be destroyed just as surely as He sent His servant to destroy another abortion mill yesterday. We pray He will not stop until he has wiped this plague against children off of our great country, yea wiped off the face of His world forever."

"*Amen!*" The crowd was whipped up to a fever pitch.

Mays words raged like a forest fire, engulfing and consuming all who heard them.

"Until that day comes, I challenge each and every one of you to pray for these murderers. Pray the Lord God softens their hearts. Pray they use their God-given talents to save lives instead of ending them. And pray they repent and beg the Lord's forgiveness before it is too late."

He was drowned out by a chorus of "*Amens!*"

Mays waited for several seconds, then pointed his index finger straight into the camera, "And for everyone who can hear my voice, I warn you, vengeance has come and every man, woman, and child should be quaking. It is not too late to drop to your knees and admit you are a sinner. It is not too late to prostrate yourself on the ground and beg God's forgiveness."

A thousand voices strong screamed in unison, "*Amen!*" at the top of their lungs. As though waiting for the Pastor Mays to finish speaking, the choirs burst forth in song, "A mighty fortress is our God, a bulwark never failing . . . "

Jackie Jefferson slumped in his chair. "Wow!" was his only comment.

Leon jumped off the couch and grabbed his hand and tried to pull him up. "Unky Jackie, can's we go right now and see's that preacher man? I's all dressed up."

"I . . . I do not know," he stammered. "Maybe we can visit his church some Sunday."

"But I wanna tell him today. I saw'd the angel too."

The close-up of Pastor Mays was replaced by a shot from a helicopter of the singing crowd which had swelled to well over four thousand. Moments later, the cameraman swung away and zoomed in on an apartment building. An announcer's voice broke in over the singing, "We've been reporting the neighborhood had been evacuated, but it seems they missed at least one resident. There is a man standing on a window ledge of a building across from the former clinic."

A moment later, Tony leapt to the street below. Several policemen swarmed him, knocking him to the ground. Even though his camera slammed into the asphalt, Channel One's logo was visible as was Mayor Gates, who stared with his mouth hanging open.

They handcuffed Tony and pulled him to his feet. When he refused to walk, two policemen dragged him to their squad car then pushed him into the back seat.

"What the heck is going on?" the announcer mumbled as two SWAT team members, dressed head-to-toe in black, came out of the same building wrestling with an elderly man, who kicked and fought them all the way to a waiting paddy wagon.

They were soon followed by four more men in black carrying a woman by her arms and legs. They threw her into the wagon as though she were a sack of flour, then slammed the door shut.

The announcer spoke. "I have no idea what those people did, but the police seem to be treating them as though they're a danger to the mayor."

Commander Washington pushed Gates towards his limousine. Three squad cars were in place in front of the car to act as an escort. The paddy wagon lined up next, followed by two more squads and a couple of municipal sedans.

"I wonder if they know how many people are waiting for them at the end of the block?" the announcer asked.

CHAPTER 24

THE YOUNG WOMAN snatched the phone and tucked it between her shoulder and ear as she continued diapering her son. "Hello."

"I hope I didn't wake you, Mrs. Morgan. It's Diane from church. Pastor Robertson activated the phone tree. He would like the choir to gather in the church parking lot as soon as you can get there."

"Choir? Now?" Isabella was confused. "Why? I have to work today."

"I'm sorry, Mrs. Morgan, but that's all Pastor said. I think it might have something to do with what's happening on TV right now. It's on all the channels."

"I'm sorry, Diane. I've been so busy getting the twins ready to go to grandma's that I haven't had a chance to watch. But I'll turn it on while I pass the word."

"Will your husband be able to attend?" the young lady asked.

"I'm not sure. He was driving a bus all night and should've been home by now."

Fred McBarker sat in his car waiting for the mayor's convoy to start moving. He had been warned by a police officer that several hundred people were blocking both ends of Elston Avenue but they didn't expect any trouble moving the crowd out of the way long enough for them to slip through. That had been well over half-an-hour ago, but they hadn't budged an inch.

The crowd actually numbered more than four thousand at the north end and slightly more than that at the south. The street and sidewalks outside the barricades were packed solid with people witnessing the power of God. Hundreds more were arriving by the minute. When police started to detour church buses away from the area, their drivers obeyed. The problem was, the traffic cops didn't tell them where to go, only, "You can't stop here," and "Keep it moving."

This added to the confusion as most were unfamiliar with the neighborhood. With no one to direct them, most followed the bus ahead in search of a very large parking space. It didn't take long for the congested side streets to become impassable.

The arterial streets weren't much better. Dozens of cars were double-parked on both sides of the road causing gaper blocks as drivers slowed to a crawl to see what was happening. Traffic cops were making a little bit of progress by rapping sharply on car windows and ordering motorists to "Keep it moving . . . there's nothing to see," until a delivery truck slammed into the rear end of the sub-compact car in front of it. That brought westbound traffic to a complete halt.

The neighborhood's residents saw the hopelessness of the traffic jam and didn't even try driving. Instead, they walked over to watch and listen to the choirs as they marched in procession. After all, you don't get many parades in the Albany neighborhood.

Most of the police who were not busy directing traffic were treating this as if it were a giant block party and joined the locals in enjoying the spectacle. That all changed when every police radio barked out Commander Washington's order to, "Clear a path for the mayor to drive through."

Even though this was the most polite and well behaved, not to mention joyful, gathering the police had ever seen, there was nowhere to move that many people. Two officers on horseback had their hands full as they tried to direct new arrivals away from the side streets. Fortunately, many bus drivers were listening to traffic reports and started parking two and three miles away. Their choirs lined up and marched in silence until they were close enough to hear the music. Then they added their voices to the thousands already making a beautiful noise.

It didn't take long for the sidewalks along Irving Park to become so crowded that bystanders spilled onto the avenues bringing eastbound traffic to a standstill. Adding to the confusion, the choirs kept singing, and their voices drowned out the police bullhorns.

Fred checked his watch every couple of minutes—it was pushing eight—and he thought for a moment about asking for a police escort so he would be on time for Reynold's press conference.

I wonder if Commander Washington is eager enough to get rid of me that he would help? He laughed out loud as he speculated on the response he would receive. *But what good would an escort do? Even the police cars aren't moving.*

He tried calling his supervisor's cell phone for the third time, but it was still being answered by voice mail. He had already left two messages and hesitated to leave another, but finally said, "Rey, I'm still stuck in traffic at the Elston Avenue collapse. Nothing is moving. I'll keep you posted."

Fred opened his door and stood up to stretch his legs. There were now three black sedans lined up behind his with their motors running. A couple of drivers leaned against their fenders smoking cigarettes. Looking in the other direction, he counted four cars plus four police cruisers leading the parade—and then there was that paddy wagon that looked so out of place behind the mayor's limousine. *I'd love to know what those people did to end up in there.*

Fred called out to a passing police officer, "Any idea when we're moving?"

The red-haired young man walked over and shrugged his shoulders as he replied, "Your guess is as good as mine. Listen to this . . . it's real goofy out there." The officer turned up the volume on his radio.

An unidentified voice asked, "Uh, where do you want us to put the marching band?"

"Which one?" was the curt response.

The cop shook his head. "Marching bands at a protest, un-freakin' believable. Somebody said the way people are coming they wouldn't be surprised if the Mormon Tabernacle Choir showed up next."

"Thanks for the update." Fred stifled a yawn. He had slept less than eight hours during the last two nights and thought, *Since we're not going anywhere for a while, I might as well take a nap. I'm sure the guy behind me will make sure I wake up when we start moving.*

Fred got back into his car, turned the motor off, and reclined the seat. He closed his eyes and tried to get comfortable, but his mind refused to relax; it kept rehashing all that had happened. A chill ran through him when he watched City Gate collapse around him. He whispered, *Thank you, God, for protecting me,* and looked at his watch again. Only two minutes had passed. *Is it too early to call Fritzi?* After the long night, he wasn't sure she would be up by now, and decided to wait awhile. *I should also call Billy and Philo and bring them up to date on the angel's latest handiwork.* He turned to look at the vacant lot. *But somehow I think they know.* He smiled.

Billy and Philo. Those guys are amazing . . . their wives too. They gave up their night to be with my Fritzi. Wow. I can't wait to thank them for all they've done for us. He looked at his watch again.

I'll close my eyes for a couple of minutes, was his last thought before sleep overtook him.

In his dream Fred saw the City Gate angel standing majestically in the clouds with his wings fully extended. Heaven's warrior was clad in polished silver armor that reflected the sun with such intensity it was hard to look at him, but Fred was so transfixed by the amazing sight that he could not look away. The angel acknowledged his admirer by raising his fiery sword and pointing the glowing tip at him. It was then Fred knew the angel was smiling at him.

It seemed like only a heartbeat later Fred's catnap was ended by his cell phone ringing.

"What the . . . I mean who?" he said as he fumbled in his pocket for the phone. "Yeah, McBarker here."

"Mr. McBarker, good morning. This is Amy McCarthy. I'm really sorry to bother you, but I'm new in Commissioner O'Dea's office, and I need to discuss your press release with you."

Fred yawned. "My press release? What press release? Is Rey there?"

"I'm sorry. I don't know who he is. I just started yesterday."

He sighed. "OK. No problem. You can transfer me to his secretary when we're done. But first, let's start with what press release?"

"The one they want me to prepare about this morning's explosion."

"And what does my press release say?" Fred sounded more than a bit annoyed.

"Well, it's not really finished, sir. And, like I said, I've never written one before, but Carol gave me a few old ones to follow as a guide. It's kinda rough," she stammered.

"Read me what you've got."

"I'm sorry, but I really haven't written anything since high school English. I didn't know what to do . . . I was hired as a receptionist. I mean I think I have the facts down but I really need to tie it all together so it makes sense. Could I please ask you a few questions?"

"No, I get the first question," Fred stated. "Who told you to write this press release?"

"I don't know."

"You don't know who told you to write it?"

"No, I know . . . but I don't know. I mean I know who he is, but I don't know his name. They took me around and introduced me yesterday, but I didn't meet him then. There's so many people here I haven't been able to remember more than a handful of names. But the way, he spoke down to me; I mean I just assumed he had to be really important."

"Did he act like you were a peon, and he was lord of the manor?"

The young lady tried not to giggle as she responded, "Yes, Sir."

"Congratulations, you have experienced Tim. But I'm sure he'll expect you to call him Mr. Stanford. Now we know who wants it, so let's move on to what he wants."

"He wants a press release, Mr. McBarker."

"Fred. Please call me Fred. Did Tim tell you what the press release should say?"

"Not really. He ripped a yellow sheet of paper off a pad he was carrying and told me to have it ready in fifteen minutes. That was over five minutes ago. I didn't know what to do . . . no one else was in the office until Carol showed up. But she's never written a press release either, so she said I should call you and ask for help. Could you please help me?"

"Sure, I'll try to help, but this is the first I'm hearing about this. OK, what did Tim write down for you?"

"They're not even full sentences . . . just words with circles around them. At the top it says 'collapse-3800? Elston Avenue-clinic-old grocery store?' The next one says, 'four-inch, medium-pressure gas line cut—two laborers on site'"

"Wait. It says a gas line was cut?"

"Yes, it says four-inch, medium-pressure gas line cut."

"Who told him that?"

"I don't know. It doesn't say. The next bubble says something like, 'no permit' then 'caused explosion-building destroyed—evacuated neighborhood—witnesses confirm explosion. No injuries or fatalities.'"

"What's next?" McBarker asked trying not to let his rising anger show.

"That's all there is. I tried to write it out so it made sense but . . . "

"Don't sweat it. It's my problem now." *Tim knows better than to try to go behind my back on something this big.* "When he comes back looking for *my* press release, tell him to call me and I'll be happy to fill in the details."

Even though he suspected Rey was behind this, he wanted to know why Tim was doing the dirty work. If Rey wanted a preliminary report to release to the press, a recital of known facts, that was his job. Tim was a nothing more than a flunky . . . a downtown desk jockey.

Could Rey be trying to cover up the angel? The police said several eyewitnesses were being interviewed. They must have seen the angel swinging his sword. It sure would be pretty hard not to tell everyone what they saw. The cops must have thought the first guy they talked to was nuts.

She rushed on, "I see Tim coming. Thank you, Mr., er. Fred. He's walking this way. I really, really appreciate this," Amy said. "Should I just hand him the phone?"

"No, it would probably be best if you told him to call me and made yourself scarce."

"Thank you, soooo much," she said before hanging up.

Now to wait for the excited phone call.

This was Fred's investigation and there was no way Tim or anyone downtown could determine the cause of this or any collapse without first talking to the field investigator. And that goes double when the cause was supernatural.

The gathering of Christians celebrating the miracle owned the lead on every news outlet in town. Radio News 710 was no exception.

"If you just tuned in, we've interrupted our regular morning programming with continuous coverage of a massive religious celebration that has broken out on the city's northwest side. My producer advised me there is a lull in the singing. We don't know how long it will last so we're going straight to traffic and, if there's time, we'll have the opening stock market report."

For the second day in a row every television and talk radio station in Chicago abandoned their usual formats to report live from the scene of a collapsed Council of Women clinic. Today, however, the story was evolving into something very different. While cynical reporters debated whether the festive atmosphere was an elaborate diversion to draw attention away from something more sinister, most agreed the presence of Mayor Gates meant City Hall was somehow behind everything that was happening.

"And why," several reporters speculated, "was a SWAT team on hand for a natural gas explosion?"

One followed another path and breathlessly announced he had overheard someone shouting into his cell phone, "Praise God, another stop on the road to perdition has been destroyed." He went on to speculate whether a Christian conspiracy similar to Islamic car bombers was afoot to destroy reproductive freedom centers.

A creative reporter concealed his tape recorder, then walked a mile and a half to the nearest fire station where he struck up a conversation with a fireman standing out front who opined, "There's no chance today was a routine construction screw up," and "Two clinic collapses in two days was more than one heck of a coincidence," before his chief saw them and ended the exchange.

His broadcast of the interview added fuel to the "cover-up" theories that many hoped would be put to rest at Commissioner O'Dea's 9:00 A.M. press conference.

Veteran reporters left wild speculations to the greenhorns as they cased the crowd to identify personalities who stood out. With no clear leaders, other than individual choir directors, they climbed on parked cars and scanned the thousands hoping to discover who was giving the crowd marching orders.

Jillian Morrow had been tipped off by her news department that a Bible-thumping preacher tore through some cable TV reporter. She scanned the crowd for him. She was certain the tall white-haired man in the black and gold robe was one of the secret leaders of the protest and intended to get him to admit the whole thing was nothing more than a staged media event. Some kind of elaborate publicity stunt. Jillian watched as the focus of the crowd shifted. Her reporter's instincts told her to grab her technician, Roberto, and find out why.

The choir was on the last line of the song, "God's truth abideth still. His kingdom is for-ev-er" when Jillian and Roberto elbowed their way to the front. Her producer had told her to, "Be ready to go the moment they stop singing." She put one foot on the pickup's bumper and vaulted the tailgate. Her tight red skirt and designer high heels made the landing awkward and Pastor Mays grabbed her arm to keep her from falling. She responded by sticking her microphone in his face. Thanks to the power of Radio News 710's signal, the entire Midwest was tuned in when he proclaimed, "The Great Reformer Martin Luther said, 'The devil, the originator of sorrowful anxieties and restless troubles, flees before the sound of music almost as much as before the Word of God.' I know your voices this beautiful morning have set him to flight."

The crowd roared a jubilant *"Amen"* in response.

Roberto listened for her producer's lead-in. He held up five fingers and began to count them down.

"We're returning live to Jillian Morrow, who is standing somewhere in the middle of a most unique crowd at Irving Park and Elston Avenue. Jillian, can you bring us up to speed on what's happening?"

When Roberto made a fist she began. "Thank you, Jack. The combined choirs just finished a rousing rendition of what I am told is an eighteenth-century English hymn of praise. Its opening line, 'Angels, from the realms of glory, wing your flight o'er all the earth' seems very apt considering every person with whom I have spoken claims to have seen a warrior angel destroy the Irving Park Women's Clinic in a dream or vision last night."

Even with three-inch heels Jillian had to look up to Mays. She clutched the microphone tight in her hand. "I have with me the senior pastor of the Church of Our Risen Lord and Savior, Dr. Lucius Mays II. Dr. Mays, I'll get right to the point. Are all of these people experiencing mass hysteria or did they really witness an angel smiting a building with a flaming sword?" She smirked as she finished her question.

"Child, the fact you would even consider asking such a question proves you have not accepted Jesus Christ as your personal Savior," Reverend Mays replied.

Jillian was rattled by his blunt answer and attempted to stare down the much taller man. *What! How dare he question my faith! I'm as religious as anyone here. I just don't believe in flaunting it like these people.* He looked back like one would at a baby.

Roberto yelled up to Jillian, "Dead air! Say something!"

The pastor's pregnant pause was only broken when hundreds of Catholics standing around them began reciting the Rosary. Mays bent over and spoke directly to Jillian, but her mike caught his every word. "Do you hear those people? They are much more than my brothers and sisters in Christ. They are soldiers in His army. And they are gathered in celebration because the Prince of Spiritual Warfare, Michael the Archangel, whose very name was the war cry of the angels that fought the devil in heaven before the creation of Adam, has joined their battle against the false morningstar and his fallen minions."

Morrow had a puzzled look on her face as she pulled the microphone back and asked, "Are you talking about waging war on abortion clinics?"

Mays' voice roared with emotion, "I am talking about God allowing His children to have the tiniest glimpse of one skirmish in a battle that began when proud Lucifer and his angelic co-conspirators led a rebellion against our Creator."

"But this is the second attack on an abortion clin . . . "

Mays did not let her complete her question. "Child, are you so naive? I am not talking about fighting a battle over bricks and mortar—I am talking about a war for people's souls. Whether you want to believe it or not, the devil is very real. And he is constantly plotting and scheming to steal your soul. The war between God's heavenly army and the legion of fallen angels didn't end with the book of Genesis. It goes on every day. Every time a husband cheats on his wife, an accountant cheats on taxes, a junkie takes drugs, or a politician sells out his constituents, the devil wins. I am talking about no less than a war where the victors earn salvation and the losers are sentenced to eternal damnation.

Morrow looked confused and flustered as she attempted to interrupt. "But did they see . . . "

Mays held his arms aloft with his palms facing skyward. "Child, look around. You are surrounded by thousands of people from every Christian denomination joining together in an ecumenical celebration to give praise and thanks to God. Look around and rejoice at Catholics standing shoulder-to-shoulder with their Presbyterian and Baptist brothers." He pointed towards a cluster praying together. "Behind you are Greek, Serbian, and Russian Orthodox praying with Methodists and Lutherans of every synod. Over there are Episcopalians praying with Calvinists, Evangelicals, and Messianic Jews. I can see believers of all of the Eastern Rite Churches including Armenians, Byzantines, Antiochenes, Chaldeans, and Coptic Alexandrians singing hymns of praise with Southern Baptists and Assemblies of God Pentecostals and dozens more that I haven't named.

"My brothers and sisters in Christ," Dr. Mays's voice boomed out to the crowd, "this young lady wants to know if you really saw an angel last night."

Several hundred voices roared their response in unison, "I saw him!"

"But why?" Morrow raised her voice to be heard over the witnesses who kept shouting, "I saw him!" "If they really saw him, why here?"

Dr. Mays held his arms up to hush the crowd before he answered, "Why here? Why not? Child, we can't begin to understand God's plan, so I hope you do not think me presumptuous if I dare answer your question. But I believe humankind is at a critical time on our road to salvation and our loving God has rewarded our faith by allowing us a tiny glimpse of His angel of destruction smiting an instrument of evil." He pantomimed swinging a sword through the air.

"We are fallen children of Adam and Eve, and our faith is weak. Our Father has given us this sign to recharge our spiritual batteries—to fill our souls with His amazing grace. He has given us this sign to remind us that we are never alone. He is always with us."

The crowd shouted *"Amen"* in unison.

"So you're saying they think they saw him," more than a hint of sarcasm had returned to her voice.

"Think they saw him!" Mays shook his head as he roared back, "They don't think they saw him. They know they saw him."

"Do you *think* you saw him too?" she asked.

"Yes, I saw him too! And if you ask me one-hundred times, I will answer one-hundred times, yes I saw God's heavenly warrior, clad in the armor of righteousness."

Scores in the crowd responded by yelling, "I saw him!"

Mays's voice rolled out over the crowd. "Yes, I saw him swinging the flaming sword of justice in his right hand."

An even larger number yelled, "I saw him!"

"Yes, I saw him brandishing a gleaming battle shield in his left—his name with *Quis ut Deus,* Who is like unto God, etched deep into it."

A roar of "I saw him," rolled through the crowd.

Again he swung an imaginary sword . . . chopping through the air as they had seen the angel do.

"Yes, I watched Archangel Michael destroying one of hell's earthly outposts. A hundred times a hundred times I will shout, Yes, I saw him!"

The roar of, "I saw him" was even more passionate.

"Yes, I witnessed the beginning of the fulfillment of Apostle Matthew's promise, 'The Son of Man will send out His angels, and they will weed out of His kingdom everything that causes sin and all who do evil. They will throw them into the fiery furnace, where there will be weeping and gnashing of teeth.'"

Quite a few people scattered throughout the crowd held up radios tuned in to the interview. Pastor Mays' huge voice echoed over the assembled masses, grabbing the crowd's attention and bringing an even louder chorus of, "I saw him!"

"A hundred times a hundred times a hundred times I will shout, 'Yes, I saw him!'" The response was deafening.

Reverend Mays waited for a moment, then gestured for silence by holding his index finger to his mouth and blowing *sssssshhhh* into the microphone. When he resumed, his voice was softer yet deeper and more reverent. And thanks to Radio New 710 every one could hear every word.

"God knows the flesh is weak. So He gave a sign to His children that He has heard their prayers." He paused for a moment. "He gave a sign to show His children they are not alone in the desert." He again paused. "He gave a sign to bring His children courage, to lift us above conflict, to infuse our spirits with strength, and brighten the dark times in which we now live."

A joyful shout of *"Amen!"* leapt from every throat.

"Yes, we were allowed a preview of the ultimate battle which is promised in the Book of Revelation." His voice seemed to escalate in emotion and size with each sentence.

"Amen!"

"Yes, we know the death grip of the devil will not cease until the final battle is fought, a battle where Archangel Michael and his celestial armies will defeat the dragon."

"Amen!"

"Yes, we were allowed a preview of the day when his razor-sharp sword will smite the great dragon—'That ancient serpent called the devil, or Satan, who leads the whole world astray.' He and all of his followers will be hurled for all eternity into the depths of hell." He flung his arm towards the ground.

"*Amen!*"

"I ask all of you, did you see Archangel Michael destroy this temple of death?"

Their roar of, "Yes!" reverberated off the buildings for several minutes, making the windows rattle.

When it finally died down, the choirs, with a dozen marching bands accompanying them, began singing, "Angels we have heard on high" with a warmth and sincerity that caused tears to form in almost every eye.

Isn't that a Christmas carol? The reporter thought.

As if reading her mind, Reverend Mays leaned over to Morrow and said, "The chorus *Gloria, in excelsis Deo!* is Latin for 'Glory to God in the highest.' These words were first sung by a multitude of the heavenly host on that miraculous night when the King of kings became man to save us from our sins."

CHAPTER 25

THREE TAXIS WERE idling at the stand in front of First Presbyterian Hospital when Granny Gates got there. She tried to get into the closest cab, a shiny yellow one, but the driver, a gruff-looking man whose face was hidden behind an untamed mass of black hair, grunted, "No" and pointed towards the first in the quay. He knew fights often broken out when a driver didn't wait his turn for a fare.

What in tarnation, Granny thought as she hobbled towards the ancient red vehicle at the head of the line. A light cloud of blue smoke hovered around the tail pipe. *I hope this crate runs better than it looks.*

The cab driver, a short, balding, middle-eastern man, with soft, chocolate brown eyes, hopped out and ran around to open the passenger side door. Granny noted he was dressed in a clean, button-down white shirt and a crisp pair of black slacks. Even his shoes were shined. *Well here goes nothing* she thought as she climbed in.

He turned around and beamed a smile that boasted three gold teeth. "Please to tell to me, to where is your destination at?"

"Skeedaddle," Granny responded.

"I do not know of this Skedaddle. You must tell to me to where it is if you wish for me to drive."

"C'mon, sonny, it's not a place. It's like 23 skidoo. Oh, never mind. Just get going. I'll tell you where to turn. Now go. Go!" Granny was nervous as she looked out the window at the hospital.

So far, so good, she thought as the cab eased away from the curb, *but this is the slowest dang getaway car I've ever ridden in.*

It had taken the century-old woman several long minutes to slide into the backseat of the cab while the driver struggled to fold up her walker.

"Is there secret button for me to compress into?"

"Just throw it in the trunk, Sonny. I'm in a bit of a hurry."

"Then it is done."

With that, Chicago Rocket cab #55 began driving eastbound in the heavy morning traffic. After they had covered a couple of blocks, Granny broke the silence, "Could you please pull this hack over, I'm a little discombobulated and I need to get my bearings."

"You use many words to which I am not known."

"Hussain?" Granny read the driver's photo ID card mounted on what was left of the bullet proof partition that used to protect him from robbers.

"You ain't from around here, are you?"

"No, Madame, but I am American citizen." The cab driver had long ago grown used to fares making jokes about his surname even though it was spelled different than the Iraqi dictator.

"Well good for you, skeeziks. Now you're one of the good guys. So let's figure out where in tarnation we are, and where I want to go. And don't call me Madame. Makes it sound like I run a bordello. The name's Granny."

"As you wish, but I must inform to you that my meter, she runs while you think."

"Now don't get all persnickety with me. I just need to remember what the angel told me last night. Yes, I do know where to go. Drive me to the Albany abortion mill."

"This too I do not know. Do you have address to give to me?"

"You have to talk louder, sonny. I turned my hearing aids as high as they go, but this clunker is so loud I can barely hear you."

"Please to be sorry to you so I speak again much louder. I do not know of where it is you speak. You must give to me address to drive to."

"I don't rightly know the address, but it's right by my house . . . over on Elston Avenue, a couple of blocks south of Irving. You do know where Irving Park and Elston are, don't you?"

"Of these I know. If this is to where you want to drive to, I will drive to straight away," the cabby responded.

"Yep, that's where I wanna go. And step on it. I'm in a bit of a hurry."

Without warning, or use of the turn signal, the cab launched from the curb and swerved between two cars. It was a credit to the second driver's quick reflexes and the Buick's ABS brakes that he was able to stop in time to avoid rear-ending them.

"Why don't you go back to where you came from you son-of-a . . . " The rest of the driver's sentence was drowned out when the car behind him laid on his horn. Unfazed, Hussain executed a U-turn into a short gap in the oncoming traffic. Several more cars had to slam on their brakes to avoid crashing into them. Horns were blowing everywhere.

Hussain ignored all the noise because he realized they were now going in the wrong direction. Since he never should have made the U turn, he continued driving in a circle and made an O turn. The Buick's driver stared in amazement as the cab completed its revolution and again cut in front of him. It then roared through a yellow light at the intersection.

Hussain turned and smiled. "We go to the right way now."

"That was some pretty fancy driving, Sonny, and, if you don't get us killed, I would like to stop at the bakery before we get to the mill. I always bring donuts for the girls," Granny said.

"Please to tell to me, where is this bakery?"

"There used to be a real good one right around here somewhere, but I can't remember where exactly. The last time I was in this neighborhood, they still had street cars. Green Hornets they called 'em. Cost a buffalo nickel. My, my, that was a long time ago and things have changed so much I don't recognize anything. It seems like they've torn down all the old buildings and built new ones . . . and they all look alike. Why don't you just stop at the first bakery we pass."

"As you wish. I do know most excellent Middle Eastern bakery. You make your friends most happy with special treats. We drive to there, no?"

"Special treats 'eh? That sounds like a plan."

"A plan? This too I do not know."

"Sonny, you may think you know English, but you sure don't know how to talk it. A plan means you had a good idea, and I agreed with you. So let's go see what kind of goodies they have at this bakery."

"OK, a plan. I know now. I will take you to it straight away."

"By the way," Granny asked, "has there been anything interesting on the radio this morning?"

He turned around again and shrugged. "There is much I do not understand."

"What about the riot? Was there anything about the riot yesterday?"

"Yes, I hear much of this. It is very much bad. But, it is where you live, no?"

He cranked his neck and shot her a quizzical look.

"Yep. Darn near in my own backyard."

"Then you are most fortunate to not to be in your backyard."

"Not there! Are you kidding?" Granny leaned forward. "Not only was I there, I started it. Got myself arrested too. Handcuffs and all." She held her right arm out to show the red mark the restraint had left.

Hussain kept weaving through traffic as he examined her wrist.

"You!" he responded in amazement. "This is not right, no?"

"I'll tell you something else that'll curl your mustache. My grandson is the mayor."

He driver cocked his head, "Now you make fun with me."

"Don't you watch TV? I'm Granny. Granny Gates. My mug's been on the news and the front page of every newspaper in this city."

"Mug?"

"My face, Sonny. Your face is your mug. My face is my mug."

Without slowing down, the driver reached over and picked through a pile of newspapers on the passenger seat. He pulled one out, unfolded the front page of yesterday's late edition across the steering wheel, and pointed to the headline "ARREST OF MAYOR'S GRANNY SPARKS RIOT."

"You?" he was skeptical.

"There. See, that's me." Granny pointed towards her photograph below the bold print. "They took that one at my one-hundredth birthday party."

"This is most strange. In my country old women stay home and are most revered."

"Sonny, this is Chicago—and watch who you're calling old—we do things our own way here. Our cops are topnotch, but if you're moping around and they tell you to beat it, you better do it. But dang if I know what I did. I've gotta ask Sidney. He'll know.

"Mind you, I'm not proud I got arrested, but I gotta admit that headline sure is a hoot. Did you know a reporter told me I was the oldest person ever arrested in the entire United States? Ever. I just thank the Lord God Almighty that nobody got killed on account of me."

"It is much like old country. Police make very much people go away. In my family, my brother, he . . . " his voice trembled with emotion as it trailed off, " . . . police take from house. We know nothing of him." He took out a tissue and dried his eyes.

"I'm sorry to hear that. Maybe I could ask my grandson to help. He's always hanging out with big whigs."

"You are much too kind." Hussain was interrupted by a staticy voice over the cab's radio.

"Drivers are advised to expect significant traffic delays on the northwest side of the city due to an unscheduled parade. The affected area stretches from the Chicago River west to the Kennedy Expressway and from Belmont Avenue north to Lawrence. No further information is available at this time."

"That sounds like one heck of a parade," Granny ventured.

"Other drivers say on radio they drive very much people to this place today."

"I wonder what kind of a parade it is. You know the Mexicans have some kind of a parade for their independence day, but that's back in May. What a sight to see, all day long hundreds of people driving up and down all the neighborhood streets with big Mexican flags on their cars. They play their radios so loud my windows shake.

"It's a shame all the other parades are downtown now. I used to go to every single one of them, riding up front in a convertible with my grandson—he's the mayor you know—but now he keeps telling me that I'm too old and frail. If it was up to him, I would never leave the house, not even to see my friends."

"Please forgive to interrupt you, Granny. I have taken now you to very much good bakery."

"Leon," Jackie called out. His attention was so glued to the TV he didn't realized his nephew was no longer in the living room. "Leon, would you please bring me my cup of coffee?"

A couple of minutes later he called out again, "Leon! Did you forget something?"

"I'm sorry, Reverend Jefferson," Mrs. White said as she entered the room. The middleaged black woman was almost as wide as she was tall and wore an immaculate apron over her paisley dress.

"The other cup was cold, so I poured you a fresh one." She handed him the steaming cup and added with a smile. "Sometimes that young man gets his mind so set on something I think he would forget his head if it weren't screwed on."

"What is he doing?"

"I'm sorry, Reverend, but I don't rightly know. He asked me to fix him a bag lunch so I assumed he was going somewhere with you."

The shiny new gunmetal gray Mercedes looked out of place surrounded by a sea of aged Chevys, Fords, and Toyotas, most of which suffered from either rust or a collision. Many from both. The graduation present had cost the driver's parents almost as much as a small house in the working class neighborhood.

Theodore Rolland Deaver II was losing patience. "OK, this ridiculous. We've been stuck in traffic for over an hour. By the time we get there, everyone will have left. We should turn around and hang out at North Avenue Beach."

"Would you shut up and drive," the young woman in the backseat moaned.

"That's easy for you to say. It's not your gas we're burning sitting here," he strummed his fingers on the leather-wrapped, burled walnut steering wheel. "And where exactly am I supposed to drive to? That car in front of me isn't moving . . . nor is the car in front of him . . . or the car in front of him . . . or . . . "

"Both of you shut up," the unkempt looking girl sitting in the shotgun seat barked. "I've had it with the two of you fighting."

The three youths were an unlikely group. The two young women were high school dropouts who imagined themselves radical feminists. Born into affluent North Shore families, both had renounced their parent's wealth and upper class lifestyles as oppressive of the working class.

They met while working at minimum-wage jobs—even revolutionaries need a few bucks in their pockets—and were attracted by the other's scruffy, non-conforming looks. Both had numerous body piercings and there were at least two tattoos visible on each.

Theodore the second, T2 to his parents, was the brother of the backseat rider. His neat haircut, shaved face, and clean clothing stood in stark contrast to his passengers.

Caroline, his younger sister, no longer looked like her father's princess. Her baggy blue jeans and hooded sweatshirt were faded, ripped, and covered with feminist slogans. She wore no makeup and her neon pink hair was a wild mess. And there was an odor that suggested she had not bathed for a while. Her friend Lee looked, dressed, and smelled no better. The only real difference was her cropped hair was glow–in–the–dark green.

Caroline talked T2 into driving in from Evanston with the promise of meeting dozens of liberated pro-choice girls at their counter protest. He assumed liberated meant promiscuous. So far the only female he had met was the masculine-looking anarchist sitting next to him—and she was not in a good mood.

"The Women's Clinic can't be that far," Lee said. Find somewhere to unload our signs and we'll walk it."

"Yeah, whatever."

It took another fifteen minutes for traffic to move far enough for him to turn onto a side street. They drove about fifty feet before slamming to a halt. He was tempted to lay on his horn, but realized, *That's strange. I haven't heard a single car honk.*

Not sure what to do, he opened his door and stood up to survey the scene. A school bus was blocking the intersection ahead. He could see a steady stream of well-dressed people getting out of the coach. At least two more buses were lined up behind it waiting to unload.

"This looks like the end of the line," he announced. "You take off and I'll catch up later," the young man said, hoping to get rid of the surly girl.

"Fine," Lee replied. "Pop the trunk, so we can get my signs out. Now! There's gotta be like a hundred Bible thumpers on this street, and I want those anti-choice bigots to see them." Their self-appointed leader raged as she made a crude gesture and shouted obscenities at a group in royal blue and gold choir robes walking by in silence. Upset at being ignored, she began chanting, "Not the church, not the state. Women will decide their fate." The choir director responded by leading his group in our Lord's Prayer.

Soon the procession of the faithful making its way down Irving Park Road was joined by the two pro-aborts. Caroline carried a homemade sign that read KEEP YOUR ROSARIES OFF OUR OVARIES while Lee banged on a drum. In unison they began to chant, "Not the church . . . "

Before they could finish, they were drowned out as every voice around them was raised in prayer. "Hail Mary, full of grace . . . "

CHAPTER 26

THREE THINGS HAPPENED the moment the clock in Fred's dashboard flashed 9:00. His cell phone rang, the choirs began singing "Joyful, joyful we adore Thee," and a police officer shouted at him, "We're rolling in one minute."

He shouted back, "Yes, sir," then pressed the green button on his phone and answered, "McBarker."

"Where are you!" O'Dea's voice was so loud Fred almost dropped the phone. "Did you forget about your press conference?" His supervisor fumed. "And shut that radio off."

"No. Rey, I called you three . . . " he started to say as he rolled the window up.

"No! Who do you think you're talking to?" O'Dea demanded.

"Rey, I mean no, I didn't forget the . . . " A stream of obscenities drowned out the rest of his response.

"Rey, I called you . . . " Fred tried to interrupt.

"Thanks to you I looked like a fool. I had to reschedule"—he made no attempt to hide his rage as he drew out the word "your"—"press conference. That's the thanks I get for sharing the spotlight with you."

"Rey, I've been calling you since before sunrise . . ."

"I don't want your excuses. I gave you an order, and I expected it . . . " The rest of his sentence was drowned out when the Chevy Suburban Command Unit parked next to Fred cranked up its 120 decibel siren.

Even with the windows closed, he couldn't make out another word. "Rey, I can't hear you. We're getting ready to move," he shouted into the phone. "I'll call you as soon as I can."

An hour-or-so earlier Mayor Gates had grown impatient and demanded Commander Washington, "Stop pussyfooting around and do something," so he could get back to City Hall.

"What about that?" Gates pointed at the police helicopter hovering overhead, "Can't he get me out?"

Washington knew Gates was terrified of flying in helicopters and must be getting pretty desperate to even consider it.

"Sid, let me have him make another sweep to see if anything opened up."

A couple of minutes later the pilot radioed back, "Sir, I reconnoitered the entire perimeter and everything around you is impassable. There are double- and triple-parked cars and buses blocking every street. I can see a couple of Streets and San tow trucks hooking cars but it'll take them all day to clear a path."

"Then Mayor Gates wants you to fly him out." Washington said.

"It's a no go on a landing, Commander. There are so many power and telephone lines I couldn't land if I had to," the pilot said.

"Then which end has smaller crowds?" Washington asked.

"It's hard to say. I'm over the south end right now and it's packed solid. The crowd spilled over onto Addison and is blocking it about three blocks in both directions. Beyond that I can see better than a dozen buses and at least fifty abandoned cars. Maybe more. I'd have to guess there's 15,000, maybe 20,000 people down there. And there's hundreds more walking towards it."

"Twenty thousand! Unbelievable. How about the north end?" Washington asked while shaking his head. "Any better?"

"Give me a second . . . I'm almost there. Sorry, Commander, that's a negative. It looks like the crowd is as least as large and they're packed shoulder-to-shoulder. Northbound Elston is a parking lot as far as I can see. Eastbound Irving is solid all the way to Kedzie. There must be twenty buses blocking everything."

"How's westbound look?" Washington asked.

"A little better." The pilot replied. "It looks like an accident blocked both lanes shy of the stop n' go light. There's a lot of people on foot but almost no abandoned vehicles. If you could get through the crowd on Elston, you would have an open road in about a block and a half."

"Any ideas on where we could herd the people to?" Washington asked.

Another voice broke in on the radio. It had a hint of an Irish brogue. "Commander, this is McMichaels. I'm standing on the roof of a church bus at the north end. I've worked crowd control at every big event in this city, but I've never seen people packed so tight. And it's almost eerie how polite everyone is. I haven't seen a single scuffle. I'm sure they would cooperate if you gave them somewhere to go—somewhere closer to the destroyed abortion mill. That's what they're all here to see. If you moved the barricades forward a couple of blocks we could spread them out enough to clear a lane."

"Why don't these people just go home?" Washington wondered aloud. There's nothing to see but a vacant lot full of broken concrete."

By the time Rocket cab #55 left the Garden of Eden Bakery, the cabbie and his fare had bonded.

"Please Granny, we are now much good friends. You call me Moiz," the cab driver displayed his collection of gold teeth when he smiled.

Granny giggled as powdered sugar fell onto her dark blue dress. *Once a klutz, always a klutz.* She opened her large leather purse and took out a handmade lace hankie and dabbed up the particles.

"OK, Moiz, one more time. What are the half moon ones with nuts called?" The elderly woman took another bite of her cookie. "They're mighty tasty."

"*Kleichat joz.* The sweet discs are *khfefiyyat* and the ones with dates are *kleichat tamur.* Do not set yourself to worry. I will write down for you all of the names," Moiz responded with another smile.

The cab driver had tried talking Granny into going inside to see the selection, but she begged off, "My dogs are barking so I'll wait here if you don't mind. Grab me a dozen of whatever looks good."

Moiz looked perplexed. "I do not hear no dogs barking. You talk Chicago to me, no?"

Granny slapped her knee and laughed, "You're a mighty quick learner." The moment he left, she took a compact out of her purse and freshened her make-up. *I've got to make myself look presentable.*

Moiz returned a few minutes later with two white cardboard boxes. He knelt down beside the door, opened the smaller box, and offered it to her. "I do not know if you ate before you leave from the hospital. Please enjoy."

"Why, thank you," she stammered. "I was getting a bit hungry."

He placed the larger box in the front seat. "I have bought much special treats for friends of my friend." He smiled and closed the door.

"Wait I forgot to pay you." She rummaged around the large purse for her wallet.

"No. It is my present to you."

"Moiz, thank you so much. You must think I'm a dumb Dora, but I've got so much on my mind. I've never been on the lam from a hospital before. And I hope I don't get you in any trouble."

"Do not apologize, my new friend. Everything is, as you teach for me to say, copasetic."

Granny settled back in the seat. "Moiz, you're a godsend."

A minute later they were on their way. The closer they got to the Irving Park Women's Clinic, the heavier traffic became. Hussain alternated between talking to Granny, questioning other drivers on the radio in Arabic, and laying on the horn. He aggressively swerved in-and-out of traffic, yet with an effortless grace, and did not hesitate to cross the double yellow line to cruise past a line of cars stopped for a red light.

"Very much roads ahead are closed. I talk to others to learn how we must drive." With that, he made a sharp turn into a restaurant's parking lot and proclaimed, "This cut is very short, no?"

Granny had no idea where they were going, but she was enjoying the ride, "Sure feels like a shortcut to me, Moiz," she replied as the car bounced over a concrete bumper before turning into the alley. If the cab had a functioning muffler they would have been able to hear the choirs boom out the opening lines of the "Hymn to Joy"—"Joyful, joyful, we adore Thee . . ." as they got closer to the former abortuary.

Three blocks later, the cab cut across a weed-filled vacant lot and made a hard left turn—the wrong way on a one-way street. The moment Moiz noticed a brown parcel van coming straight for them, he swerved onto the sidewalk—Granny was amazed no one was walking on this side of the street—and drove slowly for a couple of minutes before turning into another alley. This one was paved in bricks. The car trembled as it cruised along its uneven surface. Rocket cab again lived up to its name as they picked up speed down the alley.

"Don't they have shock absorbers in Iraq?" Granny asked after the car bottomed out in a large pothole.

He turned to face her. "Ha-ha, you make joke on me. We must drive fast before the alley fills with very much people." He honked the horn with his left hand to warn all of their approach.

At the end of the block, the cab made a violent turn into an unpaved parking lot. Gravel sprayed out of the back wheels of the cab as the rear end fishtailed. Hussain dropped his cell phone as he struggled to regain control. "Not to worry. We are very much close."

A moment later the car rejoined the asphalt, its wheels screeching as they made a tight left turn onto a narrow side street. They snaked around a couple of illegally parked cars and picked up speed until an abandoned van blocked their way. The cabby jumped the curb and clipped a fire hydrant. The sidewalk ahead, however, was filled with a choir in magenta robes marching two abreast.

"Not to worry," he smashed the brake pedal to the floor. The brakes were still screaming when he turned onto a neatly manicured front lawn. He continued driving on grass until they reached the next side street. The taxi slammed down hard when they drove off a high curb, the tires spinning on the pavement as he accelerated while turning. "Not very much more," he announced as they pulled into an alley thick with people. He hit the brakes hard and the cab backfired twice causing most to turn around to see what was making the loud noise. Without a word spoken, the crowd parted and allowed the distraction to pass. Granny smiled at the people as they crept by. All smiled back. As they neared the end of the block Moiz rolled the windows down and said, "Listen."

Granny leaned out the window and strained to hear over the low rumble of the cab's exhaust, "I know that song . . . It's 'Onward Christian Soldiers.'" Granny's eyes lit up.

"Very much soon you will join your friends to sing very much songs."

"Thanks to the swell way you handle this jalopy."

"Is jalopy good?"

"Moiz, it's the bee's knees."

"Then good. We are here, Granny," Moiz turned into a narrow gangway between two garages and brought the taxi to a stop in the well-tended backyard of a small apartment building. Several men and women turned and stared at the vehicle.

"They don't look happy to see us." Granny said. "You sure they're friends of yours?"

"They are so very much more than friends. They are our Orthodox Armenian Christian brothers and sisters from Kurdistan in northern Iraq. Listen, they are praying the Lord's Prayer in Aramaic, the language spoken by Jesus Christ."

"Well I'll be."

Moiz hopped out and hurried around to open the cab's back door while a white-haired man dressed all in black held a wheelchair for her to get into.

"What's this for? I can walk," Granny protested.

"Please, my new friend. You hire me for a ride all the way. It is still very much to walk for you, so we will finish your ride." Moiz smiled warmly as his pastor took Granny's hand and helped her into the chair.

"Welcome to my humble home, Mrs. Granny Gates. You are my honored guest." He rolled the chair to the stone patio where the prayer group continued praying. "Parts of the Bible were written in Aramaic, one of the oldest languages in the world, including the books of Ezra and Daniel. Jesus spoke His last words on the cross in our language, His native tongue, E-LEE E-LEE L-MAA-NAA-SAA-BAACH-TAA-NEE, My God, my God, why have You forsaken Me."

"We speak the language of the Son of God!" He beamed with pride."

Dr. Muhammad Ali Hammudiluh was amazed. He had been nervous he would be recognized and hoped to blend in by wearing typical middle class American clothes; blue jeans, a polo shirt, and athletic shoes. He joined an eclectic looking group walking from the west but was singled before they walked a block.

A steady stream of people sought him out to shake his hand, pray with him, and offer words of encouragement. More than a few threw their arms around their new brother and embraced him. They saw the presence of the Holy Spirit in their new brother.

"Thank you. Thank you. I promise I will never go back there," he stammered, tears streaming down his cheeks, as he gestured up the street towards the former clinic. "And thank you, Jesus, for giving me the greatest day of my life. Thank you for saving me," he shouted. "Thank you, Jesus Christ, for opening my eyes and showing me the truth. Thank you for being my Savior. Thank you for dying on the cross for my sins," he proclaimed with the zeal of a new convert.

He picked a spot on the sidewalk at the entrance to Independence Park and gave testimony to all who passed. A small group formed and invited him to read the Bible with them. He peppered them with questions, trying to learn as much as possible about his Savior. He heard the Gospel and eagerly received the message of Christ's death and resurrection. The former abortionist prostrated himself on the ground and repented for his sins.

"Son," a man knelt and placed his hand on the Hammudiluh's shoulder. "I'm Pastor Robertson. I heard you make a profession of faith in our Lord Jesus Christ and ask His forgiveness."

Hammudiluh looked up at the man in black. The pastor's steel blue eyes locked with his. "You still have much to learn, but today, you have taken your first steps. In Romans 10:9-10 we learned, 'That if thou shalt confess with thy mouth the Lord Jesus, and shalt believe in thine heart that God hath raised him from the dead, thou shalt be saved. For with the heart man believeth unto righteousness; and with the mouth confession is made unto salvation.'"

Robertson helped him to his feet.

"I ask you now in front of God and these witnesses, do you believe and publicly confess with your mouth that Jesus is Lord and believe in your heart God raised Him from the dead?"

"I believe and I confess Jesus is Lord!" he shouted. "I know God raised Him from the dead!"

"Brother, baptism symbolizes death to sin, and rising to a new life in Jesus. I see no reason why you should not be baptized."

Hammudiluh leapt for joy, "Yes! I want to be baptized. Is your church nearby?"

"Brother, all of creation is His church." Pastor Robertson replied, "John the Baptist baptized Jesus in the River Jordan. Philip baptized the Ethiopian eunuch on the side of the road from Jerusalem to Gaza" He pointed to the children's wading pool in the park. "Look, there is water."

Pastor Robertson led the group, which had swelled to more than a hundred, and stood with Hammudiluh in the shallow water. "In Matthew, Jesus Christ commanded us 'Go ye therefore, and teach all nations, baptizing them in the name of the Father, and of the Son, and of the Holy Ghost: teaching them to observe all things whatsoever I have commanded you: and, lo, I am with you always, even unto the end of the world. Amen.'"

A chorus of *amens* welcomed Chicago's newest Christian.

Even though it wasn't yet lunchtime a lot of northsiders had radios on at work to plan their drive home. Most were tuned to Radio News 710 because they had traffic and weather six times an hour on the sevens." Offices across Chicago ground to a halt as the curious gathered to listen.

"Let's go live to Robert Packard in Radio News 710's traffic copter and see if he can answer the question all of Chicago is asking. Robert, is there any relief in sight?"

"Lloyd, I hate to be the bearer of bad news but the massive traffic jam appears to be growing. Police have established roadblocks at Pulaski to the west and California to the east. All non-emergency traffic is being detoured onto these streets. Elston is shut down at Montrose to the north and Belmont to the south but backups start miles before you get that close.

And don't even think of taking a side street to get around the detours. Most are impassable because of illegally parked cars and buses.

"Closing this many major streets has had a ripple effect as far north as Touhy and as far west as Austin Avenue. If you don't absolutely have to drive somewhere on the northwest side, stay at home or take public transportation. Metra reports trains on the Union Pacific North West line are running full but on schedule. CTA reports ridership is way up on the blue line and additional trains have been added. Expect delays due to the extra time needed to board the large crowds. All buses in what the police are calling 'the exclusionary zone' have been re-routed."

"Robert, does anything appear to be happening at the scene of the collapse?"

"The police department has requested rather strongly that we do not fly over there, but, from where we're hovering, I can see a number of cars—as many as ten—have lined up behind several squad cars with their blue lights on."

"Are they going to try to drive through the crowd?"

He chuckled, "Nothing would surprise me today."

"Thanks for the update, Robert. We'll jump right back to you if the procession starts moving. Until then, let's return to Jillian Morrow on the ground and see if she can shed any light on this convoy."

"Lloyd, I'm about a half-mile from there. But even this far away the crowd is so thick on the street I can't imagine how they could get through."

"Jillian, what is the mood of the crowd?"

Even though she was convinced everything going on was part of an elaborate hoax, and was still smarting from losing control of her earlier interview, Jillian shifted to her buoyant reporter mode. "It's incredible Lloyd—a cross between going to church on Christmas morning, a family reunion, and a block party. I have never seen Chicagoans so polite, so well behaved, and so religious. In fact, I'm watching a man being baptized in a park wading pool. This is . . . " A roar of *amens* drowned out the rest of her sentence.

When it died down she shifted gears, "Well the crowd certainly seems happy with the baptism. Let me see if I can get the newly-baptized man to say a few words. Sir? Sir! Yes you." She pointed at the dripping man. "Could I ask you a question on the air?"

It took almost an hour of hard driving, but the Haynes and Clemsons were getting close.

Billy Haynes switched off the radio. "So what do you think? It sounds like traffic is so backed up we couldn't badge our way through if we had to," he referred to the routine practice of flashing a city-issued Department of Buildings badge and ID card to be allowed through a police line.

"I think we should find a parking place and walk from here," Philo said from the backseat.

"We're at least two miles away. Shouldn't I try getting a little closer?"

"C'mon, Billy. We can walk faster than traffic is moving. Turn down the next side street and find a parking space."

"What do you think, Honey?" he asked his wife.

"Don't worry, Dear. It's a beautiful day for a walk," Mauves responded, adding, "After all, this is the day which the Lord has made."

"Let us be glad and rejoice in it," the Clemsons answered in unison.

"I guess I'm overruled." The moment they turned onto the residential street, Mauves shouted, "Look. There's a car pulling out. Now tell me God didn't have that one planned."

A couple of minutes later they joined a steady stream of Christians walking east along Irving Park Road. Mauves scanned the crowd. "Do you think they're all going where we're going?"

Her husband Billy nodded. "Judging by the way they're smiling, they are."

"Do you think we'll be able to find Pastor Robertson and the choir?" Margaret Clemson wondered aloud.

"How hard could it be to find seventy people wearing white choir robes?"

"If the crowd is half as big as they're saying on the radio . . . " Margaret cupped her hand to her ear. "Listen, I hear singing."

"That's a lot of voices raised in praise," Mauves said before joining them in song.

A couple of blocks later, Philo pointed to a cluster of people in bright red choir robes and said, "Look, over there. Isn't that Pastor Mays?"

"Who's Pastor Mays?" Mauves asked.

"Oh, you know him," Margaret answered. "He's the pastor at my parent's church. You met him when mom and dad renewed their wedding vows on their fiftieth wedding anniversary."

"Oh, I remember. You said he could set the devil to flight faster than anyone you ever heard."

"And that was at a wedding . . . You should hear him when he's really preaching."

Mauves giggled. "Maybe he can help us find Pastor Robertson."

The Hansen sisters were enjoying every moment of the day's festivities. They had moved back from the frontline and were sitting on folding chairs in front of the corner donut store praying, singing, and visiting with well wishers. The owner was giving away free coffee and donuts, and, though the task seemed as impossible as feeding the multitude with five loaves and two fishes, a steady stream of smiling people were walking out with a bag of donuts and a piping hot cup of coffee.

The sisters could not get over how many strangers came up and said watching them interviewed on TV gave them the courage to admit what they had seen in their dreams.

"I thought everyone would think that either I was crazy, drunk, or had something to do with the explosion," was a frequent comment.

"Well, there's still a lot of abortion mills out there. So now that you know the truth about what takes place in these so-called women's clinics, I hope you'll get involved in witnessing for life," Kaye said. "Every mill has a group that meets on a regular basis, praying to end the slaughter."

"Have you considered sidewalk counseling?" Ruth added. "There's not a lot you can do in this life that is more rewarding than being a tool for the Holy Spirit to use to help a mother-to-be choose life for her baby."

Kaye folded her hands. "Amen to that, Sister."

Pam Romenelli pounded on the paddy wagon's doors until her knuckles bled. The metal was so thick each strike sounded like a muffled *thump*. "Help!" she shouted as loud as she could. "Phil needs a doctor."

With neither windows nor air conditioning, the temperature had soared to well over one-hundred degrees in the back of the squad roll. Phil was stretched out on the metal bench, his shirt drenched with sweat. It had been over fifteen minutes since he laid down, " . . . Just for a moment until this dizzy spell passes," and she was having trouble waking him.

He has all the signs of heat exhaustion, Pam thought back to the first aid class she had taken in college. *His forehead is burning up and he's pale and dizzy. Nausea! Oh please God, don't let him vomit.*

"Don't worry, I'll get help," she assured him as she resumed pounding with her shoe. *I wish I had worn heels instead of jogging shoes. Someone would surely hear me pounding with them.* "Help, we need a doctor!" she screamed again and again.

Pam had no idea Tony's video of her shouting, "This is Pam Romenelli, Channel One news, reporting live from the latest incident of police brutality," while being dragged away kicking and screaming, had become the network's promo for their coverage of the event.

Or that the clip of her standing up to the heavily armed SWAT team, demanding, "Which of you is brave enough to shred the First Amendment," was being shown on television stations across the globe. She also didn't know the station's lawyers were threatening to sue every bureaucrat and police official in Chicago for violating her First Amendment rights live, in front of millions of viewers.

What she did know was that Phil was getting sicker by the minute.

Father in heaven. I really need your help. This poor man is sick, maybe dying, because he helped me. I feel so helpless. It doesn't matter if they leave me in here alone . . . I'll be OK because I know You are always with me. But Father, I'm begging you to rescue Phil and bring him proper medical attention. He's a good man and deserves better than to die in the back of a truck because of me. I ask these things in your name. Our Father, who art in heaven.

Her prayer was interrupted by the dull thud of the door being unlocked, followed by a gush of cool air as it swung open. The police officer froze for a second. He stared at Pam. She squinted into the bright light, raised her limp arm, and pointed at Phil. The officer's eyes grew wide and he shouted, "Get an ambulance! The old guy doesn't look too good."

Thank you, Father.

Mrs. White sat on a kitchen chair staring at the floor. She wrung a dishtowel in her hands as her head swayed from side-to-side. "I'm so sorry, Reverend Jefferson. I would have stopped him, but I thought he was going somewhere with you. That young man never goes anywhere alone."

Jackie knelt on one knee in front of his housekeeper. "Did Leon say anything else?"

"No, sir. He asked me to make him a bag lunch, so I made him a ham on rye bread."

"Did he have any money with him?"

"I don't rightly know, Reverend." She choked the towel tighter. "Oh, this is all my fault. If anything happens to him . . . " her voice trailed off.

Jackie stood and placed his hand on her shoulder. "Not to worry, Mrs. White. We will find him. Have Samuel bring the car around, I have an idea where he might be headed."

"Praise the Lord."

It had been at least half an hour since Leon had gone missing, and Jackie was certain his nephew was trying to hear Reverend Mays in person. Today started as badly as the previous one had ended, and the last thing he wanted was to be recognized by the media. So Jackie dressed very conservatively—black slacks, a plain white shirt, deck shoes, and one of Leon's baseball caps from the hat rack in the foyer. He tucked a pair of sunglasses in his shirt pocket.

"Samuel, drive north on Clark Street and see if we can locate Leon."

Jackie violated his number one rule and drove with the Cadillac limousine's deep tinted windows rolled down. He was hoping Leon would see him.

"Samuel, you grew up in the city. How would a young man of limited means transport himself to the 3800 block of north Elston Avenue?"

"Aw, that's easy," his chauffeur replied. "He'd take the bus," the driver snickered.

Jackie held his tongue at the flip reply.

Two years ago his sister cajoled him into hiring her unemployed husband because he, "could never catch a break." Instead of being grateful, Samuel never stopped pushing the limits of family ties. *The day is nigh at hand when we settle the score and all of Caroline's tears will not save your position.* Jackie thought.

"Thank you for stating the obvious, Samuel. Do you know which Chicago Transit Authority bus route he might take to get there?"

"I guess he could walk a couple of blocks over and catch a #22 Clark Street bus and take it all the way north to Irving Park. Then he would transfer, I don't know the number of that one, and go west until he got to Elston. There's no Elston bus so he would have to walk the rest of the way." He paused and reflected for a moment. "Unless he took the Addison bus. It's kinda in the middle."

"Has Leon ever ridden public transportation?" Jackie asked.

"Yeah, last year you gave us tickets to a Cubs game. We took the bus there."

"Did you ride the Irving Park bus or the Addison bus?"

"We took the Irving bus there because I wanted to show him Graceland Cemetery. They have some real neat tombstones there including a huge statue of death, holding his cape up," Samuel held his arm sideways across his face imitating the statue. "But we took Addison home."

Jackie sighed in frustration. *Calm down Jackie. He couldn't have gone far.*

"You know, I already drove Clark Street a couple of times and all around the neighborhood and didn't see him. So he musta got on a bus."

"Then it is time to turn west."

Before leaving, Jackie instructed Mrs. White to call the CTA and inquire if Leon was a passenger on one of their buses. "Tell them he is a gifted young man who is not used to traveling on his own. He might not have known where to get off and could be sitting in a northbound Clark Street bus at the end of the line. And be very discrete . . . do not use my name. The last thing I want is for the press to find out about this."

"Yes, sir, Reverend. And I'm so sorry." She started crying. "If anything happens . . . "

While he scanned the sidewalks, Jackie called several friends and enlisted their assistance in looking for the young man. "I have reason to believe he is at the impromptu gospel fest on the city's northwest side. If you could discretely mingle with the crowd and look for Leon I would be most grateful."

Next he called his attorneys. "Gentlemen, I need your help and I trust you will not fail me again. You are familiar with my nephew Leon's unique situation. Approximately one half-hour ago he wandered from home unescorted. I have reason to believe he may either be en route—most likely on a CTA bus—or already arrived at the gospel fest. Please make discrete inquires of your contacts in the police department to learn if anyone has 'found' a lost young man. Again, I can't stress enough, your discretion in this matter is imperative."

That had been almost an hour ago, and Jefferson's limousine was hopelessly stuck in traffic about one mile east of the former women's center. It had been more than ten minutes since they moved at all.

Jackie put the baseball cap and glasses on. "Samuel, I will walk from here. You stay with the car . . . Leon might recognize it. Call me immediately if you see him."

"Yes, sir." He feigned a salute.

Jackie squeezed between two illegally parked cars and joined the steady flow of people walking westward. Three blocks later, he came across a CTA bus, its path blocked by dozens of abandoned vehicles. The door was open and the driver, a man with a beer belly so large it strained his shirt's buttons, was slouched in his seat with his hat pulled down over his eyes.

"Excuse me, sir," Jackie said as he walked up the steps. "Could you please help me?"

"Huh? What do you want?" The driver was not happy to be awakened from his catnap. "Can't you read the sign? This bus is out of service."

"Yes, sir, I did read it. And I am very sorry to have bothered you, but my nephew is missing, and I was hoping he might have been a passenger on your bus."

"Missing kid, huh. Not surprising—just look at this crowd. What's he look like?"

"Sadly, he is no longer a child. He is physically a twenty-two-year-old man, but his mental facilities are those of a ten-year-old boy. If you met him, you would surely remember him—He is always smiling and his gregarious personality overcomes his many special challenges."

"Gregarious? Nah, there weren't nobody like that on my bus. But let me make a call and see if anybody's seen him," the driver picked up the bus' two-way radio. "This is run F625. I'm looking for a lost young man. He's twenty-two years, African-American. What's he wearing?" He held the mike towards Jackie.

He leaned in and answered. "A light blue sweater and dark blue pants."

The driver continued, "He was either riding a Clark northbound, an Addison westbound, or maybe an Irving westbound about an hour ago."

A raspy woman's voice came over the speaker. "You mean Leon?"

"My nephew!" Jackie shouted, "Leon is my nephew!"

The first driver asked, "Is he still with you?"

"Not any more. But I remember him. He sat up front in the handicapped seats and asked a hundred and one questions about my bus. I let him honk the horn before he got off."

"Where are you located?"

"I'm stuck about three blocks west of you."

"Did he say where he was going?" Jackie shouted.

"Are you Unky Jackie?"

"Yes, Ma'am, I am he."

"Then he said to tell you he was going to hear the preacher man who was talking about the angel. Does that mean something to you?"

"Thank you, kind lady. It means everything to me."

It had taken a while, but April Packard was within a couple of blocks of the C of W clinic. The crowd was now so thick she had trouble moving forward. April scanned the faces around her. They looked peaceful enough.

But she was more then a little frightened to be surrounded by so many anti-choice zealots. *What if they find out who I am?* she wondered. *What if one of them is the bomber?*

Still, the haunting refrain, "How great Thou art!" echoed in her head, flooding it with memories—some happy, some sad. She closed her eyes and tried to shut out everything and focus on memories of her mother . . . her smile, how she did her hair, the perfume she used to wear. *What was that fragrance called? I remember the blue glass bottle sitting on her dresser . . . An Evening in Paris, that's the name. Oh Mom, I miss you so much. You always knew what to say when I was feeling down. It used to drive me nuts the way you could read my mind.* She began crying.

What would you think about my job? You always loved babies. I've got to get out of here . . . find someplace to get my head on straight.

She opened her eyes and saw a blonde-haired young girl dressed in a bright sun dress staring at her. "Why are you sad?" she asked.

The child's mother offered April a tissue and said, "That song always makes me cry too. It was my mother's favorite and her last request was that we sing it twice at her funeral."

April took the tissue and began sobbing uncontrollably. The stranger tried to comfort her, "There, there. You're among friends here."

Would this woman still call me a friend if she knew who I am?

Few noticed the irony of storm clouds gathering to the east as the choirs ended the first verse, "Fill us with the light of day!"

CHAPTER 27

AT GATE'S INSISTENCE Washington assembled his mounted officers to lead the convoy. "I always liked cavalry charges in the movies," Gates smirked. "And, besides, I remember you telling the City Council one cop on horseback can move a crowd better than ten on foot. Or does that only apply when we're reviewing increases in your budget?"

Five minutes later, six police horses were in place followed by two rows of squad cars lined up side by side. Gates' stretch limousine came next, then two more squad cars. Everyone else fell in line behind them. The only problem was the parade was so long the last few cars would have to line up outside the new south barricade.

The plan was to use the horses to intimidate the crowd—Washington had responded to Gates' taunt by saying, "Yes, people tend to get out of the way pretty fast when they come face-to-face with a thousand-pound horse." On Washington's signal, firemen would slide open the barricades, allowing the crowd to move two blocks closer to the former women's center. The wall of horses would march forward, creating a gap. The squad cars would then widen the lane through which the bureaucrat could escape.

Since they didn't have any more sawhorses to block the street, the new barricade consisted of several rolls of yellow POLICE LINE DO NOT CROSS tape strung across Elston Avenue. The SWAT team lined up behind it wearing full riot gear . . . helmet, shields, batons, and menacing expressions. Their orders simple: let no one but the convoy through.

"Sid, I'm not so sure this is such a good idea," Washington protested. "I don't see why we can't drive through single file."

"And have that mob swarm my limousine? Nothing doing, Max."

"But, Sid, I don't know if there'll be enough room to drive through three cars wide."

288

"Nonsense. As long as your police don't over react, everything will go fine. I know the people of Chicago and all this group of right-wing religious zealots wants is to get closer to this pancake." Gates made a sarcastic gesture towards the collapsed C of W building.

The awesome majesty of the combined choirs with full musical accompaniment made it impossible for anyone other than those closest to the front to hear the officer giving directions on a bullhorn, "In a moment we will remove the barricades. You should walk forward slowly and in an orderly manner. Do not run. There is plenty of . . . " the rest of his sentence was further drowned out when every squad car and emergency vehicle cranked up their sirens. They also turned on their emergency lights.

Another officer made a similar announcement at the southern barricade.

The police horses were well trained to ignore noise and commotion. They stood ramrod straight and awaited their rider's command.

Washington's watch flashed 9:01. Shaking his head, he gave the order by radio to begin moving. Gates stuck his head out the window and yelled, "Yee-ha! Move 'em out." More than one observer thought, *What an idiot.*

Six firemen knelt down, hefted a sawhorse onto their shoulder, and carried it away. They placed three on either side of the mayor's car. As soon as the barricades were removed, the riders gave a slight tug on the reins then tapped their mount's side with their foot. The horses took one step and stopped. The cluster of nuns saying the Rosary in front of them did not move. Instead, they stayed on their knees as a sea of silk choir robes of every color of the rainbow marched around them in a solemn procession. Their voices were raised in praise: "Thou the Father, Christ our Brother— All who live in love are Thine . . . " and their steps kept cadence with the music. They seemed oblivious to the ear-piercing wail of the sirens right next to them.

The mounted officers had never seen anything like this. In a normal crowd situation, city residents are nervous around the massive steeds and quickly gave way. Even stranger, the horses were more docile than their riders could recall, standing silent with their heads hanging down as though in respect. These were well-trained horses who responded to their riders' non-verbal commands without fail, yet the equestrian line did not move.

"What's the hold up?" Washington asked over the radio. He had walked back to his cruiser—the last vehicle—and was not happy the convoy wasn't moving.

"Sir, Chirdon here. I'm riding the lead horse. There's a line of nuns kneeling on the street in front of us praying the Rosary."

"Repeat. Did you say nuns?"

"Yes, sir, nuns. The old-fashioned kind. They're wearing brown habits with white collars and long black veils . . . the whole nun outfit.

"Franciscans . . . they would have to be Franciscans," Washington muttered as he recalled the stern nuns from his youth as an acolyte. *They wouldn't back off if the devil himself was towering over them.* "How many are there?"

"At least three dozen," Chirdon answered.

"Did you ask them to move?"

"Yes, sir," the mounted officer replied. "But they don't even seem to be aware of us. They have their heads bowed and are holding rosaries—real big rosaries—in the air while they pray. Commander, the nuns are kneeling right on the asphalt and haven't moved in over ten minutes."

Another officer broke in, "The sisters are Poor Clare nuns from their convent southwest of Chicago. They are meditating as they talk to God. That is why they do not feel pain in their knees. Look at your horses. Even they know something incredible is happening."

"Who said that?" someone demanded.

"This is Commander Washington. I want everyone off this channel. Can you go around them?"

"No, Sir." Chirdon answered. "The choir procession is on both sides of them. They're marching four wide. And the sidewalk is packed with hundreds of people headed your way."

"You've gotta be kidding! When will they be finished?"

"Can't say, Sir. There are choir robes lined up as far as I can see."

"Not the choir! The nuns!"

"Oh them. It should be soon," Chirdon shouted to make himself heard. "They just completed the last decade of the Sorrowful Mysteries and started saying the Hail Holy Queen prayer. They should be finished in about a minute."

"Then will you be able to clear the street without trampling anyone?" Washington knew several television crews were broadcasting live and had gone to great lengths to stress to his men that there would not be a repeat of the previous day's incident.

Before they lined up he had assembled his men and warned, "I want every one of you to be on your best behavior. Act like you're in church on Easter Sunday and your mother is in the pew behind you watching your every move. You will treat each and every person with the utmost respect. The reputation of the Chicago Police Department is on the line, and I will personally have the badge of any officer who brings disgrace upon it."

Washington rephrased his question. "Will the nuns get out of the way when they're finished?" He was starting to regret his decision to allow them to get this close. *I should have had the barricades set up farther away from the get go; shut down the whole neighborhood.*

"Commander," Chirdon said, "I don't know why but I'm certain they will."

"Fine, then give 'em their minute and we'll see if you're right."

Even though the crowd was very well behaved, moving that sheer volume of people was quite the undertaking. And the longer it took, the more likely it became that something would happen—sometimes all it took was for someone to trip and fall down to change the atmosphere.

Washington looked up. The sky was starting to look threatening. *All we need is a thunderstorm and there could be a stampede*, he thought as the first choir members approached his vehicle.

As soon he got back in, the radio crackled to life. A young man's voice boomed, "Commander, this is Tactical Officer Jenkins. I'm at the new north barricade and something strange is going on. The singers started to arrive, but when they get to the tape they're turning around and facing away from the clinic."

Washington clicked his mike, "Jenkins, repeat." The background noise made it difficult to hear even in a locked car.

"Sir, they're marching up to the tape, then turning on their heels and splitting off two-by-two. Then they're lining up with their backs towards me . . . they're facing away from the clinic."

"Why are they doing that?"

"I don't know, Sir. I tried asking a couple, but they don't stop singing. The civilians on the sidewalk are doing the same thing. The only answer I could get was from some old guy who pointed at the sky and said, 'Watch.'"

"Watch what? It looks like it's going to rain."

"He wouldn't say."

"What's the mood of the crowd down there?"

"I don't know . . . peaceful . . . happy. But they sure look like they're waiting for something to happen."

Washington had enough experience with crowd control to have expected a mad rush when the barricades were removed—like when a supermarket opens another cash register on a busy Saturday. Instead, the crowd not only proceeded forward in an orderly manner, they were now lining up as though they had rehearsed it a dozen times. *What the heck could they be waiting to see?*

"Good news, Sir. The nuns finished their rosary and are standing up."

"Then politely ask the good sisters if they would please step to the side so we can drive through."

"Yes, Sir."

Gates, totally oblivious to the police broadcasts his driver was monitoring, yelled, "C'mon Lucky, what's the hold up? Let's get moving."

"I can't, sir. The squad cars in front of us haven't moved yet."

"Give me your radio. If you want anything done right . . . " he muttered. "This is Mayor Gates," he shouted into the mike. "Why aren't we moving?"

"Sid, be patient," Washington answered. "We've got everything under control and should be moving in a minute. We ran into an unexpected delay, but should be rolling any second now."

"You said that five minutes ago. What's their excuse? Why aren't they doing their jobs?"

"It took a little longer to clear a path wide enough to drive through three abreast like you want. The boys on horses assure me the last group in front of them is clearing the street as we talk." *This guy is worse than a spoiled ten-year-old brat.*

"Why didn't your horses make the crowd move?"

"C'mon, Sid, the last thing we want to do is start another riot. There are thousands of people in front of your car. A lot of them are elderly—like Granny. And I'll bet most of the people in front of your car are registered voters—Democratic voters. Why don't you roll your windows down? Pretend you're in the St. Patrick's Day parade and wave to the people who elected you."

Gates' face turned red. *He must think I'm an idiot. The last thing I want to do is make it easy for some bomb-throwing anarchist to make me a notch in his belt.* He was swearing as he threw the microphone into the front seat, "Lucky, nudge the cars in front of us hard enough for them to know we're serious about moving."

Officer McCafferty bit his lip as he lifted his foot off the brake pedal.

Well, it looks like we're not going anywhere fast. Fred reclined his seat a couple of notches and tried to relax. *Take your time boys, I've got no reason to hurry.* His boss was having one of his famous meltdowns—where he rants and raves without giving you a chance to speak. When Rey finally did calm down, there would be the little matter of trying to explain how Gate Eight was destroyed by an angel.

Make that smote by an archangel, he thought with a laugh. *I don't care if we don't move until midnight because that'll be the only way I'll still have a job tomorrow.*

Besides Fred was enjoying the pageantry as the choirs marched by his car—two-by-two on his side but only single file on the passenger's side because they had to squeeze between it and the fire department's SUV parked next to him.

So how will I convince Rey I'm not crazy? I know what the truth is. I know what happened. But it's so unbelievable . . . so amazing. I wish I could reach Billy or Philo. Oh, God, I'm nervous. Please give me the strength to do the right thing. Wow, for the first time in my life I realize my life is in God's hands and here I am whining. I mean, He's got the whole world to worry about . . . wars all over the place. I wish I knew how to pray better.

Fred jumped when someone rapped on his window. *I guess it's time to roll,* he thought. He expected to see a police officer, but was surprised to see a woman with flowing blonde hair dressed in a white robe staring at him.

"Can I help you?" he asked as he rolled the window down.

The woman smiled and offered him a booklet.

Fred took it. "What's this?" he asked.

Goosebumps raced up and down his arms when he realized she had handed him a hymnal. On the front cover was printed "When You Sing You Pray Twice."

I guess I'm supposed to sing.

Monsignor Ardak Gabriel, pastor of Saint Mikaiel's Armenian Apostolic Orthodox Church, wore vestments of white and red bedecked with intricate gold embroidery. Each had a meaning and a special prayer was said as they were donned. The white surplice represented his purity while the red stole symbolized the priest being armed with the fear of the Lord. The prelate wore a headcover to remind all of the cloth with which the Lord's head was bound for His burial. In his right hand he held a gold cross and, in his left, a crosier, similar to a shepherd's staff.

He was followed by a priest holding an icon of Archangel Michael above his head as he chanted prayers in Aramaic. Fifty members of their flock, from babes in arms to a century-old new friend, lined up to progress to where they had been called.

"Moiz, that was about the finest taxi ride I've ever had. And thanks for offering to push me the rest of the way, but you can park this buggy." Granny slapped the side of the wheelchair. "I don't want people to think I'm not spry enough to walk on my own. With my walker that is."

"As you wish." Moiz folded his hands against his chest, then took a small bow. He made a hand gesture and two young men helped Granny out of the wheelchair while he held her walker.

"I can't thank you enough for getting me here. And I'm sorry to have been such a bother."

"Granny, you will never be a bother. You are now, forever, my good friend."

"Well that goes double for me. Uh, Moiz, before I forget. What are the damages?"

The cab driver cocked his head. "Damages? This I do not know."

"Damages . . . you know. What do I owe you? The fare?"

"Granny," he clasped his hands high to his chest, "it has been an honor to be of service to you. You owe me nothing." He made a sweeping motion as he again bowed.

"Well, I'll be. You sure were the answer to my prayers. You're not my guardian angel, are you?"

"Granny, you make me blush." Moiz lowered his head. "I am but a humble servant of our risen Savior."

"Well, He sure knew what He was doing when He sent me you."

It took the small group of Iraqi Christians ten minutes to catch up with the crowd of witnesses. They immediately drew the attention of a gathering of Eastern Orthodox Christians who greeted the new arrivals with outstretched arms and gave a traditional embrace: a kiss of peace on both cheeks followed by a loud proclamation of "Christ is risen" in their native tongue. They then venerated the Armenian's icon by kneeling before it and kissing it while a man wearing a long black cassock swung a large bronze incense burner over their heads.

Granny was a little surprised when these total strangers took turns "throwing a bear hug" on her. She was even more amazed when each planted a couple of kisses on her, then shouted something in a language she didn't recognize. But she felt very welcome and responded, "Granny's the name. Mighty glad to make your acquaintance."

An olive-skinned young woman wearing a simple white dress and pushing a stroller interrupted them with a smile. She gestured towards the dark clouds rolling in from the east, then at the light sweater that Granny was wearing, and draped a brightly-colored, crocheted shawl over her shoulders. She leaned over and whispered into the ear of a young boy with her. He nodded and translated, "My mother makes a present to you."

Tears welled up in Granny's eyes "I don't know what to say. Tell her thank you so very much. She has made an old woman very happy. Wait. Would you like some special treats?" The boy's eyes lit up when Granny handed him the bakery box. "I'm sorry, Moiz, but I can't remember the names of the pastries."

"Today you have much to think about. Next time we make a better day."

"I can't wait. But everyone has been so nice to me, I don't think today could get any better."

"Then look," he pointed towards the donut store.

"Sophie!" Two voices called out in harmony. The Hansen sisters spotted Granny at the same instant.

How did he know they're my friends?

Dr. Muhammad Ali Hammudiluh was giddy. His clothes were still wet from the baptismal immersion as he proclaimed to all of Chicago, "I am the worst sinner imaginable. I was an abortionist. It will forever be my shame. My hands are drenched in the blood of thousands of innocent babies. But I am saved by the blood of the Lamb. Jesus Christ died on the cross for my sins . . . me, an abortionist!" he shouted.

Jillian Morrow was mad enough to bite nails. *Aaaaaargh. I'm surrounded by crazy people!* Jillian's producer had warned against letting her mike get hijacked by another nut job and she was determined to put him in his place.

"But why were you baptized in a park fountain? Jillian asked. "There are churches for that, you know."

"I lived too long as a sinner and could wait no longer."

"There are lots of people, including the ACLU, who would object to you using a public park for a religious spectacle." She tried to bait him, but he did not receive a reply.

"You," she turned and pointed at the pastor, "you violated the separation of church and state."

Robertson shook his head, then beckoned the assembled to follow him. The new Christian praised God at the top of his lungs as they began walking east.

Jillian's technician, Roberto, tapped her on the shoulder, "Jilly, you're off the air."

She glared at him.

"Chopper Bob said the convoy is starting to move. We have to get over to Elston Avenue right away."

Jillian was not happy.

Radio News 710 was trying to strike a balance between the gospel fest, income-producing commercials, and traffic reports.

"We're returning live to flying traffic reporter Robert Parker for the latest of our continuing coverage of the event that has been tying up traffic all morning. Robert, I understand the mayor's convoy has started to move."

"Lloyd, I don't know why but it looks as if they missed their opportunity. The only movement I can see is an ocean of color surging around the mayor's convoy."

"Does it look like they will be able to move any time soon?"

"I don't see how. There are still several thousand people on the street ahead of them."

"Robert, is that thunder I hear in the background?"

"Yes, it is Lloyd. I'm watching a fast-moving storm sweeping in over the lake. The sky is turning black and I'm seeing flashes of lightning over the horizon."

"We'll have to talk to David in the weather booth about that one. He predicted sunny skies all day long."

"You might want to ask him how soon the rain will get here. There's a lot of people who are going to get soaked if the thunderstorm passes by."

"Thanks for the update, Robert. Keep us posted on the convoy's progress. After a quick commercial break, we'll have our staff meteorologist David Collins update us on the storm front forming over Lake Michigan."

Before the first ad finished, the annoying, but attention getting, emergency tone screamed out of radios throughout the Midwest.

"We interrupt this program with a special broadcast from the National Weather Service. The National Weather Service has issued a severe thunderstorm warning for northern Cook County. Doppler radar indicates a line of severe thunderstorms capable of producing golfball-sized hail and damaging winds in excess of sixty miles per hour is moving inland. These storms are located along a line extending from three miles north of downtown Chicago and are moving west at twenty-five miles per hour. This is a dangerous storm and you should prepare immediately for damaging winds, destructive hail, and deadly cloud-to-ground lightning. People outside should move to a shelter, preferably inside a strong building.

"Most affected areas can expect one- to two-inches of rainfall, and there is the potential for localized flooding. We now return you to your regularly scheduled programming."

Even with the barricades moved, Elston Avenue was packed. The northern choirs had merged into a massive chorus that filled the road from curb to curb. No one gave them direction, yet the sopranos clustered with other sopranos; the alto, tenor, and bass voices also unified with their like brethren and formed a 2,500 voice ensemble.

On the sidewalks, business men in fine silk suits rubbed elbows with factory workers and janitors in faded overalls while a pack of small children played hide-and-go-seek between their legs. Loop secretaries in expensive designer outfits talked with inner city teenagers, and grandmothers shared their lunches with former strangers. Bags of donuts were passed out by a troop of boy scouts. Every face, from newborn babes in arms to those weathered by a long life of struggle, beamed a knowing smile as they watched and waited.

Through this sea of tranquility strode the Reverend Mays, followed by a procession several hundred strong. His path took him within steps of Margaret Clemson.

"Margaret," he greeted her without breaking his stride. "What a pleasant surprise. Are your parents with you?"

"No, Pastor, but Philo is over there with Billy and Mauves Haynes."

He turned his head and acknowledged the trio with a flourish. All waved back.

"You should walk with us. But you'll need to step lively, child. Time is short."

"Time for what, Pastor?"

Mays didn't answer. Instead, he swung his right arm through the air urging the group, which swelled with each step, to walk faster.

"Where are we going in such a hurry?" Philo asked when he caught up to his wife.

"I have no idea, but I'm sure it's where we should be."

"Maybe," Mauves said, "we're going to join the choir for the next song."

"Maybe we'll find Pastor Robertson," Billy ventured.

"Shhhh." Mauves held her index finger to her husband's mouth. "I want to hear what Pastor Mays is saying."

Mays opened his leather-bound Bible and held it aloft. He had no need of the printed Word as he knew its text by heart. His voice boomed with the confidence of a man who not only knew, but loved, Scripture. "In Psalm 18, David, the servant of the Lord, spoke unto the Lord the words of this prayer on the day the Lord delivered him from the hand of all his enemies: I will love thee, O LORD, my strength. The LORD is my rock, and my fortress, and my deliverer; my God, my strength, in whom I will trust; my buckler, and the horn of my salvation, and my high tower."

The roar of rolling thunder punctuated his sentences and the sky was illuminated with flashes of lightning. Mays turned his Bible, so the pages faced those walking behind him. Many understood and read the next verse from their Bibles out loud like they did responsive psalms in church: "I will call upon the LORD, who is worthy to be praised: so shall I be saved from mine enemies."

Mays continued, "The sorrows of death compassed me about, and the floods of ungodly men made me afraid."

The thunder seemed to respect the Word and paused as each verse was read . . . only then did it echo off the buildings that lined the street with its unearthly rumble.

"The sorrows of hell compassed me about: the snares of death prevented me."

Mays shouted with great passion, "In my distress I called upon the LORD, and cried unto my God: He heard my voice out of His temple, and my cry came before him, even into his ears."

The response also grew stronger. "Then the earth shook and trembled; the foundations also of the hills moved and were shaken, because He was wroth."

The wind began to kick up dust and paper from the gutter; trees bent at its strength as Mays recited the next verse. "There went up a smoke out of his nostrils, and fire out of his mouth devoured: coals were kindled by it."

Dozens of lightning bolts flashed across the sky chasing the traffic and police helicopters away and causing the police horses to rear in terror.

Mays held his hand up with the palm open signaling stop. He was standing in the middle of Elston Avenue facing the donut store. The sky became so dark the streetlights flickered to life, but no one seemed to be paying any attention to the storm as they gathered around him. He motioned for his followers to continue reading.

"He bowed the heavens also, and came down: and darkness was under his feet."

The wind grew even stronger as Mays read the next line, "And He rode upon a cherub, and did fly: yea, He did fly upon the wings of the wind."

Leaves were stripped from branches and gnarled limbs torn from mighty oaks while lesser trees snapped in half. Their voices were so powerful the southern choir heard the words as though the speakers were standing in their midst. Above them the sky became so pitch black that even lightning bolts could not defeat it.

His congregation responded, "He made darkness his secret place; His pavilion round about Him were dark waters and thick clouds of the skies."

In an instant, a torrent of rain was unleashed from the sky, soaking everything around them—yet the faithful stayed dry. The lead squad cars, their windshield wipers on high, maneuvered around the horses—who continued to ignore their riders' commands—and began to push their way through the crowd. Gates' inexperienced limousine driver struggled to stay right behind their bumpers, while the rest of the convoy chose to wait out the savage storm.

"At the brightness that was before Him, His thick clouds passed, hailstones and coals of fire." The sky responded when Mays finished with an explosion of lightning brighter than the midday sun. Massive discharges of zigzag-shaped lightning scorched a canopy over them as hail pounded car roofs with a sound like a hundred machine guns . . . yet not a single icy stone fell on the believers.

The idle curious, small knots of pro-abortion protesters, skeptical reporters—including Jillian Morrow—and a motley assortment of non-believers standing mere feet away were drenched in an instant by the downpour. Wave after wave of hail dogged their every step as they tried to find shelter from the aerial bombardment.

The flock read the next line as the earth shook. A lightning bolt slammed into an ancient tree reducing it to a shower of flaming embers. "The LORD also thundered in the heavens, and the Highest gave His voice; hailstones and coals of fire."

Car windshields exploded from the icy onslaught. Hail was as thick as snow after a January blizzard and those fleeing God's wrath struggled to stay on their feet. Several more lightning bolts slammed into trees and telephone poles, turning them into giant flaming torches, illuminating the gathering with their flickering orange glow.

"Yea, He sent out his arrows, and scattered them; and He shot out lightnings, and discomforted them."

Two protesters holding a Keep Abortion Legal sign were incinerated by a blinding flash from heaven. They left behind nothing but a scorch mark on the pavement. Caroline Deaver used her sign as an umbrella until a screaming blast ended her life. The electricity leapt from her corpse into her friend Lee's drum. The 50,000 degree surge ran up her arms, making her blood boil. Seconds later, another who had incurred God's wrath fell to the pavement dead. Then another. The few pro-aborts still alive abandoned their companions and ran in confused terror. The vengeance from the sky followed their every step and each was struck down.

The congregation kept reading, "Then the channels of water were seen, and the foundations of the world were discovered at thy rebuke, O LORD, at the blast of the breath of thy nostrils."

Gale force winds drove the rain and hail so hard it ripped flesh from the bones of those who moments earlier had been ridiculing and taunting the faithful, driving them to their knees in horrific pain as their blood washed down the sewers. Yet not a hair was mussed on the head of any of those who had come to praise God.

Mauves pulled Billy closer; he wrapped his arms tighter around his wife.

Mays continued, "He sent from above, He took me, He drew me out of many waters."

In a hospital not far away, nurses rushed into June Dannon's room when her monitor began to emit a continuous tone. Their heroic efforts were wasted as life had been divinely taken from her, and no man could restore it.

Fred McBarker leaned against the hood of his car to keep from falling. He had been trying to think of a rational reason why he wasn't getting wet when a woman running less than ten feet away melted after being engulfed by a bolt of fire from the sky.

The congregation's response thundered. "He delivered me from my strong enemy, and from them which hated me: for they were too strong for me."

Sitting alone in his living room, Bob, the security guard from the Irving Park Women's Clinic who had borne false testimony against the prayer warriors, clutched his chest and died from a massive heart attack. It would be five days before anyone found his decomposing body.

"They prevented me in the day of my calamity: but the LORD was my stay."

Across town Michelle Holm, the abortuary's head nurse, was shopping for a new dress when she felt a sharp pain in her chest. She was dead before she hit the floor. Her assistant died the same way while riding her bicycle along the lake.

More voices were added with each verse. "He brought me forth also into a large place; He delivered me, because He delighted in me."

Ms. Diana Rhinelander, president and secretary of the C of W Intolerance Initiative, brushed off the dull chest pain as stress caused by the terrorist attacks on two of her clinics. She was busy at work in her home office arranging armed security guards for their remaining women's clinics when a thoracic aneurysm burst in her chest. She was dead for several hours before her roommate found her slumped at her desk, still clutching her cell phone.

Jillian Morrow lay face down in a puddle of mud and tried to protect her head from the constant sting of hailstones. Large black and blue welts covered her exposed flesh and blood flowed from open lesions on her scalp. *I have to make a run for it*, was her last thought before passing out

The pounding rain made it almost impossible to see and Gates' driver soon lost sight of his escorts. The mayor fumed at the incompetence of everyone around him and chided his chauffeur to drive faster, "So we can outrun this storm."

For a long moment all was silent. The rain paused. The hail stopped. The wind ceased to blow. Then the silence was shattered by a series of mighty thunderclaps that made even the earth quiver. When the air stopped trembling from the thunderclaps violence, dozens of violin players scattered throughout the crowd struck up their bows and provided an incredible introduction as the choir began to sing Handle's "Hallelujah Chorus."

"Hallelujah! Hallelujah! Hallelujah! Hallelujah!" The entire assembled orchestra, consisting of everything from high school marching bands to drum and bugle corps to concert musicians, joined in playing the great hymn of praise. Their music was so inspired it eclipsed anything that was ever played in Orchestra Hall.

The Hansen sisters and Granny sat in folding chairs holding hands in awe at the spectacle unfolding right in front of them. They had joined in reciting the psalm and now raised their frail voices in singing His glory. "For the Lord God Omnipotent reigneth" took on new meaning as they witnessed His frightening power being unleashed on the non-believers. "Hallelujah! Hallelujah!"

Dozens of people, including Granny's new Armenian friends and fellow parishioners from Our Lady of Guadeloupe, stood with them and joined in singing the refrain, "Hallelujah! Hallelujah!"

April Packard found herself drawn to the two sisters—the very women who had been a thorn in the C of W's side for so long—and walked over to them. Kaye smiled at her, then reached up and took her hand. Even though April had heard the song before, she didn't know any of the words, but soon found herself singing, "Hallelujah! Hallelujah!"

A warmth and peace came over her and she smiled back at Kaye as she squeezed her hand. Then she looked up and recognized the man standing across from her. *He's one of the doctors from the clinic. But he looks so different. It's almost like his face is glowing.* He noticed her an instant later and walked over, embracing her in his arms. "Today Jesus Christ has saved me. And, oh, I quit."

It took a lot to make Commander Washington speechless. The man served two tours as a foot soldier in Vietnam and had earned a pair of bronze stars—yet he stood with his mouth hanging open. He could see rain pouring down all around him, yet he was dry. So was the choir. About half of his SWAT team abandoned their posts when giant balls of ice began slamming into them, yet men standing right next to them were untouched.

As he listened to the psalm being read, he walked over to look at the squad car in line ahead of his. Its windshield was shattered in a half-dozen places and there were hundreds of dents where hail had struck. The driver had fled the vehicle. He looked back at his own squad—which wasn't even damp—and thought, *Why didn't he stay in the car?*

In the distance, he could hear people screaming in agony, but he was so amazed at what was happening that he made no attempt to check it out. Instead, he turned and walked in the other direction, passing three black sedans—all untouched by the calamity, their drivers looking as confused as he did—until he got to Fred's car. It too was undamaged.

"McBarker, right?" he asked.

Fred nodded.

"I don't know what's happening." He sounded frightened.

"Get in and sit down." Fred gestured towards his passenger seat. "I'm going to tell you a story I wouldn't have believed two days ago."

Pam prayed the entire time the paramedics fought to stabilize Phil. Twice they shocked his heart to get it beating normal.

"He's dehydrated, but he's going to live," the paramedic told Pam. "He's mighty lucky someone heard you pounding because I don't think he could have lasted much longer."

She knelt on the floor of the ambulance next to the gurney. "You're going to be all right, Phil." An oxygen mask covered his face. "I'm staying with you until they can get us to the hospital."

Phil gestured her to come closer. "I'm fine," he said in a soft but raspy voice. "You're a reporter. Now go report what's going on."

"Phil, I can't leave you. This is all my fault."

The elderly man shook his head. "You didn't make me do anything I didn't want to. Besides, it was the most fun I've had in years. Now go."

Pam squeezed his hand. "OK, but I'll be back to check on you."

I wonder where Tony is. She was a little nervous the police would see her. *I sure don't want to go back in that paddy wagon.*

She noticed a crowd examining a police car with a smashed windshield and hundreds of dents in the roof and hood. *What happened?* Pam thought as she compared the battered vehicle with the untouched ones in front and behind it. *I heard it raining when we were in the ambulance, but this doesn't make sense.*

A movement in a squad car ahead of her caught her eye—Tony was in it! She hesitated a moment and looked around to see if anyone was watching. *Here goes nothing.* She opened the driver's door, leaned inside, and popped the locks. Nothing. Pam didn't know squad cars lacked backseat handles and window controls to keep prisoners from escaping.

Tony pantomimed for her to open his door from the outside.

Pam glanced around and gave the handle a tug.

Tony bolted out. He was soaked in sweat and he wiped his forehead with his sleeve. "Thanks, Pam. I was baking in there. You're not going to believe this, but my camera is in the front seat. The van is close enough to pick up our signal. So, what do you say? Do you want to go back on the air?"

"Back on the air?" She hesitated.

Tony pointed to the sky. "Where have you been? We've got a front row seat to the end of the world."

Jackie heard Reverend Mays' distinctive voice long before he could see him. *Leon must be there.* He started walking faster. It began raining when he was about two blocks away, but Jackie was so worried about finding his nephew he didn't realize he wasn't getting wet. When hail started slamming into the ground, he took notice.

What is going on? he thought, as he saw people dropping to the ground after being pelted by large balls of ice. Less then ten-feet away cars' windshields were shattering from the onslaught and terrified individuals ran among them screaming in agony.

He paused in amazement and watched hundreds of people—dry and untouched by hail—praying the psalm while others in their midst were singled out for punishment. *I don't understand.*

A woman, her face beaten and bloodied, ran into Jackie as she sought shelter. He was too shocked to react. His sole concern was to find Leon and protect him from harm. His head swung from side to side as he walked through the crowd. Most stood in groups of three or four, gathered around one holding a Bible. He wanted to shout the young man's name but somehow knew he shouldn't do that.

I know he is here somewhere. He stood on his tiptoes in the middle of the street and tried to see above the crowd. Unsuccessful, he walked over to the sidewalk and climbed on a fire hydrant. Still, he couldn't see him in the large crowd.

What he did see scared him far more than anything he could imagine. Trees, that had been torn asunder, burned furiously all around them. Broken bodies lay in the gutters, their blood being washed down the sewers by the deluge of rain. Then he heard an explosion, and two young women who had been holding a sign in the middle of the street were incinerated by a bolt of lightning.

Trying not to panic, Jackie climbed down and began to run through the crowd, jumping up and down as he went, hoping to be noticed by the young man.

He almost bumped into a mother holding an infant in her arms. Her two older boys stood nearby playing catch with hail the size of a baseball. She smiled at him then pointed to her right.

What does she mean, he thought.

An ancient woman wearing a black dress and shawl stepped in front of him and pointed to her right. He turned his head and saw his nephew across the street, standing with a large group in front of a donut shop.

CHAPTER 28

THE CHOIRS IGNORED the fearsome violence the storm was unleashing all round them and continued lifting their voices in joyous praise, "For the Lord God omnipotent reigneth. Hallelujah! Hallelujah! Hallelujah! Hallelujah!"

Now even the bells in the steeple at Our Lady of Guadeloupe that hadn't rung in many years joined those from a dozen other churches in accompanying the singing.

Pam and Tony tried not to call attention to themselves as they set up to broadcast. Their plan was to film with the northern choir as their background. *I sure hope the station receives our feed before we're noticed*, Pam thought. *And I hope Tony doesn't get in any more trouble because of me.*

She needn't have worried, as Tony had no doubt they would soon be caught and returned to captivity, but there was nowhere he would rather be than filming the amazing story they were witnessing.

At their downtown studio, a technician threw his headset off and shouted, "Look!" when Tony's pictures appeared on his monitor. It took less than thirty seconds for the executive producer to preempt studio coverage of the storm and cut to the live feed.

Tony opened with a well composed establishment shot . . . a Mexican family standing together singing. The mother and daughter wore traditional embroidered folklore dresses while the father and son were bedecked in Charro suits and colorful sombreros. He framed it so the cascading torrent outlined the quartet.

Within a few seconds, two soaking-wet people ran between him and his subjects. The camera picked up the pelting rain which followed them as they fled. Pam waited for Tony's signal, then stepped in front of the camera.

305

"Good morning Chicago. This is Pam Romenelli reporting live from the Irving Park Women's Clinic gospel fest where a miracle is taking place. While a thunderstorm of biblical proportions wreaks havoc all around us, the Sanchez family has joined tens of thousands of very dry Christians raising their voices to heaven in hymns of praise."

The camera panned across row after row of choir members, their robes of many colors lined up in ramrod straight columns, singing better than they had ever sung before. Hundreds more, dressed in street clothes, stood on the sidewalk singing.

"As you can see, not a drop of rain has fallen on so much as the hem of a single choir robe." The camera zoomed out to show there wasn't any sort of covering protecting them from the deluge that was flooding down all around them. "Not a single piece of hail has touched these believers."

The camera turned and zoomed in on several inches of hail blocking the storm sewers. Tony tilted the camera up to show considerable flooding on the adjacent side street. "I can't think of any other word to describe this than 'miracle.'"

Tony tried to get her attention by jerking his head—two mounted police officers were pointing towards Pam. She nodded that she understood and began walking away from the horses while she spoke. "Even though our escape was nowhere nearly as dramatic as Apostle Peter's from King Herod's prison, we have, nonetheless, managed to escape from police custody. However, I have no idea how long we'll be able to broadcast. So far the police have ignored us, but now that we're broadcasting, we're starting to draw a little too much attention to ourselves."

Before she could start her next sentence Pam had to dive to her right to avoid being run over by a ten-thousand-pound stretch limousine. Tony's video showed City of Chicago flags mounted on both fenders as it roared by.

The choirs sang Handel's masterpiece even louder, "And He shall reign for ever and ever, for ever and ever, for ever and ever."

The inexperienced chauffeur was having a great deal of difficulty maneuvering around the large number of people standing in the street. Gates stuck his head through the limo's privacy partition and raged at his driver, "Faster, you fool. While they're busy singing! I don't want to get trapped by these fanatics again." He hadn't noticed that everyone they passed was ignoring them.

The limousine wasn't going very fast, and progress was measured in small lunges. Suddenly, one lane of Elston Avenue opened up all the way to the intersection as the crowd pressed forward to hear Reverend Mays.

"Look you fool! Over there!" Gates stuck his arm in the driver's face as he pointed. "Go that way."

McCafferty gritted his teeth and turned the heavy vehicle so hard to the left it rocked from side to side.

"Hit the gas!" The driver punched the accelerator and the rear wheels spun wildly as they lost traction in a huge water puddle, spraying water all over the sidewalk.

"Left! Turn left at the stop light . . . Irving! Turn left on Irving!" Gates was getting excited at the prospect of leaving the congestion behind. The rear end of the car began to fishtail.

While McCafferty wrestled with the steering wheel Gates screamed, "What the . . .! Turn the other way." He had spotted Granny sitting with the Hansen sisters. "Right! Turn right! Now!" He shouted. "Turn right, Lucky!"

The car's tires screamed in protest as the driver made a violent right turn—the oversized car wallowed like a row boat in a hurricane—and came face to face with a television crew. The reporter, her eyes wide with surprise, only escaped being hit by diving to her right—knocking two women over—as the driver lost control on the wet street. Incredibly, they didn't hit anyone but were now headed straight at a group of school children in uniforms.

The driver cranked the wheel as far as it would go to the right, but the rear wheel drive limousine was so heavy it took forever to respond. They were getting closer to the children by the second.

Everything seemed to be moving in slow motion . . . he could see the looks of shock on their faces as mothers lunged forward trying to place themselves between the out-of-control car and their children. After what seemed an eternity, the front tires found some dry pavement to bite on and the car swung to the right, brushing against several women as it skidded by.

The lack of traction combined with the great weight of the car caused it to continue skating forward as though on ice. Panicking, the driver over-corrected and spun the wheel to the left, causing the car to slide sideways on a forty-five degree angle. In desperation, he slammed on the brakes and fought the steering wheel for control. For a brief moment he managed to straighten the limo out, however it was now bearing down on a terrified group of people in front of a donut shop. Tony spun around and continued filming the huge car as it hydroplaned towards Granny and her friends.

Gates was swearing mad after being thrown to the floor of the car. He tried to pull himself up by grabbing his driver by the collar. "Stop this car, you fool!"

McCafferty tore his hand loose. Knowing he couldn't stop the heavy car in time, he tried a desperation maneuver to avoid hitting them—he whipped the wheel hard to the right as he accelerated, hoping to fishtail the car enough to slam broadside into the streetlight and stop the runaway. The rear end of the car started to make a graceful arc, and for a moment the driver thought everything was going to be all right. Then he heard a dull thud and felt the car bounce as they ran over something—something big.

Please God, the driver begged, *let it be the curb.*

"King of kings, and Lord of lords, King of kings, and Lord of lords."

Leon got very excited when he spotted his uncle and ran to greet him. "Unky Jackie! Unky Jackie!" He never saw the limousine careening out of control towards him.

Jackie froze in horror when he saw the out-of-control car and yelled, "Leon! Stay there!" But the young man could not hear him above the choir.

The car slammed hard into Leon, knocking him to the ground. Its rear end continued sliding around and the spinning back wheels rolled right over his body, crushing his neck with a sickening crunch. The car finally bounced off the streetlight and came to a stop right in front of April Packard.

Dr. Hammudiluh reached Leon seconds before Jackie did. Blood was pouring from his mouth as his body convulsed one last time, then grew still. Someone screamed, "Call 911."

The doctor tore open Leon's shirt and exposed his smashed throat. "I don't know what to do," he stammered. Jackie's entire body trembled as he held the young man's limp hand. There was no pulse.

Hammudiluh stared at the carnage, "I don't know what to do. Oh God, help me. I don't know what to do."

The limousine driver leapt out of the car, dropped to his knees, and pleaded with him, "You have to do something. It's all my fault. You have to help him."

Hammudiluh tried giving the young man mouth-to-mouth resuscitation, and then did chest compressions as dark red blood pooled around Leon's head.

Reverend Mays was stunned into silence for but a moment before he called out, "Everyone, bow your heads." He strode over and opened his Bible.

"'Then said Martha unto Jesus, Lord, if thou hadst been here, my brother had not died. But I know, that even now, whatsoever thou wilt ask of God, God will give it to thee. Jesus saith unto her, 'Thy brother shall rise again.' Martha saith unto him, 'I know he shall rise again in the resurrection at the last day.' Jesus said unto her, 'I am the resurrection, and the life: he that believeth in me, though he were dead, yet shall he live: and whosoever liveth and believeth in me shall never die.'"

Mays looked directly at Jackie as he asked, "Believest thou this?"

Between sobs he choked out, "Yes, I believe."

Hammudiluh collapsed next to him wailing, "I don't know what else to do."

Jackie looked the doctor in the eye and said, "Thank you for trying. It is in God's hands now." He lifted his nephew's broken body and cradled it in his arms. Tears streamed down his cheeks as he stood, looked towards heaven, and cried in pain, "Why him? Why not me? I'm the sinner . . . not him. I'm the one who deserves to die for his sins. Punish me, not him!" He dropped to his knees, clutching Leon tight against his chest, sobbing uncontrollably.

"And He shall reign forever and ever, King of kings! and Lord of lords!"

Mays continued, "Jesus saith unto her, 'Said I not unto thee, that if thou wouldst believe, thou shouldst see the glory of God?' Then they took away the stone from the place where the dead was laid. And Jesus lifted up his eyes, and said, 'Father, I thank thee that thou hast heard me. And I knew thou hearest me always: but because of the people that stand by I said it, that they may believe that thou hast sent me. And when he thus had spoken, he cried with a loud voice, Lazarus, come forth.'"

At that instant, thousand of horns, both great and small, coming from every direction of the compass, announced the arrival of the celestial choir. Repeated fanfares layered one on top of another, growing in volume and intensity until their music became a physical presence. Many thought they were announcing the return of Archangel Michael. However, his flourish of trumpets was a mere tune compared to the incredible symphony surrounding them. The mighty thunder of their music grew louder by the second, resonating as though in a great stone cathedral.

Shortly, endless scores of angels began to descend from the sky. They took their places within the human choirs, and joined them in singing, "King of kings, and Lord of lords. King of kings, and Lord of lords."

The voices of the great company of heavenly host, numbering thousands upon thousands, and ten thousand times ten thousand, surrounded them and blended in harmonies the likes of which had not been heard in this world since that miraculous night in Bethlehem. "King of kings, and Lord of lords. King of kings, and Lord of lords. And He shall reign forever and ever . . . "

The air grew thick with the sweet smell of incense from scores of angels swinging golden censers; the smoke of the incense, which came with the prayers of the saints, ascended up before God out of the angels' hands.

The earthly choir, though all-consumed with singing His praises, were made aware of the admonition God gave to Moses in Exodus 33, "Thou canst not see my face: for no man shall see me, and live."

"King of kings, forever and ever . . . "

Mays was among the first to drop to his knees and prostrate himself face down on the pavement. All with him followed his lead. Seeing what was happening around them, McBarker and Washington, though still awestruck by the arrival of the angelic choir, threw open their car doors and rolled to the pavement.

"And Lord of lords. Hallelujah! Hallelujah!!"

Tony laid face down on the sidewalk with his camera next to him—still broadcasting live, focused on the drama unfolding in front of him. Gates, however, opened his limousine door, stood up, and asked, "Why's everyone lying down?"

His driver saved his life by tackling him to the ground and demanding, "Have you no fear of God?" as he pushed his face to the asphalt.

From south to north, no man, woman, or child remained standing, yet His praises were being sung louder, and purer, by the second.

"And He shall reign forever and ever, King of kings, and Lord of lords, King of kings, and Lord of lords."

A gentle wind, not of this world, swept over the believers and all covered their faces tighter for they knew they were in the presence of God. An incredible peace swept over them as His glory passed by.

Jackie lay on the ground, clutching Leon's still body beneath his own, holding one hand over his eyes while covering his nephew's with the other. He whimpered softly, and his tears mixed with the blood that soaked their shirts.

He felt the wind blow through the young man's hair and touch his cheek as delicately as the breath of a newborn baby, yet with more awesome power then he could imagine as he proclaimed aloud, "I know my nephew will rise again in the resurrection on the last day. And I know Leon loved You and believed in You with his whole heart. I ask You because I too believe."

A terror gripped Jackie as he felt the shadow of God's brilliance fall over him, and even though his eyes were shut tight and covered, the blackness of his soul was laid bare. Cold chills caused him to tremble. He became nauseous as he was beset with an overwhelming feeling of despair.

It became hard to breathe as he felt a crushing weight against his chest—but Jackie would not relax his grip on Leon's lifeless body.

The depth of his depression over the horrific death of the young man was replaced by a hideous sorrow that engulfed him and dragged his soul to a bottomless pit. He felt the incredible anguish and hopelessness of everyone who had placed their trust in him. He began to fall, faster and deeper, being dragged down by the evil of his ways. All at once he was living the pain and agony of everyone who had looked to him for help and found none.

The awesome terror and loneliness he felt grew more gut-wrenching than anything he could imagine when he realized he had stopped falling and was alone, standing before God in judgment. He tried to look away with unimaginable revulsion as his entire life was revealed, but the images surrounded him. He opened his mouth, but no sound came out as he was shown in excruciating detail all of the times he had failed to honor the Father.

Thousands of images of him sinning—exploiting the downtrodden as the Reverend, stealing from the rich in his guise as a religious leader, and enriching himself beyond the dreams of fabled King Midas while those around him went without—caused wave after wave of fear to rip through him. Just when he thought he could take no more and his heart would surely be torn from his chest, he screamed in pain, "Father, forgive my sins."

Knowing it was the proper thing to do, the earthly choir rose up and joined in singing, "Hallelujah! Hallelujah! Hallelujah! Hallelujah! Hallelujah! Hallelujah!"

Their words were echoed by the choir of angels as they returned to heaven. "Hallelujah! Hallelujah! Hallelujah! Hallelujah! Hallelujah!"

The believers continued singing as they watched the uncountable number of angels return to heaven. Even though it was the second time in two days they had been allowed to watch God's messengers, they were no less in awe at the sight.

"Hallelujah! Hallelujah! Hallelujah!" they continued singing until the last one disappeared from sight. A flourish of unseen trumpets sounded, and the dark, cloudy sky turned bright blue in an instant as the sun erupted.

Then all became quiet as the enormity of what they had witnessed struck them speechless.

The absolute silence was broken a moment later when Leon sat up and asked in a loud voice, "Now do you believe me about the angel?"

Epilogue

The Following Week

TWO POLICE OFFICERS tried to keep traffic moving as drivers slowed to a crawl to gawk at the huge memorial. Someone spray painted "CLOSED BY GOD" in large red letters across the blue plastic tarps draped over the temporary chain-link fence the city erected around the Elston Avenue site. The yellow POLICE LINE DO NOT CROSS tape stretching back and forward from the fence to a row of wooden sawhorses was unnecessary as thousands of candles, religious pictures, baby dolls, and bouquets of flowers covered the entire length and width of the sidewalk and much of the parking lane. At both ends, a steady procession of people waited their turn to squeeze between the wooden barricades to pray at the site of the destroyed abortion mill.

The roar of chainsaws disturbed the early morning quiet as city crews finished cutting down what was left of the burned out trees. The alleys were still blocked by utility crews hanging new electric, cable TV, and telephone lines. In front of the donut shop, several women regaled passersby with the miracle they had witnessed. Otherwise, life had returned to normal in the neighborhood.

Trinity Evangelical Church looked as if it belonged on a Christmas card. Solid limestone walls, stained glass windows, and a steeple which soared towards heaven. The Pastor and elders stood on the stone stairs greeting their flock.

"Good morning, Reverend Jefferson." Pastor Christopher recognized him from television, and held out his hand in friendship. "It's a pleasure to make your acquaintance."

"Thank you, Pastor, but the pleasure is all mine. I know the agreement was I come alone, but I took the liberty of bringing with my nephew Leon because we have so much to be thankful for. I hope that meets with your approval."

"Leon, welcome to God's house," Christopher said as he shook the young man's hand.

Jefferson beamed with pride as Leon, dressed in a brand new, charcoal gray suit, replied, "Pastor, all of creation is God's house, but I must say, your building does Him great honor."

"Why thank you, Leon. I hope my service is equally as impressive. Reverend Jefferson, as visiting clergy, would you honor us by doing the first reading?"

He held his hand up. "Pastor, I must decline your request. I am afraid the foolish antics of my past make me wholly unqualified to deliver the Word with the proper reverence and respect."

"I understand and appreciate your honesty. Leon, could I ask you instead?"

"I'm sorry, Pastor, but I don't know how to read."

Christopher thought for a moment the well spoken young man was joking. Then he remembered the incredible story several members of his choir had told him.

He gasped, "You're the one, aren't you?"

"Yes, Sir." Still unaccustomed to the attention, Leon managed an awkward smile.

Sergeant Harnett spotted Jefferson the moment he rounded the corner and interrupted the conversation before the Pastor could ask him about the miracle. "Jackie, Laurie McKennae is parking her car. She'll be here with her parents in a moment. I don't have to remind you to be on your best behavior? Do I?"

"No, Sir. You have my word."

Harnett was impressed with his conservative suit. "Well I must say you're dressed mighty fine, Reverend."

"Please, that presumptuous title embarrasses me when I am standing before a man with the calling," Jefferson changed the subject. "Sergeant Harnett, I would like to introduce my nephew Leon."

"Jackie, I didn't know you had a nephew. It's nice to meet you, Leon." They shook hands. "Are you new in town?"

"No, Sir. I have lived with Uncle John for over two years."

"I'm surprised we haven't met before. Do you work for your uncle?"
"Yes, Sir. I am his valet."

It was still so hard to believe. One week earlier she was reporting on Boy Scout pinewood derby races. Tonight, Pam Romenelli became Chicago's newest news anchor. The network execs were very impressed with her calm demeanor during the siege of Phil's apartment, and getting the station's name on the air as she was being manhandled out the door by the SWAT team scored quite a few points. However, the clincher was her presence when a miracle occurred. Everyone who saw her live broadcast was moved by her sincerity and compassion while she scooped every station in town. It's not very often a television station broadcasts a man returning from the dead. And in sweeps week to boot.

She sat in the anchor's chair, closed her eyes, and recited the twenty-third Psalm to herself. After thanking God for all He had given her, she adjusted her eyes to the bright lights and waited for her cue.

"You're live in thirty seconds," came over her earpiece.

Pam thought about her conversation with Bernice, the wardrobe lady who had befriended her. "Just trying to protect my investment," she joked, referring to her $10 office pool bet that Pam would last six months. "Now don't let a little success go to your head and you'll go a long way."

"And you'll owe me lunch."

"Right, and I'll even let you super-size the fries."

They laughed together. Pam knew she had made a friend. "By the way, do you know where I can find Mike the soundman?"

"You mean Vince."

"No, Mike."

"I don't know who Mike is. Vince has been the soundman for the news longer than I've been here."

"I'm certain he said his name was Mike. We prayed together before I went on the air"

"That sure wasn't Vince. If he ever prayed, that story would lead the news."

"I must be mistaken." *I know he said his name was Mike.*

"You had a lot on your mind. Now, a little tip between us Christians. There's not a lot of believers around here. I would advise you to tuck that inside your blouse." Bernice pointed to the simple gold cross that hung around her neck.

Before Pam could protest she continued, "And just before you go live, discretely pull it out. They might be able to stop you from wearing it tomorrow, but tonight all of Chicago will see it."

Pam looked stunning in the ivory silk blouse and royal blue blazer the station had custom tailored for her. When she heard Vince say, "Ten seconds," she pretended to adjust the lapels on her blazer and moved the cross to the outside of her blouse.

"Good evening, Chicago. Welcome to the Channel One News at Five. Your number one source for news." The camera zoomed in on Pam while the station's hologram logo rotated behind her. Even though she had rehearsed her introduction to the lead story a dozen times, the soft blue glow of the teleprompter gave her confidence.

"Channel One's Jeff Sprecher was in attendance at Mayor Gates' noon press conference announcing the formation of a blue ribbon panel to investigate the City Gate and Irving Park Women's Center collapses."

Pam was replaced by a close-up of a handsome young man wearing a Channel One blazer. Not a hair was out of place as he held up a microphone and began speaking. "Good evening, Pam, and welcome to the Channel One News team. The main ballroom of the Hilton Hotel is quiet now. Two hours ago, it was a very different story as Mayor Gates' press conference turned into another of his famous media meltdowns."

A video of the mayor standing in front of six men wearing almost identical gray pinstriped suits and white shirts filled the screen. Not a one was a member of the engineering team that had determined the safety of the remaining City Gate buildings.

"This is Chicago, not Baghdad." The camera zoomed in on Gates. "If there were any terrorists in my city, I would order the police to lock them up and throw away the key." He did not look happy when no one in the audience laughed. He changed the subject.

"This distinguished panel," he gestured towards the men behind him, "is made up of some of the most respected names in their fields. And Commissioner Reynold O'Dea has kindly agreed to chair the panel." O'Dea joined Gates at the podium to a smattering of applause. "I have personally assured Rey his investigation will receive the full cooperation of every city department. I want to put my critics on notice that any rumors they hear of a City Hall cover-up of urban terrorism are nothing more than cowardly attacks from those who are trying to capitalize on these unfortunate disasters to further their political agendas.

"I will demand all of you rumor mongers—and I know who you are—apologize to the people of this great city when our thorough and far-reaching investigation shows Gate Eight collapsed because of a design flaw unique to that one building."

He then explained, "And irrefutable evidence will show the clinic building blew up when a non-union worker cut a gas line. And let this be a lesson to all of Chicago. That's what happens when you try to save a few bucks by hiring fly-by-night workers who don't get the proper permits." Gates never forgot the large donations labor unions made to his campaign.

"I am confident their investigation will also determine the timing of these two incidents was an incredible coincidence. And speaking of timing, I'm sorry, but I don't have time to take any questions. Thanks for coming." He turned and started to walk away.

"What about the archangel?" A reporter called out as the Mayor was stepping off the stage. Pam had to stifle an off-camera giggle when Gates, his face bright red, spun around and grabbed the microphone. His voice cracked as he ranted, "Archangel! What, are you people all crazy? Didn't anybody listen to what I just said?"

The thick veins in his temples were throbbing as his voice became even higher pitched. "Are you trying to create some kind of a panic like yelling fire in a crowded movie theater? I'll say this one last time, the people of Chicago are too smart to be deceived by mass hysteria fueled by irresponsible people in the media trying to sell newspapers. And that goes double for you guys on late-night talk radio too," he ranted. "This is the twentieth century, not the Old Testament. There was no angel with a flaming sword."

The camera followed Gates as he stormed out of the room. Several reporters trying to chase the mayor, were turned back by his security detail. Sprecher's face again filled the screen. "Another typical ending to a Gates press conference."

"Jeff, did the mayor give any indication when we could expect the panel to complete their investigation?"

"No, Pam, however most of the people with whom I spoke thought it would be over in a matter of weeks because Gates' statement shows he clearly expects a certain conclusion to be reached."

"Thank you, Jeff, for that amazing report. It sounds as if the mayor has fired the opening volley in his latest spin war with the media."

The camera returned to a close-up of Pam. "In a related story, State's Attorney Charles Keenan, launched an investigation into the rash of deaths of Council of Women executives and clinic employees." Small photographs of the women appeared in a box next to her.

"Even though the Cook County Coroner's office issued preliminary autopsy results showing all twelve women died of natural causes, the timing of their deaths has caused an inquest panel to be impaneled.

A press release from Marilyn Grant-Thompkins, acting president of the Council of Women, states: "The deaths of twelve healthy feminist icons within hours of two of our clinics being destroyed by reproductive terrorists is no coincidence. It is nothing short of genocide on leaders of the Freedom of Choice movement and, until the perpetrators are caught, we demand around the clock police protection at all of our women's clinics as well as all of our officers and employees."

"A Chicago Police Department spokesman declined to comment on Grant-Thompkins charges, but promised increased patrols and a heightened state of awareness around the Council of Women's four remaining clinics."

After the commercial break, Pam introduced an interview with an alderman who demanded an investigation of inadequacies in the city's emergency preparedness program after twenty-six people died in his ward from lightning strikes and hail in the recent weather event.

Their staff meteorologist followed and attempted to explain the devastating thunderstorm with a slew of textbook phrases like "elevated conduction, temperature inversion, barotropic environment, and thermodynamic convection."

Pam doubted if anyone knew what the man was talking about. She was tempted to ask how such a severe storm could appear out of nowhere, ravage a path two-miles long by a half-mile wide, then disappear without as much as a drop of rain falling on thousands of people praying on Elston Avenue. Instead, she smiled, secure in the knowledge that she knew the answer.

Fred McBarker was awake at 5:00 A.M. sharp. Old habits die hard. Ever since he graduated from high school, he left for work before sunrise and had his routine down pat. He laid out his clothes the night before and tip-toed downstairs so as not to wake his wife. The timer on the coffeemaker was set so the pot had finished brewing when he returned from walking the puppies.

This morning, however, was different. Instead of a suit, Fred had on a pair of blue jeans, and his briefcase was nowhere to be seen.

"Retired," the word kept running through Fred's mind as he poured cream and sugar into his oversized cup. "Retired."

From now on he could leisurely sip his coffee—even have a second cup—as he read the paper. The headline story announced Gates' formation of a Blue Ribbon Panel to investigate the twin collapses. "Thorough and far-reaching," he muttered under his breath. "Then how come Rey's secretary called yesterday to say there was no need for me to talk to the investigators? 'If they have any questions, they know where to find you,'" he mimicked her condescending tone.

He dialed his former boss' cell phone the moment she hung up and left a friendly message requesting a meeting. He called again at noon. "Rey, Fred. I really need to talk to you ASAP," he pronounced it *a-sap*. "You can get me on my cell phone anytime."

When he still had not heard from Rey by four o'clock, he became more forceful. "Rey, after all these years, don't I at least rate a return phone call? C'mon Rey, just five minutes." He left him a similar message on his home answering machine.

Fred slammed the phone down, "Something's going on . . . and it smells like a cover-up," he growled.

Fritzi saw how upset he was and insisted they go out to dinner and a movie. "C'mon, Honey, there's a new Italian restaurant all our friends are raving about."

And that was how he missed seeing the mayor's debacle on the evening news. The banner headline was the first he learned of the formation of the committee. He devoured both papers' coverage of the press conference. The articles mentioned Gates' verbal sparring with the reporter, but gave no details, so he turned on the TV hoping to learn more. He spun through the channels until he found an early news show that was just beginning.

"After the break, we'll recap yesterday's events including the dramatic end to the mayor's press conference." A picture of O'Dea and Gates standing in front of the committee flashed on the screen.

"Thorough and far-reaching," he repeated the words several times as he waited for the commercials to end. "Some day, Rey, you're going to have to talk to me . . . and the truth will scare the smirk right off your face."

Gates' press conference was the second story and Channel One replayed Jeff Sprecher's report in its entirety. Fred almost screamed for joy when the reporter asked about the archangel. "The truth's going to get out Rey . . . and you won't be able to spin it away this time."

He picked up the remote and hunted through the channels hoping to find another report on the press conference. Without thinking about the time, he called Billy at home. He answered on the first ring, "Haynes speaking."

"McBarker here. I hope I didn't wake you, but you sound pretty healthy for a guy too sick to work," he joked. He knew full well O'Dea had placed Billy and Philo on indefinite medical leave—with full pay—to keep them away from the office until the media was distracted by some other headline-grabbing event.

"No problem, Fred. I'm like you. I wake up before the roosters." When he was rising through the ranks at the Department of Buildings, Fred was always the first one at work—every morning—drawing the ire of his co-workers. Billy had the same work ethic and had made many of the same enemies. "I was feeling pretty good until I saw our mayor on TV last night. You should be up there heading that panel. Distinguished panel—distinguished at what? I don't even recognize most of them."

"Neither do I. The newspapers didn't even list their names let alone their credentials."

"You sure gotta love their picture. They look like clones. Did the mayor dress them?"

"I don't know, but he sure lost it when that reporter nailed him with St. Michael."

"Somehow, I don't think he'll be invited to the next press conference." Both men laughed.

"I'll see you later then. We've got a lot to talk about," Fred said as he hung up.

Fritzi startled her husband as she wrapped her arms around him. "Who'd a thunk the city would give you early retirement just to shut you up—and at full salary?" She kissed him on the head. "So, what's the young retiree going to do today?"

"Retiree. It still sounds so strange."

"Well, if you need some suggestions, the lawn needs mowing, the puppies need to have their nails trimmed, and the . . . "

"Yes, Dear." He was laughing when he kissed her. "But I actually have plans. I'm getting together with Billy and Philo. I still have so many questions to ask them."

One of the questions he had was how they could get the truth out about what they saw at Gate Eight. Billy and Philo had been threatened with immediate termination if either spoke to the press—and both had families to support. Fred had signed a confidentiality agreement that forbade him to discuss or write about either collapse with anyone other than the city. And they didn't want to talk to him.

The Council of Women was having very little success as they scoured the city for a building large enough to hold their corporate offices and a reproductive freedom clinic. With the C of W blaming terrorists for the twin collapses, very few landlords were willing to accept their assurances the Chicago Police Department would protect their building. Those who believed in God knew they couldn't.

ONE YEAR LATER

God called Granny Gates home one day after her one-hundred-first birthday. She caught a cold she couldn't shake. The family's doctor, or croaker as Granny called him, wanted to admit her to the hospital, but she stubbornly refused saying, "Hospitals are for sick people."

Complications set in and she developed pneumonia. Her obituary said she died peacefully at home in her own bed surrounded by eleven grandchildren, twenty-five great-grandchildren, and her six-month-old great-great granddaughter, Sophie Gates II. They did not mention her last words were, "The angel just told me it was time to go. I'll save you a good seat in heaven."

She went to meet her Maker with a huge smile on her face.

For the second year in a row, Granny battled City Gate for newspaper headlines. The early editions mourned her passing and recounted the full life of "Chicago's most beloved citizen." By afternoon, however, she had been relegated to a small blurb on the front page—"complete story on page 3." The headlines now proclaimed the release of City Hall's blue ribbon report, "Council of Women Structural Collapses."

It was an impressive looking book, almost two inches thick. Reporters attending the press conference were handed a bound copy along with a ten-page summation of its key points.

The entire staff of Chicago's newest civil engineering firm gathered around a portable TV set to watch Reynold O'Dea, Commissioner, Department of Buildings, read a prepared statement.

O'Dea wore a traditional mourner's black tie and white shirt with his dark blue suit.

"Citizens of the great City of Chicago, I ask all of you to join me in a moment of silence in honor of Mayor Gates' beloved Granny." After a long pause he continued, "Mayor Gates apologizes for not being here in person and asks you to keep his family in your prayers. Now, on to the reason for this press conference. I have been honored to serve as chair of the commission that investigated the collapses of two buildings owned by the Council of Women. The timing of these unique events caused many to speculate on their having a common external cause. Our thorough and far-reaching investigation has interviewed hundreds of eyewitnesses."

"Fred, did anyone interview you?" Billy Haynes asked.

Fred shook his head.

"How about you, Philo?"

Philo responded, "Nope."

"Then surely they must have interviewed me," Billy joked.

"Shhhhhh," McBarker motioned them to quiet down. "I want to hear Rey explain the Archangel."

All three men laughed. They knew the commission was only window dressing. How else would you explain their failure to interview the only eyewitnesses to the first collapse. "There's no need for you to come all the way downtown, we have your notes."

As Rey droned on about how hard he worked, Fred's mind wandered. He closed his eyes, reflected back on all that had happened since the morning of Gate Eight's collapse, and said a silent prayer of thanks to God for saving him.

The young reporter stood on the sidewalk in front of a nondescript, red brick building on Chicago's southwest side. A hand-lettered sign reading, "ALL ARE WELCOME" hung above an open door.

Tonight was Channel One News Michael Holmes' first field assignment. He took a deep breath and began, "I am standing in front of the Archangel Michael Mission which has become one of the few bright spots in this blighted community. The secret which these walls hold is as amazing as the miracles taking place in the lives of the people who come here.

"It has been one year since Jackie Jefferson, the colorful minister known to Chicagoans as 'the Reverend' apologized to all Christians and pledged to spend the rest of his life making amends."

The station played a clip of Jefferson thanking God for saving the life of his nephew.

"Renouncing his flamboyant outfits and flair for the dramatic, Jefferson sold his near north side mansion and opened this inner city mission. He dedicated his life to serving the city's forgotten. With his nephew Leon and a handful of volunteers, they have been feeding and caring for hundreds of Chicagoans every day.

"Another amazing part of this story is Dr. Ali Hammudiluh, a former abortionist, who spends every weekend providing free medical care at the mission.

"Jefferson refused our initial request for an interview, but later agreed on one condition: my crew and I join him in working an entire dinner shift." Holmes pulled a white apron over his Channel One blazer. "I found him to be a changed man and an inspiration to us all."

The view switched to a large hall where row after row of tables were being set for supper. Jefferson, wearing a spotless shop apron, placed glass dishes on a white table cloth. "We do not use paper plates, plastic forks, or styrofoam cups. People deserve the dignity of eating their meal on a real dish, with real silverware, a cloth napkin, and a real cup or glass."

Jackie's former housekeeper, Mrs. White, walked up to the reporter and said, "Excuse me, young man, but we gotta lotta hungry mouths to feed." She glared at him. "Well, are you here to help or watch?"

Without showing Holmes' answer, the picture changed to an adjacent room where Leon led a group of adults learning to read. One of his students, a gray haired man in a faded Chicago Bulls sweatshirt, stood and read a page from a primer. When he finished, Leon praised God for his student's accomplishment.

The final scene showed the tables filled with people, their heads bowed in prayer, as Jefferson praised God's mercy and thanked Him for His bounty.

"Few believed him when he held a press conference one year ago renouncing his flamboyant lifestyle, but I for one can state that John Jefferson has kept his word. Reporting from the Archangel Michael Mission, this has been Michael Holmes."

It had been a rare, quiet night at First Presbyterian Hospital and the staff gathered around the nurse's station to bring the day shift up to date on their patient load. Sally Ryun was one of the last to arrive and found her co-workers in a giddy mood. "What's so funny?" she asked in response to their giggles.

No one said a word as four orderlies standing in front of her stepped to the side so she could see Officer James Kent in uniform, down on one knee.

"Jim, what are you doing down there? Are you OK?"

He looked up and asked, "Miss Ryun, would you marry me?" He held up an open ring box.

"Yes!" she shouted, "Yes!" She almost knocked him over when she threw her arms around him.

It was one year to the day since they had met. Jim called Sally the next day. They talked for over an hour before he worked up the nerve to ask her on a date—to watch him play left field on the precinct's softball team. That night he called her his good luck charm after he went four-for-four and made a game-saving catch. They celebrated the victory with a beer at My Uncle's Place. A year later, he still called her his good luck charm, only now he also called her his fiancée.

Kaye knocked twice then entered the pitch-black bedroom. "Sister, are you asleep?"

"No," Ruth turned on the light on the nightstand next to her bed. "I've been expecting you."

"He came back."

"I know. I saw him." Ruth was smiling.

Kaye sat on the bed next to her twin and hugged her. "I knew God's avenger would come back."

PW

To order additional copies of this book call:
1-877-421-READ (7323)
or please visit our Web site at
www.pleasantwordbooks.com

If you enjoyed this quality custom-published book,

drop by our Web site for more books and information.

www.winepressgroup.com

"Your partner in custom publishing."

CPSIA information can be obtained at www.ICGtesting.com
229701LV00002B/3/P